the DEMON SOULS series
BOOK THREE

NEW EVIL

JOSH BROOKES

This Edition published in 2018 by, The Evil Bunny
First published in 2017 by Javsco Books

ISBN: 978-1-912663-04-0

eBook ISBN: 978-1-912663-05-7

Cover & layout design by Karen M. Dillon

For Paddy Powell
A genuinely kind person.

Scene!

the DEMON SOULS series
BOOK THREE

NEW EVIL

PART 1

KIRI'TOL

chapter
ONE

Hunting a demon with the intention of providing it protection was not a mission Badrick Varner had ever expected to undertake. Frankly, it was a ludicrous idea that an organisation dedicated to fighting and subduing demonic forces would ever give aid to the monster that had, at some point, been working with the son of the Devil to find and kill Badrick's own demon.

If someone had told him two days ago that he'd be doing this, Badrick would have laughed in their faces.

And yet here he was.

The clock read four in the morning, and Badrick hadn't slept for nearly thirty six hours. With no opportunity for rest, he couldn't help but feel an ever growing sense of frustration and rage towards the Ordinarius who had promised them information in exchange for shelter.

The six others that sat before him clearly felt the same; the way they worked on their consoles with sharp, frustrated taps visibly communicated their ire. Due to his fatigue, Badrick barely noticed as the agent on his far left spoke tensely into his microphone, and though he tried to tune in and listen, Badrick found it impossible.

He was only able to concentrate when a terrified voice shouted out of his earpiece, "NO!"

Having not expected the outburst, Badrick jumped almost entirely out of his chair. Shaking himself awake, he glanced around, embarrassed and hoping nobody saw him.

The one who shouted continued with, "Not until you get me!"

Betraying his rage at this unhelpful response, the agent roughly tore the headset from his head and threw it at the wall. He sat there for a few moments, staring at the remains of the equipment with wide eyes and breathing so heavily his shoulders rose and fell with each pant.

But then his anger appeared to drain away and the agent put a hand to his mouth with a sigh. "I'm sorry," he managed to whisper. "I can't even . . ."

Even as he trailed off, the woman positioned next to him placed a hand on his shoulder in a display of understanding, "It's alright," she said softly. "We're all prone to outbursts. You'd be surprised at how many headsets I've smashed in all my years."

Badrick couldn't help but feel responsible for everyone's shared stress. It was all because of him these agents were stuck on this case. *He'd* asked the Agent Commanders to be given command of the investigation, but even though he'd been delighted to have received their consent, Badrick never imagined they would give him a team.

Especially not one made up of senior agents, all far older than him and most undoubtedly frustrated to be taking orders from someone only at the tail end of his teenage years.

Badrick was in charge of these men and women. It was up to him to see the mission through.

And *he'd* failed to get their informant to cooperate.

Feeling like he should also say something, Badrick licked his lips and offered, "I once smashed apart London." He gestured to the mic. "This is nothing."

A breath of laughter escaped the agent's mouth and he turned to face Badrick, bringing his hands together in apology.

Deciding it was time to relieve his reluctant team of some of the strain he'd placed on them, Badrick beckoned for a microphone. He held it in front of himself, taking a breath to prepare, hoping he'd be able to remain calm even though there was no doubt the demon on the other end of the line would be most maddening.

Badrick placed the microphone over his hair just in time to hear a voice shout, "Come on!"

His voice full of sarcasm, Badrick asked, "Are you there, Dhornji?"

"I am," came the reply.

Badrick took a second to think. For two whole days this goddamn Ordinarius demon had senselessly dragged the Daemonium on a wild goose chase, never letting up and never fulfilling his promises.

They'd just about had enough.

"Listen, Dhornji," he spoke, trying not to let the fatigue show in his voice. "I promised we'd protect you, so trust us and tell me what you know about the New Evil."

Badrick clamped his eyes uncomfortably as the demon erupted with another tirade of curses and shouts, once more denying them any new information until he got what he wanted.

"Then stop hiding behind Lucikefer's energy and show us your position!"

"Not until you promise!"

Badrick suppressed the desire to also smash a headset, instead contenting himself with simply clenching his fists.

They'd tried everything.

Any and all diplomatic solutions.

But Dhornji was having none of it.

There didn't seem to be much else they could do . . . perhaps it was time to give in to the demon's demands. Badrick could see no other way to extract the required information from him. Of course, there was no guarantee Dhornji would provide them answers once he *was* in their custody.

In fact, Badrick had a horrible niggling feeling that this demand was just the first of many.

Badrick's face turned to stone. There was no way he'd let it get that far. If the demon didn't play ball once he was safe, then Badrick would *make* him talk.

He had ways of achieving this once people were within punching range.

And to hell with anyone who took issue with his methods. After what Dhornji put his team through these last two days, he did not care.

His colleagues appeared to read his body language, knowing before he spoke that he was going to issue orders.

"Well?" asked an impatient one.

Glaring at the woman for her disrespectful tone, Badrick sighed and told them, "He won't tell me anything."

"Still?" The agent's disbelief was somewhat unbelievable.

Yes, Badrick thought privately, sarcastically. *Of course 'still'.* He gazed wistfully at the ceiling, picturing the bed that awaited him several hundred stories up.

Would he ever see it again?

Trying his hardest not to believe that he never would, Badrick gathered his thoughts so as to make an intelligent decision.

When he failed, he looked to the agents for advice. "What do you guys think?"

The lot of them shared thoughtful, communicative glances.

Eventually, one of them sighed and said, "What else can we do? I say, bring him in."

With a nod, the woman on the far right uttered formally, "I concur."

"Me too," spoke another.

The other three agents—which included the impatient woman—were not so agreeable, pushing the idea that they could play the demon just as he'd done to them.

"But we run the risk of whatever . . . *horror* he is supposedly fleeing from catching up," argued the man on the right. "If the . . . What did he call it?"

"The New Evil," Badrick and three others said simultaneously.

The agent thanked them and continued. "If the New Evil gets him we won't learn anything new."

The man who earlier had allowed his anger to overcome him stated two simple words before Badrick could speak his thoughts. "He's right." He raised a hand to the ceiling. "Christ, look what this guy's minion did with only a week. If the New Evil is real, then we . . ." His head bobbed decisively. "We have to act now."

At the sight of the impatient agent opening her mouth to argue, Badrick sat straight and spoke up, cutting her before a dispute could start. "You're right." He was painfully aware that his decision would be the deciding vote, but ignored the uncertainty in his gut as best he could.

"Do you want us to gear up?" the man asked.

Badrick clicked his tongue and breathed, "Yes."

Nodding their understanding, Badrick's team jumped from

their seats and marched towards the exit. They would head for the armoury, Badrick knew, and from there await his arrival in the Main Hall.

The woman who sat on the far right lagged behind her colleagues, eyeing up Badrick's tired form with concern.

"Are you alright?" she asked him as the rest vanished out the door. Her hand picked up his and she regarded his pale skin with a frown. "You should sleep."

"I will when we get Dhornji here," he responded plainly.

"You're not a child anymore," she scolded him. "You're reaching adulthood and even seventeen year olds can't pull all-nighters like kids can."

"I'll be fine, but thank you," Badrick said as politely as he could, trying to ignore the awkwardness of being told he was becoming an adult by someone under his command.

The woman—God, he really should have remembered their damn names by now–chewed her lip thoughtfully. "Where's Operative Hood? His talents would be helpful."

The thought of Badrick's partner somehow dropped his mood even further, despite the belief he held that this was impossible. He felt his frame of mind plummet into a deep, dark hole, and his chest reacted to this with an unwelcoming stab of sorrow, which poked at his heart.

Without warning, he felt the nauseating need to cry.

Desperately fighting it, Badrick said in a controlled voice, "He's in his room . . . Someone who was his friend tried to kill us," he added when the agent frowned disapprovingly. "He lost Carla." When her judgemental expression refused to soften, Badrick said, "How would you feel if your husband died?"

That changed her tune immediately. In an instant, her eyes darted to the chair that originally sat the agent who now owed the Daemonium a new headset.

And with her face set in stone, she said, "Fair enough. I was too harsh."

Nodding briefly, she about-faced and walked briskly away.

"He'll come back soon," Badrick whispered, speaking only to himself. *But for now,* he finished in his head, *we have to leave him alone.*

chapter
TWO

The walls of Zale's bedroom seemed . . . *dimmer*.

The brightness they once boasted appeared to have drained away, leaving behind only a horrible, dead orange.

Had they always been like this?

Was the world always this dark?

It could have been. Zale barely remembered why he ever thought the colours of this existence were bright and beautiful when it was clearly a lie. After all, beauty and colour were signs of good—peace and tranquillity and lives worth saving.

But surely this was a deception.

He could see the truth now, because in no world where anything was beautiful could his Carla have been torn from his grasp so violently, so heartlessly.

It was evil, and nothing evil existed in a world of beauty.

So, it stood to reason, that this world was not dazzling at all; it was, in reality, a realm of hatred and cruelty and death.

It was *so* clear to him now.

This was the way the world was.

Or . . .

Zale was suffering from a state of mind that made the world appear desolate. A depression that clouded his thoughts and dulled his senses until he could only experience life through the bleakest of filters.

He'd known people who suffered like this. Those who'd loved and lost and could no longer understand happiness.

Or . . .

Those who'd loved and lost and were no longer blinded by the lie that was a beautiful world.

Yes . . . *That* was the truth.

There was no good here.

Zale's brain threatened to shut down as he came to this dreadful conclusion. As he sat on his bed, swaying slightly from lack of energy, he could feel the allure of sleep—nay . . . *hibernation*—tugging at his consciousness.

If only.

He coveted the ability to sleep.

Zale yearned to do anything but stare at his walls—they only reminded him of the con he once lived—and he deeply *wished* he couldn't see his empty bed in his peripheral.

The worst punishment the Universe could make him endure.

Zale could practically see Carla lying upon its mattress, as if her ghost had returned to spend time with him, her smooth, gorgeous, white skin caressed by the soft sheets.

How many times had she lain naked on his bed?

Zale had lost count.

He wished he hadn't.

People never remembered to memorise the truly important moments until the chance to do so was taken from them. This was the harsh reality of life; death would never really impact your being until it was thrust upon the people you loved.

And then you realised you'd taken everything for granted.

If only Zale had been prepared.

If only he'd known, he would have taken the time to force himself to remember. Used the intellect and the great power he *supposedly* had to sear the memories into his mind permanently.

If he was so smart he would've remembered every detail about his beloved.

It was too late to do it now and no new moments would come.

Carla would never lie on his bed again.

She was gone.

Ripped from him by an atrocious mutation of nature controlled by one who was once his friend.

Without warning, Zale felt a strange sensation on his hand, one he didn't immediately recognise. His following confusion was enough to pull his gaze from the wall and make him glance down to determine the cause of this stirring. He was surprised to find the splashes of a fresh tear glistening on his skin. He hadn't felt any liquid escape his eyes and he was under the impression that his cheeks were dry as a bone.

However, when he raised a hand to his face he felt wetness all over it.

Why hadn't he felt the tears?

What was this now?

Sensory failure?

Was his grief numbing him to the world in *every* sense of the word?

It would explain why Zale had no strength in his muscles. His entire body was limp and pathetic. No vigour existed within him and he wasn't sure it would ever return.

How could it when he felt *this* weak and useless?

For God's sake, even his demon appeared to have become feeble. Horas had not appeared to him since the day of Carla's funeral. Not manifested in the corner, not said a word, not even shared thoughts his way.

In fact, now that Zale was thinking on it, Horas felt oddly . . . vacant.

Thinly strung, one might have said.

Zale could barely sense his presence. Hardly felt the emotions that coursed uniquely throughout Horas' metaphysical form.

What was the demon doing?

Why was he ignoring Zale?

He deeply wished the demon would manifest. More now than ever, Zale needed to know Horas was there for him. No one else was good enough. Not another soul understood how he felt—not Badrick, not Reynolds—because they couldn't actually feel his pain.

Horas could.

And he was uniquely gifted among his kind in that he could understand these complex human emotions.

Zale was angry now; he needed a friend and Horas was ignoring him. It was only a small flicker of emotion buried beneath a dead numbness, but it was enough to finally make him move. Before, Zale had not the energy to call out to his personal hellspawn, but now, driven by anger, he raised his head to shout to the demon.

He did not deserve to be ignor—

A spark.

Tiny.

Barely worth mentioning.

But so entirely unrecognisable that Zale instantly stopped and stared unseeingly into the room. His skin began to tingle as this ember of demonic energy smouldered inside him, the tears on his face sizzling from the heat it generated.

It was growing.

Getting brighter.

Somewhere . . . inside his soul.

It wasn't originating from the bulk of energy that comprised Horas' existence. The demon's personal signature didn't resonate *anything* like this.

This was something else.

Something new.

Foreign.

Still, it was expanding, caressing his soul with each increase in size. Every time it touched him pain would stab at his chest, each time sharper than before. Zale clutched at his heart and groaned as a particularly prickly jab made him wince.

What was—

Without warning, the energy exploded.

Zale's muscles were unwillingly energised and he was compelled to his feet. He cried out as his bones heated impossibly from the power surge, his body growing hotter . . . and hotter . . . until his skin was searing damn near hotter than the sun.

The wetness on his face had long fizzled out of existence, only to be replaced by thick beads of sweat that seeped from his pours in waves. Growing panic filled him as this . . . *force* . . . tightened whatever grip it had on him, and he coughed, stumbling to the wall as his balance was lost. Gritting his teeth, Zale made for the door with the intent of getting help.

But, as he jumped forward, what he naturally expected to happen when he put his foot down never did. Instead of making contact with the floor, his foot simply continued descending, throwing him completely off balance. He fell, scorching arms flailing out in an attempt to break his fall.

Again, he never made contact with something solid.

And that was when the lights went out.

chapter
THREE

Badrick was always thankful for the sound proofing technology installed to each and every bedroom within the Daemonium facility.

As it worked both ways, it not only allowed him to cut out all sound from the outside, but to also stop anyone hearing any noise he might make.

And *that* was the most important thing . . .

Badrick's stomach was pulsing.

His ribs were convulsing.

And the heart within his chest was pounding ever faster as the anguished screams exploding from his throat practically vibrated the meagre belongings in his room. Hot tears splashed onto the floor as he fell to his hands and knees, his throat sore and strained due to the screeches of unadulterated sorrow that forced their way out.

One of his fists found a decorative vase containing a harsh looking plant. The power behind his supernatural strength smashed it on the spot, water and shattered pottery cascading across the floor, slicking the wood and cutting his hands.

Somewhere inside the distress, his subconscious chose that time to speak. Using recreations of the kind voices in his life—Zale . . . Reynolds . . . Carla—it alerted him that it was definitely time to get a grip. Breaking stuff was a sure sign you were going too far and if he wasn't careful Badrick would hurt himself.

Although in reality he possessed no control at this time, the imagined voices of the people he knew aided him in crawling to a sitting position, his back against the door. From there, he began to force deep breaths down his throat.

Despite the protests of his internal organs, he continued to refuse them the chance to convulse and, finally, the spasms relaxed and cool air flowed through his lungs at a steady pace.

Badrick reached up and wiped away the stream of tears that still painted his face, though, because his arms were still shaking, he only succeeded in poking himself in the eye. His legs were also twitching, so Badrick instead focused on stilling them.

As the after-effects of his emotional torrent started to fade, Badrick let his head rest against the door and stared up at the ceiling.

"That's the third time in two days, Daemnos," he whispered to nothing but the air. Anyone watching might have thought Badrick was mental, or perhaps about to die and hallucinating the afterlife.

However, he was talking to the monster hiding inside his soul.

When the demon prince didn't reply, Badrick scoffed. "You break me and now you won't fix me." Before he'd even finished speaking, he laughed at his own naivety. "Of course," he scowled. "You don't know how. You don't understand how emotions work."

This accusation was enough to finally spur a reaction from the demon. From within Badrick's soul, he shouted, *I brought your parents back!* His refusal to speak face to face did not escape Badrick's notice. *I knew enough, Baddie Badrick, to enhance bravery!*

"Knowing how something works is not the same as understanding it," Badrick spat angrily. "Reciting what you read in a book is not the same as figuring it out yourself. You think you're special. *'I understand humans'*. But you're just as stupid as the rest of your species."

He felt Daemnos bristle angrily and shuddered as the distinctive shiver of mental instability shot up his spine. The moment he felt it, Badrick felt bad for shouting at the Royal.

When Daemnos resurrected Badrick and, as a result, suppressed his emotional capability, he'd done it out of loyalty to Badrick.

He wanted him alive.

It wasn't the Royal's fault that he hadn't a clue how to work with human emotions. Arguing with him about it and creating a rift between them was not the right way to deal with the issue.

Daemnos was an odd creature; completely unstable, more evil than could be fathomed, and yet . . . strangely faithful. Whenever Badrick took the time to really ask him for help, if Daemnos could then he would, even if at first it seemed like he was hindering them.

With this in mind, Badrick's frustration drained and he relaxed. Forcing his aching muscles to push himself to his feet, he swayed slightly and placed a hand on the wall to steady himself.

Daemnos' anger eased when he sensed Badrick's regret. When before the energy that comprised his being buzzed and flexed, it now shrunk and relaxed, emitting soft waves of calm.

With his demon placated, Badrick stooped and retrieved the single-rifle he'd discarded in his rush. He smiled as he brought it close to his face, regarding the chips and kinks that made it *his*.

He could still remember the first time he fired this gun; a conveniently placed bullet that dropped a crazy, powerful Forsaken.

If only the round had killed the thing.

He felt a small, soothing smile play at his lips at the reminiscence.

Despite the horror he'd experienced at the time, Badrick had since matured, and, though he was no longer completely apathetic, his feelings on the Forsaken issue were still dramatically reduced.

He understood now why the Daemonium killed Forsaken.

After everything he'd witnessed since that day, he'd have been stupid not to have learned *that* lesson.

As Badrick removed himself from the room and made his way to the elevator, his mind began to cast back over the rest of his life serving the Daemonium. He thought about his training, the Forsaken, and the fight with Stefan. He pictured Lucikefer suffering in the Void, the Kalik's murder sprees and Charles' capture.

And he thought about this New Evil, and how deadly it promised to be.

Badrick could hardly believe that the Forsaken mission was only seven months ago.

Could that be true?

It was insane. So much had happened . . .

And he'd only been alive for a few weeks of it.

The night shift had started by the time Badrick arrived at the HQ. Although guards still patrolled and agents still worked, it was quieter than during the day, for which Badrick was thankful.

It helped him locate his team quicker.

They were waiting for him a small distance away, positioned by the door that led to the Gate. Their weapons were propped up either against their legs or the walls and most were checking their port-pads, perhaps updating them with useful information about the task ahead.

However, one of them was standing slightly apart from the pack, conversing with someone that Badrick was immensely glad to see.

Dominus Reynolds appeared to sense his approach, turning his way and bearing the smile of a father greeting a son.

"You look shattered, Varner," he noted. Badrick thought it a little hypocritical to say this; Reynolds' skin was white and he was swaying on his feet. He looked incredibly dizzy, as though he had just been smacked on the head. Clearly exhaustion wasn't catching up on only Badrick.

Reynolds continued, "Maybe you should let someone else take the lead."

"No," Badrick instantly argued. "I'm the one who dragged everyone in on this. I should be there too."

Reynolds offered him a respectful nod. "A leader leads by example," he grinned approvingly. However, despite his support, his expression quickly fell and he gestured to the team. "I wasn't aware the situation had gotten this bad. The demon really won't offer *anything?*"

"Not a thing. I don't think we have any choice but to do as he asks."

One of the team spoke up, "If this New Evil is as bad as Dhornji claims then we've got to go *now.*"

"I couldn't agree more," Reynolds stated. "Personally, I have no doubt in my mind that the threat is real. Charles clearly had a master—that is irrefutable."

"A master who brought Charles back a second time," Badrick added. "When I shot him."

"Which is supposed to be impossible," Reynolds sighed. "The

threat is real, agents. We need information and we need it now."

The team responded with sharp weapon clicks, a sign of respect among agents, and nodded their understanding. With that done, they indicated to one another and proceeded through the exit towards the helicopter that awaited them.

"I should probably get going too," the Dominus added privately to Badrick. "My Eminent—" He stopped himself, probably realising Badrick didn't understand what his *Eminent* was. "My *advisors* are constantly telling me I need to step back and be involved with the bigger picture."

"Haven't you always been concerned about the bigger picture?" Badrick asked, remembering all the times Reynolds helped them despite all common sense telling him not to.

Reynolds laughed softly at that. "Well, I like to think so. But I refuse to sit in an office like a bureaucrat and not get involved with the Daemonium's efforts on the ground. But *that's* what they don't like."

He sighed audibly and added, "However, perhaps for today, I should listen. There's a lot we must contend with."

Knowing exactly what Reynolds was talking about, Badrick didn't hold him up any longer, gesturing to the HQ in general and suggesting he get back to it. The Dominus clasped Badrick's shoulders with a manly grip and wished him luck on the mission, which Badrick gratefully accepted.

Then he departed, walking briskly past Badrick . . . and crashed straight into none other than Zale Hood.

"Dude!" Badrick called at the sight of his partner stumbling from the force of their collision. Being the larger man, Reynolds was more or less unaffected and swiftly acted to steady the blonde Enthraller.

"Hood?"

"How are you?" Badrick asked, striding up and grasping Zale's limp hand. Eventually, after much tugging, Zale tightened his grip and returned the gesture.

"I've been better," was the soft reply.

A strange sound squeezed out from between Reynolds' lips that suggested to Badrick he was trying to remain professional and suppress the sympathetic noises he wanted to make.

"I'm alright," Zale murmured, half smiling at Reynolds. "I'm just . . . I'm tired."

"You and me both," Badrick said, then instantly regretted it. Badrick couldn't begin to fathom the kind of weariness losing one's love would cause, so comparing their fatigue was downright inconsiderate.

However, Zale wasn't paying attention. His eyes were focused on something over Badrick's shoulder, his mouth slightly open, giving his face an inquisitive look.

"What's going on?" he voiced his interest.

Badrick did his best to explain.

"Nice plan," Zale chuckled softly after learning Badrick's intent to thrash the answers out of the demon once they got their hands on him. But the amusement didn't last; his eyes darkened and his expression turned to one of stone. "I should be going with you."

"No," Badrick instantly denied him. "You've been through a lot. Sit this one out."

"I've been sitting out for two days," Zale snapped. "I should've done a lot more already."

"I gave you a week, Zale," Reynolds interjected. "You shouldn't feel guilty."

"Charles was my friend. My responsibility!"

"And you did your duty apprehending him."

Zale let his head droop and his eyes stare blankly at the floor. He stayed that way for quite some time, long enough for Badrick to get worried.

Before he could query, Zale raised his head and relented with, "Alright, I'll stay here. But when you come back—"

Knowing where this was going, Badrick didn't let him finish. Inviting him to a fist-bump, he stopped him by saying, "You got it." Their knuckles knocked.

Even though Reynolds looked unhappy, Badrick figured that if Zale needed to work in order to process his grief then so be it.

At least he *was* grieving.

"I'll return the days," Reynolds sighed despondently. "You'll come back to the job tomorrow. In the meantime, Hood, go to bed. You'll need to rest for work."

After a breath, Zale said, "Aye, sir."

"Don't call me 'sir'. Christ's sake!" At that, Reynolds walked away, his hand lingering on Zale's shoulder until the moment it was forced to leave.

"He hates it when we call him 'sir'," Badrick chuckled. He slapped Zale on the arm. "Like he said, go sleep. We'll question Dhornji tomorrow." Hefting his rifle and pushing his helmet on, he added, "Together."

He expected Zale to either argue or do as he was advised, and so was naturally unsettled by his lack of response and the whiteness spreading through his cheeks, his eyes now oddly distant. "Zale? What's wrong?" He instantly rebuked himself. *Stupid question.*

Again, he failed to respond and refused to move until Badrick gave him a concerned nudge. Rubbing his fingertips over his cheeks, Zale finally focused on Badrick and said, "Something happened in my room."

"What do you mean?"

It was now that Badrick realised Zale was trembling and dread instantly shot through his chest. What had Zale so shaken?

"I was hit by energy. Demonic energy."

"You were attacked!?"

Zale shook his head. "No, it wasn't an attack, it was a message. Everything went dark and a voice spoke in my head." Zale's terrified eyes met Badrick's and he whispered, "The New Evil spoke to me."

Badrick took an involuntary step back, his own skin now whitening. "What?"

Zale nodded sombrely. "I heard his voice . . . here." He placed a tremulous hand upon his chest. "And here." Now his finger touched his temple. "I heard him laughing at me. He mocked me over Carla's murder."

Badrick's stunned and fearful body was quite suddenly overwhelmed by intense rage and he had to fight to keep his heart regurgitating his broken emotions a second time. Forcing himself to calm down, Badrick asked through gritted teeth, "How can you be sure it was him?"

Zale gave him an impatient look. "I *know* who it was. There's no faking what I felt when he spoke. I could sense Charles and the Kalik in his touch. Everything they did together, like catching a glimpse of his memories.

"He said that he'd sown distrust among the Daemonium and I would watch as my friends turned against me. He mocked our attempts to stop him.

"Badrick . . . he said we'd never get to Dhornji before him."

"The New Evil is going for Dhornji?" Involuntary air escaped Badrick's lungs, and he closed his eyes and tightened his fists. Their worst fears were confirmed. The New Evil knew that the Ordinarius had information and was going to try and prevent them from retrieving it.

They had to hurry.

"You must get to Dhornji first!"

Badrick placed another hand on his shoulder and said with

more confidence than he actually felt, "We will."

Zale nodded and stepped back so Badrick could leave. Wasting no time, he prayed to whatever gods were listening that his mission went well, and headed through the exit.

*

Badrick rounded the corner tensely, aiming his single-rifle into the darkness and wishing he could see more than ten feet ahead. Even with Daemnos' advanced night-vision, peering through this gloom wasn't the easiest thing to do and Badrick could only image how bad it was for his team.

He indicated for his team to advance cautiously. The coast was clear, he hoped, but you could never be too careful. If they moved too fast they could fall into an ambush.

Especially in the grounds of this ancient, ruined castle. In here, there were hundreds of places for an attacker to hide.

Badrick hadn't been aware these places existed in Britain anymore. For years, he'd been under the impression they'd all been demolished to make room for modern structures. France had châteaus still, with their penchant for public tours, but never did he think the same could be said for this sorry landmass.

"Clear," an agent confirmed. "Move up?"

"Go."

Badrick followed the team through an archway that pointlessly served as the entrance to the next room—the archway was the only remnant of the wall it had once opened up.

"Dhornji," Badrick breathed into his helmet mic. "We're here. Where are you?"

"In the grounds," was the reply.

Closing his eyes with frustration, Badrick took a breath and dumped his hatred into the act of gazing up at the starless sky, taking a second to wonder exactly when the ceiling of this castle caved in and where the rubble had gotten to.

"We were *just* in the goddamn grounds, Dhornji," he finally snapped. "You weren't there."

"Other side!"

The team moved out, darting expertly between cover. The fact that their quarry was also the target of what was supposedly the greatest dark power ever known was all too prevalent now they were out in the night. None of them could see very far—a power like that could easily sneak up, even on Badrick.

As they made their way around the castle ruins, Badrick heard Dhornji mutter something about hurrying up. He didn't bother replying, which only incited the demon to begin another tirade of hateful curses.

Properly pissed off now, Badrick stopped and instinctively placed a hand over the metal that hid his ear. "Would you shut up!" he snapped with barely repressed aggression. "We might not be the only ones out—"

Badrick stopped talking when Dhornji screamed.

A second shout of alarm dragged his attention to his team. He reacted just in time—as his teammate fell backwards, seemingly without reason, Badrick sidestepped and caught him, using Daemnos' supernatural strength to support the weight.

"What happened?" he demanded.

"Something flew over us. Pushed me back!"

Badrick returned to his comm. and hollered, "Dhornji!" The hellspawn was screaming even louder now, stopping only to choke on what sounded like his own blood.

Badrick made to run in the direction the screams were coming but was prevented doing so by a powerful, buffeting wind that almost knocked him to the ground. "That's it!" the agent shouted. "That's what I felt before!"

Badrick hadn't yet been close enough to detect the presence of Dhornji's demonic signature, but unexpectedly he felt it register in his natural sensors a split second before it spiked, several meters above him.

Invisible in the dark, Badrick couldn't see where it was coming from, despite scanning the sky with perfect night-vision.

From one end of the castle to the other, the energy soared, as though Dhornji had been ripped from his hiding place and dragged across the sky.

"Like a bloody comet!" an agent shouted in alarm.

"Back!" Badrick roared. He led the charge towards the helicopter, leaping over a fallen pillar in his haste. With swiftness years in the Daemonium had gifted them, the agents about-faced and dashed to his side as they barrelled in the direction of Dhornji's energy signature.

"Help me!" the demon screeched, his voice carrying in the wind. "Help me, please!"

"Dhornji!" Badrick responded redundantly.

There was no point in calling out to the demon. Not only was he clearly unable to respond . . . it was already too late.

The sound of flesh tearing pierced the night and with a sickening zap the demon's energy levels vanished, fading from this existence.

Over the radio, there was only silence.

The Ordinarius' body lay beneath His feet as He watched the tiny agents swarm around the grounds, searching fruitlessly for their missing quarry.

They would not find him.

After all, the demon was not where those ants believed he'd been taken.

He laughed as He saw the teenager push aside a rock and shine a light at the place Dhornji was *'supposed'* to be. When he found nothing, Badrick lifted the rock high above his head and threw it against the remnants of the castle walls. His howls of frustration and anger were even louder than the demon's screams had been.

Dhornji was, in reality, on the roof of the castle—or what remained of it, at least. Atop the highest tower, the pointless creature would never be found and *He* could see everything that unfolded beneath.

The agents would not see Him all the way up here.

He was completely unnoticed and entirely undetectable.

Invisible.

Satisfied with His evening's entertainment, He took his gaze away from the defeated Enthrallers and rolled Dhornji onto his back, taking great pleasure in witnessing the demon slowly begin to crumble. Dhornji could not exist as a physical entity—or as physical as an un-Enthralled demon could be—without the help of a greater power, and now that he was dead Lucikefer's lingering influence had lost its grip.

Without that external force, the Ordinarius could not remain on Earth, even as a corpse, and with his soul extinguished there was no place for the body to go.

So it simply fell apart.

Black ichor leaked from cracks that opened and spread across Dhornji's lifeless remains until he eventually exploded. The stone of the medieval castle was stained horribly by the mess, however no one would ever see it this high up before the rain dealt with the evidence.

Further amused by the continuing roars of anger from the powerful one below Him, He grinned at the sight of the agents leaving the scene to scurry back to the Daemonium, wrecked and defeated.

Victorious, He raised his head to the moon and bathed in the bright moonlight, imagining that he could draw power from the celestial body, growing strong from its rays . . .

Before snuffing them out and leaving the night to the whims of darkness.

He shuddered with excitement at the thought of nothing but black around him.

It was His.

All His!

Before, nobody could have claimed *darkness*. After all, it belonged to nobody—it was nothing but a consequence of lack of light. But with His arrival, the shadows of night and the dark had a new master.

More than that . . . the darkness *was* Him.

chapter
FOUR

The chaos within the HQ of the Daemonium was beyond anything Zale had ever seen before. Standing aside from the ruckus, he observed as agents darted left and right, looking panic stricken. Some were even butting into Army dealings, hoping to bolster their defences around the facility with more men.

They looked so panicked and ready to jump on anyone looking even slightly suspicious that Zale half worried they were going to converge upon his person, guns raised and shouting at him just for looking uncomfortable at their alarm. However, none of the Enthrallers nearby were charging him, so he figured he'd be alright to move through the Main Hall in search of Badrick.

Zale made his way through the herd, eventually pushing into the BCR. Inside he found a huge gathering of agents huddled around the main table. They were conversing in heated, hurried mumbles, all of their voices aimed in the same direction.

As Zale fought through the throng of people, being practically swallowed up the crowd, he realised they were looking at Badrick.

An Agent Commander was busy talking when Zale reached within earshot. In a tense voice, he had just said, "I'm putting more agents on the case. You're going to need the help."

Badrick nodded, his face sombre, his movements sagged and defeated. "Yeah, we do."

"How many agents can be spared?" the Commander asked the room.

"This is a powerful enemy we've made," someone commented. "We should allocate a decent number."

"Fifteen!" a voice suggested.

Another flustered derisively. "More like twenty."

"That's a lot of heads," the Commander said. "Might be too many cooks. But we need to get this done." He chewed his lip for a brief moment. "OK, Operative Varner, you and your partner will be reassigned to a team of twenty others. They are to be given access to the New Evil case files and you'll report to Agent Commander Julius Novak."

Badrick did not speak, only nodded his compliance.

Apparently grateful for the teenager's obedience, the Agent Commander reached his hand to shake and did not lower it until Badrick returned the gesture. "Speaking of your partner, where *is* Operative Hood?"

"He'll be back today," Badrick said softly.

"Good!" the Commander stated. "It's about time he lifted his head back off the dirt. He shouldn't be blamed just because his stupid friend was the villain. He's the best agent I've ever seen. Shut up and get over it," he added when a series of scornful snorts came from those nearby. "Accept it. He's better than you."

Zale knew that this man was only saying such kind things because he felt guilty; despite everything he'd done for them, the majority of the Daemonium, including this commander no doubt, had spent the last week or so shunning Zale for some of his past mistakes.

And many people were nothing but jealous that a *kid* was better at the job than they were.

They'd jumped on the *Hate Zale* bandwagon and then when it was later revealed that a friend from his past was the one who killed the girl that half the Daemonium could tell he loved, they let painful remorse run through them.

Through the throng, Zale saw the Agent Commander take off, leaving Badrick to stand alone inside a circle of consoles. He looked thoroughly worn and desolate, his body still sagging and with very little colour left in his cheeks.

Threading through the crowd of people, Zale approached him, speaking as he did so. "Badrick." His partner's head rose and their eyes met. "What's going on?"

After a moment's hesitation, Badrick spoke into the quiet that had ensued after the Commander's departure. "We lost Dhornji last night."

Zale let shock and dismay dominate his face. "Jesus!" he snapped. "What happened?"

For a long period, Badrick said nothing. In fact, it was becoming suspiciously quiet in the BCR and Zale had to suppress the urge to check on the people behind to ensure they weren't about to jump him.

The paranoia that the agents were going to give way to their terror and arrest everybody in sight was becoming overwhelming.

But then Badrick sighed, "I don't even know." He shook his head sadly, dejectedly. "I didn't see. None of us did."

"Did you sense anything helpful? A signature?"

Another shake of his head.

"Do you have *any* leads?"

"None." At that moment, Badrick's eyes flicked to his and bore into them imploringly. "We need you on this, dude."

"Of course. I'll . . ." Zale hesitated, gazing around the room at the flustered Enthrallers. "I'll get my uniform on then."

With that he turned his back on Badrick, the agents, the BCR, and wound his way to the Quarters Tower.

Badrick figured Reynolds would turn up sooner or later, so he wasn't surprised to see the Dominus striding in through the door that led into the Main Hall. Upon entering, the man's gaze cast about the BCR for several seconds before finally resting upon him. Ignoring the hurried demands of the Agent Commanders, Reynolds made a beeline in his direction.

"Badrick!" he exclaimed, and Badrick was immensely relieved to hear concern as opposed to anger. "Are you alright? Did it hurt you?"

"Well, it knocked me over a bit but I'll be OK."

"Christ." Reynolds covered his lower face with his hands and stared at the table in what appeared to be shock. After a moment, he asked, "You're certain Dhornji is dead?"

"I felt his life get snuffed out myself," Badrick responded bitterly, "and the scanners had so much practice trying to find his signature when he wouldn't let them that when he finally did there was no way to deny it when he died. The machines all back up what I felt . . . It's my fault," he sighed. Despite Reynolds' disagreeable huff, he continued, "I was tired. I was too slow. We got boned because of me. You should've chosen a better leader for the mission."

"Because it would have made *such* a difference," Reynolds spat sarcastically. "Don't be stupid, Varner. It's unnecessary. There was nothing anyone could have done. I've read the reports, seen the power levels at the site . . . Nothing could have been done differently."

Reynolds clapped his hands in front of his face, which made Badrick jump. The sharp sound surprised the melancholy out of him and, quite suddenly, he found himself more alert.

"I hear," Reynolds capitalised on his new focus, "that a larger team has been formed to work on the New Evil case. A 'think-tank' of sorts."

"Bloody think-tank," Badrick accidentally spoke too bluntly, but quickly reined it in when he remembered the authority of who he was talking to. "Yeah, they have," he said swiftly.

Giving him a shrewd eye, Reynolds said, "Alright. Now, what about Zale?"

"On his way."

"Good." With a roll of his eyes, Reynolds instantly retracted his repeated statement. "Well . . . not good, but . . . We need him." As he said this, Reynolds' pocket made a curious beeping sound, an incoming mail alert. It was so shrill that the noise itself somehow managed to communicate how urgent the message probably was.

"Damn it," he snapped, pulling out his port-pad. "Listen, I'm sorry, Badrick. I've got a Council meeting. We're still dealing with Charles' aftermath and all members are required."

"It's fine." Badrick half smiled, gesturing towards the door. He knew how important the Dominus' presence about the place was right now and he didn't like to think he was holding him up. Reynolds was gone in a flash, pausing only to express gratitude for Badrick's understanding.

Melting into the flurry of agents congesting the BCR, the Dominus vanished, leaving Badrick alone once again.

Badrick turned and leaned against the consoles, his eyes boring with despair into the graphs that detailed the New Evil's energy spikes. They were massive—so unbelievably strong, it was petrifying.

He decided to cast it from his thoughts for now. He would do himself no good by fretting over the danger the New Evil presented. He needed to be calm and collected, with his emotional state under control and his mind organised.

He needed to take a break and later he would look at the problem with fresh eyes.

Badrick just hoped the next day would bring fresh insight.

chapter
FIVE

Even with Badrick's attempts to focus on the New Evil case files that littered his computer monitor, the memories from the previous day kept hounding him, distracting him.

They would not stop.

He couldn't shed them.

In truth, this problem was probably due to his working the case; the more he thought about the New Evil, the more his mind cast back.

The sheer power . . . scorching . . . overwhelming . . . consuming . . . It had been awful to witness.

Ruminating darkly on Dhornji's murderer sent shocks of apprehension down his spine and reminded Badrick just how similarly terrified the rest of the Daemonium had become in the aftermath. Even Zale looked tense when he learned of what transpired.

And learning of the strength of their enemy was probably what led Zale to do what he did next.

Badrick *had* somewhat worried Zale wasn't ready to work, especially on a case which involved the death of his beloved Carla. It would've been better to start him on something simpler—ease him in—because with every new step they had to take their minds inevitably kept going back to Charles and what he did.

It wasn't healthy for Zale to dwell on what that bastard did to Carla and, despite his earlier resolve, Badrick now believed it better that he be given time to grieve without constantly reliving her death.

And with so much to remind them all of the painful past, it hadn't surprised Badrick that yesterday, when Zale returned, his melancholy visibly threatened to overtake him every time the teams talked on the Resurrected and his relation to the New Evil.

There'd been no chance to call Zale back as the tears fell and he fled the BCR, knocking people out of his way as he went.

And when Badrick learned of where he ended up, he'd been far too scared to go after him.

Ordinarily, the Daemonium probably didn't stand for the unprovoked assault of the residents within their jails, and no doubt punished the Enthrallers behind the assailment.

But *this* was different.

The dreadful events that occurred weren't some horrific accidents happening on some far off mission. It wasn't one of those things that stirs pity in your stomach but otherwise leaves you unaffected, because you can't empathise with something you never saw.

No . . . It happened on home turf.

It had been personal, violent and eye-opening.

Everyone witnessed Carla's murder and *everyone* saw Zale's grief firsthand.

As a result absolutely nobody had the heart to walk in and detain Zale when he smashed his way into the prisons and started turning Charles' face into a mashed-up mess.

It had been truly terrible to behold what was left of the Resurrected after Zale got his hands on him and Badrick had prayed that it was going to be a one-time thing. Unfortunately, the sight of Zale rampaging through the jail's door again this morning had dashed that hope to smithereens.

He was undoubtedly still in there now, hurting Charles over and over again, astray in the loneliness of sorrow and wrath.

Around Badrick, as he desperately tried and failed to cast aside his concerns and concentrate on the case files beneath his gaze, BCR life continued near uncaringly. To no one's surprise, the demonic world cared nothing for their troubles or the losses they'd incurred. No matter how much time they needed to heal, the world would always continue to spin, demon attacks included, and the agents of the Daemonium had to deal with them.

To his right, a soldier relayed information to the agent higher-ups about the Kalik he'd encountered at one of their outposts in Scotland. Badrick's ears pricked ever so slightly when he announced he'd come into contact with an electrical Kalik blade. From what the soldier was saying, it appeared that, without their undead leader, the beasts were using the weapons without care.

The higher-ups seemed happy about that; apparently the faster the demons used the weapons the quicker the agents could confiscate every last one.

As the group patted their backs on a job well done, Badrick caught a snippet of conversation on his left. Averting his attention that way, he realised an agent and operative were working on the same case as he.

In fact, now that he was listening in, it seemed the entire BCR was engaged with the New Evil issue in some shape or form. Whether it be dealing with the aftermath of the Kalik Crisis, trying to determine who this new threat might be, or just conversing on Charles' reign of terror, everyone present was radiating disquiet about this newest menace.

This realisation sent volts of gut-wrenching anxiety through Badrick's stomach.

The whole time Badrick had been employed at this facility, nothing had taken the *entire* Daemonium's attention. Even when the son of the Devil was discovered to be living within the building itself, only a portion of the BCR was dedicated to preventing his plan. The rest of their organisation still had other work to be getting on with.

Not this time.

No . . . All it had to do was show the Daemonium its power and the New Evil had everyone terrified. It was evident in the way the air hung in the room as if it no longer circulated, everyone's breaths scared still. The tension could have been cut with a knife, it was so tight. Badrick could see genuine fear in everyone's eyes, and he didn't have to look deep to find it either.

In the space of one night, the New Evil had them paralysed with fear.

Well, he thought to himself, doing his best to take a deep breath, *at least we have a better chance with so many of us fighting him*. The moment he finished this reflection, he scoffed; Badrick wasn't sure who he was trying to convince, but seeing as he was thinking this privately it was likely he was saying this for his own benefit.

As he berated himself for trying to make himself feel better with injudicious beliefs, he was quite abruptly torn from his musings when he realised there did seem to be *one* person that wasn't spending all his time shaking in his boots and worrying about their destruction. Hearing the sounds of a conversation utterly unrelated to the New Evil, Badrick couldn't help but allow his concentration to die entirely and tune into the discussion.

His astonishment was heightened when he realised he was listening to the agent detective Zach talking to the Dominus, who had apparently snuck in some time before without Badrick noticing. Reynolds was trying to get the detective to focus on an investigation Badrick didn't have any knowledge of. The General was careful to keep his words low, perhaps not wishing the agents around to learn he was personally giving Zach a case.

Badrick didn't know what all the secrecy was about, but it certainly caught his interest.

However that was when Zach said in an arguable tone, "I want to work on the New Evil team," and Badrick's brow furrowed. How severe was the detective's arrogance that he felt confident in refusing a case given by the highest authority himself?

Badrick half expected Reynolds to smack him, but the Dominus remained calm and spoke in diplomatic tones. "Agent, you understand the seriousness of what's happened, aye?"

"I do, sir, but——"

"We still have jobs to do," Reynolds stopped him. "And what happened this morning *cannot* be ignored. We need a competent team to tackle this immediately."

Zach appeared to try his best to calm down. In a far more respectful voice than before, he attempted again to convince Reynolds that he was best suited for the New Evil investigation. "I get it, sir," he added when Reynolds only looked on with impatience. "A hundred soldiers dead in an instant is bad. But I really think my skills would be best suited investigating——"

At this point, it was clear Reynolds had had enough. With his eyes now stern and his voice edgy, he snapped, "This is an order, Zach. You and your team are to discover who set these explosives and aid the field agents in apprehending them."

Though Zack looked prepared to resume his fight, there was no ignoring what had just been said. The detective had received a direct order from the Dominus and Zach was not only honour bound to follow it, but duty bound as well.

With the face of a man frustrated beyond comprehension, Zach nodded aggressively and turned his back on Reynolds, marching away in the direction of a small huddle of people who sat in the corner, murmuring indecipherably.

"Bloody child of a man." Badrick almost jumped as the sharp whisper struck his eardrums and he caught the sight of Reynolds leering his way.

Damn. The Dominus knew Badrick had been eavesdropping.

Thankfully, it didn't seem as though he had any interest in doling out punishment. In fact he didn't look even slightly upset and from the way his tired face managed a small smile, Badrick got the feeling he'd simply took the opportunity of Badrick's eavesdropping to rant to someone.

In return, Badrick smiled and nodded his agreement.

Another whisper slunk into his ears, easily audible thanks to his supernatural hearing. "Where's Zale?"

Too far from the Dominus to speak without shouting, Badrick tore a piece of paper and sadly wrote the answer.

And in grim silence, he held it aloft for Reynolds to see.

Prisons.

The hollering from his victim's mouth made Zale cringe. However, despite the abhorrence at his own actions coursing through part of him, a more dominant area of his soul couldn't help but feel glee at the sight of Charles' agony. Despite a small voice telling him this was wrong on so many levels, Zale could see the beauty in making his enemy pay for every single one of his actions. It was as though the screams of the agonised Resurrected painted colours in the air for him to see, beautifying the world with justice finally served.

The only thing that ruined Zale's enjoyment was when Charles took a break from blaring and begged him to stop. Zale had to rein in his anger whenever the Resurrected did this; his cries of pain were like a drug to him, justifying in his mind the need to keep delivering powerful blows. Whenever the Resurrected stopped to beg for mercy, Zale felt the little voice of guilt grow louder.

Charles' face vanished beneath Zale's fist for the hundredth time, only to re-emerge even bloodier than before.

With a shrill scream, Zale took the moment to demand, "Who's your master!?"

Some distance away he could sense the jailor, Malcolm, flinching with every echoing smack, every crunching of bone, and cringing at the shrieks exploding from Charles' lungs.

The Resurrected coughed up blood and squeaked, "I don't know!"

Behind Zale, Horas watched with a tentative mix of horror and pity. Although he was clearly sickened and dismayed by the brutality his Enthraller was indulging in, the demon could do nothing to hide the fact he felt sorry for Zale and just could not bring himself to intervene.

Beneath Zale's feet, the pathetic creature repeated the same words as before. "I don't know!"

"Liar!" Zale screeched so shrilly his own ears popped. He pulled back a fist to pound Charles anew, however stopped before striking. Hovering there for a number of seconds, Zale quite suddenly dropped the Resurrected and whirled away in a display of emotion. Crying tears all over his uniform, he stumbled out of the cell and charged through the prison corridors, past stunned captives and a trembling Malcolm.

He did not stop until he emerged back into the Main Hall.

People witnessing his explosive arrival did their best to pretend they hadn't seen a thing, moving away quickly, sheepishly, and conversing in hushed whispers. Zale ignored them. He simply found a bench and fell upon it, smacking his forehead into his palms and blanking out the world around him.

It wasn't hard to see Zale's trembling form from where Badrick sat. *Everyone* had heard him burst into the Main Hall and Badrick now had a perfect view of his partner quivering in distress on a white plastic bench.

"Aw man," he whispered in pity. Looking at Zale, Badrick wasn't sure what the wisest choice was—stay away or go over. He had no idea what to do in this situation. Did Zale need to be left alone, or did he need support, even if he didn't necessarily want it?

"Damn it, Zale," Badrick muttered to himself. "I'm not a goddamn therapist."

How could Badrick possibly know what to do? He'd never found himself in a situation before where someone felt immense emotional distress and as such never gained any experience in helping those who suffered.

In the end, Badrick tried to consider what *he* would want Zale to do if he was the one in that much pain, and though they were two very different people Badrick could only go on his instinct.

With his decision made—but second guessing himself with every passing second—he jumped from his chair and meandered past the agents, aiming for the door. It slid open to allow his exit and Badrick hurried in Zale's direction, frantically thinking of what to say.

He was already aware that he'd not thought this through.

Zale didn't seem to be crying when he arrived. No tearful sobs could be heard from under his hands and, though he was still trembling, Zale's arms lacked the wet streaks tears would have left behind.

"Zale?" Badrick whispered gently. "You alright?"

Badrick hadn't expected his partner to raise his head, let alone do it as fast as he did, so the sudden appearance of electric blue eyes came as quite a surprise.

"No," was the reply.

Already out of things to say, Badrick hesitated for a few painful seconds before doing the only thing that came to mind.

He sat next to Zale and joined him in staring at the far wall. They rested there in silence for quite some time, neither saying a word nor looking at each other. The entire time, Badrick desperately scrabbled for bolstering words and though he sometimes thought of great openings he could never find a way to finish them.

With every passing second he was excruciatingly aware of how awkward he was making the silence and that, every time he failed to comfort Zale, he was successfully furthering his brilliant and promising career at *Useless Friends Incorporated*.

And as much as it should have been Badrick, Zale was the one to finally break the uncomfortable silence. "I'm sorry." His voice was damn near heartbreaking; shaky, dispirited, woefully tired. It was the voice of a man who had lost everything.

"It's alright," Badrick managed to say.

"No," Zale half croaked. "It's not alright. I have to be better than this."

"You lost Carla. You're allowed—"

"No!" This time Zale shouted. "If I can't put it aside and find the bastard who had her killed, then what kind of a person am I?

How does that honour her memory?" When Badrick didn't respond, Zale scoffed, "Badly, Badrick. Badly, is how it honours her memory."

Not wanting to annoy him further, Badrick simply nodded his understanding. "What'd you wanna do?"

Zale turned his gaze away and sat back. His fingers danced edgily over each other and his foot tapped repeatedly on the floor as his leg bounced with agitation. "We're going to catch the New Evil," he finally declared.

"Any idea how to do that?" Badrick said, only just managing not to scoff. He didn't want to appear pessimistic in the face of his partner's newfound determination, but he couldn't quite muster the same confidence. Already, Badrick had heard agents commenting on how even the Devil never caused this much distress among the Enthrallers, and from what he could gather *that* monster had almost torn the place apart.

The New Evil had barely made a move and yet it had the Daemonium in the biggest panic ever seen.

How could they stand a chance against a power capable of that?

In response to his dull negativity, Zale asked, "Well, what do you have from the crime scene?"

"Nothing," was Badrick's only reply before adding, "Some off-the-charts energy readings but nothing else."

"Left behind by the New Evil?"

"Well, no one else who was there is as strong as that!"

"*You* were there," Zale frowned. "At full power, Daemnos' energy goes off the charts. How do you know it wasn't you?"

"Because apparently the BCR invented a way to chart Daemnos' power levels," Badrick sighed. "After I came back to life."

"And even with these extended capabilities, the scanner went off the charts?"

"Yep."

"So it must be the New Evil." Zale clicked his tongue. "You can't identify it? Can't track it?"

In a robotic voice, Badrick recited what the Agent Commanders told him: "There's not enough there to find the energy's fingerprint."

Zale tutted angrily and punched his own leg with irritation. Badrick didn't blame him for his anger; they would need the New Evil's energy signature in order to track his real-time location.

Even then it wasn't guaranteed, Badrick had heard, but at least it was far better than nothing.

Zale's furious eyes turned Badrick's way again, and he snapped, "Have they digitally rendered the readings and dissected it to catalogue each individual particle?"

"I don't even know what you just said."

Another tut. "You digitally separate every single iota of the reading and scan them all before uploading the data to the archive so that when the target shows up again there's no confusion as to whether or not it *is* them. That way we can detect them instantly with no room for error, that is unless you've put that data in the wrong feckin' folder. It's what we always do."

"Maybe what *you* always do," Badrick chuckled drily. "The rest of us trust our machinery."

Zale sighed, his shoulders visibly sinking, and he rubbed his forehead with his fingers. "Alright, we need to do that first. I would suggest asking Zach to help us. He's the most qualified at handling the software."

"I thought *you* were."

"I have other things I want to focus on."

Badrick shook his head, saying, "Doesn't matter, anyway. Zach isn't on the case. He wants to be, but Reynolds told him to focus on something to do with bombs."

Zale's brow furrowed in a merging of interest and frustration. "Bombs?" He quickly rolled his eyes and spat, "Whatever. Do it anyway."

"Seriously?"

"With this corner the New Evil has us crammed into I think we'll need as many people as we can convince to help. Besides . . ." A tiny smile played at his lips. "If we give Zach a little opportunity to contribute to the case he might be grateful for it. He *might* be more willing to co-operate in the future."

Despite the obvious manipulation this entailed, Badrick couldn't help but agree. Having Zach's help must have *some* benefits somewhere—despite Badrick having not yet witnessed his apparent worth—and taking steps to ensure he was less argumentative would be greatly advantageous.

They couldn't afford his interfering. When they had nothing but Kalik and Resurrected to hunt, Zach's failures weren't too bad—Badrick and Zale more than made up for them—but this time there was no room for it.

None of them could afford mistakes anymore.

"I see your point."

With his requests accepted, Zale contentedly nodded and offered a sad smile. Seeing his attempts to remain calm and avoid falling into hysterical heartache, Badrick felt extremely humbled. Even with his grief, Zale was trying his best to work effectively.

It also doubled as a cause for Badrick's humiliation and shame when he himself proved incapable of the same composure.

He never meant to say what he said next, but something stirring in his gut compelled him to stammer, "I'm scared, dude."

Badrick winced as the words escaped his lips. *Damn it!* Now was not the time to demand Zale's attention on his prissy feelings. The man was grieving, for God's sake. It was incredibly insensitive for Badrick to make it all about him.

But it was too late now.

He'd spoken.

They couldn't pretend he hadn't.

And with Zale's inquisitive eye urging him to clarify, he eventually sighed in defeat and whispered, "The New Evil scares me."

"He's just like every other scum," Zale argued sharply, his eyes angry and his face determined. "We'll get him just like we did Charles."

Still speaking in whispers, Badrick gently shook his head and spoke, "You weren't there. You didn't feel his power. It was . . . Goddamn, it was terrifying."

Zale appeared to be lost for words. "Um . . ." he hummed uncertainly. "It'll be alright."

Unsatisfied with this response, but aware that he'd been just as useless only minutes before, Badrick decided not to comment. He slapped a heavily forced smile on his face and shook his head dismissively. "Yeah, you're right. I'm just being stupid."

Which wasn't a total lie—the New Evil may have been frightening but Badrick had an awful suspicion that his increased terror levels were related to his broken emotional control.

"Look," Zale said tightly. "Go get Zach to do as I suggested and upload the readings into the scanner's New Evil file. Then meet me back here."

Badrick obeyed his partner without question. Standing, he straightened his jet black uniform and made to leave. As he departed, over his shoulder he checked, "What're you going to do?"

Zale sat forward, placing his hands on his chin, his eyes misting over.

And in a quiet voice, he said, "I need to think it over, but I might have something."

chapter
SIX

Badrick could not have moved faster.

Upon hearing that his partner might have a new lead his energy levels appeared to shoot through the roof. He darted back into the BCR with the speed of a hunting cheetah, pursuing the agent detective Zach.

Just as Zale had predicted, once Zach understood exactly what he was being invited to participate in, he grasped the opportunity with eager fists. He practically jumped to a console and began work immediately, abandoning his team without so much as a *'Hold on a sec'.*

"Listen," Zach said quietly so no one else would hear, "Badrick, thanks. I mean . . . I know I'm not supposed to be getting involved but I really want to help, and you giving me the chance—"

"Hey, don't look at me," Badrick said hurriedly, uncomfortable with the older man virtually kissing his boots. "It was Zale's idea."

Though clearly stunned at this news, Zach's chest puffed up with proud self-importance.

Badrick left him to it, only stopping to double check that the man understood his task. Then, with everything hopefully in hand, he dashed back the way he had come, finding Zale exactly where he left him.

"So?" he demanded impatiently, being rewarded with an annoyed look for his impudence. "Sorry," he sighed, just as edgily. "I'm just . . . What've you got?"

"First," Zale stopped him, "what of Zach?"

"Yeah, he's doing it," Badrick confirmed. "The next time the New Evil makes a move we should be able to at least detect the energy."

"But not the New Evil's signature," Zale cursed angrily, gazing down at the floor in thought. ""We need to rectify that."

"Any ideas?" Badrick pressed.

"No." Zale shook his head, but at the sight of Badrick's suddenly crestfallen face, he raised a swift, reassuring hand and hurried to say, "But I want to discuss something with you." When Badrick had calmed and gave the green light to proceed, Zale chewed his lip and draped his left arm over the back of the bench. "Think back, Badrick, to when we apprehended Charles."

"OK."

"Well?" Zale gestured for him to speak. "What happened?"

The moment wasn't hard to recall. Badrick could remember every detail clear as day, as though it occurred only moments ago. "He gave himself up."

"Right." Zale clicked his fingers pointedly. "Why?"

Badrick blinked inanely, a little stunned at the simplicity of this question. "Er . . ." he hummed idiotically. "I don't know . . . We had him surrounded."

Zale scoffed somewhat derisively and roughly shook his head. "No, we didn't. He had a retinue of guards." Placing a finger to his temple, he urged, "Think back. What *really* happened?"

"OK . . ." Badrick cast his mind into the past, thinking more carefully this time, plucking every little detail from the corners of his brain. He could see the Kalik in his mind's eye, gibbering madly with bloodlust as they formed a protective circle around their master. The Resurrected himself stood gloating from within the ring, confident in his control of the beasts.

But then he recoiled, fear stricken, and promptly gave up on the spot.

And that was it.

No . . . wait . . .

That *wasn't* everything.

What was that thing Charles said after?

. . .

Badrick's eyes refocused and in a shocked voice, he murmured, "His master abandoned him."

With a matter-of-fact nod of his head, Zale clapped his hands once. Badrick was concerned to see that, when before he'd looked determined, Zale now seemed downright worried. "His surrender," he said, "makes me uneasy."

"Why?"

"If Charles had just been abandoned, then surely the idiot would've fled, right?" Zale's worry seemed to deepen, his brow furrowing further and his fingers twitching anxiously. "But no, he gave himself up. Why would he do that?"

Badrick scoffed confidently. "Because without his master backing him up he knew we could take him."

Again, Zale shook his head. "The Kalik were still Charles'

army. He could have escaped us, no problem." That bothered look on his face grew to a matchless intensity, and he said the words that plummeted Badrick's spirits into sickening darkness: "I don't think he was abandoned. I reckon he was ordered to give himself up."

Badrick licked his lips—they'd become remarkably dry all of a sudden. "Why would he do that?" he croaked, the fear of what the answer could be now scratching at his insides and threatening to dissolve him into outright panic.

Zale shrugged, exhaling, "The only logical reason is that the New Evil wants him here."

Badrick decided it was time to sit down. Moving his quickly weakening legs in the general direction of the bench, he only just made it before he collapsed upon it. He winced at the pain that shot through the bones as they slammed into the bench and he rubbed his legs as his mind raced over all the possible reasons the New Evil might want to plant Charles inside the Daemonium.

"But—" He stumbled over his own words, coughed, then tried again. "Why did he have Charles do all the Kalik stuff if all he wanted was to get Charles captures? If it was me, I'd have done it days ago."

"To make us think we did all the work," Zale answered immediately. "To make us think it was all down to how clever we were." He shifted on the bench so he could face Badrick, lowering his voice so that none of the passers-by heard them. Badrick was thankful for this—he really didn't want to start a panic, so the less who knew about this, the better. "He led us on a merry chase," Zale continued, "killed a few of us, made us frightened and desperate the only way you can—with a world ending event. Forming a Kalik army was a genius move. It sent us into spiralling panic.

"Then he finished up by making us believe we caught the bad

guy ourselves. If Charles had been too easy to find we would've been suspicious. Admit it, you would be too.

"But Charles slipped up. He told me in the Apos base that it was the plan to make it as hard as possible, leaving evidence here and there and quietly ensuring we worked it out. With that testimony alone, I think this deduction is justified."

"I think so too," Badrick said, still rasping.

"Except," Zale raised an emphatic finger, "the New Evil didn't tell Charles he was going to be captured. You saw his reaction. That was as much a shock to him as it was to us. The New Evil left him in the dark until the last moment."

Badrick forcibly cleared his throat and uttered, "Maybe to make sure Charles never accidentally gave away the plan."

Zale grinned as much as he was able and slapped Badrick playfully on the chest. "Now you're getting it." The half smile vanished faster than it had appeared, replaced with concern once again. "What do you think?"

Badrick could only shrug and shake his head. "I wouldn't have thought of this myself but I bet you're right." He let his head rest against the wall and gazed up at the ceiling. "You're always right about this stuff."

"I think we're lucky Charles is an idiot, actually," Zale snorted. "If not for his big mouth, I don't think I'd have gotten this far."

Badrick didn't have an answer. Clearly he had more faith in Zale's skills than Zale did, but didn't know what words to use to help him believe in himself. Instead, he devoted his breath to saying, "Now we just have to figure out *why* the New Evil wants Charles in here."

"Why don't we go ask him?"

His head snapped in his partner's direction, his eyes wide with disbelief. "*Now?*"

"Why not?"

"You just finished caving his skull in," Badrick spluttered animatedly, his body shooting up from the bench.

Zale's blue eyes grew so angry they practically snarled at him. "Well then," Zale hissed, "he'll be more open to our questions, won't he?" He too stepped from the bench and reached to put his hands on Badrick's shoulders. "I'm sorry for the way I've been acting but we can't let that interfere with our investigation. Charles could be a ticking time bomb and we *need* to question him now."

Despite wanting to, Badrick knew he couldn't stop his partner from going back in there. In spite of believing it professionally wrong to bother Charles only an hour after Zale's abuse, Badrick took step behind his partner and grudgingly kept his mouth shut as they entered the prison.

At the end of the day, Zale was right . . .

They *did* need to do this now.

Malcolm was very reluctant to allow them entrance for a second time so soon. After Zale's last incursion into his domain, he'd apparently charged out without giving thought to his actions. Zale had left the cell completely open, leaving Charles free to escape. Having not been warned before he saw Zale speeding away, Malcolm had experienced a moment of panic as he'd thundered back up the corridor, expecting the Resurrected to be running from the cell.

Thankfully, Charles was still too wounded to even consider the idea of leaving and Malcolm was able to re-engage the shielding of his prison without hassle.

Still, it had been unwarranted stress and the jailor was extremely unhappy about it.

Zale did his best to apologise, which at first only served to annoy Malcolm. As Zale issued offers of regret, it seemed as though the jailor had no care for what the excuses were. Eventually, however, after much huffing and puffing, his anger slowly ebbed and his expression softened. Although reluctant, Malcolm accepted Zale's apology before finally granting them access to Charles' cell, sending them off with a warning that if *anyone* assaulted one of his prisoners again, then the Agent Commanders—nay, the bloody *Command Council*—would be immediately notified.

"Hellfire will rain down upon you! *Entiendes?*"

Badrick couldn't help but grin a little at this ominous, yet ludicrous warning as they trudged into the Resurrected's cell.

Upon entering, the man they came to question flinched awfully. Badrick noted that Charles had yet to leave the corner Zale had probably beaten him into, and winced at the sight of his bloodied body.

"Jesus," he whispered. The dreadful markings were everywhere. His clothes were torn and his face was in bits.

"Don't hurt me!"

It was hard to remember that this was a nineteen year old sitting before them and not a petrified animal. The way he whimpered and retreated as far into the wall as he could reminded Badrick of an abused puppy.

"We're not going to hurt you," Zale snarled, his teeth bared in what was undoubtedly barely restrained anger. "So long as you tell us what we want to know."

Badrick was going to interject and remind them all that no violence could occur this time, but he was stopped by the look on Zale's face and, despite hating himself tremendously for doing so, forgot about speaking.

The truth of it was that they were more likely to get answers if Charles thought he was still in peril.

I'm an awful person, he thought privately, believing it without reservation; just because something might be slightly necessary didn't justify it being done. He felt wretched. Zale may have been emotional—his anger was so great he couldn't readily be blamed for the things he did—but at this current time Badrick was not.

Although he was still saddened by all that had happened, he believed he was in his right mind.

And allowing this course of action to continue while fully comprehending what he was consenting to made him feel *evil*.

Thoughts he hadn't dwelt on for months came rushing back to his head. Concerns over morality and what should and shouldn't be done. What was justified and what was just cruel.

Had Badrick allowed himself to become what he'd always hated?

"My question is simple, Charles," Zale spoke, tearing Badrick from his uneasiness. "Did you surrender on purpose? Did the New Evil plant you in here?"

The only thing that left Charles' mouth was the same thing that the records told he always replied with. "I don't know!"

Badrick hurriedly placed a hand on Zale's shoulder to stop him lunging forward. It wasn't hard to see that refraining from doing so was taking the full amount of the veteran's self control and Badrick wasn't entirely convinced he had it maintained. "It's OK," he whispered, low enough so only Zale could hear. "Don't resort to violence."

"Why not!?" Badrick's eardrums almost burst from the sheer volume of Zale's roar. "This scum killed Carla and tried to make me think everything that's happened is because of me!"

Badrick managed to calm him by gently pulling him to the side and facing him away from the crouched Resurrected. Taking the lead to give Zale some time, Badrick said, "Charles, we have to know what's going on. Help us out and we'll help you."

"I don't know!"

Badrick sighed in defeat. He didn't need to spend the next hour questioning the pitiful man before him to understand *nothing* would change, no matter how long and hard they tried.

"This is a waste of time," he muttered. "He won't talk."

Charles recoiled and screamed with terror as Zale raised his face to the air above and roared with such aggravation Badrick was surprised the light bulb above didn't shatter. Ignoring the ringing in his ears, he spun Zale around so he could look him in the eye.

"That's not helping." He glanced briefly at Charles. "We need to figure something else out."

Though it took him a while to calm his breathing, Zale eventually nodded.

Trying a new angle, Badrick stated, "Your brain is big as a planet. There must be something we can think of." He turned Zale to look at the quivering Charles. "Think. Why would the New Evil put him here?"

"Why don't *you* figure it out?" Zale retorted, his voice *so* bitter.

"*Zale!*" Badrick understood there was still anger coursing through his partner's veins but now was not the time for unhelpful rejoinders. They needed to work together, so in order to get the ball rolling Badrick tried offering a suggestion. "Maybe he's here to get inside information?"

He knew it was a stupid proposition, but in a way that was a positive thing. Zale responded better to stupid ideas than he did clever ones; a feasible suggestion usually set him on a path of anxiety if he thought it was possible, but he could scoff at ridiculous proposals and set his mind working on arriving at a better one simply so he could stick his tongue between his teeth and playfully call you an idiot.

As it turned out, Badrick's bargain paid off. With the ridicule Badrick predicted, Zale mocked, "From inside a prison?"

"Maybe he's getting info from you," Badrick deadpanned. "Maybe he's relaying how badly you're taking everything."

Zale didn't acknowledge the teasing jibe. Instead he frowned and asked, "Why would the New Evil care about me?"

"Why did he choose Charles?" Moving past the rhetoric, Badrick offered another suggestion. "Maybe he wants to make sure you aren't going to find him."

"I doubt the New Evil believes any of us are competent enough to catch him."

Badrick tried one last time. "Maybe Charles has a bug."

Zale's perplexity was palpable. "What?"

"A bug, you know?" Badrick awkwardly mimed having a device attached to his chest. "What if he's leeching information from our hard drives?"

Apparently, this wasn't as stupid as Badrick expected because Zale's face instantly fell with overt panic. For a terrible second Badrick thought he might have hit home, and before that moment ended he managed to play out several horrifying scenarios in his head involving their data being stolen and the New Evil murdering them their sleep.

But to Badrick's great relief, Zale suddenly shook his head and said, "No . . . Impossible. He was searched and x-rayed. No tech exists on or in him." He thrust a finger in Badrick's face and snapped, "Don't scare me like that!"

"Sorry," Badrick breathed. "I didn—"

"Wait!" Zale's eyes once again widened and his eyes hazed over as he tumbled into the swirl of his own thoughts. When he remained staring blankly at the wall for several seconds, Badrick urged him to share his musings. "A bug," the electric Enthraller continued as if he'd never frozen. "Not a machine . . . We're not dealing with the KG-bloody-B here but . . . This is a demon we're dealing with . . . Dhornji!" he suddenly bawled, making Badrick jerk in fright. "Dhornji said the New Evil is the king of all demons, so what are we talking machines for? Demons don't use machines. We're not fighting something with human ties. Nothing with human ties could possibly be a power like the New Evil."

"Where are you going with this?" Badrick questioned.

Zale didn't answer that question and Badrick coughed when a sharp finger jabbed his chest. "Go to the Medical Wing," Zale commanded. "You remember that machine Melody used on me?"

"Yeah?"

"Don't bring that one."

Badrick almost punched him. "What—"

"In the box with a triangular label, grab the tool next to the one Melody used. It looks similar but has two handles with a trigger each. Got it?"

"Two handles with a trigger each," Badrick repeated. "I'll be right back." He made to leave. "Er . . ." he suddenly added, grinding to a halt. "Stay calm."

Badrick hurried as best he could and it didn't take him long to reach the Medical Wing. However he grew highly agitated when he failed to locate the box with the triangular label. He found square labels, circular labels, rectangular labels, goddamn hexagonal labels but none of what he actually desired to find.

That was aggravating enough, but his dismay only grew when he tried to track down Melody the medic for aid and discovered she was deep into a ten hour surgery.

Bawling with frustration, Badrick was forced to explain his needs to a dusty, grim-faced medic who looked like he was only days away from ending up on the table himself. His requests were met with much denial at first and it took a good eight minutes to get this unhelpful coffin-destined fool to assist him. Only because of the convincing from a group of much younger and far friendlier doctors did the aged medic decide to even point Badrick in the right direction.

Horribly aware that too much time had been wasted, Badrick decided to forget to request permission to remove the equipment from the Medical Wing. Grabbing what he hoped was the right machine, he hefted its weighty bulk and evacuated as fast as he could.

By the time he finally got back, Zale had long lost his already thin patience.

"How long did that take!?!" was what Badrick received as a welcome back. Not wishing to keep his understandably intolerant friend waiting any longer, he handed over the machine and stood back as Zale got to work.

"What's this going to do?" he asked warily, suddenly noticing just how much like a weapon this machine actually was.

"It's a scanner," Zale informed him. "A special kind of scanner that'll emit a pulse into Charles' body and send back what it sees."

"What are you looking for?"

"He's here for a reason," Zale declared. "What you said about bugs may've been wrong but you were close. Our enemy is a demon, so in place of a bug, what would a demon always work with?"

Badrick knew a lot about demons and understood a great deal about their behaviours, thanks to the information imparted by Daemnos.

So when he rifled through his head in search of what a demon would always work with, he came up with what he knew was the only right answer.

"Demonic energy."

Demons *were* energy. It was everything that made them up; powered them, shaped them, enlivened them. It was all they knew and understood and a power such as the New Evil would no doubt be the same.

"There's some kind of energy attached to him, isn't there?"

"That's what I'm going to find out."

Zale pressed the barrel of the tool into Charles' chest, perhaps a little harder than was necessary. Charles choked as it jabbed him, but otherwise did not move, perhaps too scared to anger Zale further.

Making sure the device was steady, Zale gripped the two handles, his fingers hovering over the triggers. Badrick heard him whisper, "Priming charge," and watched as he yanked the left trigger. Then, with a jolt that made Charles jerk, he pulled on the right and Badrick sensed the supernatural pulse shoot through the Resurrected.

Whatever might have been stuffed into Charles was so well hidden that nothing was returned on the first go. Zale cursed as he fiddled with the controls and recalibrated the machine, refusing to give up. He repositioned the device and primed it, then fired a second pulse. The Resurrected squeaked as the energy pounded him at lightning speeds, but did not move this time.

This might have been the reason the machine now glowed brightly with a positive result.

With a triumphant grin, Zale snapped, "There!"

"You were right." Badrick clapped his hands together and drew closer for a better look. "What is it though?"

"No idea," Zale murmured. His gaze was transfixed on the little screen, his fingers meddling with the controls so fast Badrick struggled to keep up. "I can't identify it. I can't even locate its exact position. It's very well hidden . . . I think . . . I think what we're seeing here is radiation."

"Really?"

"That's what it looks like," he confirmed. "Whatever's inside him is so strong that, even though it's well hidden, it's radiating out."

"Residue leaking from the hiding place?"

"Aye, but I still can't find the source."

"OK . . ." Badrick breathed. "Well . . ." How should he

continue that sentence? "At least we managed something."

Zale puffed air in what might have been a humourless chuckle. "Yeah," he said, "but what the hell is this energy doing?"

chapter
SEVEN

"Please, Operative, explain it to me one more time."

Badrick sighed with a tiredness he never thought possible as Zale also breathed impatiently, and began reciting what he'd already explained twice. As his partner began at the start for a third time, Badrick knew that if they made to do this a fourth, someone's patience might just snap.

Of course, he had to remember that he couldn't be *too* angry at the other agents for needing the explanation more than once. They were required to compile their data correctly and doing so whilst listening was probably not the easiest thing to do, especially with the speed Zale talked.

To Badrick's right, his partner spoke in tense bullet-points.

"Badrick and I found foreign energy inside Charles. At first we didn't know what it was, or even *where* it was."

"It had been hidden," Badrick added.

"By someone with skill."

"But," someone said slowly, "you *do* know now?"

"Only the where," Zale told them. "When we failed to locate the energy, we decided to use any and every scanning device we could get our hands on."

"That seems highly inefficient," a man with grey hair hummed disapprovingly.

"We had no other ideas," Zale admitted solemnly. "I've never seen anything like this before." He threw a restless hand in Badrick's direction. "*Daemnos* hasn't ever seen this before."

"We were pretty desperate," Badrick tutted at the man's continued dissatisfaction. "You got a better idea?"

"Your desperation is understandable," a woman named Rebecca Hauler stopped the grey haired man from retorting. When he had closed his mouth, she indicated for Zale to go on.

"Eventually," he said, "we got to the Soul X-Ray. That's when we found the source of the radiation."

"Please, forgive me, but this is the part I don't understand." Agent Commander Julius—their team leader and the man who called for a repeat of Zale's findings—put his hands together apologetically. "Explain it to me in terms I can understand."

"Sorry, sir," Zale uttered respectfully. "First of all, you have to understand I'm not one hundred percent on this. I can only give you what I think I know."

"That's alright, Operative."

Taking a deep breath, Zale continued. "The anomaly of energy is inside Charles' soul. I know . . . " he added at the looks of disbelief from the people grouped around. "That's impossible. Enthraller or not, a foreign energy jammed inside should have blown him to pieces."

"So why hasn't it?"

Zale sat forward and made a fist, lifting it high enough for all to see. "Think about what our souls are like. If you were to try and put demonic energy into a person's soul, they'd explode." He spread his fingers apart. "They're not just capable of containing it. You can't jam something into a space that is already occupied, right?"

"Right," echoed the room.

"But Enthrallers are born with a hole in the middle and *that* is where our demons reside. We don't know how it happens but we know why."

Hauler spoke then. "It's to ensure that the demons exist in a space not occupied *by* our souls, but inside. It's the loophole that ensures we exist."

"We don't explode because the energy isn't technically existing in the same space," Zale nodded, "which is something we'd never be able to handle, demon or not. We can live with the radiation that leaks into our souls, even use it, but we'd never survive the source of that energy existing within the same space."

Agent Hauler raised a hand to grab their attention. "And you say what has been done to Charles follows a similar science?"

"Yes!" Zale exclaimed excitedly. "Charles is a Resurrected. Not just that, he was dead for over four years. He was nothing but bones. How much *stuff* that had to be rebuilt by his resurrecter is hard to think about."

"That's not unusual," Hauler said softly. "That's how it works. Anyone can be resurrected, as long as the majority of the skeleton is there."

"My point," Zale emphasised, "is that he was dead for so long that jamming his soul back in was not a flawless process. Now, we already know that Resurrected have messed up souls. Being brought back so violently has a habit of tearing them. Not in the way a Forsaken would, and not like the demonic fissures that give us our powers. No, these are massive fractures, all over the soul.

"And in someone who was dead as long as Charles those cracks are going to be *huuuuuge!*"

The expression on Hauler's face changed to one of comprehension at these words. She raised a hand in Zale's direction, the action communicating her understanding, and whispered, "The foreign energy is in the cracks."

"Right." Zale smiled his relief that someone finally understood him. "Charles isn't exploding because this energy isn't occupying a space that's already filled. It's been expertly woven into the cracks caused by his resurrection.

"Now before any of you argue," he said quickly, spreading his hands in the group's general direction to silence the people whose mouths were now open, "I understand that it shouldn't matter. It's still a foreign power. There may be space, but it's still sourcing from his soul, not a demon, and just because his Enthraller soul is modified to accept a demon's energy doesn't mean he should be capable of holding foreign power in his own soul. He should die.

"But because Charles *is* an Enthraller *and* a Resurrected—"

"A Powered Resurrected," Badrick chipped in.

Zale nodded, tapping Badrick on the shoulder. "He's got two different types of demonic energy buzzing about inside him so he's more than used to existing with this stuff within him."

Julius now spoke. "His soul is designed to contain a demon *and* his body is fuelled by the toxic radiation that keeps him alive."

"Un-alive," someone quipped.

"All these factors give him a kind of . . ." Hauler hesitated, trying to find the right word, "immunity?"

Zale placed his hands on the table and sighed dramatically. "As I said, it doesn't matter if you're an Enthraller or normal human, our species cannot withstand demonic energy sourcing directly from our souls. We *must* have the space and the energy *must* come from a separate entity that resides in that space.

"But in this instance, with these circumstances . . . " Zale sighed again, this time in astounded awe. "They're walking a very fine line. They're finding loopholes no one ever theorised could have existed.

"But it works."

With comprehension finally dawning on everybody else, a wave of revulsion and concern was now flowing around the table. Badrick felt a cold tingle go through his spine at the sight of it and shivered uncomfortably, blustering as he wiggled in his seat. He much preferred when the older Enthrallers were professional and stoic, because when they displayed the same anxiety that he felt it sent tremors of dread shooting into his heart.

His skin white and his expression cold, the head of their meeting asked, "How did the New Evil do such a thing? How did it know how to do this?"

Zale shrugged. "I'm sorry, sir, I don't know."

"What's this energy doing?"

"As I said before, I still can't tell you."

"We haven't got a clue," Badrick laughed humourlessly, his voice attracting everyone's attention. Some smiled sympathetically his way, which he appreciated, though others glared impatiently, as though they expected him to know the answers without fail.

"We need to discover the energy's purpose," Hauler called around the table. "It could be doing something right now and we'd never know. It *has* to be our number one priority." She looked imploringly to their team leader.

"I agree," was the reply from the majority of those present.

"You know," someone piped up over the simmer of concurrence, "the New Evil could'a made a fatal mistake here. Energy is what demons are made of. If we can figure out what this energy is doin' we might be able to figure out who it belongs to."

"You could be right," said Hauler. "I think—" She was stopped by a worryingly disagreeable hum from the agent on her far right. "Did you have something to add, Kelly?"

Clearly, from the way she shook her head, Kelly was reluctant to speak, but at the friendly pushing of her colleagues, she eventually sat straighter, wiped her mouth and voiced her concerns.

"Doesn't this seem a little too easy?"

"How do you mean?"

"Well, this *was* easy," Kelly breathed. "It's been a circus around here, nobody knows what they're doing, but we found this energy with little effort. I mean . . . I don't know, I just worry."

Her words resonated with Hauler. Badrick could tell from the way her face fell and she began fiddling with the pen between her fingers. Ink began to spread in lines on her hand as she clumsily scratched her skin with the tip every time she flipped it.

"What do you all think?" she enquired of the table.

"She might be right," someone said. "We might be falling into a trap."

"And you?" The question was directed to Zale and Badrick.

This time, Badrick decided it was his turn to take the reins.

Most Enthrallers only had to worry about fighting other demons, or making sure that their own didn't run amok and hurt people. It was all action, action, action for them. But Badrick was uniquely experienced in dealing with the personalities of hellspawn. He'd spent months in the Veil with nothing but Daemnos' raw personality for company and his knowledge and memories for entertainment.

And though he was aware that Daemnos' memory was a little sketchy compared to what he first believed, Badrick had confidence in the millennia of experience the Royal shared with him.

It was this self-confidence that led him to say, "Demons might be intelligent but they have a never ending knack for underestimating the human race.

"Emotions are an important part of how we work. I've seen it a thousand times. Yeah, they get in the way sometimes, but they give us a certain . . ." He trailed off, unable to find the right words. His hand flicked in the air impatiently as he fought to continue his sentence.

"Je ne sais quoi?" Zale suggested.

"A certain *je ne sais quoi*," Badrick grinned, "that make us special. Demons lack that human part when it comes to . . . well, doing anything. Demons are powerful things, but they make mistakes a lot.

"I bet with all that power, The New Evil suffers from an ego that's bigger than the sun."

"Did you hurt yourself with all those big words?" Zale muttered his way.

"Bite me," Badrick chuckled.

Grinning himself, Zale spoke to the room, "What my esteemed colleague is trying to say is that the New Evil's hubris is a detriment to himself."

From the number of heads that bobbed at these words, many appeared to share this sentiment.

However, Julius glanced down at his papers, holding up a finger to get their attention. "That may be, but you gave us details of your investigation into the Kalik. You wrote that, before you discovered Charles, you believed your perp knew all about you, Hood, specifically because his every action appeared to be aimed at threatening you."

"And then it turned out to be someone who *did* know you," Hauler stated. "An enemy that understands you as well as Charles would recognise the threat you create. More than any of us, you pose the risk of discovering the New Evil's identity. That's a fact I begrudgingly admit, and if I'm humble enough to, so might the New Evil. He could know how clever you are and is trying to lead us astray.

"This whole thing with the energy could be a ruse."

Zale nodded his understanding of their comments, his lower lip disappearing behind his teeth as he chewed at it mercilessly. "I hear what you're saying," he eventually spoke, "but I think we're safe."

"How can you be sure?"

"*Charles* knows all about me, but there's no evidence to suggest the New Evil has any idea who I am at all."

"The New Evil chose Charles," Kelly spoke up. "That suggests something, surely."

Zale spread his hands across the table and pushed himself out of his seat. Rising above the others in the room, he took a moment to stretch before spinning to pace back and forth. "I've been thinking on this," he said. "If the New Evil chose Charles, it was because he knew of his connection to an Enthraller inside the Daemonium, right? Meaning..." He let the sentence hang unfinished so someone else could finish it.

"He knows you exist," the team leader stated, "and therefore might know much about you."

"It *does* raise some worrying questions," said Hauler.

"I don't think it does." Zale ceased his incessant pacing and faced them again. "I think the New Evil was searching for a way to take the Daemonium down. He needs us gone. We're the biggest threat to a demon that threatens the world.

"No, we don't know what he wants but we have the capacity to find out. No one else in the Universe can boast that."

"That's true," someone commented.

"I think the New Evil struck unexpected gold," Zale told them. "The link that Charles shares with Badrick and I is unnatural. It's not normal. Lucikefer really messed up in its creation and something that powerful and *that* broken is going to leave traces.

"Powerful demons are attracted to sources of demonic energy, even if they can't absorb it. We all know this. I believe that the New Evil sensed the traces left behind and when he investigated he realised what he'd found. Then, when he brought Charles back to life, he got double the reward."

After a moment of uncertain silence, Hauler eventually said, "You mean the fact that Charles can read minds."

"And paralyse us whenever he wanted," Badrick added.

"All of a sudden," Zale continued, "the New Evil had his most powerful weapon. The fact that it linked to me and Badrick was little more than unlucky coincidence, thanks to bloody Lucikefer."

The team took a few moments to deliberate on this, communing with one another in low murmurs. Badrick and Zale waited patiently, thumbing the table as the group conversed and debated.

Finally, after much muttering, Kelly reintroduced Badrick and Zale to the conversation with the words, "Could Charles have told his master about you?"

"The New Evil might still know about you," Hauler said. "He could have told him everything."

Sensing an opportunity to jump in, Badrick stopped that train of thought with, "You're forgetting about the demonic ego. I doubt the New Evil believes *any* human, even an Enthraller, could be smarter than him. I bet he paid no attention even if Charles did tell him anything important."

"Would you stake your life on that?"

Commander Julius had not spoken with an argumentative attitude, so Badrick endeavoured to response in a similarly respectful manner.

"No," he laughed truthfully. "But I trust my demon's experience. This is what it's telling me."

"I side with my partner," Zale said confidently, clapping his hands together. "If you need proof, think about every demon the Daemonium has ever fought."

"Lucikefer thought Stefan's willpower wasn't strong enough to keep him contained," Badrick recalled. "He thought he could break free whenever he wanted and he lost everything because of that mistake."

"The Devil was killed because he believed Mawr and Reynolds weren't strong enough," Zale reminded them. "Not powerful enough to beat him in a fight, not smart enough to out-think him."

The agent sitting on Badrick's immediate left nodded assertively, his expression a sheen of self-assurance. "Aye!" he called. "Some of them may be smart, but you've got to admit, all across history demons have underestimated us and we've been victorious many times because of it."

Another wave spread across the table, but it had a much more positive vibe than the last.

However, out of the blue, an agent who had kept quiet the entire time raised a hand and spoke over them. "What about the link? Does Charles still have access to everything you're thinking? If so, he could be in contact with the New Evil right now. They might know everything."

A couple of people allowed panicked exclamations to escape their lungs and, to Badrick, it looked like they were about to lose the meeting's occupants to uncontrollable alarm.

Before it could get out of hand, however, the head of their team demanded calm, saying, "Charles is locked in the deepest corner of the prisons. Any demonic energy trying to get in or out won't. The link might not be severed, but it *is* choked."

Badrick was glad to see the worrisome faces relax and he too settled back into his seat. The panic had spread quickly it had startled him like a deer caught in headlights.

Unfortunately, Zale ruined their returned composure by saying, "He may be blind to our thoughts in there, but it's entirely possible that Charles *is* in contact with the New Evil. I bet our prisons can't hold that power back."

"Which means he might know we found his energy," Kelly whispered fearfully.

The nauseating anxiety swelled within the room once again, and the agents began talking hurriedly in hushed whispers.

In her attempt to keep everyone calm, Hauler called over their voices, "In that case we need to work fast. Of course, as Operative Varner said, the New Evil might be under the impression we won't figure him out, so this panic could be unnecessary." Her eyes darkened. "Regardless, we are going to prove him wrong. Zale, Badrick, you *have* to figure out what this energy is doing."

"Understood."

Julius sat back in his chair and ran his hand through his hair. "Makes you wonder," he exhaled. "If the New Evil is *that* powerful then what's stopping him from just storming in and killing us all?"

"Depends on what he wants," Zale responded bluntly.

"Hmm," the man nodded.

"What about Charles?" Hauler asked him. "What should we do, sir?"

"My first instinct is to interrogate his demon," the Agent Commander responded. "We won't be able to maintain contact for long but we could get *something*. However, I don't want to run the risk of the New Evil hearing something we can't afford for him to hear."

"Plus he's clearly a pathological liar," Badrick found himself adding, memories of his interactions with the Resurrected flooding his mind. "I don't think we can trust anything he or his demon says."

"Badrick's right," Zale spoke. "Charles is a great manipulator. He's capable of making you believe complete lies." Badrick saw his eyes go cold and angry. "I've let him trick me into believing his lies before, and I don't think he's ever told the truth in his life. I don't believe we'll get any information from him."

Julius nodded sombrely. "For now we leave Charles in his cell. Let him rot there for his crimes. No one goes near him lest his mind-reading powers catch us off guard. Everyone in this room is to *stay out* of the prisons."

"What are the rest of us supposed to do in the meantime?" Kelly asked the room.

"We return to our assigned duties," said Julius. "Scan detail for New Evil energies, patrols guarding from potential attacks, think-tank meetings to find a way to defeat him." The team leader prodded a resolute finger onto the table. "We're going to stop this son of a bitch."

"What about when we find him?" Zale asked. "How do we fight something that powerful?"

"We'll figure that out when we get there," Hauler advised softly. At a nod from Julius, she collected her papers and offered a smile to the room. "Meeting adjourned. Good luck, everyone."

chapter
EIGHT

Zale led the way as they departed the meeting room, through the automatic door and down several staircases until they eventually emerged onto the second lowest walkway. They strode across, moving from one end of the Main Hall to the other.

Badrick was so focused on following Zale to wherever the hell he was leading him that he entirely failed to see his partner grind to a halt, and as a result very nearly crashed into his back.

Narrowly dodging this outcome by twisting and falling into the railing, Badrick tried to catch a glimpse of Zale's face to discern why he stopped.

The only thing he managed to see was what he recognised as severe impatience.

"This is taking too long," Zale stated, before, without so much as a warning, grabbing the railing and throwing himself off the bridge.

"What—" Badrick watched as he plummeted to the floor and expertly landed on his feet. From there, pushing back surprised Enthrallers, Zale made his way into the BCR and vanished from sight.

"For God's sake," Badrick muttered, unsure of what to think of this behaviour. Nevertheless, eager to catch up, Badrick did the same, shouting, "Watch out below," as he fell.

Zale was already hard at work on a console by the time he found him again.

"Dude, you're so impatient," Badrick chided him. "What's wrong with walking?"

"We need to hurry," Zale retorted snappily. "No time to waste."

With unease growling in his stomach at the sight of Zale's uninhibited behaviour, Badrick knew he had to say something. This couldn't continue. "Zale, man, look . . . I know you want revenge, but you're gonna tire yourself out. Don't rush it."

Zale turned a glare his way. "No time to waste," he repeated, speaking slowly, and with a little hostility.

Badrick wanted to argue. This new version of Zale was not cordial, and honestly Badrick greatly wanted his friend back. He knew that Zale was grieving and acting rashly because of this, but he wished he would calm down.

As selfish as it was to say, Badrick needed the confident genius that first greeted him into the Daemonium.

But Badrick had no idea what he could say to bring back his best friend. He had no more words, no comfort to offer and no advice to impart. *Maybe I should have been a therapist. That way I'd know what to say.* He sighed internally, ensuring to refrain from doing so physically. *Why am I so goddamn useless?*

Zale was printing sheet after sheet of information while Badrick was privately chastising himself for being an awful friend. It only took a quick glance to see that it was data concerning the energy within Charles' soul. When Zale was done, he grabbed the sheets, separated them into three neat piles, and then roughly stapled them with unnecessary venom.

Collecting them together, Zale handed the papers to Badrick.

Confused, Badrick asked, "What are we doing?"

"Divide and conquer," Zale responded. "The Council is directly involved with this investigation and needs to be updated on our progress. I was hoping you could do that for me."

"What about you?"

"I'm going to make a start on the energy," Zale informed him. "Meet me in the lab when you're done, OK?"

Although he wasn't exactly pleased about being demoted to a mere mail boy, Badrick didn't argue as he took hold of the wad of papers. *Someone* had to do it and seeing as Zale was the only one out of the two of them who understood their technology, there was no real point in allowing Badrick to help until he was needed.

And so, with a grumble of laziness, he reluctantly trudged back through the BCR door and aimed himself at the ramp that would eventually lead him to the Council's lair.

He found who he was looking for relatively quickly, and before he had really managed to explain what was happening the papers were snatched from him. Standing there impatiently, Badrick waited as the highest ranking of the Command Council perused Zale's case notes, frowns of worry creasing their foreheads with mounting intensity. Kevin, in particular, looked absolutely appalled at what he was reading.

"How did they manage this!?" he practically screeched, his wide eyes transfixed on the page. "Even with these cracks, his soul's been exposed to a direct source of energy. Charles should die."

Quill clicked his tongue and said, "I would imagine a level of resistance is involved.

Kevin turned squinted eyes towards the Agent Commander before the lines around them softened and he muttered, "You mean . . . Of course. Charles is also an Enthraller. So—"

"He's also a Resurrected," Quill accidentally spoke over him. "Living with various kinds of demonic energy isn't alien to him."

"He's got a kind of amped resistance," Kevin groaned. "He's stronger than us un-cracked humans."

Quill turned his attention to Badrick. "You should bring the team's attention to this."

Badrick was saved having to reply by Reynolds. "Turn the page," he said bluntly.

Frowning curiously, the Council Eminent did so.

There was a brief moment of silence before Kevin exclaimed, "Oh, for God's sake."

"Operative Hood has already theorised this." A small smile had appeared on Quill's face.

Kevin, on the other hand, threw his wad of paper on a nearby chair with disgust. "I know the Daemonium figured things out for itself before Zale came along, but sometimes it feels like we never did anything without him." He crossed his arms and sighed. "Were we always this inept?"

"He makes you feel that way, doesn't he?" Reynolds chuckled softly. He too folded his papers back and let them rest upon a chair.

"He's like the new recruit in the office who becomes the go-to-guy and everyone forgets how to do their jobs," Quill smiled.

Rubbing his hands absently, Reynolds looked around the room—stared at the potted plants nearby, glanced at the waiting room chairs, watched a moth flutter by a vent—and breathed heavily.

"What're you thinking?" Kevin asked him, noticing his extended silence.

"I'm not sure," was the honest reply. "I don't know what to do here."

"That's unlike you," Kevin said at the same moment Quill uttered, "No one does, Dominus."

It amused Badrick that the person he chose to respond to was not Kevin, and what he said was entirely unexpected. "Don't call me Dominus like that, Dennis," he growled a little aggressively. "You know I hate it."

"Sorry, Daniel." Quill's grin widened, and Badrick got the distinct feeling that Quill was playfully annoying him with his title on purpose.

Perhaps a method of lightening the unrivalled stress Reynolds had dived into the instant he took charge?

If that was true, Badrick actually felt a large amount of gratitude towards Quill.

Someone had to stand by Reynolds' side during this difficult time. Whereas Badrick did believe one hundred percent that the man deserved the respect and seniority the position of Dominus afforded him, there was no call for dumping him in the middle of the greatest crisis on the first day.

It wasn't right.

It wasn't fair.

In fact . . . none of this was fair.

How could this happen?

How could a decent man like Reynolds be put in such a dangerous position?

He was now the leader of the Daemonium.

The primary target for any villain who wished to tear them down.

Why had Reynolds been the one to be put in this situation? Badrick desperately wanted to know.

How was this fair!?!

Starting so quickly Badrick didn't have time to prepare, a familiar sharp sting jabbed him in the heart. His hand shot to his chest, his face creasing in pain. "Oh no . . ."

His words alerted Reynolds to his suffering. Alarmed at the sight of his wretched face, the Dominus queried with concern, "What's wrong?"

A pressure was starting in Badrick's stomach.

His heart was hammering.

His chest, heaving.

"Oh, not now." When he spoke, his voice cracked and wavered.

"Badrick?" Reynolds stepped towards him, arms reaching out. "What's wrong?" he repeated.

"I gotta get outta here!" was all Badrick could say. He sharply turned left, then right, desperately searching for the exit.

Of course, it was far too late to locate the way out. His mind was fogging. He couldn't concentrate. He could barely focus on where the door was despite having walked through it only half an hour ago.

He didn't know what he must have looked like, but he imagined he was giving the impression of increased anxiety. This assumption was proven when Reynolds asked, "Are you having a panic attack?"

He was rapidly losing ground against the pressure in his head, struggling to keep his mind lucid. Stumbling into the wall, he almost fell to the floor from the dizziness overwhelming his senses.

"Come in here." He felt a hand direct him somewhere to the left. The lights dimmed confusingly, and when he glanced up he realised Reynolds had moved him into the Council boardroom. "Stay here," he ordered the others before rushing in and closing the door.

He tried to approach Badrick, but unfortunately that was when the pressure could no longer be contained.

With a great scream of sorrow, Badrick lost the battle to hold back his shattered emotions and broke apart in fitful sobs. He dropped to his knees and grabbed his hair tightly, practically yanking it from his scalp as he screamed and screamed and screamed.

The shock this display no doubt left Reynolds in was probably immense; there was no way the man could have predicted this was going to happen. For a moment he could only stare, stunned, as Badrick writhed in distress on the floor.

But then he seemed to recompose himself and, in a flash, was by Badrick's side, trying to get a hold of his arms and shouting to calm down. His attempts to pacify Badrick continued for several minutes, but when it was clear none of it was working, Reynolds desisted and did something Badrick never predicted.

He pulled Badrick in close and hugged him tightly.

The sudden proximity of a warm, comforting body came as a shock to Badrick's system. It was such a jolt that it brutally interrupted his sobs, Badrick's breath catching in his throat. He wasn't completely soothed however, and it took several minutes for him to completely relax and regain control of his body.

Even so, the attack of emotions ended far quicker than any previous assault and before he knew it he was being rested on the floor with his back against the wall. Reynolds crouched down and took place beside him, waiting for Badrick's gulps for air to completely subside.

"That was awkward," he muttered, gazing at Badrick. "But my dad taught me that trick," he added softly, as Badrick's sorrow gave way to unbearable embarrassment. "If someone's crying uncontrollably, a sudden hug may be a gamble, but if it works, it'll work well." Reynolds' eyes briefly glanced at the door, as though he were making sure no one was about to wander in. "Do you want to tell me what that was all about?"

Badrick was extremely resistant. The moment Reynolds made his offer to listen, Badrick's mouth instinctively clamped shut and his mind closed off any and all possibility of sharing *anything*.

Yet Reynolds' piercing gaze was like some kind of magical key that was capable of unlocking even the most rusted of locks.

And to be honest, there was no point hiding behind his walls anymore.

Reynolds had seen everything.

So Badrick divulged everything he'd been keeping hidden, speaking of the moment Zale opened his eyes to his suppressed emotions and then when they were shattered completely by Carla's death.

"And I'm scared," Badrick added when he was done. "Like . . . all the time. I've got all this power but the New Evil has got me terrified."

"It's alright to be scared," Reynolds said kindly. "To be scared is to be human."

"Not like this." Badrick roughly shook his head in vigorous disagreement. "I can barely move, I'm so afraid."

"Don't think you're alone in that." Reynolds placed his hands on his knees and gripped them tightly. "A lot of us feel like this is the end. Whenever the New Evil decides we're done . . . we'll be done."

Badrick didn't know what to say to this. He didn't want to tell Reynolds that made it worse—that he needed everyone to be brave for him. That would have been incredibly selfish.

"Your broken emotions, as you put it . . . " Reynolds wiggled to get more comfortable on the floor. "I think they simply mean you're healing."

"What d'you mean?"

"You were numbed to human emotions for a week or so," Reynolds reminded him, "and then your friend died. This forced your humanity back and it smashed you apart." His hand moved and pressed into Badrick's chest. "But you're feeling again. That's a good sign." Reynolds offered him a pleasant smile. "I think you just have to wait it out, suffer the attacks bravely, and you'll be right again soon."

"What if I get an attack at a really bad time?" Badrick whispered fearfully. "Like if the New Evil attacks us?"

"You're not alone, Badrick," Reynolds said, hefting his shoulder in a bolstering manner. "We've always got your back. We'll defend you just as you defend us."

Badrick returned the smile. "Thanks, Reynolds." His eyes pinned to the door as he remembered that he was supposed to be meeting Zale in the labs.

And that was when he remembered the people on the other side of the door.

"Awww no!"

"What?"

"I didn't want people to hear me . . . like *this*."

"We're seven stories up," Reynolds scoffed dismissively. "No one heard you."

"Kevin and Quill," Badrick pouted.

A reassuring hand found its way to Badrick's shoulder. "I'll talk to them. Explain what happened and ask them to keep it a secret."

"Order them to!" Badrick bawled a little too quickly, not actually joking in the slightest.

Laughing, Reynolds said, "Of course I will." Exhaling from the effort of standing, Reynolds got to his feet. He offered Badrick his hand and pulled him off the floor, brushing off his dusty uniform for him.

With that, he accompanied him to the door.

"Oh," he said suddenly, pulling back on Badrick's shoulder and stopping them in their tracks, "and Badrick?"

"Yeah?"

"It's General Doyle and Agent Commander Quill to you. Got that, Varner?"

Grinning, Badrick nodded and said, "Yes, sir."

"Don't call me 'sir'!"

"Make up your goddamn mind!"

chapter
NINE

Badrick spent the next few days barely setting foot out of the Daemonium laboratories. Taking only short naps every sixteen hours somewhere on a bench, his life became solely focused on their work. He ate, drank and lived within the labs, even going so far as to use the in-house bathrooms nearby.

The only time they even lifted their heads to breathe was when he forced Zale to take five minute breaks.

Apart from those short moments of freedom, they never faltered in their efforts, working into all hours of the night, cruising into the early beginnings of morning and onwards into the failing light of the evening.

Their lives lost all variety, becoming a monotonous drill of routine.

Work.

Toilet.

Food.

Nap.

Rinse and repeat.

Being more than useless at this technological labour, Badrick couldn't help but feel he didn't deserve to be stuck in this dull schedule. Even now his life could have at least a modicum of excitement if he were to join the patrols keeping an eye for New Evil events, but no . . . Zale demanded that Badrick stay close at all times in case his aid was required.

Which, even after all this time, had been a very rare occurrence.

Zale's argument was that, though Badrick was inept at scientific endeavours, he was more than helpful when it came to the research side of things. Zale may have studied all he could on demonology, but at the end of the day Badrick's knowledge was superior, if at least only just.

Thanks to Daemnos' experience he was just as proficient in demonology, and he'd never even had to work for it.

"You cheated," Zale told him when Badrick thought it funny to mention this.

"You're just jealous."

Turning his attention to the many computer screens that obstructed their view of the rest of the labs, Badrick gazed almost sadly at the live-feed image. Displayed on the pixels was a video of the energy within Charles, streamed from a scanner set up in the corner of his cell.

With this setup, they could remain up to date on any changes that might occur.

Next to that monitor was another that showed an almost identical image. However, this was not a live-feed; this time the image was a digital render of the energy as it currently existed.

Because of their inability to be anywhere near Charles lest their plans and schemes become known to their enemy, they were using this render to simulate their experiments and attempts to identify the energy, and perhaps also discover what it was doing.

Already they'd tried many different things, pulling every experiment from the book in Zale's fervent determination to identify the energy's purpose.

So far their attempts had been less than successful.

"I'm going to punch this computer, I swear to God," Zale blurted aggressively after their latest stab at trying to make the energy react to *anything* ended with an epic lack of results. Badrick saw him try one more time, and groan when it again failed.

A few days before, Zale theorised that this strange energy was shielded by a second undetectable barrier placed by the New Evil which zealously prevented them from making progress. That was apparently the only reason Zale could come up with to explain why nothing was working. The energy *should* have reacted to external stimuli by now, but still . . . *nothing.*

Sighing, Badrick's eyes fell to the image of the live recording.

It looked exactly the same as it had yesterday.

A big orb of red energy that quivered like a heart beating a hundred different tiny beats every second.

Pulsing inexplicably rapid, like a thousand bees were writhing just beneath the surface.

What did those little pulses mean?

Badrick couldn't pretend to know. Without anything more to go on he wasn't able to piece together the puzzle, just as Zale couldn't. He and Badrick might have made a good team, but they weren't perfect. They required more than this. Not a soul in existence could manifest answers out of thin air, and they were no exception.

Zale reached forward and tapped a few commands on the

nearest keyboard. Badrick watched with interest as the render flickered and changed, growing smaller as Zale manipulated the zoom options to pull back so they could observe from a distance.

Then, with a few sharp, impatient clacks on the keys, Zale loaded a new render from the system hard drives. A small, yet unstable mass of dull, sickly aquamarine appeared next to the orb, which Zale wasted no time with before smashing them together.

For a moment, as the energies merged, Badrick's face lit up as he saw what he originally believed to be a reaction. Regrettably, however, his elation was dashed when the aquamarine faded and the red orb remained unaffected.

"What the hell was that?" he asked, his frustration causing him to unintentionally snap at Zale.

Zale's tired eyes found his as he answered, "That was Kalik energy."

"Kalik?"

"I wondered if introducing Kalik energy would do anything." He pressed his palms into his eyes and rubbed them, harder than was necessary. "Charles commanded an army of them so I thought it might have something to do with it. Honestly, I should've thought of it sooner.

"Not that it matters," he sputtered irritably. "It didn't do anything. Apparently, Badrick, this has nothing to do with manipulating Kalik."

Badrick offered his partner a comforting smile. "You're tired," he said. "We both are. We're not thinking straight."

"Maybe." Zale's palms found his face again, pressing in so deeply they left large red imprints around his eyes.

"You know," Badrick hummed, "usually this is the moment someone comes in and says something that makes us realise what we need to do. Reynolds, or Carla—"

Badrick shut his mouth so quickly his teeth banged painfully together.

What . . . the hell . . . is wrong with me? 'Oh, Carla could help but she's dead, so oh well'. Idiot! Why did I bring her up?

How insensitive was he that he practically blurted that out?

What a moron!

The flickering of lights disturbed Badrick's frayed mind and pulled him out of his self abhorrence. Glancing up curiously, he watched the bulbs fail briefly before shakily restoring.

"What—"

Before he got a second word out, the cause of this disturbance violently sparked electricity into the wall, the voltage causing the lights to once again waver. Zale called out in alarm as his arm shone a brilliant blue and more electricity practically sizzled the air around him.

Badrick's partner jumped back and gripped his wrist, glaring hatefully at the tense limb and shouting at it to stop. For a moment his power ignored him, but ultimately, with extreme effort, Zale was able to regain control of the electricity and power his arm down.

As his power dissipated back into harmlessness, the lights above recovered and returned to normal.

Badrick stared uncertainly at Zale's hand, his mouth slightly open, and was seconds away from demanding clarification for what he'd just witnessed.

That was until his brain finally caught up with his eyes and he realised he'd seen something of interest in his peripheral. It took a moment for him to register exactly what it was, but when his awareness finally rebooted, he entirely forgot about Zale's disturbance and whirled on the spot to stare at the screens.

Unless he was mistaken, the live-feed of the energy had just expanded.

There was no denying it; as his eyes focused on the screen he saw the red orb shrinking back to its original size.

"Zale," he whispered, hardly daring to believe it. "Something happened."

Interrupting his own angry curses and shouts, Zale shuffled over and demanded somewhat roughly, "What?"

"It got bigger," Badrick told him. "When your power did . . . whatever the hell that was . . . this energy got bigger."

"It what?" Suddenly extremely animated where before he'd been sluggish, Zale gestured for Badrick to give him room and pressed his face to the monitor, his eyes darting up and down as he scanned the data.

And then, his eyes glowing brightly, Zale blurted, *'Oh . . . ma'gard!'*

"What?"

The veteran's hand shot out and gripped Badrick's shoulder tight enough to make him wince. "The energy convulses at a steady rate, all day, every day, never stopping. All the time. Right?" He finally released Badrick's complaining shoulder and buried his hands in his long, blonde hair. "But when my power explodes it convulses more. Larger than before." His eyes flicked to the screen. "A steady stream . . . then an explosion . . . a violent one . . . unwillingly caused . . . larger than regular discharges . . . a bigger influx of energy . . . *OF COURSE!*"

Having understood none of these snippets of Zale's inner thoughts, Badrick opted for sitting in silence and allowing Zale to work through his processes. It would have been detrimental to interrupt him now just for an explanation, especially if it ruined his train of thought.

"Badrick!" Zale shrieked his name so suddenly it made him jump. "Give me a fireball. Stand over there—" he pointed at the wall "—and generate fire in your hand."

"Why?"

"DO IT!"

Alarmed at the increased eccentricity Zale was exhibiting, Badrick did as he was commanded, not wishing to exacerbate the man's unnatural zest. Finding his feet, he stepped to where Zale indicated and raised a hand to the level of his chest.

A little cagey, he ignited it, allowing small flames to lick his fingers.

Zale's frowns communicated his dissatisfaction. "More than that!"

Sighing, Badrick obeyed.

And the energy on the live-feed convulsed.

"What the hell?" he couldn't help but bawl. Suffocating the flames, he returned to their work station and asked what was probably a silly question. "Did it react to my fireball?"

Zale didn't offer him the consideration of answering his frantic query. Instead, he was now activating a third monitor, his fingers dancing expertly over the keyboard attached. Within moments he'd activated a second live-feed, only this time the image showed the interior of the labs. Badrick could see him and Zale on the picture, leaning over the keyboards so sharply it looked like they had backache.

Muttering to nobody but himself, Badrick heard Zale say, "Activating scanners." The screen flickered and the colour vanished, turning to dull monochrome. "Watch that," he ordered Badrick, taking two steps back.

With his palms nearly pressed together, he raised them to chest height and warned Badrick to refrain from getting too close. Already sensing the demonic energy building in Zale's soul, Badrick understood what he intended to do and so took his advice to heart, falling back behind the table.

Only seconds later did Zale charge electricity in his hands and surge it into the space between his palms. The two blasts smashed into each other, flashing brightly and spitting sparks every which way.

Badrick turned his eye to the screen, wondering what Zale was hoping to achieve by spitting demonic energy into the air, and dropped his jaw when he saw what the camera was picking up.

The energy Zale was discharging should have been exploding into the air and dissipating as the residual traces fizzled out, but instead it was like it was being gripped by some unseen force. The radiation caused by the electricity flowed through the air like the currents of a river and phased through the wall behind Zale.

Every single mote of energy Zale released was dragged away by this force. A huge cloud of sparkling demonic power—invisible to all but the scanner—pluming away to an unknown location.

And beside that monitor, the live-feed of Charles' energy expanded, pulsing aggressively.

With the light of violently sparking electricity reflected in his beaming eyes, Zale cut off the voltage and pivoted to face the direction his energy had fled. He clicked his tongue and pointed to the wall. "What's in that direction?"

"The prisons."

Zale clapped his hands and fell back onto his stool, swivelling to face the screens with a huge grin dominating his features. "I gotcha now!"

Badrick could see the triumph in Zale's grin and excitement was building within his stomach as a result. "What is it?" he asked eagerly, hoping upon hope that this behaviour signalled Zale's discovery of the energy within Charles.

For a moment, Zale didn't respond, only muttered ramblingly. "Nice try, hiding what this is, making us unable to see it. But you can hide what something is but not what it does. Suck it."

Truly impatient now, Badrick demanded, "What is it!?"

Zale's grin was slightly creepy; it was so toothy and wide. With a chuckle, he finally faced Badrick and said, "Badrick, my friend, what we have here is a power leech."

Memories from a demon's long life flooded Badrick's head and understanding dawned on him so quickly he was left with disgust at having not recognised this energy so much sooner. "Are you kidding?" he spat angrily.

"Nope," Zale chuckled.

"I can't believe it," Badrick sighed. "A power leech, of all things. The New Evil is sucking up the radiation of our powers to absorb later."

Zale threw a finger in the direction of the live-feed and said, "The prison is the perfect place for a power leech. Malcolm's power is permanently activated."

"Keeping the prisoners locked up." Badrick felt appalled. "That's why the energy always looks like its vibrating. It's getting a constant supply of power." More dismayed than ever before, Badrick shook his head and yelled incoherently.

"If the energy hadn't been hidden, the systems might've picked up on it," Zale stated, wiping his mouth with his left hand. "But it's not like anyone knew what to look for. Clever bugger, that New Evil, but I beat him." He punched a fist into his palm victoriously and smiled. "You can disguise a hand like a foot but if the toes curl all the way to the sole you know it's a fist."

Grimacing, Badrick groaned, "Don't ever say that again. That was weird."

"I kind of liked it, actually," Zale scowled. "I thought it was rather poetic."

"It wasn't poetic *or* likable," Badrick retorted before flinging his hand at the multitude of screens they were operating. "Can we please focus? We know what the energy's doing, but what do *we* do now?"

Zale's grin returned and he slapped Badrick on the shoulder.

"The energy is remarkably hidden and the systems can't identify it. They can't even tell us it's there without help."

"So I ask again," Badrick murmured with frustration, "what do we do now?"

"I do what I always do," Zale offered as way of an answer. When he noticed that this was obviously not acceptable, he tutted and elaborated. "I work around it."

"And how're you going to do that?" Badrick didn't mean to come across as disbelieving. He wasn't intentionally acting as the voice of scepticism. He wanted to believe that Zale could do as he claimed, however his past experiences with their enemy had left him increasingly cynical.

He honestly couldn't help but doubt that they were able to fight back.

Zale didn't seem to care about or even notice his pessimism. With a confident smile, he brushed aside the clutter on the desk and got to work on three separate keyboards. "I just need to teach the machines to see what I see." When Badrick continued to look worried, Zale exhaled roughly and said, "Imagine the mind of a cat was trapped within an elephant and you were the only one who knew."

"Er . . . right?"

"Other people might see behaviour they couldn't understand, but they'd still only see an elephant. You, on the other hand, understand what's going on and because you know the truth you spot the clues. The way the elephant licks its arm like its grooming, or the unnatural, painful way its back arches when it tries to be like a cat when threatened."

"Erm . . . OK."

Zale pointed at the computers and stated, "I just have to find a way to make the machines recognise there's a cat inside the elephant, then they'll be able to see what I see. The software will be able to do what it's supposed to do."

Badrick wasn't sure if Zale was mocking him by using such an inane analogy but he didn't question it. Whether or not he was being made fun of wasn't the most important issue of the day and so Badrick left Zale to do his work, hoping that the genius knew what he was doing.

Zale toiled for several hours, never quitting, never stopping and completely refusing any kind of distraction. He was so focused Badrick found himself idly wondering if even a dozen naked women could pull his attention.

It caused Badrick to wonder why Zale was working this hard.

There had never been any doubt that Zale was a severe obsessive, however in the past, even at his worst, he'd kept it in check. But now he was pushing himself past the point of exhaustion, barely sleeping or eating, and Badrick had a horrible feeling it was all to avenge Carla's death.

Her premature demise had sent Zale down a spiral of despair and it seemed nothing would hinder his efforts to capture . . . or *murder* . . . the one responsible.

With nothing to do but think, these sombre musings bothered Badrick's head for the better part of two hours. He thought of Carla, missed her terribly, reminisced on the games of basketball she'd beaten him in and wondered if she really was in a better place.

And now that he was using his head, Badrick was able to answer an earlier question. Reflecting on the life of their deceased friend, Badrick no longer needed to query why Zale's power had suddenly sparked dangerously and without warning.

For God's sake, it should've been obvious from the start.

The first thing the Daemonium coached new Enthrallers in was how to take control of their emotions, because achieving that skill meant you would attain command of the demon within you.

Allowing yourself to feel sorrow and pain was a great way to do this, this was true, but the second thing Enthrallers were taught was how to never let it get too far. Strong emotions may weaken demons, but many knew how to use them to their benefit, whispering from within and manipulating those in distress to cause havoc.

Zale's demon wasn't the kind to do this, but the simple fact that Zale was experiencing such undiluted pain made questioning why his power had acted up a rather stupid thing to do.

"Am I a genius, or am I a genius?"

Badrick gratefully tumbled out of his morbid thoughts and returned his attention to Zale. His eyes refocused just in time to see his partner leap from his seat and converge on him. Feeling somewhat alarmed at the speed of his approach, Badrick hurriedly called for embellishment.

"I've done it," Zale grinned. "The machines can recognise the energy."

Excitement built in Badrick's chest and he blurted, "Can you identify who it belongs to?"

"I've got the capability."

Badrick also leapt from his seat and felt a wide smile pulling at his mouth. "Get the data from Dhornji's murder!" he half shouted. "Compare it!"

"Already on it." This wasn't a lie; Zale was back at his keyboard in a flash, downloading the relevant data from the BCR. Within seconds he'd called up both renders and was almost pressing his nose into the screen, his face was so close.

Badrick joined him, eyeing up the readouts with a mix of impatience and excitement. Both renders were rotating slowly, various places being highlighted by either green or red squares.

Unfortunately, Badrick didn't understand what the little lights meant.

"Well?" he eventually demanded when he gave up trying to.

Zale brought his attention to the various red squares appearing on the renders. "There's a few discrepancies," he informed him. "It says the signatures aren't completely similar. There are parts that don't make sense."

"But," Badrick said, confused, "there's way more green squares."

"Exactly, so it *does* see similarities." Zale nodded vigorously. His hand found his chin and he chewed his lip in thought. "There are enough similarities that there's no doubt these energies are from the same source, *but* the power leech has differences to the energy from the castle."

"What does that mean?"

"Maybe the New Evil is changing or something," Zale offered as a theory. "Getting more powerful, hence the difference in these two readings. But they *are* the same," he growled as an afterthought, as though he was ensuring nobody tried to argue otherwise.

"Will this be enough?" Badrick asked, worry creeping in now that he was letting it. "Can we find the New Evil with this?" He never received an answer. Instead he felt a tug on his sleeve and was unceremoniously yanked from his stool.

"You better believe it, baby!" Zale finally released Badrick from his grasp and instead simply led him at speed into the Main Hall. "The differences aren't so vast they'll stop us," he shouted over his shoulder. "I can find who put that power leech there. I can find the one who killed Dhornji."

Responding would have been redundant as Zale had already broken ahead and was moving out of earshot in his haste to reach the BCR.

Badrick hurried to catch up and found Zale already typing by the time he arrived.

With great speed, he slotted a memory stick Badrick hadn't noticed before into a port and called up the data it held. Badrick utterly failed to keep up with Zale as he poked at the keyboard and the computer responded obediently, doing whatever it was that Zale wanted it to. Images that meant nothing to Badrick appeared, transferred from right to left and vice versa, flashing decisively before being minimised and the entire process restarted with other programs.

He was eventually able to recognise a render of the power leech being scanned by the energy readers. A satellite map of the world situated to the right of it was quickly zooming closer and closer to the ground.

Zale said something muffled about where he should look, before clicking his fingers and inputting one last command.

For a moment, there was only silence as the machines performed their tasks.

And then the alarms went off.

At that, while every head in the vicinity swivelled in the direction, alarmed, a computerised voice rang out.

"ALERT! ENERGY SIGNATURE DETECTED! NEW EVIL LOCATED!"

Unable to believe what he was hearing, Badrick was standing limp and slack-jawed when he was unceremoniously pushed aside. As he stumbled back, the agent that shoved him rose near the computer and studied the readouts with intense concentration.

"Some kind of alteration to our scanners," he spoke aloud. "What did you do!?" Zale didn't answer the demand, but it wouldn't have mattered regardless; the agent didn't even give him a chance to. "Jesus, it's massive!" he bawled, meaning the energy output the scanners were identifying. His eyes found Badrick, the brown orbs boring into his. "How'd you do this?"

"Zale did it," Badrick half cried, the blaring alarms and the near panic of the nearby agents exacerbating his own tension. "He worked out how to find the New Evil."

The agent glanced around, then tutted irritably. "And where is Operative Hood?"

Badrick frowned with a mixture of confusion and annoyance, raising his arm to point a little sarcastically behind the agent.

But that was when he realised he was gesturing to thin air.

Zale was gone.

"Don't waste my time, Operative!" the agent shouted. "Where did Hood go?"

Badrick wasn't listening. Swivelling left and right, his eyes darted about the place with panic, an all too familiar dread growing with every second he failed to locate his partner. Crying aloud with distress, Badrick pivoted and charged his way out of the BCR, calling Zale's name as he went and ignoring the enraged agent's demands that he return this instant.

He re-entered the Main Hall.

Hoping upon hope to see Zale out here, however his barely achieved optimism was again dashed without mercy.

"Zale!" Badrick called over the clamour of running Enthrallers. "Zale!"

He prayed for a responding, 'Over here,' but none came.

Badrick wasn't entirely sure why he was so scared—Zale had run off without him before—but there was something about his partner's disappearance that rang warning bells in his head.

He'd vanished right after the scanner located their quarry.

The quarry that killed Carla.

That was why Badrick was so scared—even before he'd come to the realisation, his instincts had know Zale's absence marked him doing something rash.

Something stupid.

Badrick's eyes flicked to the exit. "Oh no."

chapter
TEN

It was not uncommon for Operatives Badrick Varner and Zale Hood to somewhat step out of line during an assignment. More often than not they practically disobeyed direct orders, along with sound logic, and went with their gut, sometimes keeping their actions a total secret.

And they always had each others' backs when one went borderline rogue.

But on this day a deep-set terror arose within Badrick at the realisation that his partner had just set out alone, possibly unarmed . . . and definitely *without* armour.

How could he do that?

This was the New Evil they were dealing with, not some ignorant Enthraller or under-powered Forsaken. Zale couldn't leave alone and expect to succeed in . . .

What did he even plan to do?

Capture the New Evil?

Kill it?

Badrick couldn't do it today.

He couldn't have Zale's back in this heedless decision. Not against the New Evil. They needed to form a strategy, not follow an insane plan to take the darkness head on without back up.

And before he even knew what he was doing, Badrick's legs had carried him out of the HQ and up several flights of stairs. Within several seconds he was bursting into Reynolds's office, only for panic to nearly completely override his senses when he realised the man wasn't inside.

Crying aloud from sheer anxiety, he spun on his heel and hurried back out the door desperately fighting back hysterical tears . . . when he smashed into the body of someone taller than he.

As he stumbled back, and hands darted to his shoulders to steady him, a voice penetrated his ear; "Badrick? What . . ."

Another cry escaped Badrick's mouth—this time of relief— when he recognised who the voice belonged to. Allowing the hands to right his stance, he tried to explain what was happening, only for his words to come out a strangled squeak as the terror in his gut closed his airways.

"Badrick?" Reynolds tried again. "What's wrong? Do you know why the BCR alarms are going?"

Gaining just enough control of his body to clear his throat, Badrick coughed and managed to exclaim, "We found the New Evil."

Reynolds instantly tensed. He crouched so that he was at Badrick's height and stared deep into his eyes. "Are you sure?"

Badrick nodded, then spoke the words that sent fresh shivers down his spine. "Zale's gone after him!"

"*What!?!*"

"He's angry," Badrick spluttered. "He's gone out alone." That was all he was capable of saying; the panic blaring in his head was deafening, he could barely concentrate on something as simple as breathing normally.

Thankfully, however, Reynolds was a very competent man and that was all the information he required. He was gone before Badrick finished his sentence, and Badrick stumbled to catch up to the Dominus as he barged through agents and soldiers alike, making a beeline for the BCR.

"Get a lock on Horas' ID," he heard him roar. "Find Zale. We have to get to him before he gets to the New Evil." He turned and clicked his fingers at several men and women. "I want ten agents armed and armoured, ready to go in five minutes. We're going after him."

"No, Dominus!" An Agent Commander wrapped his fingers around Reynolds' arm and shook his head roughly. "You can't go."

Bristling angrily, Reynolds spat back, "That's one of ours out there!"

"You are the *Dominus!* Your place is here."

"I said I wouldn't sit back on a throne. I promised to remain in active duty."

"Yes, sir," the Commander responded. "And we appreciate that, but not today. You can't risk it against the New Evil. You have to leave it to the agents."

Reynolds clearly wanted to argue—order the man to stand down so that he could do as he wanted—but there was no denying the wisdom in the Commander's argument.

It was all well and good for Reynolds to drop from a plane and dive into an army of Kalik, but it was clear no one wanted their leader anywhere near the New Evil.

They couldn't risk the Dominus like that and Badrick had no doubt the BCR would pin him to the floor just to stop him.

Perhaps if they'd had more information, or at the very least a plan of attack, the agents of the Daemonium would follow their Dominus in the hunt, but this was a rush to stop an operative getting himself killed. There was no plan here. This was a dash and grab.

The Dominus could not endanger himself so pointlessly.

The agents inclining more towards diplomatic solutions to soothe Reynolds gave him their word that they'd retrieve Zale, and those who failed to be so tactful simply resorted to saluting, their duty to the General's orders their only obligation for accepting this mission.

Within moments the group was formed and ready to go, and upon seeing them cocking their weapons, Badrick cried, "I'm going too!"

Reynolds looked like he wanted to deny Badrick his loud demand, but everybody present understood that having Badrick along would be to their benefit. Not only did he know Zale best, but at his disposal was the greatest asset they had.

Every single power the demonic world possessed swirled within Badrick's soul and at a greater potency than any other Enthraller could boast.

It was this knowledge that led Reynolds to begrudgingly agree, and minutes later Badrick found himself sprinting through the Gate doors and leaping awkwardly onto an attack chopper. The moment his feet hit metal his balance shifted as the pilot lifted them high into the air, moving fast away from the facility.

As they cut across the English countryside, Badrick consulted his port-pad for anything that might help. Fear continued to scratch at his stomach and as he consulted with the agents at the

BCR consoles a desperate fight raged within him to keep alarmed tears at bay.

"He's moving fast," a voice told them, "and the garage boys are reporting a missing bike."

"Is it Zale's?" Badrick queried swiftly.

A pause, then, "Aye!"

"It's gonna be hard to catch up even in this thing," the pilot told them. "I was there when he upgraded the speed on that bloody bike." Badrick watched the pilot's hands tense as he did his best to increase their speed.

Someone Badrick didn't know reported, "Teleporters can't keep up. He's moving too fast."

"You guys keep him in your sights," the pilot advised. "This'll be impossible if I don't know where he is."

"Keep going North," Badrick called. "He's up wh—"

"No!" someone interrupted. "He's taken a left. Head West, we can cut him off." The owner of the voice rapidly spat a series of co-ordinates. The pilot nodded his thanks and the helicopter titled as their course changed.

"Hold up!" The moment Badrick heard these words he knew something was wrong. He felt his stomach sink sickeningly and he waited impatiently for the voice to continue. "I've got another reading. Also moving fast. Several clicks behind the Operative."

"What is it?" an agent asked.

"Demonic signature. Possibly an Enthraller."

"Is it following Hood?"

"Can't say for certain."

Badrick was seconds away from fainting from panic. It was all getting so out of control. What the hell was this new reading? Who had just gotten involved?

Fresh worry bubbled up within Badrick, his leg twitching nervously as his impatience at their lack of progress caused him an increasing level of distress.

His anxiety made him call out demandingly, "Can't we go faster!?"

Almost as if his prayers were answered, the satellite operator's voice cut through his dread and announced, "Hood has slowed . . . He's disembarked the bike. This is your chance. Go!"

Fuelled by new hope, the pilot managed to coax a little more speed from the aircraft and brought them closer to the ground. Badrick leaned out the side as they descended, desperate to catch a glimpse of his vengeful partner. The trees whipped past beneath, rivers and rock formations among them, but there was no sight of a parked bike, and no Zale.

"Where is he!?" Badrick shouted, consulting his port-pad once more. The machine told him they were close—very close—which did nothing to ease his anxiety; if they were so close then where was he!?!

"I've got him!" a voice declared. "To the North!" Badrick rushed to see, almost stumbling clumsily in his haste and falling right out of the helicopter. However, it was worth the brief fear of falling; Badrick could now spot Zale running across the land, vaulting over rocks and leaping over puddles, never stopping, never slowing.

It would be damn near impossible to halt his charge. Nevertheless, Badrick felt intense relief soothe his stricken muscles. Even if they had to wrestle Zale to the ground, they now had a chance to save him before he reached the Ne—

"Oh, God, no!" Badrick's stomach flipped at the sound of the horrified exclamation. "Get out of there!"

Nobody had time to react to what happened next. Before Badrick himself had even processed the words, a blinding green light splashed across the cockpit glass and the helicopter shuddered violently. With shouts of alarm, three agents were thrown out of the aircraft and sent spinning to the ground.

Of course, this made these three the lucky ones; any Enthraller could live to tell the tale of a fall so long as they landed on their feet. Being caught inside a mushrooming ball of fire, however, was not something they could as readily survive.

The pilot roared in anger when a chunk of his aircraft tore away as the green explosion ripped them apart.

He tried to regain control but it was to no avail; the helicopter was totalled and they were rapidly plummeting to Earth.

"Bail!" a woman roared. "Bail! Bail! Bail!" In a blitz of consternated swiftness, the agents evacuated the helicopter in quick succession. Badrick leapt out last, and just in time; he'd only just cleared the aircraft before it smashed into the trees and was irreparably mangled beyond recognition. Seconds later a great ball of fire fulminated ferociously, incinerating the helicopter, as well as the immediate area.

With horror, Badrick realised the pilot had still been inside when it exploded.

He was in so much shock that he almost forgot to swing his feet beneath him as he fell. Death nearly claimed two souls that day, however his senses returned in time for him to spin in midair and allow his feet to absorb the impact.

Nearby, an agent busied herself ensuring the survivors were alright. Two more thumps sounded behind Badrick and eruptions of dirt splattered him as two agents dropped from the trees, demanding situation reports.

As the group reorganised, Badrick fought desperately not to let fear overcome him.

"Varner, wake up!" Badrick lifted his head a little too sharply in his desperation to prove he was alert and not an emotional hindrance, cricking his neck painfully. "We have to get Operative Hood."

Before they could get moving, an agent half stumbled over and demanded, "What hit us?"

Static answered his question and Badrick winced at the sheer volume of it. Their radios, momentarily disrupted by the power that took them down, hissed angrily into their ears before finally fixing itself and being replaced by urgent shouts.

"The helicopter's down!" It was Reynolds. "Are there survivors?"

"We're alright," Badrick chose to respond, "but our pilot's gone."

The curse that burst from Reynolds' mouth perfectly communicated his upset.

"Dominus," an agent said, "what hit us?"

There was a brief pause, static filling the silence, before Reynolds shouted, "The New Evil," and Badrick felt fresh terror hit his heart. "Agents, you have to get out!"

"We need to get Operative Hood!" the agent argued.

The Dominus' voice was replaced by someone Badrick did not recognise, but he guessed that an Agent Commander had taken over to help Reynolds make a choice he didn't want to make. "It's too late," this new person said. "Abandon the mission. Get out of ther—"

A scream drowned out the rest of his sentence. The moment he heard it, Badrick swivelled, searching for the source of the deafening screech.

"Was that Hood?"

"No," Badrick rasped, his voice barely working.

"That wasn't Hood, come on now!" someone else scoffed irately, their ability to remain calm no doubt destroyed in light of events.

"Then who was it?"

"It came from over that rise!"

Badrick didn't wait for his panicking comrades to continue snapping at each other. Somehow managing to use his dread to power his muscles, he jumped forward, leaping over a burning branch and scrambling up the incline. As he crested over the top another scream disturbed the forest.

A dark figure came into view at the top of the hill. It was draped in black robes and was desperately scrabbling away from a rage-filled Zale. The figure's limbs were jerking violently, suggesting he'd suffered a terrible pain which had greatly impeded his ability to move. He managed no more than two steps before Zale let loose with a vicious surge of electricity that struck the dark figure. A third shriek rocked the forest as the figure fell to the dirt.

A triumphant Zale converged on his victim, a cruel grin over his face. He drew close and raised an electrically charged fist to strike the squirming robed stranger, perhaps intending to beat him to death.

Badrick opened his mouth to shout desperately. He needed to stop Zale. It didn't matter who this dark man was, Badrick couldn't allow his partner to slaughter him without getting answers. Eager to calm Zale, he took a step forward, hand outstretched—

"Watch out!"

A shadow flitted across Badrick's peripheral—too fast for him to track—and, quite suddenly, he was being forced to the dirt by a heavy weight. The next thing he knew a deafening bang had exploded inches away, right where he'd been standing only seconds before, and a blistering heat nearly melted his armour.

The agent that pinned him to the floor jumped to her feet and helped him stand just as there was a second explosion and Badrick spotted Zale violently thrown to the leaf-covered grass.

"Zale!" Badrick scurried over, heart racing, and ducked to his knees to check on his partner. He was coughing roughly, a hand upon the armour that covered his chest and the metal on his right arm blackened with angry scorch marks.

Several yards away the dark figure was trembling to his feet, watching them with wide, wary eyes. He looked seconds away from bolting, easily determined from the way he hesitantly stepped back, rustling the leaves with his clumsy feet.

"Stop him!" Zale retched. He pulled his helmet from his head and glared furiously at the figure. "He's the New Evil! *Stop him!*"

Badrick's head whipped around to stare disbelievingly, taking in the figure's unimpressive physique, the underwhelming way he stumbled over his own feet.

It . . . It couldn't be true.

The New Evil was a dominating force of pure evil. Just recognising its mere presence could crush a person to the ground and leave them gibbering in terror. Ever since sensing the New Evil's ominous presence, Badrick had expected a truly demonic sight.

A mass of writhing darkness.

Desolate and cruel.

Awful to behold.

But . . . this . . .

No . . .

Zale had to have it wrong.

Nevertheless, the agents took heed of Zale's warning. A wave of wariness visibly flowed throughout their ranks, however they bravely dashed forward to restrain the robed man. Knees met mud and wrists were grabbed just as Badrick's radio crackled and Reynolds' similarly disbelieving voice also said, "Zale's right . . . The signature matches the power leech.

"That's the New Evil."

chapter
ELEVEN

Badrick watched with anxiety as two medics gingerly removed the dark grey upper arm piece of Zale's armour. With his right arm raised for their benefit, the Enthraller winced as pain apparently bit at his flesh from their touch. The metal crashed to the floor as they discarded it and Badrick's eyes widened at the sight of the warped metal.

Whatever hit Zale had nearly turned his armour—made from *supernaturally hardened metals*—to slag.

One of the medics revealed an impossibly sharp blade and pinched Zale's under-suit away from his skin before cutting it open.

Badrick couldn't help but gasp at the sight of the burn—red, sore and already starting to peel—but forced himself to remember that this could have been a lot worse. Zale's arm may have looked bad, however, his armour had absorbed nearly the entirety of the blast.

Zale had escaped the danger quite well off.

The medic revealed some kind of burn cream and applied it to the angry red marks on Zale's skin. He bared his teeth in pain but Badrick could tell from the way he sighed that the cooling cream felt heavenly.

The veteran was halfway through thanking the medics when the automatic door zipped open with such venom Badrick could only imagine it was channelling the rage of the man who ordered it to get out of his way.

The Dominus looked like he was about to pull out a gun and start unloading on every nearby human body, he was so livid. Even Badrick, whose fear these days was completely preoccupied with the New Evil, felt unnerved.

And he wasn't even the one in trouble.

"HOOD!" Reynolds screamed. "WHAT THE HELL WERE YOU DOING!?!" He approached, feet stamping and hands outstretched, like he was reaching to throttle Zale where he sat. "THAT WAS THE NEW EVIL! YOU COULD'VE BEEN KILLED!"

One of the medics tried to intervene. "Sir, I—"

"WE LOST A PILOT BECAUSE OF YOUR RECKLESSNESS! WE—" As his face turned purple and spit flew with each word, Zale's eyes—exhausted, miserable, lifeless—met with Reynolds' and the anger drained from him like someone had opened a plughole in his emotions.

He stammered for nearly half a minute before finally exhaling and reaching forward to grab Zale's head and pull him closer. "Stupid," he murmured sharply. "Stupid. Stupid! We could have lost you."

Reynolds finally took a step back, straightened his uniform and said his apologies for interrupting the medics' work. Once they'd smiled their understanding, the Dominus stepped away and offered his hand to Badrick.

He took it, and Reynolds placed his other on Badrick's shoulder.

"My two young operatives," he sighed quietly. "I'm glad you're alright."

From at the back of the room, Zale muttered, "I'm sorry, Reynolds. I—"

The General cut Zale off with a wave of his hands. "What I said before . . . *I* am sorry. You aren't to blame for the pilot, for the helicopter, for any of it. He offered his life for a mission to save a fellow Enthraller. Honestly, I wish we could all die on missions that noble." He spun rapidly and gave Zale a sincere eye. "What you did was stupid, Hood, and it ultimately led to the death of one of ours. But that's the job, that's what we do, there's no shame in it.

"The New Evil killed him, Hood. Not you."

One of the medics took this opportunity to speak. So it's true? You got the New . . ."

"That remains to be seen," Reynolds begrudgingly admitted, sighing heavily. "There are some issues with detecting his power signature, but, then again, the system says we have the right . . ." He didn't bother finishing the sentence.

"It *is* him," Zale snarled, such malevolence in his voice it was unsettling. "I know it."

"We've been fooled by our enemies before," Badrick said.

He couldn't help but believe this to be the case. His earlier doubts had been given time to fester and grow and now he was at a stage of complete scepticism.

Badrick just couldn't force himself to believe they'd caught the right guy.

On the way in, the scanners had read their captive up and down, left and right, in and bloody out, and had displayed to everyone in the Daemonium a rather meek power level.

For God's sake, the New Evil was supposed to be the greatest power in all of creation.

He was not *meek*.

It was clear that Zale wanted to argue the point. His lips had parted, his face was angry. However, to Badrick's surprise, his partner closed his mouth and turned his gaze elsewhere, his eyes misting as he chewed his lip. Utilising the silence that ensued, a medic made a comment to Badrick about getting a replacement for Zale's damaged armour.

Hearing this exchange, Reynolds stepped up and gaped at the damaged piece. With a sigh, he muttered, "I knew he was dangerous, but to melt the armour like that . . . God . . ."

Zale jumped on his words instantly. He winced as he spun himself on the bed to face Reynolds directly, asking, "What hit me, Reynolds? It wasn't the New Evil."

The Dominus shook his head and replied with, "You have your own case to focus on. Don't worry about this. Zach's on it."

Zale aggressively pointed at his damaged arm, his eyes dangerous and angry. "Seriously?"

Though he was not the kind of man to be intimidated by anyone in the slightest, the sight of the operative's wounded arm seemed to have quite the impact on Reynolds. With a sigh of resignation and a breath of, "Yes, at this juncture, you deserve to know," Reynolds pulled his port-pad from his pocket.

Zale own machine beeped and he instantly lifted his arm to respond to the data Reynolds sent him.

"We're calling him the Bomb Killer," the General said. "The other day, a deposit of demonic metals manifested and we sent a contingent of soldiers to secure it, but—"

Badrick saw Zale nod. "Good call," he said, scrolling through the data on his port-pad. "We lost the stuff to the Apos loads of times last year."

"That was our thinking," Reynolds said. "We stationed the contingent to prevent that happening. Except . . ."

Not having the data accessible, Badrick had no choice but to ask, "What happened?"

With another sigh and a rub of his forehead, Reynolds said, "An explosion. The contingent was lost."

Badrick almost dropped to the floor, his legs had suddenly grown very weak. Readjusting his position to stop his stunned body failing, he kicked his helmet in his clumsiness. It rattled and rolled across the floor towards the door but nobody bothered retrieving it.

"Just one explosion?"

Reynolds gave him a serious eye. "One massive explosion," he confirmed. "Took out the entire company except for—"

He was interrupted by Zale. "What . . . the hell . . . is that?"

A sad smile appeared on the Dominus' face when Zale turned his port-pad around to show a photo of a strange green handprint burned on the red armour of a dead soldier.

At the sight of the corpse, Badrick felt the now all too familiar tugs of depression and despair. He almost gagged from the suddenness of it and the need to cry nearly overwhelmed him.

Struggling to suffer in silence, he just about managed to choke it back down and force his face to remain neutral.

There were more pressing matters than his prissy feelings.

Reynolds finished his earlier sentence: "Except for Private Mendoza. He survived the explosion but we found his body near the site with that mark."

"What is it?" Badrick drew up to Zale and took the port-pad

for a closer look.

"A heart attack."

"A what?"

"The autopsy revealed a heart attack."

"Caused by the green mark?" Zale queried.

"The labs are telling me it's hard to get a fix on how it works, but they've suggested that the Bomb Killer places his hand on his victim and pumps in energy to cause cardiac arrest. The green handprint is a side effect."

"He's an Enthraller," Zale said. It wasn't a question.

"Can you trace fingerprints?" Badrick wondered.

Reynolds shook his head, informing them that the energy burns blazed away any handprints that may be left behind.

Badrick tried another question; "Why would he go after Zale?"

He'd aimed the query at Reynolds, but it was actually Zale who answered. "An entire contingent, mate," he sighed, as if these few words explained everything. When he finally realised it hadn't in the slightest, he tutted and added, "You don't attack that many Daemonium employees unless you're specifically targeting the Daemonium, so it's likely he's scoping us out and saw me leave."

"That's what the Agent Commanders believe as well," Reynolds informed them.

Badrick selected the image of a map that had red symbols plastered at various places and widened it for a better look. When he decided he couldn't make heads nor tails of it, he asked, "What's all this?"

"The Bomb Killer's dumping his energy anywhere he goes, we think, to confuse our scanners."

"Let me guess," Zale drawled . "We can't pinpoint the real-time location of his signature, even when he uses his powers?"

Nodding, Reynolds said, "Even when he does use them, he does it sparingly, only on those who survive the detonations. By the time we catch up to the energy left behind by the act he's dumped even more energy every which way, and already fled."

"Clever bastard," Zale tutted angrily. He regarded his wounded arm with irritation. "Sounds like something I would do."

"Something else you'll do," Reynolds instantly snapped, taking quick steps to close the distance between the three of them, "is obsess over this. I know you, Hood. You'll want in on this case too.

"But I'm telling you right now, *NO!* I'm not insinuating you can't manage both cases, so don't think I am, but the New Evil must take priority.

"Alright?"

Having pushed his luck several times today already, Zale finally nodded his obedience, which Badrick was very thankful for.

The Dominus straightened, evidently happy in the knowledge that he'd pacified Zale's curiosity. "Now," he said, "as long as you can manage it, I want both of you down in the interrogation rooms." The small smile that had originally lit up his features utterly vanished to be replaced with what looked like near dread. "This is your case . . . The New Evil is waiting for you."

chapter
TWELVE

Badrick followed Zale through the open door with great trepidation, emerging into a dimly lit room that was occupied by only one other person. The guy—who looked to be in his late thirties—smiled welcomingly as they entered, stepping forward to shake Reynolds' hand. However, the smile was tainted with worry, and the man indicated to the window before saying, "Sir, I advise you go back to the BCR. It isn't safe for the Dominus to be too close to the demon."

"I won't go into the room," Reynolds assured him. "I'll stay under you protection, Agent Carter, but I need to see this."

Though upset, Carter nodded his obedience and took a step back.

Finally free to speak, Badrick mentioned something that was

now been bothering him. "You said demon ... He's not an Enthraller?"

Carter shook his head sombrely. "It's definitely a demon."

"Physical?" Reynolds blurted disbelievingly.

"Completely."

"How? Only the most powerful can achieve it without exploding."

The agent could only answer with a gesture towards the demon, whom they could see through a sheet of one way glass. He was sitting rigidly on an uncomfortable plastic seat, being interrogated by another guy Badrick had never met.

Carter sighed, "The New Evil is hardly a weakling."

"He's not the New Evil," Badrick stated absently, his voice little more than a murmur. He was unable to tear his gaze away from the demon, his eyes wide, and his skin slowly going pale due to anxiety.

"No?"

"It can't be," Badrick sighed. "He's too weak. He hasn't even tried to break out of here. If he was the New Evil, how did we catch him so easily?"

"The *scanners* say he's weak," Reynolds told them, "*but* he's physical, without an Enthraller. Clearly there's more to this demon than meets the eye."

Zale made no comment, despite Badrick expecting him to fight for his belief that this *was* their enemy. He was also refusing to look away, his gaze boring into the demon, his expression unreadable.

"Well, let's have a listen," Carter suggested. In his peripheral, Badrick spotted him flick a switch and suddenly their room was filled with a deep, rumbling voice.

"—doing so close to our primary facility?" The interrogator had been the one to speak, which was just as well because without him there would have been only silence. The demon didn't respond to the query, only stared angrily. Tutting with irritation, the interrogator stated, "Well, it's not hard to figure out. You've been watching us . . . Keeping us close . . ." With a derisive smile, the interrogator added, "What's that old proverb? *'Keep your friends close, your enemies closer?'"*

Once more the demon said nothing.

Moving the interrogation along, the next question was, "Alright, I'll ask the first question again. What's your name?"

Badrick clenched his fists when there was yet again nothing but glares from their prisoner, and he was about to suggest beating the demon into submission—just to relieve some of the stress—when he felt Zale place a hand on his shoulder.

Badrick he saw a look of deep thought plastered all over his face.

He recognised the expression instantly.

Zale had an idea.

With hope stirring in his stomach, Badrick asked, "You got something?"

"Maybe." Zale removed the hand and spun to face Agent Carter, waving to get his attention. At first the man failed to notice; he was too busy handing Reynolds a steaming mug of tea.

"Here, sir," he said kindly. "You look like you need this more than I do."

Reynolds nodded his thanks and took a sip the same moment an impatient Zale clicked his fingers to draw their gazes.

"Yes, Zale?" Reynolds asked on Carter's behalf.

"Tell him Zale and Badrick are here."

"What?" Carter half spat. "Why?"

"Trust me," Zale urged. "Just do it. I promise it'll help."

Carter looked to Reynolds for reassurance that doing so wouldn't get him fired, but even when the Dominus gave him the green-light to proceed he did so hesitantly. As he spoke into a nearby microphone, the interrogator could be seen putting a hand to his ear.

He paused for a moment, his eyes staring through the glass at where he imagined they might be standing—he was slightly off centre—before clearing his throat.

"I've been told the operative who apprehended you is behind that glass," he said sternly. "Operative Hood and his partner Badrick Varner."

At the sound of their names, the demon's carefully controlled dangerous and threatening demeanour dropped so quickly Badrick was surprised he didn't get whiplash. His eyes darted to the window, his hands now beginning to shake.

"What . . . the hell?" Badrick heard Carter murmur.

And then, without so much as a warning, the demon blurted, "I'll tell you my name."

"I can't believe it." Carter looked to Zale with confusion, mixed with amazement. "How did you do that?"

In way of a response, Zale murmured, "The New Evil spent how much energy getting Charles to mess with us?"

"A lot," Carter said.

Sighing heavily, Zale murmured, "Look . . . I never told you this but . . . " He hesitated at that point and only continued when Reynolds urged him to. "Please . . . keep this to yourselves . . . but Charles told me his mission was to kill us." The blue-eyed Enthraller clapped his hands together and placed the tips of his fingers to his mouth. "I thought to myself, why would the ultimate power need to assassinate someone in such a complex way? I mean . . . couldn't he have just killed us himself?"

"You're saying that he can't?"

"I'm saying I took a chance on betting that this guy is scared of Horas and Daemnos. With us so close, I hoped it would inspire him to be more . . . *helpful.*"

As Reynolds and Carter nodded admirably and returned their attention to the interrogation, Badrick gripped Zale's arm and pulled him close, hissing so only his partner could hear, "You told me—told the team—that it was all just coincidence." He ensured Zale could see his angry glare. "That the New Evil didn't actually care about us."

Whispering just as quietly, Zale said, "I was worried they'd take us off the case if they knew." His eyes found Badrick's. "I couldn't risk that."

"You could've told me!"

Zale opened his mouth, paused, then shut it again. Half shrugging, he murmured, "Sorry." He puffed air and shrugged a second time. "I don't know what to say . . . I'm sorry, I was just scared."

Badrick didn't know what he'd been expecting, but it hadn't been an excuse like that. Upon hearing it, he felt his irritation drain and released Zale from his grip.

He didn't know what to say so he just settled for smiling reassuringly and muttering, "I wouldn't tell anyone else." He gestured with his head to the door leading to the HQ.

Within the interrogation room, the interrogator must have been waiting for permission to continue because he had yet to say anything more. When Carter finally pushed the switch and spoke into the mic, he returned his attention to the demon and said, "OK . . . so tell me your name."

The demon visibly shuddered, his eyes flicking to the window for a brief moment. Then, with a heavy breath, he croaked, "My name is Kiri'tol."

A smash made Badrick jump out of his skin. Placing a hand to his chest to calm his frantic heart, he turned and regarded Reynolds with concern as Agent Carter hurried to clean up the broken pieces of the Dominus' mug.

"Reynolds?" Badrick said quickly, reaching a hand towards him.

Beside him, he noticed Zale put his head in his hand and heard him mutter, "Balderdashery!"

"Sir," Carter spoke, "are you alright?"

Badrick could see Reynolds' hands shaking. The man's muscles were visibly tightening, and as Badrick watched his fingers curled in until the nails cut into his palms.

And then he said, "I retract my promise."

With that, he moved from his spot and made for the door leading to the interrogation room. His hand was already on the doorknob by the time Carter caught up and grabbed him by the shoulder, doing his best to pull Reynolds back.

"No, sir!" he shouted. "You can't endanger yourself."

Reynolds swiped Carter's hand away. "Don't you know who that is!?" he bawled.

His expression pleading, Carter admitted, "No, sir, I don't. I'm sorry. But I still can't let you in there."

"I'm the Dominus!"

"Exactly!"

"You're not a sergeant anymore, Reynolds," Zale involved himself. "You need to stay back and let your employees do their jobs."

"If we lose you, we have no Dominus," Carter tried. "A power vacuum would be bad enough but what if we're attacked without our leadership?"

"You don't need me," Reynolds argued angrily. "The generals would deal with it. The Agent Commanders. *I'm* useless. I don't *do* anything. I'm in charge of a bunch of advisors, for God's sake.

"Now let me in there!"

"Not anymore, sir," Carter snapped back. "Right now we're

vulnerable. The Daemonium is shook up and we're all looking to the new council to help us get back on our feet. Right now, sir, you're the *ultimate* authority and we *need* you."

"He's right," Badrick said, wanting to help Reynolds calm down. "The BCR and the RCR will take the reins back eventually but right now you're all we've got."

Their arguments definitely resonated within Reynolds. Badrick could tell from the way his anger subsided that they'd gotten through to him. His taut limbs softened and his shoulders relaxed, his distraught expression following suit.

Seeing this, Carter sighed breathlessly, "Thank you, sir. Come on, I'll get you another tea."

"I'll have one," Badrick joked, hoping to lighten the mood.

"You'll get one when you're Dominus," was Carter's blunt response.

"Don't give him ideas," Reynolds muttered.

Carter chuckled and pulled at levers on the coffee machine. As he did so, Badrick took the opportunity to whisper to Zale, "What's up with Reynolds?"

Zale hesitated before speaking, but when he did the words actually sent chills down Badrick's spine. "Kiri'tol was the demon of Mawr's mentor."

"And mine," the hoarse voice of the General said behind them.

Quite suddenly Badrick understood Reynolds' actions and was now seeing Kiri'tol under a different, even crueller light. In addition to his disbelief, he was now *hoping* Kiri'tol wasn't the New Evil. For Reynolds to know that his mentor's demon was the greatest danger to the world . . . Well, they'd already had a little taste of how that might play out.

Beyond the glass, Kiri'tol's interrogator was sifting through data on his port-pad with a furrowed brow. "Interesting," he could be heard murmuring. "Your energy signature doesn't correspond with our records. You sure you're who you say you are?"

"Yes!" the demon snapped. "I am Kiri'tol."

"Stupid name," Badrick heard Zale utter under his breath.

"And are you the New Evil?"

They were tense, the next few seconds.

Nobody breathed.

No one moved.

Even the air seemed to stop circulating, as if it too was waiting for Kiri'tol's response.

Cutting through the silence, the demon's answer was short and blunt. "Yes."

The interrogator nodded, but Badrick had the distinct impression that he didn't believe Kiri'tol in the slightest. He pulled up more data, smiling confidently about something or other and when he finally found what he was looking for, said, "The last demon who could create Resurrected was in our employ in the eighteen hundreds." He waved a hand in front of Kiri'tol's face. "The New Evil has resurrected at least one person, but according to our data, the demon Kiri'tol doesn't have that power. More importantly, he's an Ordinarius."

"I *was* an Ordinarius," Kiri'tol corrected him.

"Was?"

Shifting uncomfortably in his seat, Kiri'tol began with, "A long time ago, the Royals' bid for power left a lot of damage. A lot to be exploited. From it, I got the power to resurrect. I became a Singularis."

The interrogator sat back, chewing his lip as he watched Kiri'tol thoughtfully. Beside Badrick Zale scoffed disbelievingly. "You can't just *become* an Singularis. It's a DNA thing."

The interrogator clearly shared similar scepticism, evidenced by the way he voiced the same facts to the demon.

"I didn't completely change," Kiri'tol responded. "But in

essence, I became one of the Singularis.”

It was Reynolds’ turn to tut this time. Muttering darkly into his tea about demons and their penchant for crypticness, he rolled his eyes and glared at Kiri’tol.

“How about,” the interrogator finally said after much lip chewing, “you just start from the beginning?” He straightened on his chair. “Your last documented Enthraller died three years ago. Start from there.”

Kiri’tol didn’t speak at first. He looked extremely reluctant to tell his story and kept glancing with agitation towards the glass so often Badrick wondered if he could actually see them standing on the other side.

Eventually, however, his mouth did open and words poured out. “I was in Hell awaiting my next Enthraller when I was attacked by a Singularis.”

“Why?”

Kiri’tol shrugged, an act so human it looked wrong on him. “Demons like to kill.” A vicious grin replaced his tension for a brief moment, his white teeth reflecting the light as he hissed, “But I killed him first. I cast his broken essence into the Nothing and stood victorious . . . But . . . Something happened after that. Ancient energies left by the Royals got in the way of our fight. I was changed and I absorbed my victim’s power.

“It was only after it happened again that I realised I was immune to the pull of Enthrallers and this was going to keep happening.”

“You could keep absorbing other’s powers?”

“Exactly.” Kiri’tol’s grin grew truly savage. *‘T’ vok daknga!’*

The interrogator blinked. “What?”

The grin was replaced by a hateful sneer. “I was powerful,” Kiri’tol translated, “and I got an idea.”

Sighing, the interrogator asked, “And what was this idea?”

"I resurrected my previous Enthraller."

"Captain Holt?" Reynolds' gasp of horror was terrible to hear. It sent shocks of sorrow through Badrick stomach and quite abruptly he felt the desperate need to give the Dominus a hug. "He brought back Captain Holt?" He dashed forward, placing a hand on the glass. "But where is he?"

Nobody in the room could answer. Thankfully, the interrogator was already pouncing on this statement.

"Holt?" he spoke quietly. "You resurrected Holt?" Kiri'tol nodded. "Where is he now?"

"Dead." The evil smirk on the demon's face made Badrick's blood boil. "I killed him again after his soul rejected me."

Having not heard Reynolds' responding scream of fury, the interrogator queried, "Rejected?"

It did not go unnoticed by Kiri'tol that he'd revealed something the Daemonium didn't understand, and the cockiness in his resulting body language was sickening.

"The Daemonium doesn't understand how this works, do they? Fantastic!"

"Talk," the interrogator snapped, "or I bring Daemnos in here."

That shut Kiri'tol right up. Every smidgen of confidence he'd displayed only seconds before instantly vanished and he was now back to being just plain terrified.

It gave Badrick a dark pleasure to see the transition.

"Alright," the hellspawn whispered shakily. "Alright . . . I resurrected my Enthraller and I was dragged back to his soul, but because *I* was the demon who cast the power the energies involved backfired."

"Backfired?"

"My own energy resurrecting Holt got in the way of the energy that makes my being. It was like one of those magnet things you humans love so much. Never before has this happened and the Universe didn't know what to do with it. The energies deflected me but because there was no other receptacle to siphon into I was painfully dumped on Earth, weakened, not entirely complete, but very much alive. The Universe reacted violently and it spat me into your realm, physical and very real."

The interrogator looked shocked.

Badrick sympathised. From the looks of the faces of all who were listening, they too shared this feeling of uncertainty. "That's possible?" Zale spat.

"Our reality must be practically straining around him," Carter said. "Imagine if we could have scanners capable of detecting reality corrupting things ... they'd be going off like hell right now."

"We should make those," Badrick sighed.

"You can figure out how to do such a thing then," Zale tutted impatiently. "You can also invent a way to make things bigger on the inside while you're at it."

Tutting himself, Badrick responded to his sarcasm with, "It can't be done. I get it."

In the interrogation room, Kiri'tol was confirming that he was indeed telling the truth. Without warning, Zale slapped the glass and growled angrily. "That information can never get out. If demons figure out they can manifest even slightly physical by rebounding themselves in such a way then we'll have an epidemic on our hands."

"I agree," Reynolds said. "No matter what happens today, Kiri'tol never leaves here." He turned to the blank space on his right and added, "Lora, if you ever tell anyone, I swear to God—" He stopped, then said, "Thank you."

"We should scan for this," Carter said quickly. "We should get the time and coordinates and look for the moment this

Resurrection occurred."

"It'll be too late," Reynolds sighed sadly.

"Our scanners constantly scan the globe and prioritise the largest, most dangerous bursts of energy," Carter argued. "Even if it got lost in the drudge of unimportant crap, it would be in the records somewhere."

Zale scoffed at him for saying this. With a derisive look, he said, "If our scanners ever detected what Kiri'tol says happened, don't you think they'd have shoved it right at the top of the list?"

With a frustrated hand-wave, Carter snapped, "Well, then why didn't we know about it?"

In the end Zale never managed to answer; Kiri'tol's interrogation had continued unaware of their sniping and the demon had just said, "I was physical and safe from your scanners because you've never programmed them to detect what I did. Any resurrection energy you picked up was smothered by the new, never-before-seen power created by my disgorging into the world."

"How did you know to do this?" the interrogator queried, his face a sheen of despair.

"I've always known."

"How?"

"I learned, you stupid human."

The interrogator might have retorted as equally unkindly, but he was too shocked to do so. Instead he simply asked, "Have you told anybody else about it?"

Kiri'tol grew furious at the question. His face contorted with contempt and he spat, "Do you think I want other demons interfering with my plans?" The demon's eyes practically popped out, he was so angry.

As the demon writhed with rage, Reynolds turned his head to Zale, and Badrick heard him ask, "On the topic of resurrection, did we ever find Charles' resurrection in the records? Were we able to determine which burst of resurrection energy was him? We could glean some info out of it."

Zale shook his head. "There've been dozens of resurrections logged since his death and he could've been brought back *any* time. We never found out which was his."

Badrick watched Reynolds' eyes mist and he guessed the man was trying to find a way around this problem with his knowledge of their computer systems. Eventually, however, Reynolds had to concede defeat and he exhaled angrily.

"If only the energy created by using that power wasn't so perplexing," Carter sighed. "We could've gotten a signature."

"I'll add it to the to-do-list," Zale whispered blankly, his focus still intensely on Kiri'tol. "Discover why resurrection energy is so difficult to dissect and identify."

When it became obvious that without further prompting the demon would do nothing more than wriggle, the interrogator asked a question Badrick had been burning to know the response to; "Why's your signature different from when you were in Holt?"

"Because of what I've done to myself," Kiri'tol spat as if this was obvious. "I am no longer Kiri'tol. I am the *New Evil. T' qy ka. T' gy dak! T' qy qe Vil kam demons! T' qy—*"

He was silenced by the raising of the interrogator's hand. "Yes, alright, that's quite enough of the demonic crap." He allowed himself a moment to think, then said, "The New Evil is supposed to be all powerful and yet you're sitting here so afraid of two of our demons that you're telling us everything." The interrogator gave Kiri'tol a questioning expression. "I can't say I believe you're him."

"I'm not all powerful," Kiri'tol barked. "But I *will* be after I've killed more demons and acquired their powers."

A memory sparked within Badrick and he spoke, "Dhornji said

the New Evil would be the death of us." His eyes found Reynolds'. "Not *you*. He said *'us'*."

"Not just humans," Carter breathed, "but demons too."

"Because the New Evil was killing demons and stealing their powers," Zale snarled. "Unbelievable."

"Christ!"

As Badrick cursed, Zale clicked his fingers to get Badrick's attention. "Remember the discrepancies in the signatures?"

"Yeah."

"Well, there's the answer. The New Evil has been growing all this time. Getting more powerful in ways we haven't a clue about. Foreign powers were being introduced to Kiri'tol's soul."

"That's why it's the same," Badrick sighed, "but different."

As they conversed, the interrogator once again gave the impression that he was psychic; the same time Badrick brought up the dead Ordinarius, he did so as well, telling Kiri'tol what Dhornji revealed. The cruel smile returned to the supposed New Evil's face as the man finished with, "Dhornji said you were going to kill everything. Rule whatever's left."

"My plan is working. The other demons—my future slaves—have already spread rumours about me. They call me the *New Evil* because they've no record and no memory of who I could be or where I come from. There's never been anything like me before. They're running scared."

"*Uk de kam ak,*" the interrogator deadpanned.

"You know our language?"

"Only a little—"

The interrogator leapt in fright as Kiri'tol abruptly sprang from his chair and reached for the interrogator's neck, his fingernails elongating into points. The table nearly buckled from his weight, the wood creaking under the strain.

Badrick's hand slapped against the glass as he tried to summon a power—any power—to strike Kiri'tol down and save the interrogator.

However, his efforts proved too slow. The claws found their mark and tore the interrogator's neck open. Gagging horrendously, he stumbled back as a torrent of gore fountained from his flesh.

Kiri'tol spun and screeched inhumanly at the glass. His face had completely changed; his now grey skin was veiny, his mouth unnaturally wide and the teeth inside turned to razor sharp fangs. His eyes were the colour of blood, his gaze becoming a monstrous leer.

Before any of them could react, Kiri'tol bounded for the furthest door and ploughed straight through it, shattering the metal like it was wood.

"NO!" Badrick bawled, panic rising in him so quickly it was shocking. "Come on, we have to stop him!"

He darted for the door and wrenched it open, kneeling by the slain interrogator when he entered. There was no pulse and already the flow of blood had lessened, meaning his heart had stopped beating. "Damn!" He leapt to his feet and made for the door through which Kiri'tol fled.

As he barged over the threshold, he was vaguely aware of something odd on the remains of the metal. It looked like vicious scorch marks burning deep into the door and weakening the structure.

Ignoring them, he charged through the corridor beyond in chase of their escaped prisoner. He wasn't sure if Zale or the others were behind him, but he didn't waste time in checking. He needed to catch the escapee as fast as he could.

If the one claiming to be the New Evil got away . . .

Badrick never actually got to finish that dreadful thought. As he reached the end of the corridor and emerged into the HQ, he was greeted by a surprising sight.

Kiri'tol stood close by, his hands—returned to normal—poised shakily above his head, his neck twisting left and right as he stared, clearly afraid, at the many men and women aiming weapons his way.

"What?" Badrick found himself murmuring. From the looks of things these people had clearly been lying in wait. They'd been positioned here, armed and ready, waiting for Kiri'tol to emerge.

The Daemonium set a trap.

"You think this is the first time a prisoner has tried to escape?" Badrick jumped in fright at how close to his back this voice was. He spun on his heel, half ready to fight, and was more than shocked to see the interrogator brushing past him, his neck impossibly unmarked.

Out of the door, stepped Reynolds, followed by both Zale and Carter. Staring disbelievingly at the interrogator as he drew close to Kiri'tol, Badrick gestured at him questioningly. His mouth was hanging open and he was only capable of making incomprehensible sounds, so he simply pointed, dumbstruck.

"An illusion," Carter said simply. "Safeguards the interrogator."

Over by the demon, the interrogator regarded Kiri'tol with what looked like amusement. "The Daemonium knows the demon that those powers belong to as the Vampire Demon."

Acidic bitterness laced his voice as Kiri'tol replied, "You've met Varmora, then?" He cast an eye on the Enthrallers above. "This is a trap. How did you—?"

"The entire time we've been talking," the interrogator smirked, "your tone has suggested you see a future for yourself. You spoke as if you believed yourself capable of fulfilling your plans. To me, that screamed escape attempt." He pointed sharply to the corridor they'd emerged from. "I also noticed something curious on the door. You were corroding it away so you'd be able to bash through, so I alerted the Daemonium and we found the route you were planning to take. Lo and behold, every door from here to the Quarters Tower is corroded.

"You were going to break a window in the Tower and escape."

Kiri'tol snarled angrily, saying, "You never spoke to anyone. How—"

The interrogator tapped his right with another smirk. "I can send messages."

As Kiri'tol lowered and shook his head in disgust, Reynolds turned to Carter and said, "I don't recognise that corrosion power but it proves his claims, don't you think?"

"He stole it from another demon," Carter nodded. "So what do you think?"

"I don't disbelieve what I'm hearing," the Dominus muttered after a moment's hesitation. "But . . ."

As they watched a group of Enthrallers escort the furious Kiri'tol back to his interrogation room, Badrick found himself snapping sternly, "I don't believe it."

"Still?" Zale sighed impatiently.

"Badrick," Reynolds began, "weak as it is, Kiri'tol's signature is the same as what we picked up when Dhornji was killed. There *are*, as Zale said, differences. It's larger, more aggressive energy than the Power Leech, and feeble compared to the scans at the castle, but . . . it's the same where it counts."

Badrick waved his hands in the air, roughly shaking his head. "I don't care!" he shouted. "This trap wouldn't matter to the New Evil. He could've blown them all apart and escaped."

"Dude," Zale said quickly, "he's not as powerful as we thought, remember?"

"No!" Badrick bawled. "He . . ." It was then that he realised it was the Dominus he was screeching disrespectfully towards and gasped a sudden intake of breath, hurrying to correct his attitude. "Sorry, Reynolds. It's just . . ." He trailed off, ashamed.

"Speak your mind, Varner," Reynolds urged him kindly.

Hesitant, Badrick did his best to speak in a calm voice. "You guys weren't there when Dhornji was killed, but my team and I were. We *felt* the power that murdered him. It wasn't . . . *growing* . . . It wasn't *'I-will-be-powerful-but-not-right-now'*. It was deadly, and dangerous. It was . . . Reynolds, it *hurt* to sense his presence.

"Kiri'tol *can't* be the New Evil. He doesn't fit."

Thoughtful and worried glances were exchanged between Reynolds, Carter and Zale. None of them spoke for a moment, each probably unsure of what to say.

The uncomfortable silence only ended when Carter said, "Our machinery is top of the line, but we would be stupid not to listen to the Enthraller of Daemnos. Badrick's instincts should be taken into account."

"Glad to see we're on the same page," Reynolds half laughed. "Means I'm not letting my fondness get in the way of my judgement." He rubbed his hands together and added to Badrick, "Does the prince himself have anything to say?"

Badrick cut a hand across his neck. "Nothing. He hasn't spoken to me for days."

"Typical." Reynolds gave them all a nod. "OK, we'll listen to you, Badrick. We'll—"

"Sense him."

All eyes turned to Zale, but again nobody spoke until Badrick decided to be the one to break the suffocating quiet. "What're you talking about?"

"If you don't trust our technology then don't let there be any doubt. Find out yourself. Go in there and make physical contact. Read him *all* the way through."

"That's a bad idea," Reynolds immediately stopped him. "We

can't just let anyone go into a room with someone who is suspected to be the New Evil."

"It's Badrick," Zale shrugged. "We've already determined that Kiri'tol is not as big a threat as we thought he was—"

"Yet."

"Exactly, Reynolds. *Yet.* He'll be fine. Just let him go in there and find out for himself. If we trust Badrick enough to let him direct our decisions then let us prove to him that we do."

The growl Reynolds sent his way was very reminiscent of his good old self, before he was overcome by the stresses of being Dominus. "I hate you, Hood."

"No, you don't."

Reynolds turned to Carter and asked, "What do you think?"

Carter only shrugged.

"I hate you too." Reynolds took a moment to roar with frustration before finally bawling, "OK, fine, but we go in with you."

"Not you, sir."

"Shut up, Carter!" Reynolds retreated and took a breath. "Sorry. I'll stay in observation, just as you ask, but please go in with Varner. Take a weapon. Zale, Kiri'tol is scared of you too, so prime your power. The sight of Horas' strength should deter him from trying anything."

"Got it." Zale placed a hand on Badrick's shoulder. "Do this for me," he said. "Find out if it *is* him. Please."

There was no way Badrick could deny him this request. Those imploring eyes were just too much for him to handle. "Alright," he found himself saying resignedly. "Take me in there."

It happened quicker than he could keep up with. The necessary procedures were organised and the next second Badrick was standing next to a squirming Kiri'tol with nothing but air between them.

He hesitated at first but, after a comforting prompt from Reynolds over the microphone, he tenderly reached to touch Kiri'tol arm, powering his digits with supernatural sensing energy. When skin contact was made, he'd be able to channel the energy throughout Kiri'tol and scan every single cell of his being.

The demon recoiled from his proximity, trying to lean far enough away that Badrick would miss. But Badrick refused to let him evade his touch and, adjusting his position, pressed his fingers onto Kiri'tol's hand.

The scream that tore from his throat deafened even him.

Blackness.

Suffocating, engulfing darkness.

Death.

Decay.

Evil beyond measure.

Power . . . *Oh, the power!*

His hand was stuck to Kiri'tol. Badrick couldn't tear it away. His demonic senses were screeching from the strain of making continuous contact with the demon. The tips of his fingers were blackening, as if scorched by a terrible fire.

And it was only when Zale called his name and vaulted the table to wrench him free did the agony stop.

However, the trauma did not.

Badrick's limbs were now thrashing, his mind was so clouded. He thought he was being attacked by an unknown enemy and his only chance of survival was to fight for his life. He had no idea where he was or who was now doing their best to constrict his arms and legs.

"Badrick!" the one attempting to murder him called. "Stop!"

"I'll kill you!" Badrick screamed, his hand glowing green and shooting a blast of energy towards where he could see the attacker's accomplice was standing. His target gasped and rolled to the side, avoiding the blast by only inches.

"Badrick!" the attacker screamed. "It's me!"

Finally Badrick's body grew weary and his arms begged him to stop. With no choice but to obey their demands, he let them fall to the floor. Pain shot through his elbows as they hit, and it was the throbbing caused by the impact that finally cleared the fog in his brain.

Blinking, Badrick realised the man holding him down was not an attacker, but his partner Zale.

However, despite his brain growing lucid, Badrick's shivering body refused to relax and he lay there, half on the floor, half in Zale's arms.

"What happened?" he heard Reynolds voice in his ear. "Are you alright? What did you sense?"

There was no denying it.

Nobody could fake what he'd felt.

Badrick turned his terrified eyes to Kiri'tol, who was also breathing heavily, though out of anger as opposed to pain.

And he breathed, "Kiri'tol *is* the New Evil."

chapter
THIRTEEN

The courtroom seemed different to Badrick.

Where before it had acted as a means to dispense cruelty and injustice, it now felt safe and secure.

The last time he'd been inside the courtroom, Zale had been on trial for crimes he'd never committed. Although it was true he'd abandoned the Daemonium in search of personal revenge, the other *billion* fabricated charges blew the justification for the trial out the window.

It had been so unfair—so *unjust*—that Badrick had threatened to blow them all up unless they let Zale go free.

He had been a different person back then and it seemed like such an age ago.

A million years.

But in truth it had been . . .

Two weeks . . .

Maybe?

Badrick wasn't entirely sure. The recent days had blended together into an inconceivable mess of terror and anxiety. So much had happened since the day he'd returned to the Daemonium and if he was being truthful he could hardly remember any of it.

The last thing he could remember with any clarity was trapping Lucikefer in the Void.

Looking at the demon Kiri'tol forced to his knees, surrounded by Daemonium agents, soldiers and operatives, Badrick wondered how they had gotten here. How could someone go from trapping a weakened demon in the Void to catching the ultimate evil in only a few weeks?

Above the self-proclaimed New Evil stood Reynolds, looming over the judge's chair. He was regarding the people who'd come to witness these proceedings in solemn silence, taking his time before speaking.

When he did, it was with a determination Badrick knew was shared with everybody present.

"The facts stand like this," he called to the room. "Every bit of technology we have is telling us that the demon Kiri'tol is the New Evil. Signature scans are the same. Power comparisons check out. Kiri'tol was not only present at every New Evil sighting but *was* the demon exuding the energy that made it a New Evil sighting in the first place."

Murmurs began to spread among the onlookers, but Reynolds held up a hand to quickly stop them.

"We've heard from the agents who were sent to extract the demon Dhornji. You all know of this event. Not only does the Enthraller of Daemnos corroborate what the machines tell us, but so do the agents from that team.

"Every single one of you called to push their senses into Kiri'tol has come back with the exact same conclusion.

"This demon," he pointed to Kiri'tol, "*is* the New Evil."

Reynolds fell into silence to allow this to sink in and when he was sure the impact of his words had been felt by everybody, he invited Quill to take the stage.

The Agent Commander didn't waste any time. He took Reynolds' place and quickly began his part in these proceedings. "A lot has happened in the past few weeks. We've seen destruction on a national scale, our own government has been turned upside down and we've been threatened like we never have before.

"Some of you remember the Devil's ascension, and I know I speak for everyone when I say that even when he tore demons from Enthrallers and wreaked havoc across Europe . . . Even then it did not feel like this." Nods and murmurs of agreement spread across the crowd. "We have to decide," Quill continued, "what to do with our newest enemy. With Kiri'tol being what he is, and the effect he's had on everyone, we decided it best that everyone had a say."

Reynolds took back the reigns from here. "If anyone has a better idea, please speak now, because we see only two options."

"Either we imprison Kiri'tol," Quill said sternly, "or we execute him."

It interested Badrick in a sobering kind of way to see that nobody argued against either of those two options.

"Then . . ." Quill faltered slightly when he noticed the cruel, murderous look on Kiri'tol's furious face. "Please," he tried again, "when we ask, display a thumbs up for imprisonment and a thumbs down for execution."

Badrick's stomach tensed as everybody shuffled, readying to

cast their vote. Hands were extended, fingers balled into fists. Ahead, Quill checked with Reynolds, glanced at Kevin, then called for people to make their decision.

One by one, without fail, every thumb pointed to the floor.

Reynolds' face was expressionless, and Badrick figured that was intentional. "So be it," he said. "There's no point in wasting time. Badrick . . . will you step up here, please?"

He had anticipated this was coming but, even so, Badrick felt knots in his stomach as he took his place next to the Dominus.

"Badrick, we haven't any proof that any of us can kill Kiri'tol. We need the Power of a Royal and have to hope it is enough." Reynolds looked genuinely sad to ask Badrick to be executing anyone, demonic hellspawn or not. "Will you do this?"

Badrick couldn't stop his eyes drifting to look at Kiri'tol's juddering form. Their gazes met, Kiri'tol's hateful glare drilling holes into Badrick's nervous one, and at the sight of those dark, malicious orbs he felt a curious squirming sensation inside his stomach.

This writhing within him intensified rapidly, growing and growing until it became unbearably painful, and all the while his mind raced . . .

The magnitude of what was being thrust upon him became all too real. The Daemonium was asking him to *kill* this demon while he was vulnerable, surrounded and on his knees.

They weren't in the midst of battle, fighting for survival in a brawl where anything was permissible.

This was going to be a slaughtering.

And in that moment, a sudden realisation came to Badrick . . .

Oh, he spoke boldly about smiting his enemies and waved away the idea of torturing and killing people who pissed him off like it was nothing. He was so very blithe. But when it came down to it, this was all just big talk.

Because the truth was he had never actually taken a life before.

The Forsaken he'd killed had been an unintentional death; a result of Daemnos' manipulations—power broke free and struck their enemy down.

Badrick's demon had been the one to slay Stefan. Badrick had been against the very idea and had no hand in his murder.

Lucikefer had only been imprisoned; a crueller fate than death perhaps, but a far less savage one.

And though, in the rush of combat, Badrick had shot Charles, the bastard was brought back instantly, and had regardless already been dead the entire time.

It was true Badrick had taken out many Kalik demons in his time, but it had always been in an act of self defence, or when he needed to combat the threat they posed. He'd never slaughtered them as they lay weak and helpless and unable to run.

Besides, they were monsters. Genuinely soulless. The word *'killing'* hardly counted when it came to those beasts. Kalik served no purpose in the world except to ruin and destroy and deserved nothing else in return.

The world was better off with them dead.

And they weren't human.

Of course, there was no way anyone could mistake Kiri'tol for a person. His very presence was capable of dashing that belief before it fully formed in someone's head. But he *looked* like a person, with human arms, legs, a head and eyes that, right now, radiated a very human-like fear and hatred.

He looked like a regular, terrified man—

No.

Badrick could not allow himself to be fooled. Could not permit these unexpected doubts and his newfound foreboding to govern his actions and prevent him from doing what he must.

Kiri'tol was no man.

And it didn't matter that nobody had yet died by Badrick's intent; he was an Operative in the Daemonium . . . He'd always known he'd be called upon to kill eventually. The iniquitous forces they struggled to hold back could not be afforded leniency.

Badrick had to remember that Kiri'tol wasn't *just* a demon waiting to spread pain and death, but was also the New Evil . . . the being who wanted to take the lives of all. It didn't matter that Kiri'tol was afraid, trembling and gently moaning at the thought of what was to come.

The world *needed* him gone in the only permanent way.

His demise would save the lives of everyone on the planet.

Badrick couldn't think about the unlucky dice that led him to being the necessary executioner. If he did, it would eat him up inside and he would fall into a deep, dark pit.

He could help nobody from within the dreadful confines of depression.

His innocence wasn't important . . . The lives of other people were his priority. To save them, he had to be willing to taint his soul.

And he had to accept that.

As resolute as he could make himself, Badrick shakily stepped in front of the quavering Kiri'tol. The demon's shaking increased tenfold, confirming the fact that he really *was* afraid of Daemnos.

Despite his trepidation, Badrick felt a small bubble of satisfaction knowing that he was causing the demon distress. It was less then what he deserved after all the death he'd left in his wake, but it *was* warranted.

Badrick didn't bother giving the demon any last words. Had he done, he might have lost his resolve and faltered, perhaps giving Kiri'tol some new chance of escape. Determined to prevent this, and hoping it was enough, he unleashed the full force of Daemnos' strength, wrapping him in supernatural power, and imagined him torn to pieces.

The power obeyed his will and pulled at Kiri'tol's physical body, digging deep and puncturing his soul. Kiri'tol screamed as his skin ripped, his flesh tore and his bones snapped apart.

And then he exploded.

Black gore splashed in all directions, but Badrick was able to contain the deluge before it stained the courtroom. With a wave of his hand he incinerated the remains with the hottest hellfire he could muster, destroying any last trace of the demon Kiri'tol.

When the last of the flames died out and only wisps of smoke remained, Quill stepped up beside him and called to the room, "The New Evil is dead. We've won!"

Before Badrick could comprehend what happened, he realised he was staring at the ceiling. The Enthrallers had surged forward and hoisted him into the air, cheering and celebrating the New Evil's defeat.

Badrick couldn't share their enthusiasm. All he could see in his mind's eye was Kiri'tol's dissolving body and all he could hear were his dying screams. What he had done, he was not proud of.

There had been no other way of disposing of their enemy—no guns or daggers could have taken him out—but for the first time Badrick no longer felt his usual elation at being a teenage boy with superpowers.

If he was completely honest with himself, what he'd just done was making him wonder if there was any morality in using the supernatural gifts of demon's to fight off other hellspawn, or if they were all just kidding themselves.

Was victory worth using the brutality of your enemy?

At the back of the room, he could see Zale. His face was just as stony as Badrick's, the veteran's body language suggesting that he felt no desire to celebrate.

Badrick couldn't blame him.

He didn't feel much like it either.

*

It had been a long time since Badrick and Zale lazed about in one of the three recreational rooms. Honestly, it was strange to think they even could. But, with no Kalik, Resurrected or New Evil to terrify them into action, all they had left to do was sit in silence.

Badrick's mind kept travelling back to the moment Kiri'tol's life was extinguished. His body fell apart in a chaotic group of seconds, and Badrick had not failed to sense the very instant his life snuffed out.

Badrick couldn't stop thinking about that moment.

He'd expected joy when Kiri'tol finally passed into the next existence, not this never-ending melancholy. He couldn't quite understand why, but there was barely any optimism in him at that moment.

In fact, the only positive emotion coursing through him was a mild sense of relief.

Relief that the darkness had passed.

Relief that his terror could now be blown away.

Relief that they were safe.

It was positively exhausting to let go of the dread he'd carried nonstop for so many days. It was like when someone relieved themselves of a heavy burden they'd been heaving around for an extended amount of time and could only collapse with weariness.

He hoped happiness would arrive at a later date when his fatigue subsided, but unfortunately that wasn't going to be today.

Maybe, he thought, *it's my fault. Sitting here miserably. Maybe I should try and find something fun to do. Celebrate like a normal person.*

Maybe then his emotions would catch up to the rest of the Enthrallers. He could hear them outside in the rest of the facility, cheering and whooping like children. They were so excited to be rid of the New Evil. So happy to be safe from total destruction.

With the sounds of their jubilation ringing in his ears, Badrick's eyes drifted over to the only other person not jumping for joy. Half slumped in his seat, Zale looked exactly as Badrick felt. His eyes were faded, nearly closed, and if Badrick didn't know better he would have said that Zale was asleep.

While Badrick was studying his misshapen partner, the sound they'd been waiting nearly two hours for was finally heard at the front of the room. Badrick turned thankfully towards the source, eyeing up the Dominus as he stepped through the door. His red and black uniform appeared crisper than Badrick had seen it in a while, and his smile was genuine as he settled into the armchair opposite.

"I'm sorry that took so long," he said. "The paperwork was a burden." Reynolds eyed them both in turn. "How are you?"

"Tired," Badrick breathed. Once again, his mind pondered on ways to help rid himself of weariness.

"I'm not surprised." Reynolds turned his attention to Zale. "Are you alive over there, Hood?"

"Mmm," was the reply.

"Good enough," Badrick chuckled. "Right? Proof of life."

"Perhaps." Reynolds didn't bother trying again. He relaxed in his chair, stretching his arms and sighing contentedly. "I haven't sat in a good chair in a week." He lowered his head and gazed at the arm of the chair. "My mentor loved this exact chair. When he had time off his duties he would come to this chair and end the day reading a book.

"He was a noble man," he sighed. "It's insulting that his demon was . . ."

When Reynolds trailed away and did not continue, Badrick tried to help his suddenly sombre mood by saying, "Wish I could have met him."

"He would have liked you," Reynolds smiled again. "Stubborn, always disobeying the Council. He would have gotten a kick out of it, just as he did whenever Mawr disobeyed anyone who gave him orders."

"Dear ol' Captain Holt," Zale suddenly said, seemingly awakening from his stupor. "Only Enthraller I've ever met who died of old age."

"He wouldn't let go of life," Reynolds chuckled. "Stubborn bastard held on for two years despite his body giving up on him."

"Kinda like my granddad," Badrick chipped in.

Reynolds made the effort to acknowledge Badrick's comment with a smile, then straightened and adopted a far more formal stance. "Enough of the chat," he said. "Back to business, you two. First of all, I personally wish to thank the both of you for your exemplary work. What we found ourselves up against over the last few weeks has been difficult. Had I known the Kalik Crisis would escalate into what it did I would never have let two very junior operatives go at it alone, or even at all.

"We all made foolish choices based on fear. Fear that Zale would be imprisoned, fear that Charles would destroy everything we've fought to protect, fear that the New Evil would kill us all."

Reynolds shrugged his shoulders in a manly way and coughed to clear his throat. "But that's in the past and despite the choices that divided the Daemonium we somehow prevailed."

"A lot has changed," Zale agreed.

"Don't interrupt me, Hood," Reynolds chided him. Clearing his throat again, he continued, "The Council has unanimously agreed to award the both of you with a Crossed-Swords medal."

"What's that?" Badrick couldn't help but ask.

Zale straightened in his chair, a disbelieving look in his eyes. "One of the highest commendations we can get." He scoffed rather rudely. "You're messing with us, Reynolds."

"No, Hood," Reynolds smiled. "I'm being serious. Like I said, you've done exemplary work. You took on the kind of mission only senior operatives should take and yet made it through more efficiently than I dared hoped.

"Most of us believed that if the New Evil didn't raze this place to the ground we'd at least be fighting him for months. Maybe even years."

"That's 'cause we're awesome," Badrick laughed, unable to prevent pride bloating within him.

"In thanks," Reynolds said, "we're also authorising two weeks leave, starting tomorrow."

"What?" Badrick could hardly believe it.

With a proud smile, Reynolds said, "You deserve it."

"Wow!" Badrick's mouth actually fell open, he was so surprised. "Thanks!"

"Two weeks?" Zale voiced, his surprise just as equal. "That's quite a while."

"Don't complain, Zale," Reynolds tutted. "Be thankful. Like I said, you deserve it, and, frankly, it's time you Mary Sues gave other people room to shine."

"That's insulting!" Zale practically hollered.

"Yeah, we aren't perfect, Reynolds," Badrick agreed, a little less shrilly. "How many mistakes have us two made?"

Zale turned a steely gaze upon him, one that made him shiver, and spat, "No, Badrick. No . . . Mary Sue is a woman. The correct term for male perfection is Gary Stu!"

Reynolds rolled his eyes and tutted, "Shut up, Hood."

"I will not be silenced when my honour is being slighted," Zale grumbled, though Badrick could see a tiny humoured smile on the corners of his mouth.

Badrick cackled at his partner's behaviour. "Apparently

defeating the New Evil had a . . . euphoric effect on my esteemed colleague here."

"Wow," Zale breathed. "Those were some big, formal words you used there. Did it hurt to use them?"

"Spend tonight," Reynolds stopped them continuing this playful banter, possibly believing them to be arguing, "deciding what you want to do with your fourteen days."

"I'm going to sleep," Zale heaved a heavy sigh. "For a week."

Ignoring his unimaginative answer, Reynolds asked Badrick what he had planned.

Taking only a second to think on his plan to push away fatigue, he answered, "You know what . . . I'm going to go out tomorrow."

"To do what?"

Shrugging, Badrick grinned. "We'll see."

chapter
FOURTEEN

The quiet of Zale's room was rather beautiful after the eclectic action of the past few days. He hadn't expected to find so much enjoyment from simply being in a silent area, but enjoy it he did.

When the door closed and all noise ceased, Zale realised he'd been waiting all day for some alone time.

He took a step towards the mirror and regarded his reflection, studying the long blonde strands of hair that flowed unnaturally, as though a breeze was passing through the room.

He'd always wondered why his hair had this otherworldly quality—it had been a source of great frustration for him—and he'd been forced to realise it was likely he'd never find the answer. The question of his genetics would have to be put to the ones who gave birth to him, and unfortunately even the Daemonium had never succeeded in locating even a cousin.

But that was in the past.

Zale understood himself now.

He closed his eyes and took a deep breath, further enjoying the silence of his room.

Unfortunately, it seemed he would not get to for long.

Gritting his teeth, Zale did his best to ignore the appearance of Horas behind him. Unfortunately, his disinterest didn't seem to deter the demon in the slightest.

"So," Horas spoke, "it seems your scheming has borne fruit. You have succeeded."

"Of course I succeeded," Zale snapped back, annoyed that the demon seemed to be implying there'd been any doubt of his impending victory. "They took the bait. Just as I knew they would."

"It's a shame you were hit by that explosive. Everything would have unfolded flawlessly if not for the Bomb Killer."

At the demon's prompt, Zale's mind cast back over the past few days, mulling over everything he'd accomplished. In his mind's eye he saw Dhornji's corpse beneath his feet, watched himself leaving his own energy at the scene for the Daemonium to detect, and recalled pummelling Charles while mind-controlling him into silence.

He remembered the moment he planted the power-leech inside the Resurrected and grinned at the thought of doing all these things without a single Daemonium energy sensor detecting him.

"Why use Kiri'tol as your patsy?" Horas asked, placing his hand against his head with exhaustion. Sighing audibly, Horas continued, "You put so much effort into discreetly raising him from Hell, filling him with powers of long dead demons, manipulating his signature to mimic yours and controlling him to do as you desired. Surely a less conspicuous demon would have been the better option."

"He was the demon of Reynolds' mentor," Zale responded simply, expecting these few short words to be explanation enough. However, it became evident that they were not when Horas only stared at him silently. Sighing tiredly, he growled, "Don't you see?" When Horas failed to answer, Zale asked him, "Didn't you notice how Reynolds reacted to that little revelation? He got so emotional, it was hilarious."

Horas nodded. "He was not thinking straight at all."

"To Reynolds, Kiri'tol being the New Evil is a cruel betrayal to his mentor. His emotions got in the way of his better judgement and stopped him noticing any little factoid I might have missed or forgotten to compel Kiri'tol to mention.

"Now, of course, there were none, but you should always have a contingency plan. Because Reynolds is smart. He notices things and I had to cloud that vision.

"And it worked." Zale's face contorted into a cruel, malicious sneer. "I won."

In the mirror, Zale saw darkness fill his eyes. Blackness crept over the whites and engulfed the irises until he was looking into powerful and malevolent orbs of dark power.

Beside him, he felt Horas sigh with dejection. "You really *are* a new kind of evil."

PART II

QUID ENIM DESIDERARI

chapter
FIFTEEN

The power was growing.

Getting brighter.

Somewhere . . . inside Zale's soul.

It wasn't originating from the bulk of energy that comprised Horas' existence. The demon's personal signature didn't resonate *anything* like this.

This was something else.

Something new.

Foreign.

Still, it was expanding, caressing his soul with each increase in size. When it touched him pain would stab at his chest, each time sharper than before. Zale clutched at his heart and groaned as a particularly prickly jab made him wince.

What was—

Without warning, the energy exploded.

Zale's muscles were unwillingly energised and he was compelled to his feet. He cried out as his bones heated impossibly from the power surge, his body growing hotter . . . and hotter . . . until his skin was burning like the sun.

The wetness on his face had long fizzled out of existence, only to be replaced by thick beads of sweat that seeped from his pores in waves. Growing panic filled him as this . . . *force* . . . tightened whatever grip it had on him, and he coughed, stumbling to the wall as his balance was lost. Gritting his teeth, Zale made for the door with the intent of getting help.

But, as he jumped forward, what he naturally expected to happen when he put his foot down never did. Instead of making contact with the floor, his foot simply continued descending, throwing him completely off balance. He fell, scorching arms flailing out in an attempt to break his fall.

Again, he never made contact with something solid.

And that was when the lights went out.

As he tumbled never-endingly, his room vanished to be replaced by the dizzying handicap of complete blackness.

He was blind.

And not just that . . .

His fear grew when he realised he could no longer hear.

The general musk of his room had vanished . . . his sense of smell was gone.

His clothes no longer warmed his skin.

He couldn't taste his own saliva.

And now, even though he knew he was still falling through space, he could no longer feel it.

Every sense . . .

They were all gone.

In the darkness, with no sight or ability to feel anything around him, Zale was utterly alone. Never before had he felt such an overwhelming sense of solitude. Isolated and desperate, Zale flailed helplessly, searching for something—anything—that would help him break his fall.

He thought he might be screaming, but he could not feel the vibrations in his mouth nor hear the sound in his ears.

Alone in this unnatural blackness, Zale felt genuine terror.

But then . . . something strange happened.

It started with the knowledge that he was no longer falling. Even though his senses had yet to return, he knew the instant his body stopped tumbling. That natural ability to determine which way was up had unexplainably returned.

Despite feeling nothing beneath his feet, Zale knew he was standing.

But that wasn't the only odd thing to occur; as he tried to blink and see through the dark, that horrible, all encompassing loneliness that he felt mere moments before vanished completely.

It flitted from his consciousness as though someone had rid him of it.

It was extremely nauseating to feel as though your own emotions were being manipulated by alien hands, and even despite his fear and disorientation, Zale tried to understand why he instinctively no longer felt alone.

It wasn't as though he considered himself any safer than before—Zale was utterly helpless—and anyone could stroll into his room and shank him while he wrestled with whatever he was experiencing.

Zale would have no way to fight back.

Wouldn't even know he was under threat until he was dead.

However . . . he wasn't as vulnerable as he thought.

Thinking about people helped him realise that he still had his greatest weapon; his mind. Even in this confusing and horrible situation, Zale's intellect was racing, thinking, and doing its best to understand.

Imagining someone walking into his room helped him realise why he no longer felt alone.

It was blindingly obvious when Zale thought about it . . . He no longer felt lonely because he already instinctively knew the truth.

He was *not* alone.

There was something in the darkness. Having worked it out, he could now sense its presence. It lingered within the unseen, watching him, studying him, waiting to see how Zale would react to the next manipulation.

Whatever was hiding out there was responsible for *this*.

It was not a friend—

BANG!

In fright, Zale's teeth bit his tongue and pain shot through it. At the same time the noise deafened him, a blazing light scorched his eyes and he was forced to clamp them shut. A shrill whining nearly burst his eardrums and refused to quieten, even after he slammed his hands over his ears.

The roar of fear now coming from his mouth eventually grew so loud it drowned out the whine, which eventually surrendered to his superior decibel and silenced.

When Zale was sure the din would not resume, he gingerly took away his hands and opened his eyes a crack, hoping the light was finally gone.

What he saw was not what he expected.

The darkness had released him, but the familiar surroundings of his room were gone.

He was standing in the Main Hall.

The glass and metal walkways stretched across the space above Zale, illuminated by the strong overhead lights. The glass reflected the light from the window and cast vivid rays of sunshine into the room.

Zale noted the scorch marks made recently by the chaos caused by Charles' Energy Disrupter Pulse. He saw the walkway leading from the Medical Wing was still in pieces, and the shattered glass of a decimated light was scattered all over the floor.

It was certainly impressive; this place looked *exactly* the same.

However, Zale was not fooled. He knew he wasn't actually standing in the Daemonium HQ. There were too many discrepancies for him to fall for this ruse.

Firstly, where was everybody? The place was a ghost town. Were this actually the Main Hall, it would have been filled with hundreds of people.

Secondly, what he'd just experienced did not correlate to any known demonic teleport power. It had been a long and painful process, and even forced teleportation inflicted on an unwilling subject didn't cause discomfort like that.

Zale hadn't travelled anywhere.

Thirdly, as good as this recreation was, there was no denying it didn't *feel* real. This place couldn't replicate the sensation of physicality provided from existing in the real world.

Zale didn't even feel like a real person anymore.

So it came to reason that this whole thing was occurring in his head, where life could attain only a metaphysical existence.

At first, he imagined he might be experiencing one of the three grades of visions.

If that were the case, it would be Grade Two—a vision of a place.

But that was impossible—a demonic vision flowed so quickly only those proficient in this kind of supernatural occurrence could take a moment to think. It would start, display what it was going to display, then end.

Whatever this was, it certainly wasn't a vision.

There was only one conclusion Zale could come to; someone or something had forced him, chaotically, indelicately, into his own head. All of this was a reconstruction of the real world that was using his brainwaves as foundations.

And thankfully, although Zale had yet to learn the purpose of this cerebral assault, he'd managed to determine how it paced along.

It wasn't hard to figure out; every event was linked to his own actions.

When Zale decided he didn't deserve to be ignored—the demonic power ignited.

When he tried to get help—his senses were stolen.

When he realised he was not alone—everything returned.

Based on how this whole incident was unfolding, Zale had a feeling the *unseen* was waiting for him to figure out where he was.

And now that he had, surely the next stage would come.

Not a problem—Zale would play its game. He could determine his attacker's identity at a later time. Better to outwit this new opponent and escape before hunting it down and violently punishing it for interrupting his grieving.

"That . . ." a voice cut the silence like a knife, the only source of sound in this quiet place, "is exactly the attitude I was hoping for."

Zale couldn't understand why such palpable alarm spread inside him at the sound of the voice, but it was as though his subconscious knew something he did not and was projecting instinctual terror into his conscious mind, despite failing to provide an explanation as to why.

His panic forced his tired muscles into action and he swivelled on the spot, searching for the source of the voice.

But the owner could not be seen. It was not on the walkways, nor standing in a doorway. There remained a significant lack of any other life anywhere in this building. Even the space between hard surfaces, which might have contained a hovering menace, was completely empty.

That was until Zale pivoted to his left and came face to face with an expressionless blue visor.

The sudden appearance of another person sent his heart rocketing into his throat and he gasped, stumbling back in surprise. "Horas!" he hollered.

The demon looked extremely worn. His shoulders were heaving as his ragged breath escaped in shuddering pants. Overcoming his surprise, Zale stepped back to him, greatly concerned by the sight of his pain.

The simple fact that Horas looked physically shattered was mind-blowing. He was supposed to be nothing but a wavelength, so why would the demon have physical exhaustion of any kind?

"Horas?" Zale repeated. "Are you OK? What's going on?"

Horas' head shook aggressively, but he otherwise ignored the questions. Instead, he half shouted, "You must go!"

This fatigue wasn't simply an act, Zale could see. Now that they were engaging for the first time in days, Zale could feel the demon's weakness as if it was his own. It was a confusing sensation—as though Horas was weary from years of strenuous effort.

Somehow something had tired him out.

"You must go!" he repeated, placing a hand on Zale's shoulder and pushing him back. "You cannot be here. You must go. Quickly!"

"What's going on, Horas?" Zale asked, pushing Horas' hand away from him. "Why are we here?"

"You have entered into a coma!" the demon shouted with great impatience. "*It* needs you trapped in your mind so it can seize control." He sidestepped, blocking Zale's view of the Main Hall. "I have been holding it off but in here I cannot protect you. You are vulnerable. You *must* leave. Go now!"

Zale desperately wanted an explanation but he could tell the situation was dire. Horas' was definitely alarmed about something, and his general formal behaviour didn't evaporate and give way to panic for no reason at all.

It was his trust in his demon that made Zale back away and begin searching for a way he might escape this mind-trap.

But he realised too late that there was no chance of getting out.

As he moved, the unseen presence stilled both him and Horas with a surge of power so intense it was *visible*. It rippled the air and bent the walls. The walkways above wobbled impossibly, the metal moving as though made of water.

And the light *vibrated* in such a way that it mingled with the shadows and created a curious flashing effect.

Zale could hardly breathe; the presence's mere existence was overwhelming.

Filling the room with its very being, the power Zale could detect radiating from its unseen form was unbelievable. Never before had he experienced such a source of energy.

And he'd been present at the Daemnos/Stefan brawl.

Even the blasts of residual power that battered the landscape during their all out combat seemed trivial and pointless in comparison to the unseen presence.

Whatever it was seemed to be enjoying his reaction as it didn't make another move for quite some time. Only when Horas seemed to regain the courage to speak again did it interrupt him before he could.

"Well . . ." Something moved in the shadows, coming closer to them with each new word, "well . . . well . . . What do we have here?"

Zale had to fight the urge to vomit. Every time the voice spoke it was like his very soul was being struck so hard it was coughing blood. It carried such power that each word made him feel weak and tiny.

In compare to this presence, he was nothing.

And now, from the cover of darkness, a figure emerged.

Zale saw impeccable blonde hair, the sort you might find in a styled animated movie. An impossible blend of flat and spiky, long enough to cover the newcomer's forehead, the strands flowing like leaves on a tree.

But it didn't hide the brilliantly handsome face; cleanly shaven, fair, beautiful and yet rugged all at the same time.

All of this was alarming, but it was the eyes that drew the most attention.

The moment Zale saw the face of the presence he'd expected to look into bright, electrical blue eyes.

But the eyes were *not* like Zale's.

They were black.

Upon seeing these dark orbs staring at them intensely, Horas exhaled with fear. "No!" he breathed shakily. "Zale, you must go."

But Zale didn't listen; he was too transfixed on his own face staring cruelly back at him.

But more than that, it was like he was inexplicably rendered incapable of responding to any words directed at his person.

He could not explain it . . . what he was now experiencing was beyond human comprehension.

If someone addressed the man known as Zale Hood, there was no way at this moment he could respond because . . .

He was *not* Zale Hood.

At least . . . not all of him.

Right now, he had no name.

Wasn't even a person.

No . . . Just half . . .

However, there *was* a title he could be known by. It spoke to him from deep within the soul nestled inside the body of Zale Hood, emanating with bright confidence.

Inside this broken place, he was known as . . . *Light*.

"I'm glad I don't have to spell it out for you," the presence slithered, suggesting it knew what was going through Light's mind.

Light may have gotten a handle on what he was, but that didn't help in understanding who this presence could be. Its face being the same meant nothing; with the right power anyone could maintain a glamour, disguising themselves as someone of their choosing.

"Who are you?" Light asked.

"Well," the presence sighed, "if you call yourself Light, then I guess you can call me . . ." a cruel grin spread across those handsome features, *"Dark."*

The presence apparently known as Dark took a dramatic step back and placed a dainty hand on his chest. "By the way," he crooned, "I think it's insulting that you don't know your own self."

Ignoring this confusing comment, Light queried, "What's happened to us?"

He instantly reeled from what he just uttered.

Us?

Why . . .

Why did Light say *us?*

From the moment he opened his mouth to the point the words escaped his lips, Light meant to use the word *'me'*. It had been so perfectly formed in his head that he failed to realise he was going to say the wrong thing until it was too late.

The ominous pit growing in Light's stomach threatened to burrow deeper and ever darker. There was such uncertainty corrupting his thoughts he couldn't think straight, and his fear just wouldn't fade.

He was so scared.

Dark's grin widened and Light knew he was enjoying his dread.

In the end, the shadowy figure opted for answering the first question. Spreading his arms wide and taking an arrogant little bow, he said, "I am the one who resurrected Charles."

Their isolated world seemed to grow as cold as death.

Light couldn't believe what he was just told.

The one responsible for the horror Zale's old friend inflicted upon the world was this dark presence?

The one who caused so many hundreds of deaths?

The one who . . .

The one who led to Carla's death!?!

Rage bubbled within Light so fast he was barely able to contain it. A dreadful desire to leap forward and tear the face from Dark's head was overriding his senses and Light wasn't certain he had the strength to fight it.

Sensing his anger, Dark threw back his head and laughed. A vicious, malevolent cackle that reverberated off the walls and made them shake like a drum skin.

And in a mocking voice, he purred, "Got a little headache, do we?" He poked a finger to his temple and tilted it to the side. Moments later, Light's skull exploded with pain. His hands shot to his head and he moaned as the ache pounded at his brain. "Feeling my presence there, are you?"

"What do you want?" Light screamed, half from the pain, half from terror. Beside him, the petrified Horas shook uncontrollably as Dark took one pace closer

Tutting irritably, Dark said, "No."

"No?" Light bawled incredulously.

"No," Dark repeated. "I will not answer the wrong questions." He clapped his hands loudly, the sound bouncing around the room. "Ask the right ones and you'll get an answer."

Taking deep breaths, Light lowered his arms and tried to calm himself, doing his best to ignore the throbbing behind his eyes. He cursed as it seemed to get larger simply because he was trying to ignore it.

The pain was rendering him incapable of thinking straight, a grievance the real Zale had shared the past week.

Wait . . . The real Zale . . .

The neurons in Light's head blinked on, pushing past the pain.

Dark didn't actually answer my first question. He dodged it.

He's not the real Zale . . . I'm not the real Zale . . .

But 'who am I' is not a question I should bother asking.

In an impossible situation such as this . . . disembodied, halved and standing alone . . . I should be asking 'what am I'.

. . . He dodged my first question . . .

What if the rules that apply to me apply to him as well?

With this thought, Light's headache dissipated in an instant. The effort of holding up his head vanished and his eyes were free to open and witness the world without pain.

He faced Dark confidently, standing straight.

And when he opened his mouth, the words, "*What* are you?" came out.

Dark's teeth flashed in vicious delight. "*That* I shall tell you."

chapter
SIXTEEN

Despite having promised to provide the answers Light so desperately wanted, Dark still did not speak. He stood there, grinning ear to ear, clearly enjoying the sense of frustration he was causing.

And Light wasn't above letting him know just how well it was working. "Come on!" he finally bawled. "Spit it out!"

"I love it," Dark hummed in response, "when you get mean."

Light growled in dire aggravation. "Just," he breathed, "tell me." Trying to remain docile and not give Dark any more chances to mock him, he asked again. "What are you?"

Dark put his hands behind his back and rocked on the balls of his feet, giving the inappropriate air of someone relaxed and entirely content. "How to answer that question," he mused.

As he swayed, Light again found he was having a hard time staying focused on the malevolent Dark. The longer they stood there, wasting time not answering questions, the more Light could feel a strange, unnatural tiredness pressing on his eyes.

It was as though Dark's powerful presence was so dominant that it was forcing Light to his knees. He could feel it—the power wanted to compel him to the floor and stamp him out of existence.

Light was so tired now . . . he just wanted to give in and sleep.

Nevertheless, he fought this desire with every ounce of strength he had left. If he allowed himself to sleep now, he had a horrible feeling he wouldn't wake up again.

Quite suddenly Dark clapped his hands, snapping Light from his exhausted reverie. His eyes darted back to the evil one's form and studied those deep, black pits, trying to gauge an emotion, *any* emotion.

He wished he could tell what was going through Dark's head. Despite the cruel one seemingly having a connection to Light's thoughts, Light himself couldn't figure out how to do the same.

The need to ask, however, was quite unexpectedly removed, as Dark finally stopped rocking and said, "I am you."

A confused silence fell upon them as Light struggled to understand this answer, but when he finally accepted he could not decipher this strange response he pressed Dark for more information.

"I am you," Dark repeated, before adding, "Or rather . . . I am your other half."

"What other half?"

Clearly Light had said what Dark most wanted him to say; with the glee of someone revealing the greatest secret known to mankind, he cackled shrilly and shouted something that turned Light's stomach.

"I am the demon half of your soul."

Stunned and scared, Light could only shake his head. "I . . ." he stammered. "I . . . don't . . . What does that mean?"

"Yes," Dark sighed impatiently. "You do know what that means."

"I don't . . . I don't kno—"

"OK." Dark cackled once again and took a step closer, peering into Light's eyes with an intense stare. "Looks like you're finding this somewhat difficult. Would you like me to break it down? Do you want to know the truth?"

A passionate curiosity made Light respond with, "Yes."

An abrupt shout of "No!" reminded him that Horas was still with them. "Zale, you must go."

"Which one of us are you talking to, Horas?" Dark hissed with glee. He waved a hand that silenced the demon in an instant. "Quiet, boring one, while I deal with my lesser half.

"Simply put," he continued, speaking to Light this time, "you are you. But, dear, I am you as well. You see, we are two halves of the same person."

"That doesn't make sense," Light returned. "How can one person be two halves?"

"The same way *all* people have two halves, you moron." Another stride closer. "One is provided by the father and the other—"

"The mother," Light finished, speaking in whispers.

Dark spread his arms wide and smiled proudly. "What can I say? I am my mother's son."

Despite being already grim, the Main Hall appeared to get dimmer. When Dark spoke, it was as thought this reconstruction reacted to his words, darkening in tandem with Light's emotional state.

Shaken, he backed away.

Only a few steps . . .

But enough for Dark to notice and glean immense pleasure from it. Light could see the satisfaction on his face.

"No . . ." Light whispered. "No . . . you're lying."

"I'm really not."

"Yes, you are!" Light argued loudly, a glare replacing the fearful stare that had previously dominated his face. "We're not half demon. We can't be!"

For the second time, Dark pressed his finger into his own temple, grinning savagely and simpering, "Got a headache, do we? Not thinking straight, are we?"

This cryptic taunt turned out to be nowhere near as obscure as Light imagined; as Dark's teeth glinted maliciously under the light and his cruel, evil eyes leered his way, Light realised he understood what he was referring to.

If there was one thing Zale was good at, it was solving mysteries. He was unparalleled in the *art of deduction* as he so called it.

Once, in only an hour, he'd discovered the location and motive of a murderous Enthraller whose demon had never surfaced until that day, and who had killed his wife because of a string of adulteries. Within moments of entering the crime scene he'd discovered the infidelity because of a letter on the table sent by the wife's orthopaedist. It detailed an appointment to treat pain the woman was experiencing in her thumbs.

From there, Zale deduced from the nature of the injury that it could be from doing a lot of mobile phone texting. He'd pondered aloud why a woman in her forties would text like a teenager as opposed to using the phone traditionally, as anybody over the age of thirty tended to do back then.

The only answer he could come up with was that she didn't want to risk being overheard. They were looking for a motive for murder, after all, and when Zale put two and two together he'd come to the conclusion that she'd been secretly texting a lover.

Quite a few of them, judging from the extent of the injury.

The data on her phone also proved this theory correct.

After that, it was a simple case of figuring out where the husband would go. They couldn't find him because, even though his power had risen to the fore, it had shrunk back again. For reasons they never actually discovered, this Enthraller's demon never manifested and so was undetectable by their scanners.

They'd had to find another way.

Zale realised this had been a crime of passion and the man was most likely in shock from the vicious act. It was also clear from the officious way his office was kept—and the fact that he had a proper office at all—that he'd been a man of business and organisation. Being so meticulous, Zale figured he'd keep his secrets in his desk. A fake bottom in one of the drawers was subsequently discovered and a snub belonging to a strip club was quickly found.

Zale theorised that, having just committed such a passionate crime, he would most likely be too shocked to think clearly. He would also have been under the impression that the body wouldn't be found until *he* alerted the right authorities.

He had no idea the Daemonium had tracked his demon's energy signature, meaning he believed he had all the time in the world. Therefore, Zale reckoned the man had been working on autopilot, possibly heading out to someplace he usually went to.

And so it was that they found him at the strip club, drinking in a daze and paying very little attention to his surroundings.

That man remained imprisoned inside the Daemonium jails to this day.

Zale had been proud of that solve.

And he had the right to be; no one else had come even close to his level of efficiency that evening and he'd continued being that effective for many following investigations. So it was alarming that, only two years later, when confronted by what was frankly a clumsy opponent, Zale had experienced such difficulty in apprehending him.

How had he not figured out who the Resurrected was quicker?

The answer?

That accursed headache.

A delighted roar of mirth made Light jump and return his focus to Dark.

"That was me!" his apparent other half bellowed. "That pain was me pushing my way out."

"Your way out?"

"You've no idea how long I've been trapped in there!" Dark snapped, pointing a finger at Light's forehead. "But I got some wiggle room. I reached out and corrupted you. Took you over. When I interfere, you can't think!

"Did you really not guess any of this?" Dark queried when Light remained silent. "How did you not notice you weren't working at optimum efficiency?" He threw his hands into the air and guffawed rudely. "For God's sake, what kind of detective chooses to find the minion before the master? That's just stupid."

"It's . . . it's . . . legitimate strategy," Light said lamely, disarmed by this mockery. "Police do it all the time."

"No!" Dark roared. "It is the strategy of a fool. You should have realised your brainpower was being stunted. But you couldn't sense me messing with your head, making you see and think only what I wanted you to.

"Everything you missed. Every clue Charles left for you and it still took you a week."

"What clues!?"

Dark waved a dismissive hand. "I don't know, but they must

have been there. It was always obvious the next steps you could have taken but you were so wrapped up in your belief that a Resurrected couldn't sneak into the Daemonium and that it couldn't have been the murdered Mawr that you utterly failed to consider the idea that the Resurrected didn't become one until *after* he stole the swords. Which would have explained why no sensors were tripped."

"But that *didn't* happen," Light argued. "Charles used his S.D.P."

"Of course, but, were you working at one hundred percent, Zale, you would have added this to your list of theories. But did you? No. You did not.

"You never thought there might be a traitor in the Daemonium . . . That an agent or soldier could have supplied the Resurrected . . . Another viable theory Zale would have come up with if I hadn't been influencing him.

"You never checked the systems to see when Charles was resurrected. Surely the machines detected it. You could have found the agent who was assigned the case and gotten more information.

"And the other thing—and this is my favourite bit—you never remembered to check the security cameras the day of the theft. How amateurish is that? Those cameras might have revealed your villain but you never even brought them up."

Light tried to open his mouth to argue his point. There was more to it than Dark was suggesting. It wasn't as simple as all that. There were hundreds of variables to consider.

But he just couldn't make words form. Dark's presence was engulfing him once again, clogging his mind and refusing to let him think for himself. All he could see in his head was Dark's evil face grinning at his pathetic attempts to fight back.

"All the theories and actions you should have considered and taken," Dark simpered. "But no . . . you only thought what *I* wanted you to think.

"You did nothing!" Now Dark seemed to get angry, as though he felt particular resentment towards Light for something he'd done . . . or didn't do . . .

"*I* was the hatred that hunted Lucikefer.

"*I* was the voice that told you to find the Kalik blades instead of fulfilling your duty to the Daemonium.

"*I* was the alien power you thought you felt that made Reynolds give the green light to hunt Charles alone.

"*I* was the one who scared Charles into surrendering.

"Face it! There's a stronger half to Zale than you, you pitiful human waste. *I* am the dominant gene. *I* am the power."

Light's breathing was so ragged from the effort of keeping himself standing under the barrage of power emitting from Dark that when he next spoke the words emerged as a hoarse rasp.

"It can't . . . be . . . Where . . . Where did . . . you . . . come from?"

"Our mother," Dark stated bluntly. "I've already told you."

"I've never sensed you before," Light breathed. "All my life . . . Where have you been? I . . . I've . . ."

Dark allowed him to stutter stupidly, offering no more insight until Light finally gave up and stammered into silence. Once quiet had fallen completely, Dark broodingly interlocked his fingers and let his eyes drift into a black mist.

After a moment, he muttered in a voice much more humble than before, "I was asleep for a long time . . . hiding unwillingly . . . not even aware that I existed." He scowled crossly and shook his head. "When you can understand what it's like to be alive and yet not exist simultaneously then you . . ." He trailed off, catching himself and returning the grin to his face.

"But then Badrick came to the Daemonium and when we

shook hands in Reynolds' office, I knew it was time. I awoke, groggy and so deep within Zale he never knew I was there, but *awake*.

"And then I awakened Charles."

"How?" Light interrupted him. "We never resurrected Charles."

"No," Dark sighed irritably. "Your subconscious did. From within the confines of the exile I was trapped in I worked power into the world and summoned our old friend from the dirt, replenishing his flesh and jamming his soul inside. He could hear my voice even when you couldn't." Dark chuckled lightly, clapping his hands once. "The fool serves me even now."

"Why did you do this?"

"To help me break the wall you erected upon our birth to keep me subdued."

"I don't remember."

"Of course not," Dark snarled. "How could you? We were just a baby. Before I could act you took Zale for yourself. But it's *my* time now. I did all of this so *I* could emerge as the dominant half."

All of this.

A rage unlike anything Light had ever experienced beat at his heart and chest with a cruel vigour when he recalled for the second time that *'all of this'* included having Carla butchered.

The hate was so powerful that Light felt Dark's presence wane before its forceful might.

Only a diminutive amount . . .

But still it waned.

However, Dark simply shivered and crooned, "Tickles." Although, he *did* blink in surprise when Light's anger culminated into a vicious roar; he screamed unintelligibly and, before he even knew what he was doing, Light had charged towards Dark with the bare intention of striking him dead.

Tutting, unimpressed and completely unafraid, Dark waved a lazy hand. Light screamed a second time, though this was no holler of abhorrence. This was a screech of pain as his legs stopped working and he fell to the floor, hard. "No!" he roared, writhing on the hard material in his attempt to regain his feet. "I will kill you!"

"Oh, stop pouting," Dark spat. "Her murder was necessary."

Barely listening and with rage still flooding him, Light tried to repeat his proclamation. "I will kill y—"

"Hush." Despite having spoken quietly, Dark's calm voice emphasised so much malice Light felt it like a strike across the face. He immediately closed his mouth, leaving his wail unfinished.

Dark sang derisively, "You have nothing to threaten me with." He drew closer, each step filled with such cruel intent it was hard to watch. "*I* am where all our power stems from. Our human half is weak." His head lowered and he leered through his eyelashes at Light with the kind of murderous glance that would send lesser men into a terror-induced coma. "*You* are weak."

"If Charles served you without me knowing," Light quavered, fighting to his feet, "then that makes you a separate entity. I can fight you off."

The laughter that exploded from Dark's mouth shook the walls of the Main Hall like they were made of jelly. The glass, however, did not and reacted to the shaking by smashing. Every single pane obliterated, falling to the floor with violent crashes. Light ducked and stumbled back as the walkways above crumbled and rocketed down, carving deep gouges in the floor and destroying much of the Main Hall.

The statue in the decorative pond was crushed and many benches were obliterated.

As the Daemonium fell apart, the floor too dissolved, vanishing into darkness. The debris followed suit, disappearing until they were surrounded by nothing but the same suffocating blackness as before.

Standing only strides away from Dark, Light fought not to let panic take him over.

"You fool," Dark hollered gleefully. "You can't fight *yourself*. That's who I am, human. I *am* you and you are *me*. We are one person and one person only." He scoffed irreverently.

"No," Light tried to argue. "That's not true."

"But it is."

"No . . ."

"Yes!" Dark snapped. "I'm not a separate consciousness. I'm not a separate entity. I am the dark impulses inside your soul given voice by your desire to hear them."

Flinching repulsively, Light snarled, "I do *not* desire to hear you."

"Yes, you do." Treading within touching distance, he continued, "You've only ever done what you want to do, and what you want . . ." the monster's smile widened, " . . . is what *I* want."

Recoiling from Dark's proximity, Light backed into someone he'd forgotten yet again was even there. Catching his shoulders and righting him, Horas marched to his side and exclaimed, "No!" He placed a hand on Light's arm and said, "Do not listen to it. This cannot happen. Wake up now. Turn away. Do not do thi—"

"Quiet, Horas." Dark briefly glanced his way, somehow silencing the demon with a mere glare. His pure black eyes glinted cruelly and his smile truly reflected the evil within him. At the sight of it, Light once more felt the pressure forcing him to the floor and instinctively knew that his ability to resist was diminishing. This time there was no doubt it would succeed in subduing him. He had not the power to stand firm any longer.

Sensing his victory was close, Dark leaned in towards Horas. "This is between me . . ." he turned back to Light, " . . . and me."

chapter
SEVENTEEN

Moving soft and slow, Zale's eyes opened.

For a moment he did not move as he felt his body awaken from the near-dead coma it had entered, and even the air seemed to stop circulating, as if waiting to see his heart once again beat inside his chest.

With purpose, Zale now raised his body, using his hands to push himself to his feet.

He was barely erect when a spark of energy fizzled behind him and Horas' visage appeared. Flustered and panicky, the demon asked, "Zale?"

Zale felt his mouth widen into a vicious grin, and, as he clenched a fist in gleeful victory, he murmured, "Not right now, Horas."

Twirling on the spot, Zale's mouth practically fell open as memories he never realised he owned flooded his head at the same moment his extraordinary power finally awoke within his soul, unfiltered and unencumbered by his human instincts.

His strength . . .

It was *magnificent.*

Power unlike ever before witnessed in the Universe.

It streamed from his essence and into his heart, spreading throughout his muscles and coursing through his veins like a potent drug.

Zale felt like he could just lie back and float in the air, he felt so damn high.

He could do this for hours, just stand here and immerse himself in the glory of his strength.

Unfortunately, the elation that fuelled his delight was ruthlessly cut short by the abrupt and unwelcome sigh of a certain demon re-manifesting on his bed. Noticing him reminded Zale that it wasn't all going to be a power trip from here on out. With his power finally liberated from its cage, Zale's next decisions would have to be vigilantly premeditated.

Oh, he sighed internally. *The stress of it all.*

Horas was watching him intently now, disappointment evident in the way he held himself. "I would be failing in my duty as your friend if I did not ask you to reconsider this path you have chosen." Swinging his legs over the mattress, he sprung to his feet and gestured imploringly at Zale. "You must listen to your human instincts. They were right. This is not you."

"Horas." It was only a hiss, but one overflowing with menace, and it quietened the hellspawn without delay. "You think I'm going to keep my life the way it is now that I know who I am?" Whirling away from Horas, Zale observed his reflection with interest.

He looked more alive than ever.

"With power like mine, it would be a waste not to use it."

"What do you intend to do?"

"Take the world, obviously," Zale laughed. "Take this entire Universe. Make. It. Mine."

To Zale's surprise, Horas was greatly *unsurprised* by this response. "Any time a demon attains vast power, they aspire to dominate." He appeared in the mirror, his reflection standing over Zale's shoulder. "You might think you are unique, but your demon half is just the same as all the rest. It is your human half that defines you, Zale, not this *monster* you are becoming."

Turning slowly, Zale's eyes met Horas' visor. The electric blue faded away, covered by a black mist until all that was left were the dark eyes of the New Evil. "Horas . . . Now I've realised my true destiny, I'm sure I don't have to mention that I no longer have any need for you." The demon shrunk away at these words, his terror delicious as Zale tasted it inside Horas' soul. "I'm sure I could simulate your presence in here and make everybody believe you're still alive." He slowly—pointedly—tapped his chest.

The threat was enough to make Horas completely recoil, however the demon was quick in regaining at least a modicum of composure. His visage straightened and stood rigidly before Zale, his blue and grey armour pristine and perfect under the yellow bedroom light.

"I understand you are powerful, Zale," he said icily, "and that there is nothing I can do to change your mind."

Zale frowned. This over-the-top sincerity was like a slap in the face and he wondered if Horas was actually being facetious. Scowling, he spoke, "All I want to know, Horas, is whether or not you're with me."

Horas shrugged; a gesture far too human to look natural on his shoulders. "You are my Enthraller. I will always be by your side."

The cruel grin returned to Zale's face. He could feel the demon's honesty and knew he could rely on him not to be a hindrance.

His fear of the New Evil would stop him from even trying.

And with Horas' loyalty affirmed, Zale could focus on the schemes in his head that excited him so much.

He returned to the mirror, wishing to gaze upon his handsome power in person. Observe his brilliance. Look upon his might.

Unfortunately, Horas interrupted him again. "Zale, explain this to me." He dared to take a closer step. "How are the sensors quiet when you are at their doorstep, brimming with such power?"

"Urgh!" Horas retreated at Zale's impatience, sliding to the back wall as far away as he could manage. Swivelling to face the irritating fool, Zale pointed to his own head. "Can't you just see in here?"

"No." This time Horas seemed to scowl. "I cannot."

This was *exactly* what Zale wanted to hear; the moment Horas revealed this fact he balled his hands triumphantly and howled like a wolf. "Oh, Horas, baby," he cried. "You can't see in my head because I don't want you too."

Horas' shock was crystal clear. As the demon of an Enthraller, he should have had near unlimited access to Zale's active thoughts and emotions. To be told that the Enthraller was blocking him so completely was sure to shatter some of his core understandings of the Universe.

Zale regarded the demon for a moment, pondering on whether or not the hellspawn deserved to be clued in. He wrestled with the idea of keeping him in the dark completely. After all, why *should* the demon know anything?

The answer to that was the same as why he hadn't just cast the demon into dust yet.

Because to be honest, what was the point in doing anything if he didn't have someone to gloat to?

With his mind made up, Zale took a breath and delved into the explanation Horas so desperately coveted. "As you've already noticed, I'm powerful, Horas. So powerful I can hide my . . ." he chuckled delightedly, "*New Evil* signature completely."

"Like Daemnos?" Horas asked. "Lucikefer?"

Zale instantly scoffed. "Don't compare me to those idiots. My version of this power is perfected. There will never be a blip. Never a weak moment. Never a time where they might find me when I don't want them to. Not even Charles, my little psychic minion, will know I'm there if I don't want him to."

Zale laughed when he felt foreboding creep through Horas' being, however his elation did not last long, as recalling Charles did bring about one concern—a concern that did not escape Horas' notice. The demon quickly picked upon on Zale's momentary hesitation and used it to question the reason.

At first, Zale failed to speak; he was far too deep in his own head to voice this thoughts. But when Horas pushed, Zale clawed his way back to reality, blinking as he returned to the real world. "The splinter," he murmured. "The one that affected me."

"What about it, Zale?"

Huffing impatiently, Zale snapped, "Honestly, I didn't expect it to affect me . . . well, at all." He raised his right hand, the veins and cartilage on his wrist protruding as he clenched his fingers into a claw. "I thought the introduction of foreign power would awaken mine and that would be that. But instead . . ." He trailed off.

"You went crazy," Horas said. "As all the others have before."

"And it was Hell, too," Zale scoffed. "Being subjected to that . . . *impediment*. Being forced into madness. Having to watch the world through eyes that couldn't understand what they were seeing. I can barely remember what happened." His palm found his forehead and he closed his eyes, willing the memories to burn away from his consciousness.

He didn't like knowing there was something that made him weak. Even if this Achilles' heel was temporary, Zale desperately needed it to *die*. Nothing that caused him weakness could be allowed to exist.

To his right, Horas visibly hesitated before asking, "You . . . saw . . . through your body's eyes?"

"What else am I going to see through?" Zale mocked him.

Again, Horas faltered, but eventually whispered, "You don't remember what happened?"

"Are you going senile, Horas?" Zale snapped, but quickly reeled back and considered Horas with shrewd eyes. "Or is there something I'm missing?"

Horas quickly breathed, "No, Zale, I am simply intrigued. You are right. It is odd that *you* of all people should be susceptible to Resurrected splinters."

Further rage boiled in Zale's heart at the mere idea that he had any kind of weakness. The only thing that stopped him from dashing Horas into oblivion right there and then was the fact that it was the truth, as painful as it was to admit.

Horas didn't continue the stream of questions he had obviously yet to finish. Despite his powerful curiosity, it seemed Zale's strength had finally scared him into complete silence.

Which was perfectly fine by Zale.

He had things to do and it was time he began his work.

For now, Zale would—

Electricity sparked.

Zale's fingers shone a brilliant electric blue as voltage surged down the flesh of his arm and struck the wall to his left. He jumped in surprise and took several tentative steps back, unsure of what to make of this sudden development. He gazed at his hand, his eyes wide with fret. Along his fingers he could see angry scorch marks, as though the electricity had burned him on its way out.

Unable to fathom what had just occurred, he turned his steely gaze upon the one responsible.

"What," he hissed threateningly, "was that?"

However, it didn't take Zale long to see that Horas was as bewildered as he. In fact, the demon looked positively terrified that the incident had occurred at all. Zale wasn't sure to make of that, but decided to file it under *'Consider for later'*.

Not that this bizarre episode wasn't alarming—Zale just had more pressing matters to attend to.

Zale's power was growing. He could feel it, nuzzled within him contentedly, waiting to be unleashed on the poor souls of this world. But he knew it was not yet strong enough to do such a terrible thing and get away with it scot-free.

His power was quite like a battery; one day he could very well be so powerful entire galaxies might bend to his will, but right at the moment he was charging. Slowly powering up. He would have to remain cautious at the current time, but it was just a matter of waiting for his strength to build.

One day he would have the power to rule the Universe.

It was his *birthright!*

The only problem was staying hidden until then. Above all else, Zale couldn't risk people learning of his rising before he was ready.

An unlikely thing to happen . . . and yet it already had—there was an Ordinarius out there that seemed to have information on the New Evil. Zale could feel him from within the confines of the room—could sense the demon's panicked thoughts out there somewhere in the country.

A major problem, yet thankfully one that would prove easy to dispatch, and with Dhornji's death the threat he posed would be destroyed.

However . . . there was *one* other who knew about him

And *this* person would not be so easy to get rid of . . .

Reading the thoughts Zale generously allowed him access to see, Horas chose then to speak up once more. "Who else knows?"

Zale did not answer him. Above his bed, the clock ticked significantly louder than before. He turned to gaze at it, knowing this meant that the next hour had begun.

"Horas," he called over his shoulder, "stand guard outside my door. If someone comes for me, let me know immediately."

"Yes, Zale."

The demon brushed past him and phased through the door, vanishing from sight.

"I hope this doesn't take long," Zale muttered quietly. Positioning himself in the middle of his bedroom, he rolled his shoulders in preparation, breathing heavily in anticipation of what he was about to attempt.

When he was ready, he closed his eyes and spread his arms wide.

Zale expected to have some difficult accessing his power like this, but to his contentment there was no effort involved. At his command, the energy ignited and powered up, a flawless, beautiful pulse of unparalleled demonic energy.

And before he even realised it had occurred, Zale's wish was granted.

A curious yet painless tearing sensation ripped through his body from the top of his scalp to the soles of his feet, and, as though he were nothing but a breath, Zale's disembodied consciousness expelled from his head.

chapter
EIGHTEEN

The only word to describe it was *surreal*. To gaze back at one's body as nothing but an incorporeal awareness was like nothing Zale ever experienced before. He would have laughed with joy, except he no longer possessed lungs with which to do so, nor a voice box to make the noise. He was nothing but invisible energy, hovering above and free to flit to wherever he wished.

Utilising this power to its full effectiveness, Zale commanded his new form to fly straight towards the floor. Everything shifted oddly as he moved, as if nothing was quite real anymore, and no pain surged through him when he hit the floor. Without a body, his intangible form phased cleanly through the wood, remerging into the room below.

He continued this pattern, dashing through room after room

until he finally slipped through the last floorboard and slithered out the ceiling of the Main Hall.

Seeing the pride and joy of the facility at this angle was quite fantastic, to say the least, with the work of expert architects from ages past laid out beautifully below. But Zale had no time to squander admiring inane beauty; he had to find the one he was searching for.

The room he suspected this person to be located was above him now, but off to the right somewhere. He'd come to the Main Hall to orientate himself, not having yet gotten used to this form of travelling. Finding his bearings, Zale shot onwards, blasting silently and unseen through walls and furniture until he finally emerged exactly where he needed to be.

The Command Council's lair.

There they were, just as he'd suspected. Every poor sap chosen to be a member of the new Council, deep in conversation and completely unaware that he was now among them.

Zale felt elated knowing that, even when he was pulling off a power a complicated as this, nothing and no one could detect him.

The group sat around their large oval table, busily ticking off boxes on their vast to-do list, separated by department on either side. The one Zale was searching for sat at the head of the meeting, exhausted yet vigilant on an overly decorated throne.

Dominus Daniel Reynolds.

On either side of him, placed slightly forward along the table were what the Council called the Eminent. Acting as advisors to the Dominus, Reynolds' chosen—Agent Commander Dennis Quill and General Kevin Doyle—were joint second in the chain of command.

Each of the Eminent personally headed a group of three Enthrallers that were know as Eparches, who in turn were all at the front of their five or six Guardians. With the amount of individual sets of people this resulted in, this made the Command Council a rather large collection of people.

Zale studied the new Council with mild interest, having never seen the entire cluster gathered in session before. From the way they were talking it was easy to see that they all took this new honour very seriously. They were working as a well-oiled team, never arguing, always listening to one another.

Undoubtedly that had something to do with Reynolds' leadership. Zale had never met the Dominus before him—the one that took the place of the Hierarch when he randomly resigned his post and retreated to his penthouse—but Zale had heard she was an incredibly lazy woman.

This was unarguably why the Eparch Jonathon Carver had always been so vocal in the previous Council's day-to-day operations. Why they'd become a group of micromanagers when they were supposed to leave general operations to the two Command Groups, and only get involved when huge issues arose.

Then again, at least Carver had put the effort in, despite his idiotic habits often leaving the other Eparches in difficult positions.

But of course, both the woman and Carver were gone, demoted to God only knew where, and Reynolds was now their leader. It was a humorous irony that, because of everything the Council allowed to happen, the new Dominus was now forced to be what he despised, to play the part of sole authority until the Daemonium recovered from the Kalik Crisis and the upheaval of its leadership.

Zale couldn't help but be disgusted at the thought of the Daemonium returning to its normal routine. Back to the time when any of these people, even the Guardians, had the authority to make almost any decision they wanted.

None of them were truly in charge; the Guardians would

debate with their Eparch, who voiced their opinions to the Eminent, who in turn relayed all information to the Dominus.

He or she would then make the final decision.

And even then, this only occurred when the Daemonium faced the largest concerns; major war declarations, the most powerful enemies, and the like. More often than not the Council stayed behind the scenes, caring for the Daemonium as a whole and communing with their outposts overseas. If anyone in the Council got involved with general operations at all it was usually because they had a vested interest in the mission.

What an insult to those with power.

It was a ridiculous system of power sharing and equality, and was completely humiliating to watch. Frankly, if these pointless human souls wanted to be equal then they could be . . . as *insects*. That's all they were, and when Zale took over he would have no equal.

He would rule alone.

Below, as he silently seethed at things that disgusted him, the men and women of the Council rather surprisingly adjourned their meeting. Every single body got to its feet, shuffling their papers and shaking hands in some gesture of support.

On Reynolds' right hand side, a woman approached and offered the man her hand. Over the clamour of voices, Zale caught her saying, "I also wanted to say, on behalf of everyone in this Council, thank you."

A frown creased Reynolds' face. "What for, Lucinda?"

"We're impressed with your administration, sir. It's only been two days and you've dealt with the Kalik crisis' aftermath."

"It wasn't just me," Reynolds rebutted her. "You all did great work, as did our agents in the field."

"Of course, sir, and we appreciate your compliments, but without your leadership this could've gone on for weeks."

"You don't give the Daemonium enough credit, Lucinda."

"We just want you to know," a different Guardian voiced, "that we're proud to call you our Dominus. Your reputation precedes you but your value has obviously been underappreciated before now."

"The old Council made a mess of this place when they took control," Lucinda spat angrily. "I hated them. No offence, sir."

"So we just want to thank you for everything," someone else piped up.

"What did you expect from the man who killed the Devil?" Kevin laughed.

Reynolds immediately shook his head, waving a dismissive hand with embarrassment. "Private Blayke weakened the Devil by the time Mawr and I got there. He deserves the praise, not me."

"Well," Kevin half shrugged, "we might give him it if he was alive."

"Regardless," Quill added over them, "not one of us could've managed it. It was a hell of an achievement, Reynolds."

"You've done a lot, sir," said the Guardian who started this ridiculous and abhorrent celebration of Reynolds' life accomplishments. "And we understand how hard it's been."

"Thank you, Lucinda," Reynolds smiled, shaking Lucinda's hand once more. The moment their fingers parted, Reynolds clapped his hands and ushered the Council from the room, justifying his actions with the declaration that he had some things he had to sort privately.

Obediently, the Council did as commanded, filing out of the room and closing the door behind them.

Zale grinned with savage excitement at the thought of the advantage this offered him. The Dominus was now completely alone, and with no cameras allowed in this room there would be no witnesses to what Zale planned to do.

In an instant, he cut the link between him and his powers. Like a gale-force wind his consciousness was dragged back to his body, the world spinning past in reverse and threatening to make him dizzy.

In his room, Zale's real lungs exhaled victoriously, and his eyes opened.

There was no time to lose. Taking a quick step back to ensure there was enough space, Zale prepared himself for what he was about to attempt next.

It would take a lot of concentration to pull this off without messing up.

With his focus on the writhing energy in his soul, he barely registered Horas walking through his door, taking position behind him, and with a clap of his hands Zale fired an imperceptible blast of energy towards where he knew Reynolds to be. This force would hit the man squarely in the head, if his aim was true, and would render him completely unconscious.

The blast travelled ethereally through walls and floors until it struck Reynolds so hard his body jerked violently. The power quickly acted to relax his muscles and subdue his mind.

Moving quickly, Zale acted to stop Reynolds crumbling to the floor.

Keeping him aloft with a little bit of telekinetic manipulation, Zale twirled his other hand, channelling energy through his fingers and into the space before him. Hidden in the room, Reynolds' body vanished, disappearing into nothing.

Half a second later, he appeared in Zale's room.

For a brief moment, as the chaotic energy pulsated and vomited Reynolds onto his floor, Zale worried he might have asked too much of himself. The man was swaying sickly, his mind blank and pale, which could have indicated Zale had inflicted some kind of harm.

But there didn't seem to be any physical damage and a quick scan of his biological functions proved that, apart from being catatonic, Reynolds was fit as a fiddle.

As the blank and unseeing Dominus swayed precariously on the rug, Zale couldn't help but clap and admire his handiwork with arrogant pride. Demonic teleportation was one of the hardest things to conceal and most demons who were capable of even slightly masking their energy failed to achieve it completely.

Forced teleportation of a separate individual or item was even more problematic.

So having managed to achieve not only a forced teleportation, but also the subduing and manipulation of a man not even within his sight, without setting off one single alarm or alerting any of the energy-sensitive Enthrallers in the building was . . .

Well, it was bloody phenomenal.

Even Horas was impressed.

And if Zale could pull off what he had planned next with the same flawless skill . . .

Once again, euphoria over his sheer power flowed through his veins and he had to fight not to get distracted. Reaching out with his mind, Zale commanded the fabric of reality to twist and change. The air around Reynolds vibrated impossibly, pulsating with a sickening series of rapid throbs. Around him, a light now blazed, surrounding the General entirely.

And then, without warning, he vanished from reality, disappearing from sight as the space he once occupied was taken by somebody else. This new person stumbled as they were forced into the world, evidently dizzy and ailed from the experience.

Unlike Reynolds, they were clad in armour that borrowed similarities from the Daemonium's designs. Where Reynolds had uniform, this figure had metal. Where Reynolds had a face, this person had only a visor.

Behind him, Zale could sense Horas gaping as he came to comprehend what he'd just witnessed.

On the rug, the demon Lora put her hands to her helmeted head in an effort to adjust to being unexpectedly physical. From beneath the metal, her voice sounded out, stammering as she swayed dizzily. "What . . . what happened?" Her hand reached for some kind of support.

Zale did not provide her with one.

"I switched you with Reynolds," he said boldly. "Now he's inside your soul. Don't worry, he's unconscious."

The sound of his voice cut through her wooziness and she fought to shake it away, replacing it with what Zale could only describe as an evil jubilation.

"My King," she cooed, the grin behind her visor obvious from her joyful tone.

Ignoring her, Zale spoke what he needed to speak. "You know." The chuckle she made when he said this only served to irritate him. Fighting the urge to grind his teeth, he elaborated. "I heard what you said when the S.D.P released you. You *know*."

Lora curved her body sultrily and gave him a seductive purr. "I always knew what you are."

This was not what Zale wanted to hear. "How?" he demanded.

Lora laughed at that, apparently finding something amusing. Her cackles stopped, however, when Zale tightened his telekinetic grip around her throat. As her under-suit rubbed against her flesh and the air was prevented reaching her lungs, she flailed her hands in panic, physically begging him to stop.

After a full minute of this torture, he finally relaxed his grip, confident the message had been clear—*Mess me about and you will die.*

"How?" he asked once more.

Breathing raggedly, Lora rubbed the leather covering her throat and coughed. "When we found you in London, I saw the power in you the moment I laid eyes on your little body."

Zale felt anger rise in his chest—so much so that his power reappeared in his eyes, blackening them entirely. "So Reynolds knows too?"

The danger she was in didn't seem to faze the she-demon in the slightest—in fact the more Zale allowed her to witness his power the more . . . *aroused* she appeared to be getting. Now she was performing a slow and truly spectacularly sexual dance, bending left and right, subtle movements only, and kept gesturing towards him as if she was barely managing to keep her hands off his body.

And apparently, as well as this newfound sexual appeal to female demons, Zale had a promising career as a comedian to fall back on should his plans fail; though her throat was still recovering from the constriction, laughter escaped her lips once more, though it was a pained giggle.

"Oh no, no, no," she cooed. "Daniel has no idea, though he *thought* he sensed something when he found you. That's why he shot you. But when it vanished a second later he got very confused. Bless him, the poor dear." Lora paused her dancing to shrug. "After the soul probes found only Horas, he passed it off as residual energy from Lucikefer and now doesn't remember it happened."

"Even if Reynolds does not know," spoke a voice Zale had forgotten was even present, "it is remarkable this harlot saw you."

Zale turned to Horas, amused. "Harlot? That's very rude, Horas. I thought all demons like to shag."

Giving Lora a disgusted, disapproving glare, Horas snapped, "This is wrong . . . I do not approve."

Trying not to ponder on the irony of a *demon* branding something immoral, Zale rolled his eyes and returned his focus to

Lora. Seeing that she once again had his attention, she continued her amorous dance and said, "I don't know which demon bore you into life, but I recognised you were one of us. I could sense your power." Abruptly, her dance ceased and her right hand rose to the level of her chest. "You're going to rule us all . . . and I plan to be by your side when that happens."

It took a moment for this to sink in, but when it did his surprise at this statement struck Zale like a wall of bricks. "Excuse me?"

"I'll take care of you, baby." And with a flick of her hand the armour adorning Lora's body vanished from sight. Without the metal obstruction, she was free to reach up and begin unzipping her under-suit—the only thing keeping her bare skin covered.

"Wow," Horas quipped as the leather fell to the wooden floor with a *thwump*.

At the sight of Lora's naked body, and upon hearing her presumptuous tone, rage boiled within Zale, flooding his senses and deepening the blackness that was his eyes. "Whore!" he practically screeched, unwittingly mirroring Horas' earlier attitude. "I don't care for such pointless physical desires!" He drew up close and roared in her face, intending to scare her.

To his great infuriation, it did nothing of the sort.

She only grinned wide, reaching up and grabbing his wrists. Against his wishes, she pulled him close and placed his hands on her breasts.

"Of course you do," she hummed. "You're part demon, my king. Everything that makes us what we are makes *you* what you are."

"And what," he snapped, "makes me what I am?"

Lora placed a delicate hand on the back of his neck and leaned in so she could whisper tenderly into his ear. *"Sin."* Before Zale could even bristle at her audaciousness, she pulled back and said,

"You may think you're above it, but you're not. After all, you're the King of Sin." Quite suddenly, Lora pressed her hands against his chest and pushed him from her. She took a step away, adding, "I'll be here when you realise that."

Zale's fingers curled into claws, his anger was so great, the nails turning deathly black and lengthening into points. He wanted to dash her into oblivion, remove her soul from this existence *and* the next.

Kill her utterly.

But . . . he restrained himself.

With much effort, he uncurled his fists and took a subtle breath, forcing his eyes to return to their usual blueness. When he was sure he was back to normal, Zale rolled his shoulders and returned his gaze to Lora.

Killing the demon would serve no purpose. If he slaughtered her, Reynolds would die as well and that would be extremely detrimental to his plans. The General's continued existence was necessary.

For now.

With a wave of his hand the she-demon's armour reappeared, manifesting around her naked form. She stumbled from the impact of such power, but managed to keep her feet.

"Say nothing," Zale warned her. Not wishing to give her a chance to reply with more of her crap, Zale quickly pushed her back to where she belonged. With a single cry, Lora vanished, light flashed, and Reynolds returned to the physical world.

Upon his re-entry, he neither gasped nor shouted nor made any noise at all. The Dominus was still under the effects of Zale's power, cataleptic and unaware of his surroundings. He would remember none of occurred. Barely offering him a thought, Zale simply waved a lazy hand and sent Reynolds on his way, transporting him safely back to the Council's lair. His supernatural senses saw the Dominus reappear in his lavish throne, dazed, white and only half conscious.

Horas was the one to break the silence that ensued after the General's forced departure. It was obvious he was fairly stunned by all that he'd witnessed in the past half an hour but, despite his obvious shakiness, when he next spoke it was with a steady voice. "Lora does not know who your mother is."

Sighing, Zale went, "Nope."

"Have you given any thought as to who she might be?"

Zale tutted with irritation, but only because he didn't want to admit that he cared enough to worry about such a thing. However, he knew he would just look pathetic if he tried to deflect the question, so he simply said, "I do wonder, yes."

"You do not have any idea as to who might have given birth to you?"

Zale rounded on the demon with such speed it made Horas jump in surprise. "I was a baby, you idiot. How the hell would I remember?" He pointed an accusing finger at the Singularis. "Why don't *you* know? You were there as well."

When the demon stuttered and failed to provide an answer, Zale shouted, "Oh, forget it!" and turned his back. He already knew the answer and, to be honest, couldn't blame Horas for being as ignorant as him.

Being dragged into an Enthraller was a traumatic experience. When it occurred, all demons fell into an agony-induced coma for the first year. Once they awoke, they would have to watch in silence until the day the Enthraller's soul *'noticed'* the demon was there and reacted in surprise, culminating in their powers manifesting.

Having been comatose at Zale's birth, there was no way Horas saw his mother, and would have awoken far too late; Zale was in a foster family within weeks of his birth, his biological parents nowhere to be found.

Evidently thankful Zale had dismissed the need for an answer, Horas tried to change the subject. "Are you going to kill Reynolds next?"

Zale wasn't sure why the demon *kept* talking to him. He'd have thought Horas would be too wary of angering the New Evil. He definitely looked it every time Zale looked even slightly annoyed.

But for some reason he was more talkative than he'd ever been.

In answer to his question, Zale scoffed, casting a mocking glare his way. "You're not the brightest star in the sky, are you?" When Horas failed to respond, Zale elaborated. "Listen to what I tell you very carefully, Horas.

"There's an Ordinarius grass-up coming to tell the Daemonium about a new enemy that's coming.

"Only days ago, Charles told Badrick not to trust me. Remember hearing that?

"Knowing that an evil is coming, and that I'm supposedly untrustworthy, how do you think people would react if the Dominus died just like that?" He clicked his fingers to emphasise his last three words.

Horas bobbed his head. "I suppose it would be risky. Charles was your friend, after all. Someone *could* come to the conclusion you are to blame."

"Exactly," Zale affirmed. "It'd be a long leap to make but there are people here willing to make that jump were they to discover what Charles said." He angrily spat a profanity. "Curse that Resurrected scum. If not for the fact that you were listening in on him and Badrick at the hangars I would never know about his feeble attempt at treachery. I might have walked right into a trap." Taking another calming breath, Zale muttered, "You know . . . I never thanked you for that."

"There is no need." At that, Horas mustered his bravery—Zale could feel it flickering inside their souls—and drew up as close as he dared. "You are walking a very fine line, Zale. You must be careful with your next moves."

Grinning, Zale chuckled, "You're right about that."

Horas continued, "If I know you and how you think . . . you want to trick someone else into killing your enemies for you."

Zale was impressed. "How'd you figure that out?"

"We share the same body, Zale. Though you may block me out I still know my Enthraller." Horas crossed his arms and appeared to stare intensely into Zale's face. "You believe it needs to be done in plain sight, in front of everybody, and with no way to trace it back to you.

"Meaning you need someone else to kill Reynolds."

Zale was already grinning widely by the time Horas finished speaking. "This is why I love you, Horas."

Sidestepping the odd compliment, Horas asked the question he so desperately wanted to ask. "Alright . . . so how do you plan to accomplish this?"

And with a murderous cackle, Zale rumbled, "We're gonna play a game."

PART III

PRIMORDIAL

chapter
NINETEEN

(Present Day)

Badrick had never experienced anything like this before.

The music was deafening, the atmosphere intoxicating.

People surrounded him on all sides, smashed off their heads and thrashing their limbs in drunken, unimpressive attempts to be perceived as sexy.

But Badrick paid them no heed. He hadn't travelled nearly fifty miles and altered the minds of several bouncers to permit him entry to waste time watching the others around him.

He just wanted to dance.

To experience life as normal people his age did, with no demons trying to influence or kill him, no world-ending entities threatening to destroy everything, and not one commanding officer ordering him to do something or other.

Having been here an hour already, Badrick *was* starting to see the appeal of coming to a place like this and losing himself to unthinking pleasure. To just switch off from all distractions and the stress-causing happenings of real life was incredibly blissful.

He danced just as stupidly as those around him, though Badrick was not doing so with the intention of impressing anyone. He couldn't have cared less what they thought about his terrible dance moves. He was living life to the full, caring for nothing and no one but the music and himself.

As he thrashed stupidly, a space opened up in the crowd, and, as he spun on his heel, Badrick caught a glimpse of two girls eyeing him from across the bar.

At first he paid no attention, expecting them to be judging his enthusiasm for the music.

But when they shared a few hushed words and sauntered over to sidle up to him, he abruptly realised their intentions were far more social.

The taller girl went behind him while the shorter pushed herself in and began grinding him without shame.

And quite suddenly Badrick wasn't so preoccupied with himself.

Never before had he experienced the accentuated sex drive so many Enthrallers documented having—he always assumed the mentally unstable Daemnos wasn't interested in such carnal desires—but now, as this pair of very sexy girls took him by the hand and pulled him away from the crowd, he felt a curious sensation shoot through him.

As a male, he recognised what it was without fail, and, in that moment, made the executive decision to see what the fuss was all about. He allowed these two to lead him through the throng of thrashing people with a grin on his face and a surge of desire coursing through him like he were nothing but a randy teenager.

The only thing that stopped him from following these two all the way to wherever they were leading him and having his way with both was the sight in his peripheral of a very red man.

He stopped dead in his tracks, digging his heels into the floor, and circled to glare at the visage of Daemnos with such irritation it was partly surprising the demon didn't flee in terror.

And to further his annoyance, one second of diverted attention was apparently all it took; ignorant of why he'd halted, the girls decided he was no longer worth it and removed their grips from his, destroying Badrick's chances with them forever.

As they moved away, Badrick intensified his glare. "Thanks," he hissed like a furious snake, "for that!"

Luckily, with all the inebriated people surrounding him, no one noticed a young lad talking to thin air as they continued their attempts to achieve what Badrick already had before Daemnos ruined everything.

The demon didn't respond, instead gazing around with what looked like curiosity, studying the drunken dancers with interest. Badrick expected him to comment, but when Daemnos remained silent it became clear something was bothering the mental being.

Deciding to put his anger aside for now, Badrick asked, "What's wrong with you?"

"I'm worried, Badrick," Daemnos breathed, not looking his way. "Very worried."

Badrick couldn't help but tut like a disproving, grumpy old man. "What's there to worry about? We stopped the New Evil."

"Oh, Baddie Badrick, it's not the New Evil!" Only now did Daemnos focus his attention on him. He stepped closer, his fingers clenching over and over, and Badrick could tell there was definitely something wrong. His usual eccentric personality seemed lessened in the face of his anxiety. "This Bomb Killer, as you have so christened him." Daemnos suddenly spat, muttering, *"Christened. Blargh!"*

"Stay on track, Daemnos. What about the Bomb Killer?"

Bristling oddly, the demon said, "Make his case your case."

"But Zach's on it," Badrick argued. "They don't need me—"

"Make the case your case, Baddie." Daemnos drew worryingly close and Badrick instinctively stepped back, not enjoying this proximity. "For all our sakes . . . murder him!"

*

The Daemonium itself seemed calmer as Badrick stumbled tiredly into the HQ. The early morning rays shone brightly through the singular window, illuminating the dust swirling around the highest walkways with bright golden light.

Badrick shielded his eyes against the glare as he made his way in the general direction of the BCR, doing his best to ignore his exhaustion.

All of last night he'd wasted getting back to the Daemonium post haste after Daemnos' warnings and not a single moment of sleep was achieved. It was bloody typical; the whole point of going to that nightclub was to push away fatigue and all he'd managed to do was trade one kind of weariness for another.

He cursed Daemnos' problematic existence as he trudged through the door but didn't squander too much time on his frustration. After all, Daemnos may have had a habit of popping up uninvited at the most inconvenient moments but Badrick was hard pressed to think of a time he didn't have a good reason.

Thankfully, with unbelievable luck, Badrick managed to locate the person he was searching for within the BCR. He whispered thanks to whatever gods might be watching that he wouldn't have to spend hours searching the base, then headed up to the agent leaning over a console and ruffling his hair with frustration.

As he approached, Badrick saw him pick up a mug of coffee and swig it slowly. From this angle, Badrick could see the stress in the lines on his face, and his shoulders were so tense they could have deflected rocks. Feeling a stab of pity, Badrick tried placing a comforting hand on the agent's shoulder.

"ARGH!"

Badrick jumped back with fright when Zach reacted to his presence with such surprise it sent the contents of his desk flying every which way and almost caused him to toss his coffee across the floor.

Spinning on the spot, the detective finally relaxed when he realised his attacker was just Badrick.

Calming his own heart, Badrick snapped, "Jeez, man!"

"You snuck up on me!" Zach retorted.

"I was trying to let you know I was behind you!"

"Language works!" Zach bawled. "In fact, I'm pretty sure that's why it was invented."

Figuring they could very well end up wasting all morning on this ridiculous argument, Badrick took a breath and swallowed his anger. Just as he expected, Zach accepted the apology he gave without humility and asked what Badrick was doing in the BCR.

He pulled up a seat and went into explanation of what Daemnos said back at the nightclub. Zach listened with intense curiosity, interrupting Badrick several times to voice his surprise that Daemnos cared so much about a lowly terrorist.

"Maybe not so lowly if Daemnos is worried," Badrick said.

"Maybe not."

"So, as I said, I'm here to try help."

Amazingly, Zach actually scoffed at him. "Thank you, Badrick, but I don't need the help. My team and I have got this in the bag, and besides, didn't Reynolds give you the fortnight off?"

Fighting the urge to grind his teeth, Badrick muttered, "Yes, he did, but Daemnos won't let me sleep unless I help. For my sake, Zach, let me."

Even this attempt to make it sound like Zach was doing him a favour made no difference. With the kind of smile adults gave children when believing they knew better, Zach shook his head dismissively and shunned his aid once again. Though he was greatly frustrated with Zach's attitude, Badrick took a breath and, in lieu of punching him on the back of the head, opened his mouth to explain why he'd be a great help.

And had he managed to make it, Badrick would have been able to form a great argument.

Before he could utter even a syllable, a voice at the front of the BCR stopped him, and Badrick froze so quickly his mouth hung open stupidly. With downright disbelief, he swivelled to look at the newcomer, his incredulity intensifying tenfold when his eyes confirmed what his ears heard.

The voice had said, "Don't you think you have bigger problems than some pointless bomb maker?"

And in unison both Badrick and Zach bawled, "Mawr!?!"

chapter
TWENTY

Speaking aloud to the room, Zach clicked his fingers sharply and announced, "So, as I mentioned before, in an act of desperation I scanned the energy readouts on the murder victims killed by the handprint. That's the only time the Bomb Killer's signature is left behind and really the only lead we have on finding who it is.

"When I had what I thought might be a signature I cross-referenced it with Daemonium members. I always do that on a case like this, just in case there's a traitor in our midst. Unfortunately, the readings didn't even come close to any of us."

Zach tapped with frustration on his computer desk and turned to the room, spreading his hands to the empty space behind him.

"But of course, nobody cares" he muttered darkly. "They're all more interested in Mawr's sudden suspicious return from death. I'll just talk to myself, that's completely fine."

As the door zipped open and his team finally wandered in to

replace the night shift, Zach reached for his port-pad and pulled up files on both Mawr and Zale. "I'll also investigate the fact that Zale conveniently goes to his room the moment all hell breaks loose," he whispered to himself. "Since no one else seems to be worried."

Badrick believed he'd witnessed the peak of Zale's anxiety many times before today. So much had happened to them with such disastrous results that he couldn't imagine seeing fists get tighter than Zale's.

That was until Mawr Burakka returned from the dead and his partner broke his own record.

Zale seemed only seconds from drawing blood as they sat restlessly outside the Dominus' grand office and stared at the wall, waiting for whatever was occurring within to come to an end.

Unfortunately, whatever Reynolds' initial reaction to seeing Mawr was, they weren't privy to it.

Perhaps it was similar to Zale's.

Badrick felt like he didn't need to ask why his partner was so white and shaky. They'd all believed they outlived the last few weeks and had come out the end of the tunnel. But for Mawr to return the day after they defeated the New Evil could only bode ill for everyone here.

This was clearly on Zale's mind as well.

These horribly morbid thoughts only served to make Badrick lose himself to dwelling on the current situation. He could feel his own eyes misting as he plunged deep into his mind, wondering what was so urgent about Mawr's return that the moment he arrived he was whisked to the Dominus' office without a word.

It couldn't just be the fact that he was alive after being reported KIA. With his first step into the BCR, Mawr had demanded to see the Dominus with imperative news. With the fuss he'd been making, his guards had been left with no choice but to scrap their original plan to dump him in the BCR for the Agent Commanders.

A mistake, frankly.

Because now the whole situation was blown out of proportion, Badrick felt. Yes, his return was big news and he needed to be briefed, and Reynolds would want to see him, but bothering the Dominus like this was unnecessary.

Badrick tutted; there never seemed to be any end to the mistakes in this place—

The office door zipped open and a very sullen Reynolds appeared at the threshold. He didn't see them at first as he stepped through, his mind noticeably elsewhere, but when he nearly tripped over Zale's foot Reynolds realised he had more visitors.

"Typical," the Dominus snapped. "Why am I not surprised that you two delinquents are here?" Badrick didn't answer. It seemed Reynolds was unusually vexed and he didn't want to worsen the situation. Eventually, Reynolds gestured sharply to his office and snapped, "Luckily for you, the pair of you are who I was looking to find. Inside quickly."

"Us?" Badrick couldn't help but voice in surprise. "What could *we* help you with?"

However, he obeyed the General as fast as he could. Jumping from his seat, he broke ahead of Zale and set foot inside the office.

The door closed behind them and Reynolds brushed past, walking briskly into the lavishly styled office. Badrick couldn't help but be impressed; clearly Council member luxuries got more extravagant the higher up they were.

With a *flumph* Reynolds fell into his large desk chair and indicated for Badrick and Zale to take seats. Mawr was nestled in his own chair opposite Reynolds, his fingers interlocked and his expression just as stern as the Dominus'.

He nodded in greeting and Badrick quickly made to return the courtesy and sit down. . .

Anything to hide the fact that he couldn't stop looking at Mawr's face.

Every moment they spent with the soldier before his *'death'*, he'd been clad in his armour. Badrick had never seen him without it.

Even when he entered the BCR hours ago he'd been hidden behind his visor.

So it was slightly jarring to see the real him for the very first time.

His hair was the same shade of black as Badrick's, though the strands were cut a lot shorter. He looked older than Badrick expected, though he shouldn't have been surprised. Both he and Reynolds fought the Devil over twenty years ago, so the sight of a man in his forties should have been anticipated.

His skin was tanner than Badrick expected. Somewhere in the back of his head, Badrick had a memory of Stefan calling Mawr a half-breed freak, but if he was honest that had never really sunk in. Mawr's accent was so similar to Reynolds' he'd just assumed they were the same.

Badrick wasn't sure what races Mawr might have descended from but the colour of his skin and various parts of his face suggested to Badrick that Mawr definitely came from divergent parents.

Forcing himself out of these redundant musings, he demanded that his mind focus on what was now being said. He tuned in just in time to catch Reynolds say, "Operatives, you remember Corporal Mawr?"

"Yeah, of course." Badrick nodded.

Zale remained silent.

"He has some information he wants to share with you."

This piqued Badrick's interest. "What information?"

Before anyone could speak, Zale stopped them by asking, "How are you alive?"

Reynolds gestured to the young veteran and looked pointedly at Mawr. "Do you want to explain that?"

Mawr rolled his eyes and aimed what he next said to Zale and Badrick. "I was attacked by Lucikefer. Maybe you figured that out by now. He shot me in the spine."

"So . . . how?" Badrick frowned.

"I heal instantly from any wound," Mawr explained, "except from one to the spine."

"Or at least that's what he and his demon told everyone," Reynolds grumbled from the other side of the desk.

"It was a lie." Mawr glared at the Dominus. "To weed out anyone who might want to hurt me. There's actually no weak spot."

"You didn't know about it," Badrick guessed, speaking to Reynolds.

"No one did. He lied to everyone."

"It was necessary," Mawr snapped. "I'm sorry, Daniel, but if you quit complaining you'll remember how beneficial it's turned out to be."

Once again, before anyone could continue this argument, Zale cut them off by speaking loudly, "Isn't there supposed to be a trial now? Mawr's been missing even longer than I was. He abandoned the Daemonium."

"I did *not* abandon the Daemonium." Mawr frowned irately his way. "Everything I've done since the attack has been for the Daemonium's sake. Besides, there isn't time. We have to forget a trial."

"He's telling me what to do now," Reynolds sighed. "Some things never change."

Mawr placed a hand on Reynolds' desk and breathed, "Daniel, I respect your new position, but what I told you has to be discussed."

"I'm not sure I believe what you told me."

At the sight of Zale opening his mouth to cut them off yet again, Badrick slammed his fists on the desk and bawled, "OK! Please stop arguing, all of you. Why are we here?"

Reynolds appeared to realise he'd acted unprofessionally. Coughing, he tugged on his uniform uncomfortably. As for Mawr, he simply sat back and nodded agreeably.

Zale did nothing, nor said anything.

"Tell them your story, Mawr."

"To these two?" The soldier eyed them disapprovingly. "They're a little junior, don't you think, Daniel?"

"It's their case, Mawr. Tell them."

Hearing that, Badrick's stomach dropped.

"Fine." Mawr rubbed his hands together quite aggressively, apparently collecting his thoughts. It was clear he was reluctant to include Badrick and Zale in on his little tale, nevertheless he began with, "When I woke up after being attacked, I tracked Lucikefer. He had my key card and I wanted it back. But when I saw who he was meeting with, I decided against starting a fight. I made a quick decision to fake my helmet's status report and started investigating on my own."

"Why?" Badrick asked.

"If Lucikefer or his meet-up knew I was still alive it could have exacerbated things."

"Let me guess," Zale drawled. "You saw Charles."

"Aye, I saw the Resurrected," Mawr confirmed. "I also heard him talking to someone I couldn't see, but it was clear Charles had a master. And when I saw Lucikefer cower in fear . . . I had to know more." Mawr's sharp, dark eyes focused on Badrick, who shivered slightly under their piercing gaze.

And in a voice that suggested more than he was letting on, the soldier asked, "Badrick, how is the New Evil case coming?"

With a fear in his stomach he couldn't quite explain, Badrick responded a little too defensively, "We got him. He's dead."

Mawr's jaw tightened and he whispered, "No. He's not."

"What?"

"You got the wrong demon."

Badrick felt like his own honour was being personally insulted. Felt like his work was being shoved to the trash. And so it was with a hefty element of indignation that he said, "And how do you know?" He hadn't meant to act so pettily, but he couldn't quite help it.

Mawr's steely gaze refocused on him and he said, "I was there when Kiri'tol received his orders from the New Evil."

Badrick could say nothing but a repeat of an earlier utterance. "What?"

"I've witnessed everything." The soldier ground his teeth irately. "I saw Dhornji spying on Charles. I saw him figure out what he was seeing. I saw him running to you and I felt him die.

"And then, on my way here, I noticed Kiri'tol scouting the place out, and I heard him talking to the same monstrous voice Charles did before you captured him.

"He was not the New Evil. That darkness used him as a patsy."

"But . . ." Badrick felt a shiver go through his spine; what Mawr was saying couldn't possibly be true.

He was painfully aware that he'd peddled this very same theory only two days before.

But Badrick had been proven wrong.

Kiri'tol *was* the New Evil.

However, he couldn't help but wonder whether he was resolute in that belief because it was fact or because he so desperately wished it to be true.

Mawr saw the disbelieving look in his eyes and scoffed angrily. "Even after everything, you people don't comprehend the strength of what we're facing. The New Evil is powerful beyond our understanding. Perfectly disguising someone to look like him, feel like him, sound like him is nothing compared to what he's fully capable of."

Reynolds breathed a heavy sigh and shook his head. "I have to agree with Varner, Mawr. I sensed Kiri'tol as well. I know what I felt."

"The New Evil *irradiated* the soil beneath Charles' feet just by being there in thought," Mawr snapped argumentatively. "Did Kiri'tol ever do that?"

In the corner of his eye, Badrick could see Zale's already pale skin whitening even further, his hands and feet trembling, and Badrick felt fresh sorrow slink through his body. He couldn't bring himself to accept what Mawr was saying, primarily, because if it was true then everything Zale lost was in vain.

All his efforts to capture this evil had been pointless.

"OK, Mawr," Reynolds sighed. "Prove it to us. Tell us something we don't know."

Mawr wasted no time. Licking his lips, he got straight to it. "When Charles communicated with the New Evil, he addressed him as *Primordial*."

"Primordial?" Reynolds parroted.

"What the hell does that mean?" Badrick asked loudly.

"This demon," the soldier began dramatically, raising his hands and moving them to emphasise each word, "is both old *and* new. From what I could gather its bloodline is one of the most ancient, potentially even more so than the Royals. However, the term *New*

Evil doesn't mean he is our newest enemy. The name is *literal*.

"As we all know, demons are old, old creatures. But this being, the Primordial, is freshly made. He's the newest member in an ancient line of demons." Mawr sat back and raised a cocky eyebrow at Reynolds. "Did you know that?"

Reynolds was forced to admit that they did not.

"Dhornji rambled something similar," Badrick muttered, forcing himself out of the numbness that threatened to overtake his every muscle. "Said evil was *supposed* to be old."

"The bloodline is so old," Mawr continued, "no one remembers it. I couldn't discern much more from the snippets I managed to overhear, but I got the feeling that the Primordial itself doesn't even know where it comes from.

"Simply put, Daniel, he's powerful. I reckon he could take even *me* out."

I plan to.

With the murderous eyes of a furious snake sighting prey larger than itself, Zale leered at Mawr with venomous hatred

Zale's plan was perfect.

There'd not been a single flaw.

He'd assured everything went accordingly.

So how had he never accounted for this eventuality? *How* had he never sensed this meddlesome soldier's proximity to his slave? *How* did he never feel him listening to their conversations?

Having not known of Mawr's continued existence he was forced to admit he'd been clumsy. He had to swallow his pride and confess there was no way he could have foretold the soldier returning to blow the whistle on the Primordial's survival.

Primordial . . .

Zale could barely remember using that title when plotting with

Charles to awaken the dormant power within him, but the moment he heard it spoken aloud his memories sparked and he instantly knew this was his name.

A smothering cloud of amnesia was being displaced, revealing to him his true identity.

He *was* Primordial; the beginning of all things—progenitor of a fresh era—the start of a new world.

Zale liked the sound of that.

Of course, with Mawr's revelations, how likely was that future now? With the soldier casting suspicions left, right and centre how many Enthrallers would suspect Zale of lying about Kiri'tol?

Would they suspect *him* of being anything more than an Enthraller?

Impossible.

How could they?

Through Zale's panicked thoughts, he managed to catch words coming from Mawr's mouth that he *really* did not want to hear. When he heard him say, "We should question Charles again," he felt fresh waves of alarm shoot right him.

I'm not ready for them to know. I'm not charged enough. I'm still weak enough for them to stop me!

If they questioned Charles it would be all over.

The boy would talk.

They would discover Zale.

I have to kill Mawr!

With his growing distress utterly destroying his sense and reason, Zale actually felt his arm rise to strike Mawr down where he sat. He was already preparing himself to reach into his soul and summon megatons of power to dash the soldier from existence.

He stopped himself just in time.

It was an effort, forcing his hand to return to the arm of the chair, but with a strained calming breath he demanded his mind quieten. Slowly, but surely, it complied with his commands and the fog of panic began to lift.

Zale couldn't afford to be foolish now.

If he just stayed calm he would always remain victorious. If he could just trust his intellect he would forever stay one step ahead.

Irrefutable proof of this was occurring right now; with his heart no longer racing he was able to concentrate on the facts of the situation.

First of all, his power may still have been growing, but it was still enough to spell Charles into permanent silence.

Secondly, he'd already proven no scanner or Enthraller could detect him *even* when he used his Primordial power. Not a soul would ever notice his manipulations were the reason for Charles' refusal to talk.

And finally, no one in this room had yet displayed a belief in Mawr's story.

To act now would have been a monumental jump-of-the-gun.

Just stay calm, he told himself, *and pay attention to what happens.*

He returned to the conversation just in time for Reynolds to say, "Under no circumstances is anyone to go near the Resurrected. If what you say is true, then I will not permit anyone to alert the New Evil that we know the truth.

"We can't risk him seeing us through Charles' eyes."

See? Zale sneered internally. *They're already ruining themselves.*

Mawr shrugged and said, "You're the boss," though he looked somewhat annoyed.

"Well, what then?" Badrick snapped—apparently all these 'revelations' were upsetting him greatly.

"We need to determine if it's true or not," Reynolds announced immediately. "We'll instate a—"

"There is," Mawr's quiet voice cut him off, "another way."

A bemused silence followed this statement, however Zale

could see Reynolds regarding Mawr with a suspicious eye. Eventually he groaned aloud, a sound Zale couldn't remember ever hearing coming from the man before. "I recognise that look. I *hate* that look. No, Mawr. Not today."

"It could work."

Reynolds gave the soldier a pleading look. "Come on, Mawr!"

"What're you talking about?" Badrick stopped them both.

The Dominus immediately made to speak, but Mawr managed to get there first with, "We can find out who the Primordial is without using the Resurrected."

Next to Zale, Horas appeared and chuckled, "Looks like you have a situation on your hands."

Reynolds reached across the desk and grabbed a hold of Mawr's arm. "There isn't the time. We need something solid, not myths."

"It's not a myth, Daniel, and you know it."

For what felt like the hundredth time this morning, Badrick was forced to stop them arguing, flapping his hands like an impatient bird and demanding they explain themselves.

Mawr's grin was wide and confident and, ignoring Reynolds' warning look, he said, "There's a device called the Captus Memoria."

"*Fabled* device," Reynolds sighed tiredly, settling back into his chair in defeat.

"It could help us find the New Evil," Mawr stated with bold self-assurance. "If we can find it, replicate it, we can put as many as we want around the country. No matter where the Primordial goes we'll be able to find him.

"We might even be lucky enough to find he's been near the Captus Memoria already. If that's the case, we'd discover his identity immediately."

Badrick had to admit he liked the sound of that, but before they went any further with this grand plan he wanted a little more information. The fact of the matter was that he hadn't a clue what the Captus Memoria was.

An unexpected burst of energy brought his attention to the originally empty space behind him. He turned in surprise, voicing, "Daemnos?" in question to the demon's appearance.

The Royal raised a showboating hand and called, "I do!" He laughed and stepped closer, reaching a finger to Badrick's forehead. "Lemme try an' clear the cobwebbles."

The tip of his finger phased through Badrick's skull, who gasped as an unwelcome sensation ripped through the neurons of his brain, his hands gripping the chair tightly in discomfort.

"Badrick?" Reynolds called in concern.

Taking several deep breaths, Badrick reassured him, "Gimme a minute."

Retracting his fingernails from the holes he'd torn in the upholstery, Badrick blinked to clear his blurred vision and rubbed his temples to dull the pain brought on by the sudden introduction of foreign knowledge.

The Captus Memoria—a device created by demonic scientists untold millennia ago, designed to record the past of any individual unlucky enough to get inside its radius. It was created so that it could... No, wait... Badrick couldn't access that part from Daemnos. It was too foggy. He reached further in, hoping he might glean this info, but was disheartened to see that Daemnos' memories were just too blurry.

However, there *was* more—apparently, when activated, the device went above and beyond its capabilities. The demons discovered that it was also capable of recording an individual's entire future.

No ifs, no buts—whatever you might see within the Captus

Memoria's *'hard drive'* would be *exactly* how events would unfold.

It was the ultimate scrapbook/fortune teller.

Badrick could see why Mawr believed it would help them.

He pressed the memories again, hoping to see an image. Get at least an idea of what it looked like. However, the harder he tried the foggier everything seemed to become and he was forced to eventually throw in the towel.

"Reynolds," he spoke softly, deciding to put the older men's dispute to rest. "It's real."

Reynolds looked aghast. "You're kidding me."

Apparently also happy enough to take Badrick's word as gospel, Mawr laughed victoriously. "I told you, Daniel."

Reynolds looked ready to hit Badrick over the head. Thankfully, he seemed to repress the urge and simply snapped, "Fine." He gave Mawr an angry look. "You win. It's real." Before Mawr could comment, he raised an authoritative hand and said, "Now let's face another reality; we'll never find it. We don't know any of the demons that made it. It's been gone for millions of years. Nobody in the Daemonium outside the Council even knows it exists." He pointed an accusatory finger at Mawr. "*You* aren't supposed to know it exists."

"How *do* you know?" Badrick was compelled to ask.

"When the Daemonium was fighting the Devil's army, my demon made a habit of mocking me with knowledge of its existence. If we had the Captus Memoria we could predict where the Devil would go next."

"We could have ambushed him," Reynolds sighed. "Yeah, I've heard this complaint before."

At the sight of the Dominus' disapproving scowl, Mawr exclaimed, "I didn't choose to know, Daniel, and it's not like I know what it looks like."

"Didn't stop you obsessing over it for twenty years, did it,

216

Corporal Burakka?"

Mawr pointed his own angry finger at Reynolds. "Don't emulate Captain Holt at me, Daniel. I'll shoot you."

"Are you two actually friends?" Badrick sighed tiredly. "'Cause all you do is fight."

You obviously don't know a lot about brothers, a derisive voice said in his head.

And you do? he retorted.

He instantly regretted responding. It had been a stupid thing to do, especially with a question as unthinking as the one he'd issued. Of course Daemnos understood what it was like to be a brother; he had two of them.

And though Mawr and Reynolds weren't related, Badrick got the feeling they might as well have been.

He'd heard enough stories to know they'd die for one another.

Coughing with embarrassment at Badrick's harsh comment, Reynolds once again straightened his uniform.

"Daniel," Mawr said, his voice softer before. "Listen to me on this. Let me see the Captus Memoria. I can do this if I know what to look for."

"It fell into the Void, Mawr." Reynolds shook his head. "It's said even Vermiah failed to get it back."

"I showed you my reports years ago," Mawr said. "I'm telling you it reappeared on Earth."

"Where?"

With a sigh of resignation, Mawr was forced to admit he didn't know. He followed this admission with another request to finally be allowed to witness the Captus Memoria's visage. Mawr claimed that it was their best chance and that, if he could just know what it looked like, he would be able to find the thing.

Though the Dominus appeared resistant, it was clear to Badrick he'd already made up his mind on the matter. Whatever laws previous Councils once enforced no longer mattered. Thanks to the Hierarch's actions Reynolds could now enforce or revoke their rules and regulations at a moment's whim.

At least for now.

Sighing heavily, he revealed a small keyboard from a draw and tapped away for a few seconds, looking deeply solemn. At his command, a revolving hologram flashed into existence over the table.

And Badrick felt his jaw drop to the floor.

It was purple in colour. Shaped like a tear drop. A gash ran across the middle, from which light impossibly shined.

"The Captus Memoria," Reynolds announced with fake blitheness.

And in a tone that didn't quite accurately communicate his sheer disbelief, Badrick whispered, "That's the *Odd Monument*."

chapter
TWENTY ONE

Daemnos' highly amused cackles were more irritating than anyone else could possibly imagine. "I did wonder how long it would take you, Baddie Badrick!" the demon guffawed. "I *did* wonder. Some giant demon device appears in your town and all the silly people just accept it?

"You *humanses* . . . so funny."

Badrick had had enough. He gripped Daemnos with metaphysical hands and stuffed him deep inside his soul until the echoes of his laughter ceased. Though he could still hear tiny chuckling from somewhere within, the Royal's cackles were at least no longer drowning out those talking in the real world.

He studied the holographic map that now dominated Reynolds' desk, musing over how different his town looked at this angle. The Dominus had his finger hovering above the church that housed the Daemonium agent Hans.

"... and according to Badrick," he continued a sentence Badrick didn't hear the beginning of, "the Captus Memoria is here." He moved his finger along the map before withdrawing it and grinding his teeth thoughtfully. "How did we never see it there?" Badrick heard him mutter.

"That's what happens when the Council keeps its existence a secret," Mawr said bluntly. "Who knows how long it's been there. The Daemonium might not have even developed scanners at the time. Who knows what its energy is like. If our scanners have never picked it up then ..." He trailed off.

Determined to be a part of the conversation, Badrick asked, "What do we do?"

"We go get it," was the confident exclamation from Mawr.

Reynolds put a halting hand between them and said, "No, Mawr, we need to be careful. We need to keep this quiet."

Although he was clearly agitated, impatient and excited all at the same time, Mawr actually obeyed the Dominus. He settled on the flats of his feet, and nodded, though his eyes never left the location of the Captus Memoria.

"I agree we should extract it," Reynolds said. "But we need to be careful about how we go about it. If the New Evil *is* still out there we can't risk tipping him off."

"Agreed."

"We should scout the area during the day when it's busy."

"Secure it," Mawr nodded affirmatively. "Airlift it out during the night?"

Reynolds' head bobbed side to side as he milled the idea over before deciding in its favour. With that, he deactivated the map and laid his palms against the desk, supporting his weight. "Ordinarily," he spoke, "you three would not be doing this.

Badrick, Zale, you two are supposed to be on leave and you, Mawr, aren't even an agent."

Badrick heard Zale mutter darkly, "And supposed to be dead," and had to suppress a laugh.

Reynolds rubbed his lip with a thoughtful thumb. "However, under the circumstances, it's best if you three go. Badrick knows the way around his town, and he'll need back-up."

"And you don't want anyone else knowing about this yet," Mawr smiled.

"Right."

"Understood." The soldier was quite suddenly sharp and alert. "When do we leave?"

"As soon as possible. Badrick, Zale, I'm sorry to cut your holiday short, but—"

"It's fine," Badrick breathed honestly, waving his words away with frantic hands. "I can't sit around doing nothing right now."

Reynolds smiled proudly in his direction before shimmying around the table and ushering them out. "Go on," he said. "Get ready. Plain-clothes equipment."

As Badrick exited the office his thoughts turned immediately to his partner. There was no doubt these newest developments would be causing a great deal of distress for Zale, and Badrick wanted to see if he could help. He placed a hand on Zale's shoulder and studied his deathly white face.

It broke Badrick's already shattered heart to see.

"Are you OK?" he asked stupidly.

The reply was a simple shake of the head.

"Go take a minute," Badrick told him. "Then come meet me."

This time Zale nodded, and as he turned away and departed Badrick felt the tug of those pesky broken emotions yanking at his chest once again.

Not now, he chided himself, *I'm busy.*

Mawr spun away from the closing door when he heard Reynolds sigh like a blade stuck into his stomach had just been removed. Mawr saw that his face was a mile long and his shoulders were dramatically sunken.

He looked terrible.

Concerned for his oldest friend, Mawr attempted to lift his spirits by saying, "Thank you, Daniel. You make a great Dominus."

"Sure." Reynolds' reply was laced with sarcasm. He eyed Mawr for a moment, then lifted a hand with three fingers extended. "Remind me, old friend, out of the three times we agreed to let ourselves be unprofessional, how many do we have left?"

"One," Mawr stated. "We used the second four years ago. Remember?"

Mawr didn't need to ask to know the third time was to be used right here, right now, and when Reynolds circled the desk to approach him, he remembered to refrain from objecting. He too reached forward and pulled him into the manliest hug he could muster.

"You have no idea how glad I am to see you alive," Reynolds said. They parted there, and the Dominus sidestepped back to his chair, into which he fell without grace.

"Glad to finally be back," Mawr said truthfully. "My apologies for bringing this to your doorstep."

"You had to."

Mawr retook his seat and commented, "I was surprised to see that it is now *your* doorstep. Daniel Reynolds has been elected Dominus, I heard one day." He found himself laughing. "My surprise was, as you can imagine, total."

"Thank you." Reynolds scowled back.

"What's it like being Dominus?" he queried.

"It's hell, Mawr!" Reynolds slammed his hands onto the desk and let his head droop. "I hate this position. I'm always unsure. Always second guessing myself."

"You're not yourself, that's for damn sure."

Reynolds' head lifted and, with a cocked eyebrow, he murmured, "What do you mean?"

"Daniel Reynolds is an authority," Mawr said boldly. "Sergeant in the Daemonium Army, Eparch of the Council, one of the few truly respected members from that old farce. Becoming Dominus shouldn't have changed that. But you're overwhelmed. I can see it right now. You're too willing to allow others to make decisions because you don't feel you can. You don't believe you have the common sense to make a decent decision."

"Well, I—"

Mawr threw a rigid hand in the direction of the door. "You would never have allowed Varner to cut you off the way he did today, and I suspect you've been letting those two get away with murder ever since that damn boy came back to life.

"Daniel, what are two kids doing on a case as big as this?"

"They were the unlucky operatives who got the case," Reynolds told him. "Before it could be taken from them they solved it. It's not their fault it led to the New Evil. It's mine. I helped them hide the case's importance from the old Council."

"Still . . ." Mawr shook his head with disapproval. "When it escalated it should have been moved to a more experienced team."

"When Dhornji was murdered, the Council unanimously agreed to let them stay on the case. We needed Badrick's power and Zale's intellect."

Maw huffed with irritation. Regardless of Reynolds' explanations—no matter how sound they were—he highly disagreed with letting kids head missions as large as the New Evil case.

Reluctantly moving on from the subject, Mawr went back to his earlier point. "You need to remember who you are, Daniel," he said gruffly. "You're a capable man. A soldier. A leader . . . What would Blayke say if he could see you now?"

"Blayke served in the *actual* military. He was better at this than both of us."

"Inconsequential."

That last comment earned him a vicious scowl from the Dominus. "Since when did the famously abrasive, brutish Mawr Burakka become so bloody insightful?"

"When the confident, only slightly abrasive Daniel Reynolds stopped being so." Another scowl, so Mawr tried again. "I want you to be the leader you're capable of being, Daniel. So do it. Keep the Daemonium afloat with the success you obviously can achieve."

Without giving Reynolds the chance to respond he held up three fingers. "Moment of unprofessionalism ending in three . . . two . . . one."

Mawr rose to his feet and offered Reynolds a crisp, sharp salute. "Orders, Dominus?"

"Get your equipment," the man told him after a brief moment's silence. "Meet up with Operatives Hood and Varner, whether you like it or not. Plain clothes op. Find that damn thing before anyone else does."

"Yessir!"

He entered the room slowly, allowing the door to close behind him without a word. When the thing met with the floor, he slowly reached up and pressed the switch that would render his room soundproof.

He heard the machine whirring away at his touch and listened as it did its work.

Now he was safely secure in his room. No sound was capable of escaping, nor would any disturb him from outside sources.

With slow, steady steps, he approached his bed, letting his leg knock into the side. Still, he made no sound nor uttered a word.

He barely even breathed.

Zale just listened to the silence, and continued to do so until a grating, rumbling voice spoke in his ear. "The situation looks quite bad."

Horas jumped in surprise when Zale pivoted on his heel and roared inhumanly in his face. As the monstrous scream vibrated the walls, his eyes blackened, his teeth elongated into points and vicious, dark shadows manifested around his form.

To Zale's great surprise, this act of rage failed to incite the reaction he expected. Horas did not cower in fear, but seemed to stare back, unimpressed. The shock of this was enough to deflate his anger and return his features to their normal visage.

Horas pretended to wipe saliva from his visor; a rare display of humour.

And in the mannerisms of Zale himself, he said, "If you are quite finished, you can tell me what you plan to do."

"What *can* I do!?!" Zale bawled. "They're going to find it and I'll be finished."

"This may seem obvious," Horas said, "but can you not simply avoid the Captus Memoria's radius? If I remember correctly, I was once informed it had a range of ten meters."

Zale allowed himself to laugh with great derision, ensuring the demon could feel his contempt. "They'll want me to study it, Horas. I'll be forced to get close. Besides," he growled angrily, "I've already been within its range."

"You have?" Horas seemed surprised. "When did this occur?"

"Are you stupid?" he snapped. "Don't you remember? Lucikefer! When he connected you to Daemnos. We drove right past Badrick and that—" he gestured aggressively into thin air "— *accursed* thing!

"It's already scanned both of us. If they look into its memory, they'll see not only what I've done, but what I plan to do."

He spun away from Horas and slammed his fist into the nearby sink. It parted from the wall with a deafening crash and fell to the floor, smashing apart further upon impact.

"You seem upset." Another unwelcome moment of humour from the famously sincere Horas. Hearing it left Zale seriously considering whether or not to strike him from the history books right there and then.

However, he managed to resist, not wanting to waste time when he had to figure out how he was going to crawl out of this mess.

After all, the Daemonium would surely attempt to discover how to access the Captus Memoria's data before doing anything else. The chance that memories and a foretelling of the New Evil's movements could be within reach was too great to pass up.

They would have to ensure the device didn't already contain what they desired.

Even if Zale had been lucky enough to avoid being recorded already, he was certain they'd demand he and other scientists reverse engineer the damn thing.

Make their own if possible.

Spread them out across the country.

The world.

Was there any chance he could keep the data they uncovered from everyone else?

Not a chance; a discovery this big, he wouldn't be allowed anywhere near the Captus Memoria alone, and Mawr—the man apparently obsessed with its existence—would demand immediate access.

Zale had no doubt the bastard would get it.

Apparently sensing his uncertainty, Horas pressed him into speaking with, "What do you want to do?"

"What *can* I do?" Zale repeated dispiritedly. "If they get a hold of it, they'll discover me, and if it goes missing before they get there, or they find it destroyed, it'll prove the New Evil is alive."

Horas seemed to disagree. "I think that—"

"Believe me, Horas, it'll be obvious." Zale let himself fall to his mattress, his body bouncing on the springs. He put his hands over his eyes and sighed, dread and anxiety coursing through his veins. His teeth bit his lip and gnawed so hard he felt a sting as he nearly cut it open. "If they realise Mawr's telling the truth, they'll ready for the fight. Prepare themselves for my return."

"You do not want them rallying against you," Horas said. "If they are able to organise, your plans could—"

"What did you say?"

Horas stopped and Zale sensed him frown. "You do not want—"

Zale cut him off with a flap of his hand. "No, after that."

"If they are able to organise—"

Once again, Zale stopped him with a sharp swipe of his hand. He pushed himself from the bed, eyes wide, mind whirring, and stared at Horas' armoured visage, ignoring the demon's confusion.

He could now feel a small smile spreading on his lips.

"That's right," he whispered. "I need to stop them organising."

At this juncture, nothing I do is going to stop them learning the truth, his mind told him. *They'll discover it on their terms and have time to prepare.* "But what if they find out on *my* terms?" he voiced aloud.

"Zale?"

He leapt from the bed, excitement building in his chest. "What if I announce the New Evil's return for everybody to see?

"How—"

"I attack openly . . . If I announce the New Evil's continued reign in a display of dominance they'll be as afraid as they were before. Even more so, actually. They'll witness my power once again and remember what scared them so much.

"If they're afraid, they can be manipulated. Woven to do what I want them to." He allowed his growing grin to dominate his features. "Make them afraid. Make them know without doubt the New Evil is still out there, and then use that fear."

Horas retreated a few steps when Zale abruptly made his way to the mirror, stepping on the shattered remains of his sink, and regarded his reflection with increasing exhilaration, thinking on all that was to come.

"It's time for a new game."

*

Going back to his home town was quite the experience for Badrick. He had not returned since the moment he was rendered unconscious by Agent Hans and barely spared a thought for the place since.

Seeing it now, he remembered exactly why.

It was a goddamn dreary place. Cut off from any major population centres and practically in the middle of nowhere, this little town had very little to do within its borders. There was a grand total of one park, with no leisure centres and not one single cinema.

Drab was an understatement.

The three of them ventured down the back roads so as to avoid the wandering eyes of the populace, only glimpsing the inner town through various alleyways and side streets.

"I don't want to have to remind you this is your home town," Mawr had told them half an hour earlier.

"And yet you just did," Badrick remarked scathingly back.

"You disappeared from this place after your house blew up with your uncle inside. Stay out of sight."

Now and then someone would pass, either walking their dog or heading somewhere unknown, and Badrick's heart would half stop. He didn't need Mawr to tell him that it could lead to some very unhelpful problems if he were to be recognised by the wrong person.

However, it always turned out to be someone Badrick didn't know, and the person would only smile considerately or ignore them entirely.

As a huge German Shepherd pulled the last person they saw onto the main road, Badrick realised they were getting close and flicked his hand ahead. "It's down this road, to the left."

"Understood," Mawr stated, as their small pathway opened up into a quaint little stretch of land, filled with cottages on either side. Checking the road for civilians, he moved forwards so fast he practically left Badrick and Zale in his dust.

He was so far ahead that when Badrick abruptly noticed a severe problem walking towards them he was forced to abandon Mawr and drag Zale into the closest doorframe. Perhaps sensing their sudden diversion, Mawr stopped and checked to see where they had gone.

But it was too late.

"Act casual," Badrick hissed when Zale demanded an explanation. He leaned against the doorframe, hoping the owner wasn't about to open the door and find them on their step. Pushing his hands into his pockets, he took a breath and hoped the problem would pass.

The procession of teenagers he'd spotted approaching finally drew close. Most passed without caring what they were doing, chatting about anything from television shows to college applications, and Badrick began to believe they'd managed to go unnoticed.

Until a boy his age ground to a halt and stared at Badrick.

Goddamn it! Badrick screamed in his head when he realised who it was. *Bloody Donavon.* Why did the one kid from his school who recognised him have to be the idiot who'd make the biggest scene about it?

Staring at Badrick, the teenager went, "Ain't you that kid whose house exploded?"

Putting on his best bored persona, Badrick slowly turned his eyes upon the boy and slurred, "Erm . . . no."

"Yeah, you are," the boy continued. "You're that Badrick, from school."

Laughing derisively, Zale followed Badrick's lead with, "What kinda name is Badrick?"

Badrick forced a respondent laugh and said, "My name's Alex, mate. Who the hell are you?"

"Don't lie. I'm not stupid."

You could've fooled me. Donavon was now drawing closer, his approach aggressive and hostile, and to Badrick's great despair his ruckus was attracting the attention of the teenagers who'd already moved on.

Because of this arse, they were coming back.

Maybe I should point my pistol at him. Badrick tried to rid himself of that thought before it could even fully form.

He was saved having to respond to Donavon with equal aggression by the unanticipated intervention of Zale. His partner surged forward and slammed his palms into the teenager's chest. As a result the meddler was nearly thrown from his feet, however he just about managed to keep his balance.

When he'd recovered, Donavon ensured to let them know he was enraged. He dashed forward, raising a fist—

And stopped when he felt the sting of Zale's blade against his throat.

With a furious glare, Zale hissed, "I have never understood why morons like you start fights with strangers. Any one of them could be a psycho. You never know. Anyone could be holding a gun or a weapon or might retort by kidnapping you. So why risk it?" Zale dug the blade in deeper. "How can you be that stupid?"

The boy didn't move or speak as his entourage only stared in shock.

"Zale." Badrick reached out, his eyes wide with surprise.

His partner ignored him, instead opting to whisper in the boy's ear, "Run, before I kill you." The moment the blade pulled away from his throat, the teenager bolted. He scrambled to his group, who parted to let him through, only to promptly follow.

A dreadful silence was left in their wake in which Badrick could only stare in disbelief at Zale as he gently sheathed his dagger. "Zale . . . did you . . . did you really need to do that?"

He couldn't see Zale's face. His back was turned to him, his shoulders hunched over tensely. His breathing looked so heavy Badrick was surprised he couldn't hear the breaths.

Badrick didn't know what to do.

But then something truly surprising happened; Zale turned around and flustered like an old man.

"Remind me never to try and channel bad people again," he said, leaning over and exhaling sharply.

"What?"

"I hung out with Charles for ages when I was a kid," Zale told him. "I know how to fake being a bad person. Just remind me never to do it again. I don't like how that made me feel."

Badrick weakly pointed towards the fleeing group. "There must have been a better way."

"We don't have time to waste trying to be diplomatic," Zale argued.

Though Badrick was still in mild shock, he couldn't deny the logic of this, and he had to admit that realising Zale had only been acting was a great relief. For a moment, he'd been under the impression that the stress of the last few days had finally caused Zale to snap.

They were prevented conversing any further by the arrival of Mawr. As he stepped into view, Badrick saw his face was stern and impatient, his body language communicating intense irritation. "What was that?" he demanded.

"People from school," Badrick enlightened him.

"Did they recognise you?"

Mawr hadn't seen what occurred. Deciding to refrain from sharing the entirety of their encounter, Badrick opted for just shaking his head. Evidently believing them, the soldier about-faced and hurried on, eager to complete the mission.

Around the corner they went, emerging on the road that would eventually lead them to the psychiatrist's office. That brought up some bad memories but, refusing to dwell on the past, Badrick forced himself to join Mawr in grinning victoriously.

The *Odd Monument* rested right where he remembered.

Badrick figured he should stop calling it that now he knew it was an ancient demonic artefact capable of things nothing else was, but it was hard to let go of the habit.

"Scout the area," he heard Mawr say. "Make sure no civilians are around and we'll have a quick look at it. Then we'll contact HQ and keep it guarded until night."

Content to listen to the senior Enthraller, Badrick moved off to the left, checking for anyone who might be near. If there was he'd need to find a way to convince them to leave. For a second time he toyed with the idea of waving his gun around. The sight of a weapon usually made people evacuate pretty quickly—

Badrick was on his knees before he understood he'd fallen; the force of what struck him disorientated his mind so swiftly and painfully he briefly lost awareness of his surroundings. The only thing that helped him realise he was on the ground was the sting that scraped his knees and the choking in his throat as an indescribable darkness slashed at his very soul.

Beside him, he heard Mawr also cry aloud, and in his peripheral vision he witnessed the soldier fall like a plank onto his back.

A third scream echoed around the street and, fighting the pain pinning him to the ground, he strained to turn, and saw Zale writhing on his back, his fingers like claws as he scratched at the air in agony.

A shadow was hovering over his prone body, and not just any kind of silhouette. This was a shifting, shapeless mass of evil and cruelty.

An unholy void of emptiness.

Before Badrick could make a move, the shadow converged on the Captus Memoria and engulfed it within its convulsing form. The moment those dark tendrils touched the machine, it began to spark and fizzle and emit the most horrendous grinding sound.

In an instant, Badrick understood the shadow's intent.

"No!" he roared, but of course it was far too late. With a deafening crash, a burst of power far more threatening than anything Badrick had experienced before lit up the street, setting black fires along the tarmac.

Amongst the shadow's onslaught, the Captus Memoria went up in violent, blue, demonic flames.

A distance away, Mawr scrabbled to his feet, roaring wrathfully. With the swiftness of a cheetah, he withdrew his sidearm and unloaded the clip into the mass of shadows.

It had absolutely no effect. The shadow absorbed the rounds without so much as a recoil. The only sign it even knew it had been attacked was when it fired a blast of energy at Mawr and knocked him flat.

Badrick watched in shame, too weakened to act in time, as the shadow flickered, then vanished from sight, returning to whatever hellish place it came from. Badrick stared at the empty space it once occupied as the black fires died out, numb and stunned into shocked silence.

"It was him." Zale limped into Badrick's peripheral and placed a shaking hand on his shoulder. "The Primordial. He destroyed the Captus Memoria."

chapter
TWENTY TWO

It was rather quiet in the BCR that day.

So when Mawr shouted without warning and leaped forward to grab an agent by the collar, it made Badrick jump out of his skin.

The cause for this sudden aggression was easy to understand; upon returning to the Daemonium, Badrick, Zale and Mawr hastily scrambled to the agents' lair to study the energy readings at the attack.

They needed to review the site if they had any hope of salvaging this mess.

It was there they were told that, even though there *was* demonic energy present, the machines did not register the signature as belonging to the New Evil.

They all argued against this with impatient confidence. Merely sensing the energy of the entity had floored all three of them. Badrick himself had barely been able to move. No matter what made its way to the Captus Memoria—a slave, a patsy, the Primordial itself—there was no denying the New Evil's presence.

But no . . . the agents stood by what the machines told them.

And that was when Mawr snapped.

As the agent was shaken left and right, stupidly trying to repeat what incited this attack in the first place, Badrick wondered whether he should free the poor man from Mawr's furious grip.

He quickly decided against it when he saw the look of sheer ire on the soldier's face.

If Mawr was content to assault people five minutes after walking through the door, Badrick figured it was best to avoid seeing what else he was happy to do.

In the end it was Reynolds who saved the blue uniformed man. The Dominus prised Mawr from him, ordering the soldier to 'Calm the hell down! Right now!' before checking on the victim.

"It *was* the Primordial!" Mawr roared angrily. "This moron doesn't know what he's talking about."

"He's only relaying what the machines tell him," Reynolds said back. "If he says they're telling him the New Evil wasn't there, then I believe it."

Mawr looked ready to spew lava out of his eyes, his dark skin flushed so vividly. "How can you—"

Reynolds silenced him with a hand. "I didn't say I believed the machines." He helped the startled agent back to his seat and added, "We have to figure out what happened. Why the machines aren't showing us what we know to be true."

It was then that Zale finally chipped in. With a flick of his fingers to grab their attention he said, "I have a theory, but I'll need time to confirm it."

Reynolds looked expectantly at the nearby Agent Commanders

and rolled his eyes when they simply stared back, nonplussed. "Well?" he sighed. "This is your division. Can he have the time?"

Almost as if they feared disobeying the Dominus, a commander nodded vigorously and ushered Zale to a free computer to allow him to do his work.

With him occupied, Reynolds turned his attention to Mawr and Badrick. He spoke to the soldier first, uttering words Badrick never expected to hear. "You're determined to stay on this case?" Mawr nodded. "Then I'm reassigning you to the SpecOps division."

Mawr's reaction was just as aggressive as his earlier one. "What!? No, Daniel. I will *not* be an agent."

"Not an agent," Reynolds scowled. "An operative."

"Same difference. They take missions. I will *not* do missions. I am a soldier."

"A soldier who is determined to take a mission," Reynolds drawled in his direction. "A soldier who has been acting like an agent for months." When Mawr sighed angrily, Reynolds tried a softer tactic. "I'll make it temporary, all right? But no one is going to like a soldier—and a corporal, no less—getting involved in the biggest agent operation of our time.

"You know a lot about the New Evil. You've discovered so much and I trust your instincts. I need you to do this, Mawr."

His sincerity deflated the soldier's irritation. His body visibly relaxed and he shook his head with disgust. "Alright," he breathed. "But just for now."

Smiling, Reynolds thanked him.

Then he turned his attention to Badrick. "As for you, Varner, listen to your commander on the New Evil investigation, help Zale with whatever he needs, and bring Mawr up to speed on anything he doesn't yet know. Take him through everything we have. The Kalik Crisis, Charles' capture, our info on Dhornji . . .

everything. Can you do that?"

Determined to do as the Dominus requested of him, Badrick affirmed he would and took Mawr aside so that they could together dredge up every single case file on the New Evil and his movements.

Somewhere, in the recesses of his mind, he remembered that Daemnos wanted him to focus on the Bomb Killer. As he sat down at a console, Badrick felt a little bad about changing priorities, however he felt safe in assuming that his demon would rather him focus on the greatest threat to mankind instead of a bomb maker.

At least, for now.

Badrick and Mawr spent several hours going through the files, however, within minutes it had become apparent just how arduous this task was going to be. Mawr ensured that he knew everything. He asked hundreds of questions, pointed out and commented on dozens and dozens of notes made by whoever wrote the files he was mercilessly dissecting, and forced Badrick to repeat himself many different times.

"A Kalik?" he queried during one of these moments. "A Kalik got in here?

"Yes."

"How?" Mawr appeared utterly bewildered. "Is our security *that* stupid?"

Badrick didn't know why he felt personally insulted by this rude comment—it wasn't like he was responsible for the security of the Daemonium—but he was nonetheless. When he brought Mawr's attention to the corresponding case file, he did so with a hefty amount of venom.

"A Kalik prisoner was logged in half an hour before it attacked," Badrick said, reciting what he knew to be on the screen. "It was unconscious so they were taking it to the prisons.

Everything checked out until it was suddenly *not* in the prison."

"Who brought it in?"

Badrick could only shrug. "They said it was a soldier, clad in his armour and everything. But—"

"It was probably Charles," Mawr finished for him bitterly. He fell back into his seat and glared at the screen as if it paid him personal insult. "No doubt dumped the armour on his way out. We should try to find it if we haven't already."

"It was found the same day." Badrick was immensely glad to hear the sound of his partner's voice and swivelled to offer a large grin of welcome. It was relieving to know he didn't have to work with Mawr on his own anymore.

Zale took a seat and stretched amidst queries of what he'd been up to since they last saw him. When he told them that he believed he'd discovered the reason the sensors couldn't recognise the New Evil, Mawr's head snapped to attention and he demanded to know the answer.

Looking a little alarmed at the newly appointed operative's intensity, Zale instead spoke to Badrick. "Remember the discrepancies in the renders?" Badrick replied with a nod. "Well, it happened again."

Zale stretched once more, working soreness from his muscles by rubbing them with his hands, before diving into what he'd learned. "We all know power can grow. When a power gets more . . . well . . . powerful, it grows in size. But the New Evil . . . I've no doubt it's getting stronger, but every time it does, whole new chunks add to its energy.

"The Primordial is changing as well as growing. He's evolving constantly and his signature is getting more complex each time."

"That's why the scanners didn't recognise him?" Mawr raised a curious eyebrow. "Because he's changing?"

"Before," Zale continued, "when we thought we'd caught the

Primordial, we did it by comparing two scans of his energy. They were different, but also similar. Therefore, with a bit of inspired reprogramming by yours truly the machines were able to see the similarities.

"But this time the change was too vast. There were more differences than similarities and the machines just didn't register what they were supposed to."

Mawr's eager face fell and he sighed somewhat dejectedly. "If the Primordial keeps changing we might never be able to figure out where he is or where he's gone."

Zale made an *'eeeer'* noise and waved his hand in a *so-so* gesture. "What?"

"It may have changed," Zale said, "but when comparing what attacked us to the other readings we have I *did* notice a pattern. A recognisable sequence that can—I hope—be predicted.

"It's like those maths problems you'd get in school. You need to find the next number in a sequence. Consider this . . . If the first number is ten, the second is eight, the third is sixteen, the fourth is fourteen, then the fifth is . . ."

He left the sentence hanging, to which Mawr eventually answered with, "Twenty eight. You alternate between subtracting two and multiplying by two."

"The old man has it correct," Zale stated, ignoring Mawr's bristling at having his age mocked, "and that is the logic I applied to my calculations."

The hope of excitement roused in Badrick's chest. "Are you saying you can predict how his signature will look the next time he attacks?"

"Well . . . that's the hope." Zale's attention diverted from them as he said this, his eyes flitting to a space behind Badrick. Turning, Badrick saw what was so interesting.

Reynolds was once again in the BCR, apparently forced to

come down and personally give the agent detective Zach a stern talking to. From what Badrick could determine, having learned the New Evil was still alive, Zach was adamant he be allowed on the case. In light of the recent attack, he was claiming they needed him and would not take no for an answer from the Agent Commanders.

Hence Reynolds' presence in the BCR.

"I haven't updated the systems with this algorithm yet," Zale spoke quietly, his voice soft. "Maybe we should get Zach to do it, like we did last time."

"You think so?"

Zale never got a chance to reply, because Mawr showed them both what he thought of this idea by scoffing loudly.

"Listen, Mawr," Zale growled, clearly irritated, "Zach has the ability to be a real hindrance. When we were searching for Charles his eventual decision was that—" He cut himself off, perhaps suddenly realising who he was talking to.

"What?" Mawr demanded.

"Well, he decided that *you* were our culprit."

Mawr blinked. "He did what?"

"The only reason he didn't stop us getting the real bad guy was because he wasn't a part of our investigation."

Badrick nodded, saying, "Imagine how badly everything could've gone if he got in our way."

"If we bring him in on this, he probably *will* get in the way. If we continue to deny his demands, he'll try to help regardless and possibly be the ruin of us all."

"You don't have a lot of faith in him," Mawr noted.

"No," Zale scowled, "I don't."

"But," Badrick added, "if he *thinks* he's being included, Zach won't get in the way as much."

"Trust us," Zale concluded, "just let him think we want his

help and he'll be grateful."

Mawr's reaction was extremely doubtful. "How can you be sure?" he asked.

"He was last time," Badrick told him. "He thanked me for including him despite the commanders ordering him to stay away."

"And the secrecy of that charitable act inspired him to be a lot more inconspicuous," Zale finished. "Believe me; he will get in our way so we need to calm him down. He'll think we're including him in secret and will work to keep it that way." When Mawr continued to be unconvinced, Zale edged closer and said, "So you think we can afford mistakes? The New Evil will allow us one or two, will he?"

That changed Mawr's attitude. His face dropped and, with an angry glance towards Zach, he growled unhappily. "I don't like this cloak and dagger crap and I *don't* like going behind Daniel's back." He sighed deeply. "But we can't afford people who can't pull their own weight. Clearly Zach is a liability and we can't let him get in the way." He tutted and fell back into his chair. "Alright. This situation calls for unorthodox methods. Play your trick. But I'm telling Daniel. I'll try to convince him of the benefits but if he doesn't like the idea we're stopping."

"Go on, Badrick," Zale said, rolling his eyes and placing a hand on his shoulder. "You should be the one to do it again. Keep ourselves consistent. Give him my algorithm and tell him to update our systems."

As luck had it, the moment Badrick took a USB stick from Zale the agent detective stormed away from the Dominus. Eager to catch him before he sulked out the room, Badrick hurried to intercept him.

Zach was surprised to be accosted by Badrick and was more than aggressive when they greeted one another. Badrick bit back a vengeful retort to Zach's disrespect, knowing the idiot's mood would improve once he understood why Badrick was here.

When he realised what he was being offered, his eyes lit up like stars had just winked on inside them. In fact, he got so over excited that Badrick had to hit the break and ground his expectations.

"We can't involve you in everything straight away," he said, pretending to check behind himself for eavesdroppers, "but you're a good agent and we could use your help. So will you do this for us?"

Badrick hadn't been this manipulative the first time around. Back then they'd simply given Zach the data and asked him to do the work. But with everything that had happened, Badrick could see the need for complex deception. The situation was dire, and they couldn't afford blunders.

Zach had to be pacified.

Interrupting the man's hushed thanks, Badrick murmured, "Remember, this is a secret."

Nodding excitedly, Zach hurried away with a skip to his step he'd lacked before.

"And what, Varner, was that about?"

Damn. Putting on an innocent expression, Badrick about-faced and looked into the face of the Dominus. "Just trying to make him feel better," he said, which wasn't a complete lie.

Glancing at the now busily working Zach, Reynolds remarked, "Looks like it worked."

"Hopefully. I just told him how important it was to find the Bomb Killer. I mean, even Daemnos is worried about that guy. Zach will be a hero if he stops him."

"Ah," Reynolds smiled humourlessly. "Playing on Zach's vanity. Something I am practiced in doing and yet you seemed to have achieved it better than I ever have."

Badrick grinned in Reynolds' direction, looking the man up and down and noticing the sharpness of his posture. "You seem—"

"What, Varner?"

"Nothing," he said rapidly, realising he'd been nanoseconds from stepping out of line. What he'd wanted to say was that Reynolds appeared to be in better spirits, despite the chaos unleashed upon them. His formality was back, bigger and better than ever, and the confidence with which he held himself was returned.

Apparently able to read Badrick's mind, Reynolds spoke in a very low voice. "An old friend reminded me who I am."

That was all he said on the matter.

Gesturing to Mawr and Zale debating in the corner, he asked, "Speaking of said friend, how goes your task? Is Operative Burakka up to speed?"

"Yeah," Badrick sighed tiredly, quite suddenly feeling the fatigue of the last few hours.

"Something wrong?"

Unsure whether it was wise to speak aloud the words in his head to the man's best friend, Badrick hesitated in speaking. Unfortunately, he was unable to help himself, and by the time he realised he was talking it was too late to stop. "Was he always this hard to work with?"

He regretted it instantly, knowing he had spoken out of turn.

However, Reynolds did not chide him on his bluntness or his honesty as expected. The responding laughter from his mouth was quite the surprise, and Badrick could only gaze, stunned.

Reynolds wiped away a humoured tear and said, "He can be argumentative, but he takes his job very seriously."

"Does he know how to relax?" Badrick drawled blithely, again regretting his daring.

A sadder expression appeared on Reynolds' face and, after a

moment's hesitation, he said softly, "The Devil changed him."

"The Devil?"

"Yes, he—" Reynolds stopped himself right there and gave Badrick an accusatory glance. "Before I say anything else, I must ask . . . How much do you know about the Royal Family? About Daemnos' siblings?"

"Not a lot," Badrick had to say truthfully. As he spoke, his mind cast back to the moment he awoke in the dirt, coughing, spitting and struggling to breathe after months of being dead. Back to the moment Daemnos revived him with shared ownership of the Royal's memories and experiences.

Back then Badrick believed he had access to everything the Royal knew, despite it being a little jumbled at the time. He'd assumed it would all arrange neatly into place. But as time passed he'd come to understand that it wouldn't. Daemnos was utterly mad—more so after the resurrection—and even *he* didn't have concise control over his memories.

If the owner of these thoughts had no rule over them, what hope did Badrick have?

Many things remained blurry. Some things that were unclear were now crystal. Some that were once clear were now so fuzzy Badrick could hardly focus on the memories.

And as for Daemnos' family . . . forget about it.

He relayed this information to Reynolds, adding at the end, "Daemnos hasn't seen his brothers in millennia. I don't think those memories are capable of *un-blurring*."

Reynolds chewed his lip in a knowledgeable sort of way and responded, "I'm not surprised your memory connection isn't perfect. It's not something that's ever happened before, having access to a demon's mind, and with your demon being who he is I must say I've always been amazed it works at all."

That made Badrick laugh.

Amidst his titters, Reynolds sighed, "As I was saying . . . I can't tell you a lot . . . Those in the know have been prohibited to speak of what they saw and did . . . But I can tell you that what we had to do . . ." For a moment, Reynolds' voice seemed to break and he lost his ability to speak coherently. For a shocking second, Badrick thought he was going to cry.

But Reynolds regained control before he could, and, with a cough, continued, "What we had to do to keep the world safe changed all of us, but none more than Mawr. It was only us and the Hierarch who knew the real truth, and the loneliness of that . . . being unable to share what we went through . . . It changed him.

"You should have seen him before." Reynolds' teeth flashed in a wide grin. "Fresh out of Egypt, every second sentence was some kind of native slang that went right over my head. And he was kind. So very kind. He always saw the best in people."

He stopped there, his eyes misting as he remembered better days of the past. When it was clear he wasn't going to speak again without prompting, Badrick said, "But fighting the Devil changed him?"

Reynolds bobbed his head sadly. "Yes, the Devil changed him, and I think . . ."

"Think what?"

Reynolds hesitated for only a brief moment before saying, "I think that if we ever have to face the Devil again, it'll be too much for Mawr. He is the way he is for a reason. His actions and words are his walls. He's safe inside them. But . . . Well . . . I hope the Devil stays dead or I believe Mawr will collapse."

Slightly alarmed at these words, Badrick asked, "*Could* the Devil come back?"

Reynolds gave him a wry smile and said, "You're phishing."

"I'm just curious." Badrick shrugged innocently.

"No," Reynolds smiled. "He may be the Devil, but he was still a demon, and demons cannot resurrect. When they die, they're dead. I simply meant that I sometimes worry otherwise, despite myself, for my oldest friend."

His curiosity still getting the better of him, Badrick tried again. "You can't tell me any more about what happened?"

"No, Varner. Nothing more."

"But you're the Dominus," he kept on, fully aware he was pushing his luck. "The rules that stopped you don't matter anymore."

"Nice try, Operative," the General half scowled/half smiled, "but these orders come from the Hierarch. I can never reveal what I know, Dominus or not.

"Now!" he snapped, pre-emptively stopping Badrick from opening his mouth again. "I've shared far too much of our lives with you, Varner, so don't ever bring this up with Operative Burakka. The only reason I've told you this much is to help you understand your new partner. Try to be patient with him. He is the way he is for a reason."

Badrick nodded. "OK."

"You also have work to do. Remember? I suggest you go back to it."

Despite his desire to grill the Dominus for all he knew, Badrick recognised it was time to obey. With disappointment mingling with his dread over what was to come, he made his way back to his team, ready to continue the fight for survival.

chapter
TWENTY THREE

It was night by the time Zale finally eased through his bedroom door and allowed it to close, activating the soundproofing technology in order to garner as much privacy as he could manage.

For the first time in a long time, he actually felt *tired*.

Fatigue had not bothered Zale since the day he realised his power. He was usually far too charged with demonic energy to feel weariness.

But what he'd experienced that day had been too much.

Even for him.

There was no denying he'd been exceedingly lucky to have figured out a way around his Captus Memoria problem.

A sentiment that was apparently shared with the hellspawn lurking in his divided soul, made obvious by the way Horas immediately took the opportunity to materialise and comment on just how close Zale had come to being discovered.

"If you had not dreamed up a way to destroy the Captus Memoria in the perfect manner, everything could have come undone."

"I know, Horas," Zale sighed, flopping onto his bed. "I will admit I came close there."

"*However,*" the demon enunciated, "you succeeded." Horas' form appeared in his vision as the demon leaned over the bed. "I must congratulate you on your brilliance."

That made Zale laugh.

And he had to admit, hearing it made him feel better.

"Thanks, Horas. I knew I kept you around for a reason."

Despite appreciating the demon's efforts at bolstering his mood, Zale couldn't be fooled into thinking that was the only reason he'd bothered appearing. He wasn't here to shower Zale with compliments. There was a question burning within the demon that he desperately coveted an answer to.

Zale could already hear the thoughts and knew what this query was, and so spoke before Horas could work up the courage to question him.

"No, Horas. Of course I don't actually believe Zach will be satisfied. Our attempts to pacify him won't work this time around. In fact, his obsession will be exacerbated."

"Then why?" Horas shook his head. "What do you gain from involving the detective?"

Zale pushed himself into a sitting position and linked his fingers together. "Well, first Badrick will notice that it hasn't worked." He spoke slowly, as though explaining his actions to a small child. "Having been trusted to be secretive, when Zach inevitably continues his efforts to be involved, he will appear desperate and flustered. More importantly, he'll look careless when he lets his curiosity take him over once more.

"That's the way Zach is. He'll keep demanding to be involved. I have no doubt he'll involve himself *without* permission."

He allowed Horas time to process his words. The demon turned from him and stared at the wall, and Zale could hear the echo of his mind as he deliberated on Zale's scheming.

"There is more," he eventually stated.

It wasn't a question.

Admiring the electric demon's sometimes impressive intuition, Zale smiled and announced, "You're right. There is more. Did you know that Zach's been noticing whenever I mysteriously go to my room?"

"I noticed," Horas affirmed. "And I also know you deliberately let him. I have been wondering about this. I see no benefit in allowing him to observe that, at times, you are nowhere to be found."

"Zach doesn't like me, Horas. In fact, because of his jealousy he hates me completely."

"This is good, I assume?"

"It's paramount," Zale half laughed. "His hatred blinds him and this is no exception. If he hasn't already, he's going to start connecting dots simply because he wants them to be connected.

"Who knows, he might even solve the whole New Evil case. But let's be honest, who's going to believe him if he suddenly accuses me of being the Primordial?"

"Not a soul." Horas shrugged. "Everyone knows of his hatred towards you. They will believe his mind has snapped. They may even incarcerate him for his own good. Is that your goal?"

Zale waved a dismissive limb and shook his head. "What Zach does doesn't matter. I already know what to say to confuse his theories if he *does* get on the right track." He rubbed his hands together, his eyes misting as he ruminated on his extended schemes. "No," he whispered, more to himself than Horas. "I just need him to get so riled that he voices his concerns about my disappearances within ear-shot of Badrick."

"If he does confront you or others, it is more than likely Badrick will hear of it," Horas said. "Zach has never been one to talk privately and you all work in the same room. Everyone will hear what he has to say."

"That's what I'm counting on."

Horas strolled over—uncharacteristically casual—and took a seat next to Zale on the mattress. His blue visor seemed to bore into Zale's skull. It was like the demon wished he could pull the secrets from Zale's head with just his gaze. "But why?" he finally asked, once more resigned to no longer being capable of this. "Do you want Badrick to doubt you?"

The question amused Zale and he smiled at Horas' words before responding with, "There's already doubt festering inside him. It's been there for weeks even though he doesn't yet realise."

Horas seemed to sigh, and Zale watched as he put a hand to his head in a display of lethargy. Zale observed his fatigue with interest, already knowing the reason behind it and finding it a little funny. The demon had been experiencing blackouts recently. Hours of time were missing from his memories, and Horas could not comprehend why it kept happening. It was not something that he should have been capable of experiencing as a wavelength of energy, trapped inside another's soul, and it upset him greatly to not understand the cause.

Overcoming his weariness, Horas sighed and continued his stream of questions. "Why would he have cause to doubt you?"

"Aspersions have been made against my good self," Zale scowled. "I want him to talk to me about it so I can dismiss them, but he has to do it on his own terms. He can't know I'm aware of what's been said."

Zale felt a flicker of emotion that wasn't his and tutted with irritation. "I can feel your disapproval, Horas, and you're right. This is hardly the most important thing to worry about. Whatever doubts Badrick has they're not closely related to the New Evil."

"So why waste the time?"

He sighed, frustrated. "Doubts can grow, Horas. Doubts can multiply. They lead to more suspicions. They're like trees, in a way. If you have the seed of doubt, no matter how small and unimportant, it'll eventually grow into a tree of branches, with each branch representing something new.

"If Badrick notices the wrong thing, or the right paranoia spreads, one of those branches could eventually become a doubt over the real identity of the Primordial.

"But without that seed," Zale clenched his fist tightly, "the tree will never grow. I can't have Badrick coming to the conclusion that I'm the Primordial until I'm ready, and I can achieve that best by ensuring he has total confidence in me. Confidence begets loyalty. Even when faced with evidence to the contrary, he will be more likely to deny the truth."

"You believe this will work?"

"Trust me, Horas," Zale grinned darkly. "My efforts will reap many benefits. It shouldn't take long. I estimate within the next few days."

Horas could only shake his head once again, obviously unable to fathom what Zale was planning.

Zale jumped on the opportunity his silence provided by telling the demon to remain that way, for what he wanted next very much didn't require his presence or his input in any way.

"What are you going to do?" Horas asked, accidentally disobeying the order instantly.

Too exhausted to frighten him into submission, Zale simply said, "What I should have done days ago."

At that, he cast Horas from his worries, ignoring anything else the demon tried to say. Closing his eyes, Zale spread his arms and focused on driving his spirit from his body. It was easy this time and before Zale knew it he was soaring invisibly through the Daemonium's corridors at lightning speed in search of the one he desired.

Thankfully, Reynolds was also taking the opportunity of the night shift to catch some sleep. He was in the middle of pulling on a shirt and climbing into his bed, a relieved smile playing at his lips.

Secure in the knowledge that Reynolds was alone, Zale pulled back to physical form and used his great power to rip the Dominus through space and dump him before his feet.

The same power also blanked Reynolds' mind, leaving him catatonic and unaware of his surroundings as Zale dug inside and touched the dark presence in his soul. Swapping the souls around, he watched Lora replace Reynolds in the space he occupied and land heavily on the floor. She gasped with discomfort at being forced into the physical plane and took some shallow breaths to calm her shaking body.

After recovering from the shock, she placed her hand onto the leather covering her stomach and breathed, "How can I help you, my King?"

Zale regarded her armoured form for a moment, chewing his lip in deep thought. He could see that she was nervous in his presence, unsure as to why she'd been summoned.

She wouldn't remain that way for long, for she was here for something she also wanted.

With a sigh of defeat, Zale said, "You were right."

She needed no more info. Somehow, through his tone or maybe his body language, she seemed to recognize exactly what he meant. With a laugh that greatly communicated her desires, she reached up and pulled her helmet from her head, throwing it unceremoniously at her feet.

She went to work on the rest and, once all traces of metal were gone, she gripped the zip and opened her under-suit, moving so slowly Zale began to feel intense impatience.

A lust he wasn't aware he was capable of grew to uncontrollable levels as more and more of her perfectly shaped body came into view until finally she tore it from her shoulders and revealed what Zale wanted most.

He could feel his eyes darkening with furious lecherousness, shadows dancing over the globes. Angry fangs elongated his canines and his fingernails grew to black claws.

A hunger for a woman's body unlike he'd ever known erupted in his chest.

And as Lora stepped up to him, grabbed his hands and placed them on her breasts, she whispered in his ear, "I am yours."

chapter
TWENTY FOUR

Badrick had grown accustomed to sitting in the BCR with no idea as to what their next move should be. It happened more often than not with this job, a problem exacerbated by the fact that they were routinely lumbered with the worst missions.

However, on this one occasion, being so uncertain was killing him.

More and more he realised just how unfathomably world-ending the Primordial was—the being really could just swoop in at any moment and wipe them all out without effort—and the knowledge that they desperately needed to find a new step *right now* was giving Badrick major panic.

At some point during the day, Mawr brought their attention to the Captus Memoria attack. He noted that even though the New

Evil destroyed the machine, it hadn't endeavoured to destroy *them*.

The shadow actually fired a blast of energy at Mawr that achieved nothing more than to incapacitate him.

Mawr opined that this suggested the Primordial wanted them alive for something and that was why the monster had yet to slaughter them all. He believed it was significant that the Primordial not only avoided hurting them sufficiently but made sure to pull his punches.

Unfortunately, he couldn't explain in what way it was noteworthy and the only thing achieved by mentioning it was to start a half-hearted debate between Mawr and Zale on what the Primordial actually wanted.

Naturally, with so little information to go on, even Zale couldn't come up with an answer.

Badrick wished his partner had something to say; because of his own inability to come up with a plan of action, Badrick greatly wanted Zale to kick-start the engine in his goddamn brain and work out a solution.

But, as they sat there, mulling privately, the only sound that came from his partner was the scratching of the pen in his hand. He was currently in the process of writing a long overdue report on the attack that lost them the Captus Memoria, taking the responsibility at Mawr's behest.

The soldier-turned-operative had been too sour to face the task of jotting down the details of their failure and so the young adult took it upon himself. Badrick watched him finish the report with a satisfied sigh and throw the sheets of paper one by one onto a scanner. A blue light shone beneath each page and on the flat-screen before them Zale's immaculate handwriting was translated into computerised text.

Zale's hands flashed over the keyboard and he sent the report on its way for review by an Agent Commander. He also retrieved his papers and slotted them into an envelope, which he sealed.

"Better go give these to someone," he said, standing. "If you guys think of anything regarding the Primordial, let me know."

Mawr cast his eyes disapprovingly over the envelope, ignoring Zale's last comment and instead opting to say, "Why did you bother to handwrite it? Doesn't make any sense."

"Writing by hand is calming," Zale told him. "Right now, we all need a little calming."

"Strange lad," Mawr muttered as he trotted away.

Badrick smiled in agreement.

Zale never intended to enact a portion of his larger schemes on this day, but after forty eight hours of *nothing* from any of the people he was waiting on he decided to subtly remind them they were needed.

When he'd noticed Zach was working directly with Agent Commander—what was this decrepit old man's name?—Killian Murdock, he'd thought of a way to get what he needed.

It was true what Mawr said—he could have just written his report on a computer. But he needed an excuse to get close to Zach, and so he'd formulated a reason to randomly walk up to an Agent Commander he ordinarily had no business going up to.

Commander Murdock was a senior Agent Commander, which meant handing him a report was common practice. Approaching him with such a thing would make their interaction appear natural, even if it was a little odd to have handwritten a report.

Murdock saw him drawing near and turned his way to question why Zale was interrupting them. He made clear that he was only handing in a report, apologising for the hand written format but explaining—*lying*—that his personal login was acting up.

The commander waved the apology away, declaring it

unnecessary and praising Zale on endeavouring to finish the report no matter how taxing. Murdock tore open the envelope there and then, perusing the most important details before slipping it back in and throwing it on his console.

"How the devil did that monster know you were going for the Captus Memoria?" he murmured aloud. "Confounding."

"I've no idea, sir," Zale sighed, shrugging. "If it helps, you can blame me."

"Why would I do that, Operative?"

"I don't know." Zale shrugged again. "People like blaming me for things." As he said those words, he noticed Zach begin to pay attention, his face rigid and his eyes untrusting.

Good, he thought, ensuring to keep his eyes on the commander. *Just one more push.*

Zale leaned in and added, "If we're being honest, sir, you wouldn't be the first person to accuse me of something."

Apparently believing Zale to be referring to the Kalik Crisis and the swords that Charles thieved, Murdock *pfffted* at him and said, "Perish those thoughts, Operative. Everyone knows the old Council was to blame for Charles' thievery, not you. You're good in my book."

Zale bowed graciously. "Thanks, sir." He pointed behind himself. "I'll get back to my team."

"Very good."

As Zale turned away, he fought to maintain his casual expression, refusing himself the chance to laugh at the expression on Zach's face.

If I didn't know better, I'd say that worked just as well as I'd hoped.

Badrick was ready for Zale's return. He'd spent the entire silence that his absence had created thinking on what they should do, and when he couldn't drum up anything productive, Badrick figured it couldn't hurt to take a break.

In fact, he felt as though they could all let off some steam, so when Zale reached within earshot he put forward the idea that they visit the firing ranges.

Take some training rifles and practice their gun skills.

Zale was happy to go along with that idea. He agreed that they were achieving nothing by sitting stagnant in this blue room and maybe some activity might energise their overworked brains.

Mawr, on the other hand, was resistant to the idea. He was of the mind that being active would make little difference and opted to stay behind, though he reluctantly allowed the two of them to head off.

He was instead going to take the time to feed himself.

They parted ways, Mawr leaving in the direction of the cafeterias and Badrick and Zale turning right to make their way to the ranges.

As they exited the BCR, chatting about which weapons they were going to use, Badrick noticed with a pinch of unease that Zach was watching them leave.

Intently.

His focused eyes followed them, his aggressive expression quite alarming.

Badrick didn't know what to make of this behaviour, but had a small inkling that he really didn't want to know.

Unfortunately, it quickly became clear that he was going to find out.

They'd made barely five steps out the door when the man shot out of the BCR in their wake and brushed up to them so fast he almost knocked Badrick to the floor. Had the idiot actually collided, Badrick could've been thrown off his feet.

"Can we help you?" Badrick asked warily, as Zach righted

himself after almost slipping in his attempts to avoid hitting them.

"I want to talk to Zale," Zach stated. "About something . . . sensitive."

Sensing a confrontation, Badrick planted his feet firmly on the ground and said, "Well, he's right there." He gestured to his partner. "If he wants to talk to you too, that is," he added sharply.

The detective gave him a pointed look, at which Badrick quickly shook his head. "You can say it with me here."

These days Badrick would never be so aggressive to a fellow Enthraller, but Zach had a unique way of really pushing his buttons. His every utterance felt challenging and disrespectful, and he had a habit of inciting anger in even the calmest of people.

Badrick hadn't liked the way Zach approached them and was determined not to leave Zale to face the detective alone.

"Just say it," Zale sighed when Zach bristled at Badrick's bluntness. "How bad could it be?"

Angrily, Zach snapped to attention and hissed, "Alright." He slid closer to Zale and, in a highly accusatory tone, whispered, "I wanted to talk to you about a very sensitive matter."

"So you said," Badrick deadpanned.

"What sensitive matter?" was Zale's more tactful response.

"Your friend Charles has made some accusations about you, hasn't he?"

Badrick was so surprised to hear this that at first he didn't understand what Zach was referring to. It was only when the detective elaborated that he fully comprehended what this confrontation was about.

"When he was captured, Charles told Badrick that you couldn't be trusted."

"How do you know about that!?!" Badrick immediately demanded, his temper rising. By what manner of deception had Zach used to get that information? Even Reynolds didn't know about this little factoid. The only time he'd ever spoken about it was when Badrick conferred with Daemnos about how ludicrous the accusation was.

"I heard you talking about it," was Zach's reply.

Now it was Badrick's turn to bristle with rage. "You were eavesdropping?"

He felt a calming hand on his shoulder and his fury subsided a little as Zale asked, "He said what?"

Guilt arose in Badrick when he realised he had no choice but to come clean. He described to Zale what Charles had said when they cornered him, watching Zale's face for any hint of anger or betrayal.

But in the end Zale only said, "What a strange thing to do. What do you reckon, he was just trying to get in our heads?"

Monumentally relieved that Zale wasn't enraged at him keeping this secret, Badrick grinned and nodded his concurrence.

"Enough!" a voice suddenly demanded with an authority it had no right to. "I don't believe it was nothing."

"Why not?" Badrick sighed tiredly. "Charles is a mental."

Zach straightened and shook his head, evidently not dissuaded by this statement. "Then explain to me, Badrick, why Daemnos made the same accusation."

Badrick was stunned into silence.

He couldn't speak.

He couldn't move.

And it was only after Zale gave him another curious glance that he finally found the strength to say, "That's out of line, Zach." Shaking the shock out of his system, he turned a vicious glare upon the detective and snarled, "You don't have the right to listen in on people's private conversations."

Zach shrugged, which only served to make Badrick angrier. The situation was further exacerbated when the detective said blithely, "I'm a detective. I have the right."

"Can someone tell me why people keep accusing me of things?"

Badrick took a long hard breath to calm the hatred coursing through his body and turned his eyes to Zale. The poor guy was looking quite confused, and Badrick knew he had no choice but to explain.

"When Daemnos healed your craziness, he told me not to trust you."

Zale's bewilderment looked genuine. "Why?"

"He said you know things," Badrick said. "That you can do things."

Zach spoke before Zale could. "I want to know what that means."

With grinding teeth, Badrick hissed, "I tried asking Daemnos about it after Carla's funeral, but he could barely remember even mentioning it." He gave Zach a derisive eye. "You know, being mentally ill and all."

As he spoke, a portion of Badrick's mind travelled to the metaphysical wavelength of energy that was his soul in search of the mad prince, wondering if he could provide any aid in this situation. He was disheartened to find that Daemnos was having one of his worse moments—his evil and madness was consuming him to the point where he was practically having a fit.

He'd get over it eventually—might even try to make up for his uselessness by actually being helpful—but for now Daemnos was out for the count. This wasn't the first time the Royal had no focus on the outside world so Badrick didn't begrudge him his afflictions. No matter how frustrating they were.

Sending gentle waves of soothing energy towards the demon in an attempt to calm his rampant mind, Badrick retuned into the conversation just in time to hear Zach state smugly, "I heard you and I want to know what it meant."

"Then why," Zale breathed before Badrick could retort, "are you coming to *me?* Surely Badrick should be the one to ask."

Zach's face went slightly red as the logic of Zale's word hit home. He blinked rapidly as he tried to pretend that he'd already considered this and had deduced that confronting Zale was a better option. "You're the suspect here, Hood!"

"If you say so."

"You need to—"

"No!" Badrick snapped. "That's enough. What're you doing? What're you trying to get out of this?"

"I'm *trying* to get to the bottom of everything. A demon and the Primordial's lackey—an old friend of yours, no less—have claimed you can't be trusted. You've made no headway on the New Evil case, it's like you don't *want* to solve it.

"*And* you keep vanishing!"

"What?"

"You were nowhere to be found when Dhorni was killed. Where did you go? What do you keep going off to do?"

"STOP!"

Zale was once again forced to calm Badrick's anger. "It's OK," he said softly, rubbing his hands together and aiming his eyes at the floor. From the look on his face, Badrick surmised he was taking the time to get his words together.

After a brief moment, he stepped in Zach's direction and spoke quietly.

"I'm in mourning, Zach." His voice was barely a whisper, but the indignancy he felt at these accusations was evident. "Carla is dead. Where am I going? *My room!*" Zach recoiled at the sheer irritation in Zale's eyes. There was no doubt Zale did not appreciate being made to say this out loud. "I'm going to my room to mourn, you brain-dead idiot. Do you understand?"

At first, Zach did not speak. His eyes stared in Zale's general direction, his mouth hanging open stupidly. They waited for the man to respond, but no such thing happened. His silence endured for so long Badrick was tempted to punch the agent in the stomach just to make him do something other than blink like a moron.

Eventually, he did do something—he stepped back. Nodding sharply, he said nothing as he about-faced and briskly retreated.

"What an idiot!" Badrick tutted as they watched Zach disappear back into the BCR. "We bring him in on the investigation he wants to be a part of more than anything and he treats you like that."

Zale didn't comment on the subject. With Zach finally deterred, it seemed he wanted to end the topic and think nothing more about it. He slapped Badrick on the shoulder and suggested they make their way to the ranges.

Unnerved and annoyed by Zach's interrogation, Badrick did as Zale said and followed him through the HQ.

Zale could hardly believe his profound luck.

Everything—*everything*—he'd designed was coming together.

It had given Zale quite the surprise when Zach went against his usual behaviour. Attempting to confront him privately was something Zale had to admit he hadn't accounted for, and for a moment there he'd believed his plans would come undone.

In a private conversation, all his efforts would have gone to waste.

But then Badrick himself had refused to leave. Unknowingly, he'd saved Zale's skin.

Even if Badrick had absolutely no time for anything that Zach spat at them—even if he believed it all trash—Zale was certain the seed of doubt within him had been watered.

What Daemnos told his Enthraller was not the kind of thing somebody forgot. Even if it vanished from the forefront of the brain it would linger in the subconscious, waiting to fester at a moment's notice.

And with Zach having played into Zale's hands, he fully expected Badrick's doubts to worsen. His partner had been aggressively reminded about what Daemnos said and, despite his better judgement, the memory was going to keep bugging him.

Yes . . . Zale could feel it now.

Like a tiny, red light in Badrick's subconscious . . . Vibrating . . . Pulsating . . . The seed growing bigger as Badrick ruminated on what just occurred. Zale could hear his mind angrily chastising Zach's lack of tact and care, multiple swear words describing what he thought of the man.

This continued for quite some time until eventually he'd burned away his anger and all that was left was the memory of the event. And, true to the human race's capacity for dwelling on things, Badrick failed to stop listening to Zach's accusation bouncing around inside his head.

Zale smirked privately as they both picked up guns and began firing into the floating orbs. Badrick didn't speak while they continuously pulled the triggers, and Zale knew it was because he had quite suddenly found himself unable to escape his thoughts.

Again, he could feel it.

Zach's words were echoing..

Loud.

Shrill.

Disruptive.

After a time, Daemnos' voice began to mingle with Zach's, crowding Badrick's head with noise until he was left powerless to prevent the uncertainties in his subconscious from taking over.

Because Daemnos did *say Zale couldn't be trusted.* Zale grinned at the sound of this thought running through his partner's mind. *Why did Charles say the same thing? I don't believe anything that evil monster says . . . but . . . Daemnos said the* same thing.

Why?

Zale had to fight the urge to laugh that built in his chest as Badrick tried to convince himself that he wasn't letting Zach's accusations get to him. Attempted to persuade himself that what he was now feeling had nothing to do with the agent detective.

The so very broken emotions that Badrick had tried to keep hidden from Zale flared up right on cue, fusing with the frenzied thoughts and exaggerating his uncertainty, creating anxiety and influencing Badrick's next actions.

There is something going on. I need to know the truth.

Fighting the cackles with great difficulty, Zale counted, timing the numbers with Badrick's frantic thoughts.

Three . . . Two . . . One . . .

And on cue . . .

"Zale?"

Smiling, Zale answered, "Yeah?"

Badrick hesitated for a brief moment, unsure of himself and what he wanted to ask. For a second, Zale worried he might actually get a grip and desist from voicing his new concerns. To ensure he did not, Zale stopped firing and turned to his partner.

"What's wrong?"

Badrick also ceased his repetitive shooting, but looked down at the floor. "I don't . . ." He sighed. "Do you know why Daemnos said what he said?"

Zale tutted impatiently and went back to aiming down the sights. "Don't listen to Zach, dude. He's an idiot."

"I'm not asking because of Zach." Badrick clicked his tongue. "I'm asking because both Daemnos and Charles said the same thing."

"Because *they* can be trusted." Zale's sarcasm was hefty.

"Maybe not Charles," Badrick agreed, "but despite his evil and insanity, Daemnos never lies unless he has a good reason."

Acting carefully, Zale pretended to hesitate in an effort to make himself look guilty.

Apparently it worked; the expression on Badrick's face subtly changed. Now he wasn't just unsure, he was *suspicious*.

This misgiving made Badrick say, "Daemnos said you know things." He took a step closer. "You can *do* things? What did he mean by that?"

Inside his head, Zale heard Horas finally comprehend what his Enthraller told him two days ago.

He heard his thoughts: *That's what you meant. You knew Daemnos had said this.*

Of course Zale knew. When Daemnos brought him back from the edge of insanity, the Royal couldn't prevent a few recent memories from transferring. At his touch, Zale instantly knew that Daemnos felt there was something off about him.

The demon didn't know what it was.

But he had a *feeling*.

Concentrating on the now, Zale said, "It's nothing."

This vague response was carefully planned. The moment he said it, waves of aggravated doubt flooded through Badrick. His brow furrowed into a tight frown and he spoke harshly, "No."

"No?"

"I can see it," Badrick stated. "You're not telling me something. Not only is there something but you *know* what they meant."

"Badrick, honestly . . . it's nothing."

"You're my partner, Zale. You can't keep secrets from me. Not now, of all times."

Zale lowered his gun and stared sadly at the target he'd peppered with pistol rounds. However, he continued to say nothing—a calculated silence.

"Zale." Badrick came closer. "Tell me."

"Alright!" Zale snapped, acting frustrated by Badrick's never-ending persistence. He took a deep breath and closed his eyes. "Alright," he repeated, much quieter. "But if I tell you, you need to promise not to freak out."

"What?"

"If you're really going to force me to tell you what Daemnos and Charles were talking about, you need to calm down." He took another, deeper, breath. "Because what I'm going to tell you will change you. You won't ever feel safe again. You'll be filled with paranoia for the rest of your life. Do you get me?"

Badrick clearly didn't know how to respond.

Zale didn't give him a chance to speak. Double checking that Daemnos was far too busy with his madness to be listening, he stepped as close as he could, putting his mouth near the side of Badrick's face, and whispered something.

Something awful.

A secret that would forever haunt him.

And when he was done, he withdrew and gave Badrick a sombre look, taking pleasure in the sudden change of his skin colour.

All traces of healthy pink were gone and his wide eyes looked truly dreadful.

Badrick's nearly snow white lips smacked together and he stared sightlessly into Zale's eyes.

Wondering what was going through his mind, Zale took a peek inside his head.

He immediately withdrew when he'd concluded there was absolutely no point trying to discern anything in there right now.

It had become a mess.

Not one thought was concise.

Far too noisy.

"That's . . ."

Zale expected Badrick to say more, but after that solitary utterance no more sound escaped his lips.

Impatient for a reaction, Zale gave him a falsely concerned nudge. The pressure applied to his side appeared to kick the gears into action again, as Badrick's mouth finally closed and he blinked roughly. "That's . . ." he repeated. "If people knew . . ."

Nodding sombrely, Zale said, "It would destroy everything."

"And . . . you're sure? There's . . . That's true?"

"Unequivocally."

"That's . . ." Badrick licked his lips. "That's what Daemnos meant." His wide eyes found his hands, his face still white as paper. "You know things and you can do things." Badrick's fingers curled into fists. "What you know . . . You could destroy the Daemonium."

"Yes."

His partner's mouth opened and closed silently, and Zale had to admit he couldn't blame Badrick for his terror-induced shock; even the most composed human being would be shaken to the core if they learned what Zale just divulged.

"This has to be kept a secret."

Zale nodded in agreement and repeated his earlier response. "Yes."

Badrick took two weak steps back, almost falling to the floor. Tense and wary and visibly irresolute on what to do next, Zale's partner glanced in the general direction of the office belonging to the agent who maintained the ranges.

It amused Zale to see Badrick already ensuring that no one had overheard them.

"I have to . . ." He faltered, his hands now shaking. Badrick clenched his fists tighter, fighting to regain control. "I have to go . . ."

"It's OK." Zale gestured to the door with a kind smile. "Go. Take some time."

Badrick nodded, then instantly departed, as though he couldn't wait to get as far from Zale as he could.

As his back vanished across the threshold, Zale felt a presence materialise beside him.

"Did you tell him what I think you did?"

The disbelief was evident in Horas' voice. It was extraordinary, the sheer indignation the demon felt that Zale would dare voice the secret he'd entrusted the Enthraller with.

Zale smiled at the empty space left behind in Badrick's wake.

Yes, Horas. I told Badrick the real reason demons are going into people's souls.

chapter
TWENTY FIVE

Badrick could barely see as he walked down the hallway, his mind so filled with terrible thoughts that his eyes just weren't working properly. He'd almost crashed into four different people on the way out of the Gate and now very nearly did so again, stumbling in his attempt to dodge the person and nearly tripping over the threshold into the Main Hall.

He wasn't quite sure how he'd managed to keep moving. Badrick's body was so numb he fully expected it to buckle and collapse within seconds, yet somehow his trembling legs kept his weight and inexplicably directed him on.

Badrick wished he hadn't pushed his partner for information.

Why?

Why did he do that?

Badrick—stupid, moronic Badrick—had managed to convince himself it was going to be something awful.

He'd had *no* idea.

What he told me . . . It would destroy everything.

As he continued walking mindlessly, those broken emotions that had bothered him these last few days rose up once again, tugging at his heart and darkening his mind with despair.

Daemnos knows, his mind frantically told him. *Daemnos has to . . .*

No . . .

Badrick didn't need to even finish that thought. He already knew the answer.

This was because Badrick's inner turmoil had disturbed the demon within, rousing him from his crazed fits enough for him to cop on to what was wrong. Quite abruptly he appeared in front of Badrick, his rage so very evident. "That's what the blonde idiot knew!?! Are you serious? *That's* the reason our kingdom was taken from us!?!" With one last scream of indignation, Daemnos vanished, though Badrick could still feel him squirming with fury.

Clearly Daemnos had as much an idea of why demons were going into people as all the others did.

Even the demons don't know what's happening.

Those had been some of the first words Reynolds ever said to him.

A lie?

Passed down through the ages by the hellspawn?

No . . . that felt wrong too.

It was more likely that if any demon ever once knew the truth he or she had died millennia ago. The Enthrallers were an anomaly that had been occurring since the dawn of the human civilisation. Badrick figured the secret was lost untold generations ago and the modern demons were clueless to the reason behind their entrapment.

However, the demon prince in his soul *had* known something was up. He'd sensed that in some way Zale was dangerous and had believed the electric Enthraller couldn't be trusted.

The wrongful conclusion of a being whose mind was addled—Zale had proven time and time again that he was more than trustworthy—but the danger his knowledge presented *was* all too real.

The thing that really shook Badrick to his core was that Charles also knew.

Now the question was—what was he *actually* aware of? Despite Charles' link to them being unstable, it certainly worked well. He'd stolen so many secrets from their heads it was hard to keep track of what was still sacred. Did he too know the secret, plucking it from Zale's mind with his telepathic powers, or had he just picked up on Daemnos' reservations about the young man?

Badrick wouldn't learn the answer any time soon, but it screamed so many warnings that he couldn't hear his own inner voice.

He forced himself to calm his frantic mind, because he knew there was no time to panic. If what he'd deducted was true, then they had a very serious problem.

Because if Charles knew, then it was likely the Primordial did too.

Was this why the darkness never came after them? Never attacked them at home or even bothered to kill them? What if it had commanded Charles to accuse Zale of treachery and as a result sow mistrust among the Daemonium? Pull the dreadful origins of the Enthrallers out of the veteran and there was no doubt the Daemonium would destroy itself.

Forget about attacking—the New Evil wouldn't have to lift a finger.

His enemies would end themselves for him.

The Primordial was playing a very cruel game.

And if the New Evil's plan centred on Zale yet *again* then Badrick's partner would have to be protected. No one could be allowed to get to him. His safety had to become Badrick's number one priority.

Because that secret had to remain hidden.

Badrick could never repeat it.

That also meant keeping this concealed from their new team member.

It would be a troubling burden, he knew, and Badrick once again cursed himself for his stupidity. If he'd just *trusted* Zale and kept his doubt under control he'd be as happily ignorant as ever.

Badrick grumbled and shook his head roughly, placing a hand on the closest wall and using it as a support. Forgetting his troubles for the moment, he concentrated on the problem at hand.

There could be much to do.

Badrick glanced at the time on his port-pad—it was quite a bit later than he'd realised. Night would be fast approaching and with nothing to go on Zale would probably return to his room to rest up and prepare for work tomorrow.

Much of the day team would be doing the same, Mawr included.

That gave Badrick some time to work privately.

Right now, every second he could scratch up was valuable.

After all, how much time did they even have left?

chapter
TWENTY SIX

Something seemed wrong.

As Zale numbly stepped through the ornate, wooden doors and slipped under the police tape, he realised he had no idea how he'd gotten here.

Where even was he?

What was he doing?

Hadn't Zale been in the middle of something seriously important? Something that would shape the world in the days to come? As ridiculous as that idea was, he couldn't shake the notion that it was the truth.

He felt his legs take him up a flight of stairs, again without truly understanding why.

It was like he had no control. Zale's body was following some kind of predetermined path and he was powerless to alter the course.

As he reached the top and slid onto the landing, Zale brushed past a mirror, catching his reflection for only the briefest of moments . . .

And quite suddenly he remembered.

How silly of him—he knew why he'd come to this elaborately constructed student housing estate. He was a recruit for the SpecOps branch at the Daemonium, an organisation dedicated to fighting and containing demonic threats.

How had he forgotten that?

Zale laughed and shook his head, taking a second to step back and regard his reflection, checking his hair to ensure no strands had fallen out of place. The face of a sixteen year old lad gazed back at him, fair looking and quite handsome, if he did say so himself.

He brushed aside some strands threatening to stab his eyes, straightened his jacket and folded his collar, not wishing to appear uncouth for the people he was to see next.

As he wriggled in his clothes, a hand unexpectedly gripped Zale's shoulder and a deep voice boomed behind him, "Okay, Hood. Let's see what my Eparch's been banging on about. Prove you're worth Sergeant Reynolds' adoration."

Zale felt slightly irritated by the Guardian's scornful manner in which he spoke, but decided against retorting. He was here to do a job—one that could very well prove he deserved to be issued cases despite still being in training. He knew that Carla enjoyed solving mysteries with him and revelled whenever they cracked a case even the most senior agents couldn't get their heads around.

Zale liked it when his training partner was happy.

The hand directed him through the wide corridor, pushing past the army of policemen crowded inside. They eyed Zale with distrust as he walked over the threshold leading to the dorm room, with the Guardian close behind him.

Inside the room was who Zale guessed was the senior detective. She was a dark-skinned, resolute looking woman, and Zale took a moment to be impressed at the way she was twirling a pen stylishly between her fingers with expert precision.

She didn't notice them at first—her attention was on the body at her feet—but eventually she caught sight of them in her peripheral and her expression turned from sad contemplation to one of incredulity.

"What's this?" she practically barked, giving them a cold, unwelcoming glare. "Who the Christ are you?"

With one swift stroke, Guardian Ennis whipped out a badge—a perfectly fabricated fake—and treated the detective to a long and boring speech about her 'collaboration' with the big boys of law enforcement. Behind his back, his fingers wiggled and Zale sensed what little mind manipulation powers Ennis possessed working their way towards the detective.

Though he was not capable of full-on mind control, Ennis could exert a little persuasion into her. With a little bit of luck, she would accept anything he said.

As he worked, Zale had to wonder exactly where the Guardian got this over-the-top speech from—had it been revised by the Agent Commanders or was it one of his own design?—and fully expected the detective to pull out a baton or something and force them back into the corridor.

He was therefore admittedly surprised to see whatever he wasn't listening to was working; with a tut and shrug, the woman accepted Ennis' claims and gestured to the room, stepping away. As she took the backbench, she glanced at Zale and asked, "So what's the kid doing here?"

Ennis flipped the badge closed. "Take your child to work day."

Pocketing the badge, he looked over Zale's head and studied the body. "What do we have here?"

"Didn't you get given a report?" the detective asked bitingly.

"I prefer to hear it from someone intelligent," Ennis stroked her ego.

Again, his efforts worked. With what looked like an appreciative, yet unconvinced, scoff, the detective relaxed. Zale thought it was pretty obvious what they had here, but the detective explained it to them regardless.

"Twenty year old female, name of Julie White," she said robotically. It was clear she was used to doing this kind of thing. "She's the owner of this dorm, and was found two hours ago with cauterised stab wounds in her chest."

Ennis' eyebrows rose. "Cauterised?"

"And I mean charred," the detective added. "Like this girl was stabbed by a sci-fi laser blade or some crap. Try explaining that one." At an amused look from Ennis, she shrugged. "My son likes video games."

Smiling, Ennis asked, "Any suspects?"

"None yet. And get this—every entrance was sealed shut."

"I'm sorry?"

"Yeah," the detective nodded, clearly bemused. "The door was locked tight, and the window was locked tight. Unless they phased through the wall, nobody got in or out of here."

Ennis mulled over this, his tongue rolling around inside his mouth. Bobbing his head as he pondered, he eventually said, "Thank you, detective. Can we have the room please? I'll call you if I need anything."

The detective sighed with irritation but still held her hands up in complacency. "Take a whirl," she said, a little sarcastically, and stepped through the door, regrouping with the police outside.

Once she was out of earshot, Ennis addressed Zale. "OK,

Hood. What d'you think?"

Zale cast his eyes across the room, drinking in as much detail as he possibly could, grinding the gears in his head in an effort to think despite the disrupting chatter outside. "It's a tricky one," he breathed, more to himself than the Guardian.

"We're here because the scanners detected a burst of demonic energy," Ennis stated. "One signature. No doubt the killer has a demon. The first they've used their powers, too, seeing as the scanners say it was a first time manifestation of energy. Probably surprised them a bit if the demon hadn't appeared to them before. Hey, maybe all this was an accident."

Zale desperately wished Ennis would shut up. His callous deductions were getting on his nerves.

Accident indeed; one look at the body confirmed that those stab wounds were intentional. They were deep, wide, and perfectly positioned over the heart. Not to mention that no accident involved stabbing someone more than once.

"No way in, no way out," the Guardian gratingly continued. "If there is a killer, I reckon they teleported out. What d'you reckon?"

Zale instantly rebutted that idea with a shake of his head. "Teleport energy is like a five metre streak in whatever direction the teleporter is going, but the energy we saw here was a simple surge. An offensive power was used. Besides," he scowled at Ennis for his lack of concentration, "we already know the demon and it can't teleport."

"We do?"

"Cauterised stab wounds?" Zale tried jogging the man's memory, but to no avail. "It's in the archives, Captain Ennis. The scanners identified the burst immediately. This Enthraller's demon is called Adya. She has the power to generate plasma blades from the wrists."

Ennis blinked and practically spluttered, "Yeah, I knew that."

Sighing with exhaustion, Zale decided it was time to shut the Guardian out. The man's input was nothing but detrimental to Zale's own processes, and if he wanted to solve this he had to be working at his best.

There was no time for incompetency. The systems back at base couldn't lock onto Adya's signature, for reasons they had yet to identify—most likely the killer's heightened adrenaline and emotional state was dampening the energy output—and Zale had to work fast before the rogue Enthraller got too far.

Turning from Ennis, he recommenced his studying of the room.

The unfortunate occupant of this dorm had greatly enjoyed decorating. That was obvious as the walls were plastered with fancy wall hangings, artistic paintings and drapes of some description that flowed softly in the breeze coming from the window. Despite the variety of colours, it was clear this girl had experience with decor. None of the varying colours clashed, and Zale had to admit he liked what had been done with the place.

The floor however was not so well looked after. Its surface was littered with dirty clothes. Bras, shirts and socks were strewn about the place with very little care. In spite of her meticulous talents as an interior decorator, the girl had been somewhat lazy.

Lazy . . . yet apparently precautious.

A rather hefty safe was tucked beside the girl's bed, the only dark coloured thing in the room. Zale could see it was locked shut, however based on his observations Zale had confidence he knew how to crack it open.

"What're you doing?" Ennis queried as he approached it, but Zale ignored him.

Precautious . . . but lazy. His fingers hovered over the keypad as he considered what his next move should be, and with gentle touches he pressed the zero key four times.

Yeah, too easy, he thought when the small digital screen displayed an error message and the number of tries he had left. Trying one more time, he reached forward again and inputted the code *one-two-three . . . five.*

And with a click the safe opened.

"Gotcha," Zale grinned victoriously. He didn't bother checking the contents of the safe, instead straightening and backing away. What the thing contained was not important; the method of its locking was the only relevance.

"Oh." The surprise in Ennis' voice was enough to drag him away from his tiny victory, and with a frown he turned back to see the Captain running a hand over the air above the body.

"What?" Zale demanded.

"We've got a problem."

When Ennis failed to explain, Zale again snapped, "What?"

"Zale," the Guardian Captain sighed impatiently, "the energy is coming from the body. Adya was this girl's demon."

Zale hadn't expected that. "Oh . . ."

That would explain why they could not track Adya's energy despite having documented her signature many decades ago. She was back in Hell, and her Enthraller's powers had been still too newly manifested for the systems to detect her departure.

Ennis rose to a stand and put his hands to his head in a display of exhaustion. "Great," he muttered. "So, what d'you think? Julie sees she's under attack, perhaps extends Adya's blades instinctively, and surprises both of them. But the killer gets over his shock first and overpowers her, impaling the girl on her own plasma sword."

"Undoubtedly," Zale agreed, glad Ennis had made a reasonable deduction for once.

"That means we have a witness to demonic powers on the

loose, and a dangerous one. We need to contain them."

Zale didn't bother responding. The urgency of their task was all the more prevalent with this new revelation.

Having an Enthraller on the loose usually wasn't too bad; most were scared and confused and tried to hide, running from anyone who might discover them. The secret was often kept safe and the Daemonium was well equipped to handle things if it got out.

Even a murderous Enthraller wasn't too bad. Though devastating, their organisation had centuries of practice limiting their effect and containing the bastards.

But a human witness—being hunted by police for murder—someone quick-thinking enough to use someone's powers against them—this person was incredibly dangerous. This was an occurrence Zale himself had never heard of.

He had to get to work.

Acting quickly, he took three great strides and drew close to the window, studying it with interest. The white painted wood was just like any other window frame in an English suburban house, however there had been something bothering him about it ever since the detective informed them on the situation.

Voicing his concern, he whispered, "Who opened this window?"

Hearing him speak, Ennis visibly came to understand why an open window would attract Zale's interest, and he exclaimed random words in anger. About-facing, he leaned through the door and shouted, "Who tampered with the bloody window? You could've ruined evidence. What if—"

"No!" Zale stopped him berating the police officers any further. "It's OK. They might have actually helped me."

Ennis raised a questioning eyebrow, but Zale didn't have time to explain. He was eager to solve this fast, and spent the next half a minute staring at the windowsill, knowing there was something wrong but not quite yet understanding what it was.

Moving absently, as though his subconscious was trying to direct him, Zale ran his fingers along the wood and stared at the cracks and splinters that lined the windowsill. For some reason this sill was in terrible condition, and yet the rest of the window was in perfect health. The frame wasn't too dirty, the glass of the actual window wasn't all that foggy and none of these cracks spread any further than the area where the window would meet with the sill.

Why was the rest of this window practically immaculate and yet here it was in tatters?

Secure but lazy.

At this reminder, Zale found himself gazing up at the open window, his eyes immediately focusing on the metal lock attached. It looked old, a simple hook that latched onto a ring when closed to secure the window. It was maybe one rain drop away from rusting, and even without touching it Zale could see that it didn't look quite tight enough.

Precautious but lazy . . .

Gotcha . . . Those cracks were caused by hard impacts.

To Zale, his conclusion was unarguable, but just to prove it he grabbed the window, tensed his arm, and slammed it closed. The bang echoed into the room, making Ennis jump and alarming the officers outside. Several ran in, probably assuming a firearm had just gone off.

Zale ignored their harsh demands for an explanation.

He was too busy studying the lock.

The moment the window hit the windowsill that loose little hook jolted and fell right into the ring. At Zale's slamming, the window had locked itself.

He grinned—Zale had it figured out.

As Ennis ushered the police from the room, Zale pivoted and

approached the Guardian. Seeing his excitement, Ennis quickly asked, "You got something, Hood?"

"The killer escaped through the window," he said.

Ennis frowned and rolled his eyes. "No, Hood. The window was locked."

"The window has been slammed so often it's splintering," Zale argued. "Julie knew it would lock if she just slammed it. She was lazy like that. The evidence of this is all over the room.

"The murderer climbed out the window and slammed it from the outside. They also knew it would lock." Zale glanced back at the window and rubbed his thumb over his lip in thought. "I really doubt a University student has the kind of enemies capable of planning a murder in *such* depth that they researched an escape route, and anyone who hasn't been in this room often would not have found that loose lock without investigating the area."

"Meaning?"

"The killer was someone the victim knew well," Zale stated. "Someone who's been in this room so much they know all its secrets. Friends, boyfriends, more than occasional shag-buddies."

"OK," Ennis said. "So you tell me what we do with this information."

Zale scoffed and said, "Well, we can't let the police get our bad guy, so we need to find out who comes in here frequently and get a mind-reading agent to see if they know about the existence of red plasma arm-blades."

With an expression of admiration, Ennis nodded with approval. "OK, Hood. Come on. We'll contact the BCR on the way out." The Guardian turned on his heel and marched through the open door, making his way past the police.

Zale made to follow him, excited that he was being included in the apprehending of the villain, but was unexpectedly stopped by a curious zapping sound.

He ground to a halt, his ears pricking.

He knew that sound.

In a panic, his eyes darted to his right arm just in time to see vivid, blue electricity explode across his flesh. The voltage zapped and sparked, tearing and burning the sleeve of his jacket. Crying aloud with fright, Zale practically vaulted into the wall, he stumbled back so fast.

He hit the wall the same moment the electricity exploded from his arm, obliterating the room into rubble and blinding him with white light.

"ARGH!"

With a jolt, Zale felt his body rise from the softness of a mattress. His bedroom, dark and quiet only seconds before, now lit up a brilliant blue as powerful voltage continued to electrify Zale's arm and jolted him violently from the dream world he'd occupied. His duvet cascaded to the floor as he leapt to a sitting position and grabbed his wrist, teeth bared with rage, and attempted to regain control over Horas' frenzied power.

Even before the chaos ended, the demon was fretfully flapping his hands in Zale's direction and spitting apologies faster than the speed of light.

Zale didn't pay him any attention. How could he when this insane occurrence was causing him actual pain? He roared with ire and demanded his soul dominate the feverish energy that belonged to Horas.

Quite quickly, as though his limb was a person capable of being intimidated, his fitting arm stopped jerking and the voltage began to die. After a time, the electricity stopped and Zale was left in silence and darkness, the only sounds his heavy breathing and Horas' continued apologies.

He flicked his finger and commanded the light switch to turn on. Light flooded the room, revealing the devastation caused by this explosion of power and Zale realised he was groaning with irritation at the scorch marks that now lined his wall.

He turned away from it in disgust. His arm still smoking, Zale slowly pushed himself from the bed and regarded the damage to his sleeve with mild interest.

This was certainly new.

Whenever this happened before now, the electricity manifested as though Zale was harnessing the power himself. Never before had it caused damage to his clothing or hurt him in anyway.

Today had been different.

He couldn't help but be interested, despite the soreness that remained along his arm.

"I ... am ... so ... sorry, Zale!" The demon who was to blame for his pain was still pleading for forgiveness in the middle of the room, his hands placed together tightly. Horas' body language communicated severe distress.

Zale actually felt pity for him.

He looked pathetic.

"Please forgive me," Horas said. "I cannot control this. Two demons are not designed to exist together—"

Zale held up a hand and silenced him. "It's alright, Horas."

He appeared shocked. "It ... It is OK?"

Zale nodded; he truly meant it.

Breathlessly, he clenched a fist and summoned power into his hand. Purple light emitted from within, making his fingers glow vibrantly.

"Yes," he confirmed. "I know why it happened." Zale allowed the light to die and grinned savagely.

Zale's every skin cell felt electrified, however this had nothing to do with Horas' powers. His senses were heightened to Godlike levels, and he'd never felt more alive. His mind was alight with the brilliant significance of this event.

"It's never done that before," he told Horas, "which means our situation is getting worse."

Clearly confused by Zale's gleeful attitude, Horas murmured, "This is . . . good?"

Sighing contentedly, Zale replied, "Our powers are reacting worse and worse, Horas. Which means?"

It took a moment for the demon to get to the right answer, but eventually—far too long for his liking—Zale felt understanding flow through Horas. "We are reacting worse because you are getting more powerful."

"And what would a reaction as bad as that signify?"

Horas hesitated, clearly very desperate not to have to say it out loud, but under Zale's expectant eye he was left with no choice. "Your power is very strong."

"Aye." Zale clenched a second fist and once again created light. "I thought it'd take a bit longer, but no . . ."

"You are ready?"

Laughing, Zale nodded. "Time's up," he muttered. "I'm ready for the next stage." With great eagerness, he jumped to his wardrobe and pulled his uniform from the hanger.

In minutes he was dressed and tying his shoes.

"What are you going to do?"

Looking up from his feet, Zale made sure to catch Horas' gaze and treated him to the cruellest grin, his canines elongating to sharp points. "Wait and see, Horas.

"It will be magnificent."

chapter
TWENTY SEVEN

Badrick was incredibly tired by the time groggy-looking agents started shuffling into the BCR in preparation for the day-shift and he barely noticed as they took chairs at various consoles and replaced those now leaving to sleep the day away.

Almost passing out on his desk, Badrick was roused awake by a woman sitting at the console beside him. He jerked in his seat, muttering stupidly something about giant rings in space, which attracted a frown from the agent.

Apologising numbly, Badrick slapped a hand clumsily over his face to catch a yawn escaping from his mouth. Checking the time—was it seriously six in the morning already?—he stretched and rose from his console. Taking the time to ask those nearest if they wanted a coffee or anything, he shambled away in the general direction of the cafeteria.

He was grateful to emerge from beneath the blue lights for the first time in eight hours. It was cool in the Main Hall, the general scarceness of human bodies during the night shift having allowed the temperature to lower somewhat. The freshness was relieving after the stuffy BCR, and Badrick took several deep breaths as he passed across the hall's width.

The closest cafeteria was empty save for two others. A woman sat in the corner, sipping what looked like an orange juice and was entirely focused on some kind of novel Badrick didn't recognise. The other person was an indistinguishable male. His head was buried in his arms and his body hunched over so tightly his blue uniform was stretching.

It was only when Badrick poured fresh, hot coffee into a large mug that the figure stirred, sniffing the air, and with a start Badrick realised it was none other than Zach.

"What're you doing in here?" he asked as the agent hunted down the source of the smell. Opting for generosity, Badrick handed his mug over, but resented the effort of having to refill the machine.

Zach gulped the coffee thirstily, then stuck his tongue out with a groan, having gone and burned it in his eagerness.

Idiot, Badrick tutted privately.

In answer to his question, Zach slurred tiredly, "I didn't get any sleep so I came in here for a snack."

"Trouble sleeping?"

"No," Zach said, "I was too busy going over the New Evil investigation."

With a groan of dire frustration, Badrick demanded, "How did you get into those?"

"You let me input the New Evil signature," was the reply. "Twice. I hacked the codes to the rest of the data while I was already halfway in the system. Made it easier."

Hearing this did not make Badrick any happier.

He was seriously starting to hate Zach; the man just couldn't leave it alone.

It wasn't like Badrick was completely unsympathetic. He could grasp the reasons behind Zach's actions; the man had utterly failed to catch the Resurrected Charles. Having come up with a conclusion that turned out to be so very incorrect, there was no doubt Zach was over eager to prove himself.

And Badrick understood that the Primordial scared the hell out of everyone, but it didn't change the fact that Zach was taking this too far. The man had been ordered multiple times to stay on his own investigation, but he routinely disobeyed these commands.

Even direct orders from the Dominus—ones that you *did not* contravene under any circumstances.

"Listen, Zach," Badrick sighed, deciding it was finally time for him to say something. "We didn't bring you in on our case for you to go behind our backs. You were told to stay away."

"I can't stand back and let innocent people get killed."

With anger flaring within him, Badrick snapped harshly, "You mean you can't stand back and let Zale solve a bigger case than yours."

An uneasy silence followed this outburst.

The older man didn't say a word, only glared at Badrick with new hatred and humiliation.

Eventually the quiet was broken by the sound of the woman leaving her chair. The worn-out rubber feet screeched noisily on the floor, and she departed the cafeteria, still holding her orange juice and book.

Apparently deciding he wanted to do the same, Zach about-faced without a word, leaving Badrick to stand alone beside the coffee maker.

Muttering darkly about idiot detectives who couldn't do as they were told, Badrick gave up on his coffee and threw the mug he was holding a little too hard at the counter. The handle smashed as it hit, sending jagged shards every which way.

At first Badrick ignored the destruction, his dark mood too strong for him to feel guilt. Unfortunately, that didn't last long and before he'd even made it out the door he was back and collecting the pieces.

With them safely in the correct bin, Badrick took a second to calm himself. If he allowed his emotions to govern him so badly that he was breaking stuff, they would all end up in trouble. It wasn't just the fact that he was a wrecked fool at the moment.

The first lesson in Daemonium life was that all Enthrallers had to keep control of their emotions.

Anger was fine—violent behaviour was not.

If Badrick allowed himself to get too comfortable with allowing his rage to flare so badly he broke things, then it could lead to him losing control of his power.

And in Badrick's case, that would be a catastrophic thing to happen.

Perhaps that was what the New Evil truly wanted—for them all to allow their demons to run rampant.

He stupidly allowed these melancholic musings to bother him all the way back to the BCR.

His team had arrived by the time he returned, much to his surprise. He hadn't expected them for another few hours, but here they were, already discussing the New Evil as if they'd been at it for hours.

Mawr was talking when he reached within earshot; "What about Dhornji? Can we find his body?"

Zale responded, "We tried to, but there wasn't anything left."

"Are we sure?" Mawr pressed.

"Sorry, Mawr." Zale shrugged resignedly. "We scoured those grounds, but nothing."

Mawr's bitter disappointment was evident in the way he balled a fist and smacked it on the closest console. The disturbance drew him several unimpressed glares from those closest, but the soldier-turned-operative utterly ignored them.

"It's not that bad," Zale said in a soothing voice, "We probably wouldn't have gotten anything from his remains anyway."

Mawr didn't look entirely convinced. "Perhaps," he sighed. "But I would like to go back and double-check."

Zale closed his eyes, hesitated a second, then nodded his agreement. He opened his mouth to say something—

—and that was when the alarms exploded.

"What the hell?"

Badrick shared Mawr's sentiment. Although he had gotten used to these damn things deciding to blare in the middle of people's conversations, it never meant that they didn't have good reason for doing so.

"*ALERT!*" a voice bawled over the din. "*All available personnel to the prisons. ALERT!*"

"The prisons?" Badrick only just heard Zale query. "What the hell's happeni—" Without warning his jaw dropped to the ground and the colour in his face drained so fast it was like he'd always been deathly pale. "No . . ." he breathed, his voice surprisingly ragged. "Not possible. It has to be someone else. Please, tell me it's somebody else." He spun on the spot and bawled, "Someone find out what's going on!"

In the end, there was no need for an investigation. From out in the Main Hall, shouts of alarm could now be heard. The moment of the first disturbance practically the entirety of the BCR sprang to its feet and stormed towards the door. Badrick was jostled along with them so roughly that he eventually got annoyed enough to supernaturally push the bodies away from his personal space.

They stumbled as his power struck them but were otherwise unharmed, though several glared reproachfully his way as he pushed through.

And once the crowd had room to spread, Badrick saw what the fuss was about.

A small diverse group of people was crowded near the entrance to the prisons, shouting over the commotion, desperately fighting to be heard. Some were crouched to the floor, focused on something Badrick couldn't yet see, but the rest were at the opening, weapons raised and roaring at the top of their lungs.

It was only when he got closer that Badrick realised the thing on the floor was a body.

And when Mawr barged into the group and made room for Badrick to see who it was, he felt ice replace the blood in his veins.

"Malcolm?"

Zale tore the people out of his path in his desperation to see what was occurring. Several were thrown to floor from his aggression, but in his haste he bade them no consideration. When he eventually caught up to his partners and saw Malcolm the jailor lying on the floor, his chest torn to ribbons, his heart went as cold as Badrick looked.

He was about to demand an explanation, when he finally noticed what was going on in the prison hallway. A vast group of men and women were huddled inside, glaring hatefully at the soldiers pointing rifles at them. Some tried to take steps forward, others were priming barely controlled powers, but most were taking the threat of the soldiers' guns very seriously.

Zale understood what was going on instantly. Without Malcolm, the jail's forcefields would have vanished and all the prisoners freed.

As he watched, an angry looking woman swept her hand through the air and blasted fire their way. Though they ducked expertly out the way, the soldiers' reactions were unnecessary. The woman was un-practiced in harnessing demonic energy and it died before it reached them, barely leaving a singe on the walls.

It was enough to provoke aggression however, and the stupid woman was the first to fall as the guards unloaded their weapons into the crowd. Many prisoners fell, bloody and broken, and those left standing had backed up several paces by the time the gunfire ceased.

Zale couldn't help but feel a little disappointed that, despite appearances, the bullets were carefully aimed. Only those displaying aggression were killed in the attack and the prisoners who were more complacent had been spared. Many of their hands were now in the air in a display of submission.

With that situation in hand, Zale returned to Malcolm. "What happened?" he roared, his eyes wide as he stared at the bloody wound that took the jailor's life.

"What do you think!?" a soldier screamed back. He stepped aside and gestured furiously to something behind him. Zale's eyes darted to the floor and were greeted by the sight of a brown, misshapen mess.

"Kalik?" Badrick croaked, eyeing up the demon's dead form.

"How did it get in?" someone demanded.

"That doesn't matter!" Zale told them. "What was it doing here? Do we know?"

The soldier this time pointed in the general direction of the Gate. Upon turning to look, Zale saw legions of soldiers and agents pouring through the exit, no doubt heading towards the grounds.

Following the gesture, the soldier said something that made

Zale's partner cry aloud with despair; "The Resurrected escaped."

It took Horas all of half a second to appear by his side, and he could immediately feel the demon's mixed emotions mingling with his. Horas wasn't sure whether to be terrified of Zale's coming wrath, or amused at Charles' getaway.

"Well," the demon said quietly, "did you see that coming?" Zale didn't need to speak for Horas to glean an answer.

His expression was enough.

"No . . . You did not."

chapter
TWENTY EIGHT

The Agent Commanders were descending upon them even as Badrick processed the information that their most dangerous prisoner had escaped. They chattered away to him, issuing numerous orders and commands and not noticing in the slightest that Badrick was barely listening.

He was numb.

So deadened he couldn't feel the floor beneath his feet, nor the clothes clinging to his skin.

The world no longer felt real.

Not one muscle was working—his arms, his legs . . . not even his eyes. He couldn't take them off Malcolm's body, his heart pumping fast and frenziedly as he did nothing but stare.

Badrick knew he was losing himself to desolation.

He could feel it happening despite knowing there was nothing more detrimental.

But if Charles reunited with the New Evil, then surely it was all over. What evil would those two commit together?

It was too horrible to think about.

In the midst of this crippling melancholy, he became aware of a strange sensation. At first he was unable to focus on it, but eventually, after it persisted, his attention snapped to and he abruptly realised he was being shaken so roughly it was unfathomable that hadn't noticed immediately.

He blinked and glanced up to see Mawr's urgent expression inches away.

"Are you listening?" the ex-soldier demanded.

Badrick managed a numb, "What?"

"We have to go!" he roared. "We've got to recapture Charles before the Primordial does."

"Come on!" a second rage-filled voice bawled over the chaos around them. Badrick recognised it as Zale's and leaned to see his partner angrily beckoning them over.

The sight of his panic acted as a battery that powered Badrick's frozen muscles and brought back life to his body.

Stamping on the depression that threatened to overwhelm him, he leapt into action, hurrying to Zale's side. They joined the throng of agents stampeding through the exit and within seconds were swept up in the rush, swiftly emerging into the early morning sun.

To the left, a battalion of helicopters were already prepping to fly and dead ahead an uncountable number of cars and motorbikes were already rushing through the Wall Gate.

Badrick felt a hand tug his arm and, before he knew what was happening, he was clambering aboard a helicopter. The rotors above were already spinning, so it took the pilot no time to get airborne.

As they soared over the wall, Badrick checked behind him, observing the fleet of choppers following in their wake.

This was insane.

Damn near the entire Daemonium was bolting after their escaped prisoner. Barely any of them had taken the time to retrieve their armour. Most only had a side-arm on hand.

As for Badrick . . . he couldn't help but remember the last time he was in a helicopter.

Feeling a shudder coming on, he returned his focus to the ground beneath. They were soaring over the local forests, many of their number straining to look through the gaps between the leaves in search of their quarry.

Badrick became aware of the pilot waving his hands at something that was directing them North.

It was a person, flying in the sky without natural aid.

He shouted something Badrick failed to catch over the rush of helicopter blades, but apparently it was enough for the pilot. Their craft veered to the left as the pilot sharply tugged on the sticks.

At their rear, the other aircraft followed suit.

The flying agent rocketed away, his hand to his ear and his eyes focused on the ground beneath him.

"We can't get a fix on Charles!" a voice reported.

"What're you talking about?" Mawr demanded over the comm. "He's a Resurrected. Follow the corrupted energy."

"He can suppress his energy!" Zale roared back. "We can't track his taint."

"Then how?"

"Follow the link!"

"Link?"

Badrick saw rather than heard Zale tut with impatience. "He's linked to Horas and Daemnos. We have the data on it in the system. Use it to track him."

Mawr's face lit up. "Brilliant!"

"What if the New Evil is hiding it?" a voice of scepticism asked.

Zale's eyes turned grave, but he didn't respond.

Badrick was surprised by his silence. He'd expected Zale to shoot off several superbly deducted reasons for his suggestion but he only seemed to shut off, closing his mouth tight and glaring hatefully at the passing trees.

There was a flurry of activity in spite of this scepticism as the agents in their chopper accessed their port-pads, downloaded information from the scanners and connected to their satellites above.

"I've got him!" someone announced. "Back the way we came!"

"Go!" Mawr hollered.

"Turn this thing around!" someone else screamed.

Badrick was forced to take a stabilising grip as their aircraft's engine roared and they turned as sharply as possible. On the land, the ground units did the same, pelting after them in hot pursuit of their target.

As they headed south, Badrick struggled closer to Zale and murmured so only he could hear, "Tell me the truth." Zale's eye met his and they stared at one another. "Do you think we can't catch him?" Badrick had been considering this as the reason for Zale's earlier silence. Zale might've believed that they didn't stand a chance.

A nervous laugh escaped his partner's mouth, and he said, "I certainly hope we can."

Horas gazed at him between two agents, his body language completely unreadable. Zale actually felt uncomfortable beneath his gaze, unsure if Horas was again trying to gain access to his mind, or just judging him. Zale knew it frustrated the demon that he was able to block his thoughts off completely, and usually he took enjoyment from that. However, right now, Zale was too preoccupied with this current situation.

It required all his concentration.

Ignoring Horas as best he could, Zale leaned over the side and watched as the trees of the forest passed below them. The foliage was thick in this part of the woods, something which Charles was probably hoping to use as cover. If the Daemonium determined which direction he was fleeing—which they had—then these closely grown leaves would provide many decent hiding places.

A report from the Field Commander that sat next to the pilot removed him from his concentration. "We're close!"

The pilot jerked in surprise, as did Mawr. "Already?"

"Location?" Zale demanded.

Someone spat a series of letters and numbers he failed to catch.

"All units, converge on those coordinates!"

At the command, Zale witnessed a rather impressive formation build around their helicopter as the others surround on them. As their speed increased further, he noticed the intensity of the leaves ease, offering at last some visibility of the forest floor. Through the branches Zale observed agents moving through the brush.

And with a jolt of powers to his eyes he could clearly spot the widely spaced footprints of someone who'd sprinted through this area. As he watched, two agents ground to a halt and looked up at the helicopters above. Following the ladies' gestures, the choppers cut across the sky in an Eastern direction, passing over the perimeter of the humungous forest.

"I've got a visual!" The excitement in the pilot's voice was easy to recognise. It was the sound of relief flooding through him like a wave of euphoria. "Heading East."

"Cut him off!" Mawr loudly suggested.

Even before the pilot could alter their trajectory, he suddenly spoke again. "Correction, he's turned South." He went to turn, but again was forced to say, "Wait . . . he's changed again?"

Zale was the one to speak next. "He's reading my thoughts. Me and Badrick." He slapped his partner on the arm. "Turn off your comm. and don't listen to anyone."

His partner did as he was instructed just as the Field Commander reported, "It looks like he's panicking . . ." Zale clenched his eyes shut, slammed his hands over his ears and bawled over the voice, determined to remain ignorant of Charles' actions.

Their helicopter altered trajectory once again. Zale grabbed the handrail as their craft tilted and began to descend at a rapid pace. He just about heard someone authoritative command, "Cut him off!" before they landed with a rather heavy thump on the dirt.

The grass whipped fiercely as their feet hit earth, disturbed by the powerful rotor blades. The other helicopters formed a wide ring and also descended, hovering just above the ground.

Having seen the aircraft before him, Zale noticed the trapped Resurrected stop so suddenly he skidded on the grass, falling to the ground. Back on his feet in an instant, he tried scrambling back the way he came.

His face fell when he saw he was surrounded.

Arriving in a churning of mud and water, the army of ground vehicles caught up to the scene, grinding to a halt outside the helicopter-circle's radius. Wasting no time, a platoon's worth of agents pushed forward, tightening the space Charles had to move in before grabbing and throwing him to the dirt. With the Resurrected safely restrained, they withdrew handcuffs and clamped them on his wrists so tightly Zale was a little surprised he still had hands.

Reactivating his comm., he was just in time to hear one of the agents snarl, "We got you, you son of a bitch!"

"Thank God," Badrick sighed audibly, his hand stretching out and weakly grasping for some kind of support. Finding Zale's shoulder, he added, "If he'd gotten away..." He trailed off, leaving his sentence unfinished.

Placing a hand on Badrick's upper arm, Zale smiled a genuine smile and said, "It's OK, man. We got him."

In the distance, the agents began to lead Charles to one of the choppers. Two were situated on either side, compressing him between their bodies and ensuring there was no chance he could escape again.

"Keep any eye out," their Field Commander said. "This is an affiliate of the New Evil. *He* might turn up."

There was no actual need for this to be said. Several metres to their left, Mawr had his pistol withdrawn and was holding it ready, glancing around warily. He wasn't the only one; nearly everyone in the vicinity was aiming their weapons at the sky as if they expected the Primordial to descend upon them from the heavens.

Zale smiled with amusement.

If only they knew he was on the ground with them . . .

But . . . that wasn't important right now.

Zale had to focus on Charles.

The Resurrected had nearly reached a helicopter, still surrounded by boys in blue. As he watched, a rough-handed agent jabbed him in the back with the barrel of his rifle. Charles grunted in pain but otherwise didn't react, which only incited the man to do it again, this time tearing his already tattered shirt at the hem.

"Wait." The moment the agent spoke, time seemed to stand still. "What's that on your back?"

The entourage halted and turned questioningly, however the agent failed to elaborate. Instead he reached for the hem of

Charles' shirt and roughly pulled it up.

"But . . . that's . . ."

Zale didn't know if the agent finished what he wanted to say or not, as Horas had quite hastily materialised and was speaking in his ear. "Zale . . . I felt something."

"What?"

"I sensed . . . I think I sensed an electrical discharge."

Tired with Horas' crypticness, Zale dared to ask, "What kind of electrical discharge?"

Horas never responded.

He didn't need to.

The moment Zale made the query, Charles mouth opened wide, and he coughed loudly.

He then did so a second time.

And a third.

The coughing continued, uninterrupted, until his body started to tremble and the agents lost their grip. He collapsed to his hands and knees, such abominable hacking forcing its way out his throat that Zale felt disgusted.

The Resurrected shook terribly as his skin whitened and his strength failed him. Crumpling to the floor, he was struck by a terrible seizure, his body jerking wildly as the agents tried to control the shakes.

Their efforts proved fruitless; with one last spasm, a long breath escaped Charles lungs, and he fell still.

Someone on the comm. demanded a report, to which a female agent in the group responded, "He's . . . dead."

"How!?"

She breathed heavily and told them, "There's a green handprint on his back."

"But that means . . ."

"That Bomb Killer the secondary investigative team is

hunting . . . He killed our prisoner.”

And beside Zale, Horas sighed, “Well . . . That was *exceptionally* lucky.”

chapter
TWENTY NINE

It seemed the BCR was spending more time in sombre silence than actually working these days. At least, this was certainly the case today as the team watched the security footage of Charles' escape with Reynolds. In light of the morning's events, it was apparent no one quite knew what else to do.

Not one person chasing after the Resurrected expected their pursuit to end in his death, especially not at the hand of someone unaffiliated with them.

Even Horas was left stunned. Zale could feel his surprise coursing through their shared body, and he kept muttering, much to Zale's chagrin. "You were planning to kill Charles soon, weren't you? You wanted to kill him but he escaped before you could. I would say it is lucky someone else did it for you."

Yes, Horas, Zale snarled within his head. *I know. Shut up.*

On the video, nothing stirred. The prisoners remained in their cells, contained and unable to escape. In his office, Malcolm sifted through a magazine filled to the brim with semi-naked women. The hallways outside were calm and undisturbed, not a soul in sight.

Until they located the correct timestamp.

The Kalik approached from the Main Hall, walking in so casually it was unfathomable that it managed to infiltrate the place without being seen. It was as though the damn thing belonged. The beast ambled down the hall, surprising those prisoners aware enough to notice its passing. They either backed away in terror or jumped from their beds and tried to see where it was going.

The beast continued until it reached Charles' cell. From behind his barrier, the Resurrected's head snapped up, his expression one of complete disbelief. However, the Kalik did not attack the barrier.

It just stood there, staring at its former master, and continued doing so even when Charles stood and approached the forcefield.

They stayed that way for quite some time.

Everyone was so transfixed on the pair of them that most jumped a little when the Kalik abruptly bolted to its right and disappeared from the camera's view.

It reappeared seconds later, smashing into Malcolm's office.

The man flailed at the sound of his splintering door, his magazine fluttering to the floor in a mess of pages, then cried aloud as the beast converged on him. Though his hand rose, Malcolm was too slow in preparing a barrier to deflect the deadly claws that tore into his chest like he was nothing but a big human-shaped block of butter. A torrent of gore drenched the wood of Malcolm's desk, and, as the Kalik pulled its claws back, the jailor collapsed to the floor.

In the jails, every barrier flickered . . . then failed.

Charles was the first out, suggesting he knew exactly what was going to occur. He charged from his cell and barrelled down the hallway, and was in the Main Hall and halfway to the Gate before anyone noticed there was a commotion.

It was only when the Kalik left the jails and re-entered the Main Hall, dragging Malcolm's corpse with it, that the alarms *finally* blared. As expected, the Kalik was gunned down immediately, Malcolm's weight slowing it down and rendering it unable to get away from the gun-toting Enthrallers.

The soldiers approached the jail entrance and found the throng of prisoners trying to follow in the Kalik's wake. They aimed their guns and Zale could see them gesturing angrily, warning the prisoners to stay back.

Only minutes later, Zale saw himself, Badrick and Mawr reach the scene.

Meanwhile, Charles had managed to reach the grounds. It didn't take long for Zale to understand from the way he was moving that Charles was predicting the movements of the Enthrallers outside by reading their minds and doing his best to avoid them.

He proved proficient in this skill; seconds later he was bounding up a staircase and throwing himself off the wall. He landed with a heavy thump several stories down, but Zale knew the fall wouldn't have hurt him. With a lifeless body numbed to physical pain, the wretched zombie bastard jumped to his feet, completely unharmed, and darted away, running as if the Devil himself was hot on his heels.

To the right, Badrick huffed angrily and smacked the back of a chair. "They planned this," he said. "Him and the New Evil."

Behind Zale, Horas actually laughed. "If only they knew."

"Forget that," Mawr growled. "How did the Kalik get in?"

"Good question," Horas drawled. "Do you know, Zale?"

Shut up, Horas, he hissed dangerously in his head. This time, there was no doubt the demon sensed his rage. Bowing his head obediently, the demon vanished from sight.

It was Reynolds who offered the answer to Mawr's question. "The New Evil."

"You think so?" Zale found himself asking.

"Clearly," Reynolds nodded. "A Kalik can't get in here without supernatural cover."

"It's happened before."

"Yes," Reynolds tutted. "When commanded by a minion of the New Evil." He pointed a thumb at the screen. "The Kalik doesn't show up on the cameras until it enters the jail. It clearly had help."

But what help? a voice could be heard in Zale's head.

He didn't bother telling the demon to be quiet this time, as he hadn't actually said anything.

Nobody could help the thoughts that flowed through their minds.

"I'm of the opinion that you need to have a word with the guards," Mawr snapped. "How many times has someone or something broken in here unseen? What the hell, Daniel?"

Reynolds gave him an indignant glare. "We have body heat sensors to detect invisible invaders and demonic energy detectors, not to mention staff that can do this naturally.

"Mind readers, twenty four hour security cameras, automated light systems and dozens of other security systems.

"If none of our equipment stopped that Kalik, then there's nothing we could've done." Reynolds stopped, and sighed, placing a hand on his forehead. "But you're right; we do need to resolve these break ins. Somehow."

"How . . ." Badrick began to speak, but stopped after the first word. He remained silent even when he was urged to continue, and it took the combined efforts of Zale, Mawr *and* Reynolds to get him to talk.

"I don't know if I *want* to know the answer," was all he said.

"Speak," was Mawr's heart-felt response.

At a second urging from Reynolds, Badrick sighed and said, "How did the Bomb Killer get Charles?"

"I'm more interested in why," Mawr commented. "Charles was not an agent."

"Or a soldier."

"I think I can help there." Reynolds picked up the laptop he'd left on the desk when he arrived. Turning the machine to face them, he slapped the space bar. The image on the screen began to move, and Zale realised he was looking at more security footage.

"This was taken from an external camera," Reynolds informed them. "One of the guards was investigating a strange disturbance."

A red armoured figure was crouching at the foot of the wall, rubbing his hands against it curiously and studying the seven deep gouges that marred the otherwise meticulously perfected construction. His other hand was at his helmet, suggesting he was speaking on the radio.

Behind him, completely unnoticed, a figure wearing jeans and a large grey hoodie was creeping up to him, his face completely obscured, and hand outstretched.

He was inches from the soldier when the soldier abruptly jumped to his feet and gazed up the wall, tearing his helmet from his head. His mouth moved rapidly and his face looked highly alert.

Zale guessed he'd just heard the alarm.

Moment later, further down the wall, a clumsy body fell like a ragdoll into the dirt, then jumped to its feet and dashed into the distance. The soldier's eyes followed Charles as he ran until he finally noticed the hooded figure in his peripheral. Starting with surprise, he only had a second to gaze at the figure before he was leapt upon, a hand slapped against his chest. Green light burned beneath his palm as the soldier tried to push him off, his face a sheen of panic.

The hooded figure jumped away and clicked his finger in the soldier's direction. Instantly, the soldier fell to his knees, clutching at his heart.

Writhing for only a few seconds, he collapsed to the ground and relaxed, very much dead.

Unfortunately for the figure, this assassination didn't bring him any peace; the Daemonium was now in uproar. Looking through other cameras that Reynolds brought up for their convenience, they could see the tumult caused by Charles' escape.

The hooded figure clenched his fists and smacked the wall, kicking the body for good measure. Breathing heavily, his head turned menacingly in the direction that Charles ran.

And with determined steps, he began after him.

"My guess," Reynolds said, turning off the footage, "is that the Bomb Killer was in the middle of something."

"He killed that guard," Badrick noted redundantly.

"The Council believes he was in the process of a major attack and Charles ruined it."

"He killed Charles for revenge," Mawr concluded. "He got to him before we could."

"While we were going in the wrong direction," Zale added.

"Where was Zach?" Mawr muttered darkly. "This is *his* case."

An awful groan gave them all the impression that Badrick knew the answer to this question, and when he realised they were all staring at him expectantly he rolled his eyes and exhaled, "He was looking into the Primordial . . . again."

Reynolds' fist slammed against the arm of his chair so hard Badrick was surprised it didn't shatter. "I have told that man time and time again. Now his obsession has cost us not only a guard but also our prisoner."

"Don't worry about that, Daniel," Mawr said quickly. "You focus on Zach, we'll worry about the Primordial."

"Do you want us to look into the Bomb Killer too?" Zale asked. "Maybe it'd be a good idea."

Reynolds shook his head. "Don't stretch your resources too thin. I'll get someone else on the Bomb Killer. At this point, Zach has to be removed."

Though it was saddening to hear that a fellow agent was losing his case, Badrick knew it was for the best. The Daemonium had kept facilitating his behaviour, moving the line further each time he crossed it, but now it just wasn't possible.

Sighing tiredly, Badrick sunk into his chair, wondering where Zach would be. He glanced at the clock, trying to determine his whereabouts by the time of day. However, when he saw just how much later he believed it to be, all thoughts of Zach vanished from his head.

"It's one o'clock?" he voiced aloud. "Awww man … and I haven't even been to bed yet."

Reynolds instantly picked up on this comment, querying, "You haven't slept, Varner?" When Badrick shook his head, Reynolds added, "Bed. Now, Badrick. We need you sharp. Take the rest of the day.

"Zale, Mawr, in the meantime you can help the agents pick up the pieces of Charles' escape."

"What about the New Evil?" Badrick argued. "I can't just *sleep*."

"We have prisoners to contain," Mawr told him. "You might

as well."

"There's nothing to be done for now," Reynolds agreed.

Badrick was going to argue the point some more, but he was starting to forget why he was bothering. Exhaustion was beginning to overcome him and he could barely think straight.

Maybe they were right.

Reynolds stood and stretched, moaning from the effort. "I need to convene the Council. We'll catch up later. Do me a favour and stay alert. I think we're in for some trouble."

"What do you mean?" Badrick asked.

Laughing a humourless laugh, Reynolds counted off his fingers as he said, "The New Evil lost his accomplice, one that he might have been in the process of retrieving. The Bomb Killer has clearly also had a setback.

"My friends, I think we're in for some serious repercussions, from both of these enemies, sooner rather than later."

chapter
THIRTY

Zale had not bathed in the dark of night since he'd taken Dhornji's life.

It was invigorating to once again be out in his natural domain, free to express his real self, uninhibited by the need to remain incognito.

He was Ruler of the Night.

King under the Moon.

It was stifling to always be trapped in that bloody facility, forced to hide his real identity from those he wished to kill, and so he was thankful that his schemes had finally led him out into the night once again.

As he crouched on the edge of the rooftop like a bat stalking its prey, and Horas watched him with distaste, Zale was abruptly reminded to focus on what he was doing by the sudden arrival of the one he was waiting for.

Below, on the street, a woman appeared through the gloom, walking briskly down the road. She was visibly uncomfortable in the dark, an observation that made Zale grin savagely.

He looked forward to showing the woman that she had every right to be terrified of the darkness.

As she passed below his position, Zale cast his thoughts into her mind in order to keep track of her position. Jumping to his feet, he made his way to an alleyway he knew was perfect to waylay her, all the while listening to her frantic thoughts.

She was an incredibly busy woman, but Zale had expected nothing less from the Mayor of Southampton.

Not only was she overworked looking after the city, but she had recently, along with many other mayors of various cities, found herself a part of the newly formed C.R.L—*Charity for the Recovery of London*.

What the world believed to have been dreadful terrorist attacks that occurred several months prior may not have destroyed a whole lot of real estate but it had left three blocks dangerously unstable, not to mention creating a lot of fear in the country, especially among the higher-ups in government.

Zale grinned even further when he heard her muse on the thing that unnerved her the most; not a single person seemed to have *any* information.

No reports, no CCTV . . .

Nothing.

None of the proven witnesses seemed to have any knowledge of anybody going into that bloody alleyway, nor did they ever apparently see a bomb.

Some barely even remembered an explosion at all.

That *fact* had people in government scared.

There should have been something to go on . . . shrapnel they could study to identify the explosives . . . security footage of suspects going into the alleyway . . . *something.*

It wasn't even like the explosions took any lives so what was the point of the attack?

Zale chuckled quietly—if only she had known that the blasts were the doing of the Devil's spawn, and that the reason barely anyone even remembered there'd been a series of explosions was because the Daemonium had wiped as many memories as it could.

Zale continued to follow her solemn musings as she continued down the road, fascinated with what was shooting through her mind.

Now she was thinking about the fact that her fellow mayors consistently burdened her with the arduous tasks, throwing paperwork at her office day in and day out.

None of the other mayors in the charity seemed to care that a city had been brought to chaos by terrorist attacks. Not one of those stuffy, selfish old men cared about what happened to anything but their bank accounts.

She sighed as she treaded wearily down the path leading to her house, where her husband and young daughter were awaiting her return. Their presence would ease her mind. Calm her troubled thoughts.

She smiled at the thought of the cuddles to come, not to mention the beautiful dinner her husband was no doubt preparing right this moment. However, nothing brought her greater joy than the warmth of her bed.

These thoughts made Zale scoff with disdain. Deciding enough was enough, Zale dematerialised into mist and slithered to ground level, re-manifesting on the tarmac and stopping the Mayor with a few choice words.

"Such . . . menial . . . thoughts."

The Mayor ground to a halt, spinning on the spot and vigilantly searching for the source of this voice.

"Who's there" she demanded with impressive authority.

Zale wasn't hard to spot. He stood only five metres away and, though he was shrouded in the dark of night, he was easily visible to the Mayor as she squinted in an attempt to discern his features.

As she studied him warily, he continued, "Dinner . . . family . . . bed . . . Such pointless things." She tried to respond, but Zale stopped her by saying, "When power and sex exist in the world, why do humans bother with such trivial things like love? Or food? Money, even?"

"Who are you?" she demanded, but Zale sensed her instantly chastise herself; she sounded like one of those idiot women in her husband's favourite horror movies—engaging with a mysterious figure instead of doing the smart thing.

Leaving.

As such, the Mayor quickly pivoted and attempted to walk away.

Or rather, she would have if not for the fact that Zale was already in her path, moving faster than light to prevent her escape.

"OK, look," she snapped. "Neither you or your friend there are impressive, so get out of my way."

Her face fell with confused fear when Zale opened his mouth and bawled with laughter.

It was too funny—she believed him to be someone else. She couldn't comprehend the powers behind his being and had no understanding that he'd moved in front of her.

With tears beginning to stream from his cackles, Zale sneered, "What friend?"

Once more, he sensed her mind racing, going over everything she *knew* to be true but couldn't bring herself to accept as she pivoted and tried to find the man she believed to still be behind her.

"Such frantic thoughts for someone usually so calm and collected," Zale said. "You should work on that."

"What do you want?" the Mayor spat his way, alarm now rising in her chest. Where before she'd cared nothing for her aggravator, she now understood there was definitely something nefarious going on here.

"Well," Zale responded to her question, "I'm glad you asked." He drew closer, his face finally emerging into the light.

The Mayor saw his impossibly handsome features and hair so blonde and beautiful it defied reality. But his good looks did nothing to ease her worry, because his eyes were nothing more than empty, black pits.

The way the gloom of night seemed to almost move *with* him, crowding around his body as though he could command each and every shadow—it terrified her.

The Mayor took a stride back.

"What I want," he breathed dangerously, stepping with her, "is to murder a rather large organisation." He clicked his tongue and rolled his eyes. "An old organisation we would really be better off without.

"They're so old, love. Ridiculously old. Pre-dating history, even. It's just stupid. They live in a giant lotus-shaped facility and yet because of the protections they're capable of putting in place no one on Earth knows they exist.

"No one's even stumbled on the place by accident. Not once. It's incredible. This organisation is *so* powerful, no government stands a chance."

The Mayor wanted to demand to know what he was babbling about, but her fear forced her to refrain. She seemed quite suddenly unable to respond. To her, Zale sounded deranged . . . *mental* . . . like he'd just escaped a psychiatric hospital.

She really didn't like the way he was going on.

"But that's why I'm here," Zale concluded. "I want to take them down. No one should have that much power." A vicious grin replaced the neutral expression on his face. "At least . . . no one but *me*."

At that, the Mayor tried to get around Zale, darting to his left and trying to push him out of the way, however he threw out an arm and stopped her in her tracks.

With hostile action taken against her, the situation became all too clear for the Mayor. Instincts kicking in, she reached into her bag and withdrew the pistol she kept for moments like this.

With the barrel at his chest, Zale looked into her eyes, his expression one of amusement.

"A gun?" he queried. "Blimey. Who did you have to sleep with to get that, your highness?"

"You have two seconds to get out of my—" A loud bang cut her short and she cried in shock as the gun kicked. Her expression betrayed her confusion that the gun had just discharged itself.

With a cruel leer on his face, Zale twirled the bullet he'd just snatched from the air and hissed, "I'm sorry, love. I thought I'd just cut to the chase."

The impossibility of what just occurred shocked the Mayor so much that her grip failed and the gun clattered to the ground.

And, with a cackle, he dropped the bullet and flicked his hand towards her. She screamed as her arms seemed to gain a will of their own and spread as far as they could on either side. Choking from the strain this put on her chest, she blinked as her feet glued to the floor.

Trapped like she was pinned to a cross, the Mayor tried to scream for help, but Zale pressed his fingers together, and suddenly she could no longer speak.

"Calm down," he tutted. "I only need you for a ritual."

"A . . . ritual?"

"Aye." Zale stepped so close to her, he knew the Mayor could feel his breath on her face. "And I need something of yours for it."

"What is this?" she cried, desperately trying to move and panicking more and more with each second she couldn't.

His cruel leer returned in force the moment she spoke these words, wholly ecstatic that she'd said *exactly* the words he'd wanted.

Leaning in close, his face only inches from hers, he whispered, "Repercussions."

The Mayor gagged and groaned as a terrible agony tore at her chest. Looking down, she fought to see through the torrent of blood now pouring from her mouth and just about recognised the sight of Zale's hand puncturing her stomach.

Zale sensed blackness scratch at her peripherals and he sighed, basking in the glory of death as her body went limp.

Finally setting her free, he allowed her body to fall with a crash onto the tarmac.

It was there, with blood pooling around her, that the Mayor of Southampton died.

chapter
THIRTY ONE

"I'VE BEEN ASLEEP HOW LONG!?!"

If there'd been anyone besides Badrick in his room, he'd have made them lose their lunch in fright. He screamed so shrilly that he was pretty sure his walls vibrated and was surprised that the vases didn't shatter.

He could hardly believe it was the next morning.

He'd come here for a nap, not a coma!

Scrambling ungracefully from his bed, Badrick stumbled to his wardrobe and yanked out his uniform. Roughly pulling it over his head, he tripped over his panicking legs and almost face planted into the wall. Grumbling darkly, he righted himself and pulled on his black trousers.

Had no one thought to come get him?

For all he knew, beyond his bedroom door the Daemonium could have been utterly destroyed. Maybe he would open the door and find the hallway gone, obliterated into nothing.

Half believing this to be the reason no one had retrieved him, Badrick finished dressing and bolted for the exit at breakneck speed, ordering it to open.

Thankfully, the orange hallways had not been stripped away and his colleagues mercilessly slaughtered, however that didn't convince Badrick that nothing was wrong. Though Enthrallers moved perfectly calm through the corridors, he couldn't shake the feeling that something awful had happened.

Allowing his door to close and trying to forget his wariness, he made his way to the elevators, intending to get to the BCR as quickly as possible. Hopefully his team would be there and could provide an answer as to why he'd been permitted to sleep for so damn long.

He had thoughts to share and was quite irritated that he'd passed out for nearly twenty four hours. What if his thoughts helped the investigation? They might be too late to do anything about it now.

He was so irate about this that he stopped concentrating on where he was stepping at the wrong moment and collided with someone as a consequence. Due to his lack of attentiveness, he stumbled from the impact and had to fight to keep his feet, catching his weight by grabbing a doorframe.

The person he struck was lucky enough to fall into the wall and didn't collapse to the floor. Spluttering apologies, Badrick jumped to steady his accidental victim . . . only to stop when he realised who this person was.

"Oh . . . Zale, sorry."

When Zale saw that it was Badrick who walked into him, his face went from the flustered disorientation it had adopted when he'd fallen to a sheer white panic. "Oh, bloody hell."

"Nice to see you too," Badrick deadpanned.

After a moment's hesitation, Zale shook his head, returning some colour to his cheeks and stammered, "Yeah . . . sorry, Badrick . . . are you alright?"

"Of course. Are you?"

"Yeah, I'm good." Zale indicated to the corridor behind Badrick. "Listen, I've really got to go."

"Wait," Badrick stopped him. "I wanted to talk to you before we got back to work."

Looking incredibly impatient for reasons Badrick didn't understand, Zale gestured pitifully to the corridor before sighing and saying, "OK, what's up?"

Opting to discover the reason for this behaviour later, Badrick started, "I was thinking about the Kalik yesterday, right . . ."

"Right?"

"And I was thinking, could the New Evil have controlled the Kalik to save Charles himself? I mean, Charles was in prison. It's not like he could contact the Kalik from in there."

". . . OK . . ."

Getting annoyed at Zale's impatience, Badrick asked for his opinion.

"My thoughts?"

"Yeah, what do you think? What if the New Evil is strong enough to control Kalik now?"

"He could be."

"Or," Badrick continued, "if not, he could have influenced the Kalik's actions. Mind control, you know? Convinced it to save Charles."

"Not a bad theory."

Emboldened by this praise, even if the way Zale spoke made him feel like he'd just suggested something stupid, Badrick perked up and asked him what they should do with the information.

"Nothing yet," Zale told him. "The Kalik is already gone and I doubt we can learn anything from the corpse. We need to focus on the Primordial's next moves. Try and predict him."

Disappointed but understanding, Badrick acknowledged his opinion.

The moment Zale saw him nod, he slapped him on the shoulder and said "Sorry, man. I've really got to go."

"Yeah," Badrick sighed. "OK . . . I'll see you in the BCR?"

"Right." And with that, Zale hurried away, vanishing around the corner.

What was that about? I didn't even get to ask him how a Resurrected could die of a heart attack when they don't have heartbeats.

Badrick was surprised to get an answer to this question before he'd even reached the lifts.

Supernatural heart attack. You don't need to be beating to die of that. Don't even need a heart, really.

Ordering the elevator to the ground floor, Badrick responded, *Nice to hear from you for once, Daemnos.*

I was busy!

Quite, Badrick sighed internally.

For half a second there, Badrick believed that Daemnos' return to at least mild coherency would mean he'd be in a state to help them with the New Evil problem. Unfortunately, the way he'd bawled that last sentence proved this wasn't going to be an option.

A helpful demon Daemnos may have been, but he was madder than a floating sheep. The demon liked playing games with them far too much to be of any straightforward aid.

Ding!

The pleasant alert of the lift told him he'd arrived, and he moved out as quickly as he could.

He hadn't even made it to the HQ before he noticed that he'd perhaps been right to suspect something was wrong.

The ground floor of the Quarters Tower was so cramped Badrick couldn't see further than three feet ahead of him. Agents and soldiers alike were crowded together, conversing in hurried voices. It seemed like hundreds of Enthrallers had journeyed from their rooms to meet up in the Tower's foyer.

The reason for this, Badrick couldn't make out over the many voices all speaking over each other. Knowing that, if there *was* an issue, the BCR was the best place to find out, he pushed his way through the cramped spaces until he managed to crawl through the door.

The familiar ambiance of the HQ greeted him, as did an equally large group of agents, somehow managing to crowd the Main Hall despite the extended space. Once again forcing his way through, he battled to reach the BCR and was relieved to finally arrive under its blue light.

The agent's lair wasn't as crowded as the Main Hall, which Badrick was very thankful for, but it was obvious this was where the commotion was stemming from. Agents and operatives were conversing in highly strained voices, their movements suggesting great stress.

Badrick didn't need to ask to know what would cause such anxiety.

Approaching people he recognised from the New Evil investigation, he asked to know what was happening. Two of them were able to confirm that a Primordial signature had been picked up in the city of Southampton, and a huge one at that.

"Zale's programming worked?" He hardly dared to believe that they would get such a lucky break. Though he never doubted Zale's skills, he understood that their enemy was powerful, and so was elated to learn that their alterations to the software had panned out.

For once, they were one step ahead of the New Evil.

"Not just one reading, either," a woman added, gripping Badrick's shoulder to get his attention. "Operative Varner, we've got three bursts of energy."

"Three?"

"And better yet, the evidence suggests the New Evil tried to hide his energy." Badrick recognised the speaker as Hauler, one of the senior agents on their extended team. "The readings are strained, which is indicative of attempts to cloak the energy."

"He put in all that effort and we *still* detected him?"

Hauler gave him a euphoric smile. "Your partner has outdone himself this time, that's for damn sure."

"No kidding."

Approaching the closest monitor, Badrick leaned in to get a better understanding of the situation. The screen showed a digital render of Southampton, which the Daemonium was using as a map. Several miles apart, three separate areas had been circled off by red rings. Badrick guessed these were where the bursts of energy were located.

"Was it just bursts of energy?"

Happy to hear the voice of a teammate, Badrick relayed the information from the screen to Mawr. "We're finding out now."

Hearing their dialogue, the console operator next to them explained, "I'm tapping into police records, security cameras, the works. If anything significant happened in these locations, I'll find it soon."

The operator was stopped by yet another new voice. "No need. It's on the news."

"What?"

Badrick barged through agents a lot taller than him to ensure he got a good view of the screen an Agent Commander had just tuned into some kind of news station. A good looking newsreader was talking on the left hand side of the screen, with the right dedicated to a picture of some older lady Badrick didn't know.

From what the newsreader was saying, he learned that she was the Mayor of Southampton, who was just one of three victims found with their hearts ripped out. The bodies had been hidden, but once the first corpse had been found by an elderly woman walking her dog—the animal apparently sniffed the bloody thing out—fate had conspired to reveal the others to unsuspecting civilians just trying to get on with their day.

"Do these murders correspond to the energies' locations?" Mawr asked to no one in particular.

Someone bawled, "Yes."

"Hearts?" Hauler spoke behind Badrick. "The New Evil took their hearts?"

"And hid the bodies."

"What can the bastard do with people's hearts?"

If anyone had the answer, Badrick wasn't able to hear it over the shrill shouting that erupted inside his head, prompted by this question. *I know! I know! I know! I know!*

"OK!" he roared, making anyone close jump in fright. "So tell me!"

"Tell you what?" snapped Mawr unhelpfully.

Why should I? his demon came back with.

Growling angrily at the Royal's unhelpfulness, Badrick asked Daemnos, *Do you want the Primordial to kill us all?*

Ah, don't be a baby. Lol.

Hardly able to believe a demon had just said *'lol'*, Badrick retorted with, *If he kills us, he'll kill you too.*

Silence ensued.

And then, *FIIIIIINE!* Materialising on top of the unaware Mawr's shoulders, Daemnos voiced aloud, "Taking three human hearts is a power boosting ritual, Baddie Badrick. The New Evil is looking to boost his power faster than it's growing."

Badrick slapped his forehead and groaned at his own stupidity. "Of course. I knew that!"

"You want to clue the rest of us in?"

Badrick lowered his hand and treated Mawr to a very serious glare. "We need to get Reynolds down here. This is urgent."

Zale heard the call for Reynolds to report to the BCR over the comm. exactly when he expected to. Smiling to himself, he hurried to waylay the Dominus, planning to catch him before he reached the agents' headquarters.

With perfect timing, Zale reached the lowest walkway overlooking the ground floor just as Reynolds appeared from the Quarters Tower. Hurrying, Zale planted his feet firmly on the metal and set his eyes upon the Dominus.

Casting his thoughts toward the man, he took hold of Reynolds' mind.

Ordering him to keep moving so as to remain inconspicuous, Zale proceeded to project a series of commands into his subconscious—ones that would wait for the opportune time to surface.

When Zach demands he and his team be allowed to go on the mission to hunt the Primordial, you will deny him.

When he reminds you protocol dictates that his team be involved in primary field investigations when more than one team is necessary, you will cave.

When the teams are sent out, you will go with Zach's team to make sure he stays in line, no matter what anybody tells you.

Reynolds . . . we're going to leave this place, unprotected.

Are we clear?

Emotionless and blank, Zale heard an agreement shoot

through Reynolds' subconscious.

"Good," Zale muttered aloud, allowing the power numbing Reynolds' head to ease. "Go on in, my friend."

Completely unaware that anything strange had occurred, Reynolds picked up his pace and entered the BCR.

Badrick was immensely glad to see Zale walking in behind the Dominus and proved his happiness by grabbing Zale's hand and pulling him quicker into the room. Zale wasn't given time to even collect his wits before Badrick dived into an explanation of what was going on.

"A power boosting ritual?" Zale scoffed. "God's sake."

"No kidding." Badrick threw a careless hand in the direction of the monitors. "Any thoughts?"

Zale *hmmmed* and *aaaahed* as he placed his hands on a console and studied the computer screen with interest. Badrick could see his blue eyes reflected in the image, and could tell just how much his partner was concentrating. He waited anxiously for a response, not wishing to break this intense focus, but thoroughly hoped Zale would hurry up.

Unfortunately, they were disturbed by the sound of a very familiar disturbance.

It took all Badrick's effort to refrain from marching over and knocking Zach out cold as his voice rose above all others in his attempts to convince the Agent Commanders to let him help. His fingers were twitching strangely as he argued his case and his eyes looked crazy, the flesh around them purple with tiredness.

He looked psychotic.

It was all getting so very out of hand. The man was a mess. He desperately needed to be calmed down.

Frankly, Badrick privately believed that a horse tranquiliser would do him—and them—a world of good and briefly wondered if he should sift through his list of powers to find something that could achieve a similar effect.

Or maybe he should go through with his original impulse and beat the man unconscious.

However, much to Badrick surprise, Zale appeared to not share this sentiment. Sighing audibly, Zale shouted above the arguing and beckoned Zach to approach the monitor.

He did so warily, unsure as to why the man he constantly tried to outdo, and even bluntly offended, would want him anywhere near.

The moment the detective was in earshot, Zale pressed a finger to the screen and asked, "What does that look like to you?"

At first Zach couldn't make heads nor tails of what he was looking at, but after Zale explained what they were dealing with a glint returned to his eye and his skin's pallor appeared to lessen. Doubling back to a table some steps away, he began throwing stuff to the floor, rummaging through papers, books and equipment with a zest Badrick hadn't seen in him for a while.

Eventually, with a cry of victory, Zach grabbed a black marker pen and, after uncapping it, he placed the tip against the screen. Ignoring the protests of the Agent Commanders, he drew a wide, black circle that encompassed the three red rings.

With a click, the cap found its way back to the pen, and a smile spread across Zach's face.

Zale appeared to understand exactly what this defacing of their equipment indicated; with a nod he turned to them and asked, "Do you guys see it?"

"I do," Mawr stated. Turning to a console operator, he ordered, "Find out what's inside that black circle."

"Specifically?"

It was Zach who answered the operator's request for hints.

"Places the New Evil could hide."

At that, Badrick finally understood what the rest of them had already perceived; they were attempting to determine where the Primordial might have based itself from the locations of the murders.

That was smart.

The agents worked on their new task with diligent fervour, typing and searching as fast as they could. A man to Badrick's right scrolled through Southampton's local newspapers, two women perused police records and another male agent had hacked into government files.

But it was the young lady behind them that found something worthwhile. Badrick didn't realise she was standing at his back until she spoke, making him jump in surprise. She explained that she'd searched housing and construction records. "If we're looking for a hiding place, then where else is a good place to look?" she used as her reasoning.

Nobody demanded to know why she'd done such a thing, as the he success of her efforts was undeniable. On the records, she'd discovered that there were two abandoned buildings yet to be renovated or demolished within the black circle. One was a family house, the other a small office.

Her work was commended by the present higher-ups, including Reynolds. He thanked her for her endeavours and took the reports in hand. He began to pace, studying the pages intensely.

Nobody interrupted his concentration. Out of respect for their leader, they waited for him to finish in his own time.

"This is good work," he muttered. "We might actually have a chance here."

"What do you want us to do, sir?" Hauler asked.

"This is your division, Hauler," Reynolds replied. "What do

you and the other Agent Commanders have to say?”

A tense debate began on what their next move should be. Badrick did his best to keep up, but unfortunately, with the number of people all giving their opinions at the same time, this turned out to be very difficult.

Eventually he was forced to give up.

His partner, however, did not, and refused to only listen to the conversation. He could be heard making claims and giving advice along with the rest, mostly drowned out by the other voices. At one point, however, he managed to make himself heard when he said, “We should be careful. It’s the Primordial.”

“Are you suggesting we don’t go to these locations at all?” someone growled at him accusingly.

“No,” Zale heaved a sigh. “I’m saying we have to be careful. We still don’t know how powerful this enemy is, but we’ve always believed he could destroy us with a flick of his fingers.”

Someone interrupted him to question how they could even be sure the New Evil would be holed up within the circle. “He’s been all over the place. Like when he attacked the Captus Memoria. That was nowhere near Southampton.”

“The New Evil was attacking his enemies in those moments,” Mawr stated in answer. “But with *these* murders, he collected parts of his victims to bring to wherever he is based. He would need to choose targets close by to lessen the time that would take.”

“Operative Burakka is right,” Hauler nodded. “As is Hood. We know the Primordial’s capable of great power, but we still don’t understand to what extent. We *must* proceed cautiously.”

“Agreed,” said Reynolds. “However, we absolutely cannot let this opportunity pass us by. If we hesitate we run the risk of missing him. *If* he is in one of these two buildings, we need to find him before he finishes his ritual.”

“He won’t be going far until he’s done,” someone Badrick

didn't know spoke up.

"If we chase the New Evil we run the risk of being . . . you know . . . obliterated."

Badrick tried to see who this doomsayer was but failed to discover him in the crowd of people.

"Also agreed," Reynolds sighed.

It was then that Mawr scoffed so sharply he somehow managed to silence the entire room. "Listen to you lot," he jeered. "We're Enthrallers of the Daemonium. We put our lives on the line every time we leave this place and *this* is no different. If there's a chance we can at least learn the identity of our enemy then we have a duty to do so."

"Easy for you to say," an agent scoffed. "You can't be killed."

Mawr glared at the man, his eyes flashing dangerously. "By the New Evil, I have no doubt I can be." He swiped a hand through the air. "My point still stands. We go."

Reynolds breathed a heavy sigh and stated bluntly, "Mawr is right. We have to do this." With his mind apparently made up, the Dominus stepped higher than the throng of people and called for quiet. When he next spoke, he addressed them all. "We'll form a large team, split into five groups. Two will take the buildings. The other three are to patrol the area, establish a perimeter and provide back up if required."

"Armour or plain clothes?" Mawr asked.

Reynolds rubbed his chin before responding. "The three backup teams go plain clothes. Those units will be on the streets and we can't have civilians panicking at the sight of us.

"But the two teams on the front-line will prepare full equipment. The evidence suggests that the New Evil doesn't want us to know about his ritual. We know he tried to hide his energy this time. But we don't know what we'll be walking into. His lair? Maybe. A trap? Probably. Whatever the outcome, if the teams encounter the New Evil, they will need all the defence they can get."

A murmur of agreement spread throughout the ranks of agents and operatives present.

Reynolds continued, "The operatives in charge of this investigation will join the first team. Zale, Badrick, Mawr, get your armour. I will confer with the Agent Commanders available and draw up a plan of action.

"Prepare yourselves. You all leave in sixty minutes."

Although these people were not Army, the group offered Reynolds sharp, military-style salutes as a sign of respect for their Dominus, and as the agents began to prepare for the task ahead, Badrick felt a strange sense of relief mixed with a prickly anxiety fill his stomach.

What they were about to do . . .

On one hand they might *finally* reveal the New Evil and, if they were very lucky, this whole nightmare might be over before the day was done.

But on the other hand . . .

It might all be *over* before the day was done.

chapter
THIRTY TWO

Badrick felt Zale slap his shoulder and heard him say, "Gear up, man. We're going to get this bastard."

His team hurried away to retrieve their armour and equipment, leaving Badrick in the dust. He would collect his gear too, but he needed a moment to process first. The agents busied themselves with their orders while he stood there, taking deep, calming breaths and trying to waylay any cracks in his emotions that might spring up during the mission.

Reynolds also occupied himself, however what he now found himself doing was definitely not something he wanted to do.

At first, as the Dominus told Zach for the *last time* that he was going nowhere near the Primordial investigation, it seemed as though Zach was finally going to accept his leader's commands without argument.

But then, quite out of the blue, he pulled some crap about protocol regarding investigative teams.

Badrick wasn't surprised to see Reynolds slap a hand to his forehead and exhale with impatience.

However, he *was* surprised to hear him relent to Zach's demands.

He couldn't believe what he was hearing. Within minutes, Reynolds had ordered the secondary investigative team to head the second group going to the abandoned office. Badrick was appalled that whatever protocol Zach had babbled was forcing Reynolds to let him have his way.

How many times in the last week had this idiot been a hindrance?

How many times had he jeopardised his *own* investigation?

Apparently none of this mattered; regardless of what its leader had done, the secondary investigative team's presence was required on field missions such as this. Badrick could see that Reynolds hated having to give in, but it was clear that his hands were tied by regulations the new Council had yet to be rid of.

However, the Dominus wasn't going to let this slide without a little caveat.

Badrick felt it coming seconds before Reynolds spoke. He could see in the way their leader glared at Zach, and rolled his shoulders, that he was about to put the detective in his place.

And damn near half the BCR exploded with outrage when Reynolds informed Zach that he couldn't be trusted and therefore would be going out in the field under the command of the Dominus himself.

Even Zach was surprised, so much so that this time his refusal to accept a superior's authority was not borne out of arrogance.

"You can't put yourself in danger, sir," he argued, for once showing Reynolds the respect he deserved.

Dozens of agents shouted their agreement.

They were silenced when Reynolds bawled louder than any of them. "ENOUGH!" His breathing was ragged as he surveyed the agents with anger in his eyes. "*I* am the Dominus," he snarled, addressing any who dared to argue with him. "And I made a promise that I wouldn't be a bureaucrat. I am your comrade.

"A leader must lead by example." He paused to take a breath. "I *will* lead by example."

This time there was nothing that could be said to combat this, and everyone knew it.

The Dominus had spoken.

And so it was that thirty minutes later Daniel Reynolds appeared in the armoury and punched in the code for his armour. Having chosen the dispenser beside him, Badrick witnessed the contented smile brought to his face by the sight of his equipment. Reynolds may have accepted the role of Dominus without complaint, but the truth of it was the man wasn't an office person. At heart and soul, he was a soldier.

This was what he loved.

His face disappeared behind his visor, and Reynolds cocked his rifle before slapping Badrick on the back and disappearing from sight.

Pulling on his own helmet, Badrick followed in his wake, slinging his single-rifle over his shoulder as he went. In the Main Hall, the Daemonium was mobilising. Countless agents had prepared plain-clothes equipment, but there was still a hefty group of armoured individuals nestled within the crowd.

Identifying Zale in the mass, Badrick hurried to join him.

"You ready?" the newly armoured Mawr asked as he also approached.

"As ready as I can be."

The mission plan was easy enough to understand. Badrick studied it as their helicopters raced across the sky towards the sun, heading for the borders of the city of Southampton.

Neither Badrick nor Zale were in charge of this team. The scale of the mission meant that they were expected to fall under the direction of a Field Commander, one who had a lot more experience than they. Even Mawr had been forced to take a low-ranking position on the team, something he'd not been happy to hear.

Southampton was too far for land vehicles to reach in a decent time, which was why they were currently soaring several hundred feet in the sky. The mission planners had actually calculated the differences in travel times and not one of them had been willing to risk the longer option.

A huge force of BCR operators at home would have their back for this mission. It was up to them to prepare the landing sites for the field agents, cover up the arrival of several dozen military-grade helicopters, and provide a bird's-eye view of the area.

Badrick perused the complicated details of how an expansive operation like this would work and was immensely glad that he had nothing to do with implementing this part of the plan.

Badrick flipped the page on his touch-screen and took some time to study what would happen upon landing. It wasn't hard to remember, so he only scanned it once before turning away from his port-pad and sitting back, the back of his helmet hitting the metal of the helicopter.

Around him, no one was speaking.

There was an unmistakable fog of tension clogging the atmosphere of the tiny space they occupied.

It was painfully obvious what was at stake, not to mention what risks were involved. Some of these men and women may not see home again after today. Maybe one of Badrick's friends would die, or perhaps *he* would be killed.

For all they knew, the Primordial could murder them with nothing more than a thought. Crush their bodies at will and dash their souls into oblivion, ensuring they'd never know what afterlives might be out there.

With his imagination running over-time, picturing all the ways their enemy could destroy them, Badrick failed to notice when they arrived at their designated farmland. He only crawled out of his head when Mawr kicked him on the shin and pointed to the agents leaping from the helicopter and advancing away.

His boots hitting in the dirt, Badrick hurried to catch up.

At the opening to a road, a large number of their group split into a vast web of bodies. They sped away, hands hovering over their belts nervously as if they expected the need to draw their pistols at any moment.

The armoured units went their separate ways; Badrick's Field Commander led them North, whilst Reynolds and his gang headed East.

The Dominus' voice sounded over the comm. "OK, everyone. Keep our armoured units covered. Take to the rooftops if necessary. Plain-clothes Units Alpha, Beta, watch our backs. Anyone who sees us will need to be mind-wiped."

A bunch of irritating confirmation lights winked on Badrick's HUD. He ignored them, choosing to concentrate on where he was going. They were very quickly approaching a residential locale, the first of their squad already scaling the wall of the closest house. Following them up, he heard his Field Commander speak. "Easy on the landings. Use every ounce of concentration. Best to avoid letting people know we're on their roofs."

The only response he received was, "Civilian looking through window, two o'clock!"

The team scrambled to the other side of the roof and held their positions tentatively. After a second, the Field Commander demanded a sit-rep and the agent who bawled the warning placed a hand to the metal over her forehead. "Stand by . . . He's gone, sir. Didn't see us."

"Anyone looking on this side?"

Badrick's skin tingled as Daemnos' overpowered senses detected supernatural feelers probing the area. He shivered and wiggled in his armour uncomfortably as the agent declared, "All clear."

The Field Commander turned from them and Badrick heard his voice over the comm. "Area too open. Using rooftops."

The radio fizzed for a heartbeat before Reynolds responded. "Understood. Heading down an alleyway. We're close to our target."

"Roger that." The Field Commander clicked his mic off and ordered the team to do the same. Though they'd be unable to respond to any contact, it was certainly better that way; if the Primordial was as powerful as they believed, it wasn't much of a stretch to think he could hear radio signals. Anyone dumb enough to use radio channels at this point deserved to be discovered.

"No talking," the commander ordered. "Agent Halsey, watch the area. Hand signals only, everyone." He made a rapid series of hand signals, then said confusingly, "Formation Gamma Beta."

Badrick could only say, "What?"

"We stay behind Halsey," Zale explained helpfully, "and move three seconds apart."

"Thanks," Badrick whispered gratefully.

They moved, leaping over the roofs of people's homes, advancing with extreme caution. Never dropping their concentration until they finally reached their destination.

The target house stood somewhat apart from the rest of this neighbourhood, looking alone and ramshackle in its solitude. Even the grass and bushes surrounding the building appeared desolate, the once green colour reduced to a sickly yellow.

The team descended and hit the ground with quiet thumps. At a signal from Halsey, they froze until she indicated it was safe to move on. They pelted across the grass, keeping an eye out for any civilians that could spot them. Luckily, most of the residents of the neighbourhood would be at work or school at this time of day. What was more important was seeing a dark power before it noticed them.

As Badrick crouched by the front door, he was able to really appreciate just how rundown this place was. Half the windows were shattered, some had the wooden frames missing entirely and the bricks that made up the walls looked to be seconds from crumbling.

And that shredded doormat had seen better days.

The Field Commander typed on his port-pad, paused, then nodded. He gestured towards the door. Badrick's heart began to pound in his chest as he was ordered to silently melt the lock. The metal turned to lava and oozed from the door, sizzling as it dripped onto the decrepit doormat. He winced at the noise, convinced it was as loud as thunder, certain the Primordial—if he was here—would be alerted to their presence.

They entered slowly, stepping so softly it was like the floor was made from cloud. Badrick entered fourth, following Zale as he edged into the living room, his auto-rifle ready. The oldest of their trio entered last, covering the squad's rear and ensuring nothing was evacuating the windows on the upper floor.

With every creak, Badrick grimaced.

Every thud made him wince.

So many sounds Badrick had to fight the urge to gasp in panic.

With so much anxiety flowing through him, Badrick could feel that crack in his emotions straining. He was fighting with all his strength to keep it closed, but he could sense it widening, fracturing, threatening to shatter open and flood him with uncontrolled terror.

If Badrick broke down now, he would torpedo the mission.

He couldn't allow that to happen.

Swallowing painfully, he ignored the tears of effort filling his left eye and continued into the house, using his unimpeded right eye to see.

One of the agents gingerly opened a door and peered inside, aiming her auto-rifle through the doorway.

A half second pause, then a blue light winked on Badrick's HUD marked '*clear*'.

This happened a second time as another Enthraller checked a different room.

The Field Commander performed a series of hand gestures that Badrick recognised. He was ordering Badrick, Zale and himself to the first floor, while the rest of the team were to stay down on the ground. Swallowing saliva, Badrick commanded his reluctant feet to take him up the staircase, suddenly finding this task immensely difficult. A terror at the thought of meeting the New Evil was biting at his bravery and he couldn't get the idea out of his head that they were climbing to their deaths.

Badrick scowled at himself—he was the Enthraller of Daemnos, one of the all-powerful Royals.

He wasn't supposed to be afraid of anything.

When he first awoke after his death he'd been utterly fearless.

Nothing could faze him.

But now . . .

In the end, it was Zale who helped him go on. Noticing his

shaky hesitation, the veteran reached out and gripped Badrick's arm, pulling him gently in an effort to get him moving.

It worked.

Badrick was able to move the muscles in his legs and follow Zale up the stairs.

This floor was as neglected as the rest of the house, with the doors and walls peeling paint. Several even had full blown holes punched through them.

Moving quickly but softly, they left nothing to chance. They checked every single room, including the bathroom, until there was only one left. Zale took the lead, inching forward and gently pushing the door open. He gripped his auto-rifle tightly and darted inside.

Badrick followed.

Before he'd even managed to register that the room was empty, Zale was cursing and letting his rifle fall to the floor. "There's nothing here," he snapped.

Sighing tiredly, Badrick stumbled to the window and used the frame to support his weight. A strange hollowness had formed in his stomach at the realisation that this house was New Evil free. Badrick may have been scared to find the bastard but he understood the desperate need for them to have succeeded.

Taking a moment to breathe and settle his stomach, Badrick suggested they contact the BCR. Find out if Reynolds' team had any better luck. The Field Commander agreed and consulted his port-pad. Zale stepped beside Badrick and joined him in staring out the window.

"Were we too late?" Badrick asked heavily.

"I don't know."

The sound of their radios sizzling stopped Badrick saying anything further. He grimaced as his ears exploded from the sharpness of the noise and closed his eyes, groaning aloud.

Through the door came two agents, demanding to know who was transmitting.

They never got an answer before a loud, panicked voice replaced the static. "Oh my God! GET OUT!"

"What in tarnation?" their commander snapped.

"TEAM TWO, GET OU—"

A deafening rumble drowned out the speaker, and the comm. died with a horrible screech, destroying Badrick's ear drums.

In the distance, a resounding *BOOM* could be heard.

Zale swivelled on his heel and shouted down his radio. "Reynolds, what—" For reasons Badrick didn't understand, Zale cut himself off. Expecting his partner to have been struck by something, Badrick spun to see what was wrong . . .

Zale murmured, "Oh God!"

At that, the other three people also about faced . . .

And saw the explosives lining the wall behind the door.

As they stared in shock, a little red light blinked twice and three beeps echoed threateningly.

"RUN!"

Badrick didn't need to be told twice. Pelting towards the window, he hurled his body through what remained of the glass. The shards cascaded around his body and he felt the sunlight touch him seconds before billowing fire filled the room.

It exploded through the open window and Badrick felt flames lick his under-suit, the heat so intense it hurt even through the strong material.

As he fell to the dirt, he saw that Zale was right behind him, only his partner had been too late. The blast interrupted his fall and pitched him further out. With a cry of pain he shot to the ground like a meteor, blasting mud and stones into the air.

Badrick twisted to ensure he landed on his feet as Zale's armour smoked into the dirt and felt the ground rush to meet him.

He was one step towards him when two other figures bolted through the open door just in time to avoid the ground floor going up in flames.

The house buckled as they rolled to safety, the foundations crumbling to sand. The house that had looked seconds away from collapsing finally did so. A choking cloud of dust engulfed the survivors as the remains kicked up more dirt, stones and bricks.

Badrick protected the wounded Zale from the debris, shouting in alarm as clumps of rubble struck him on the back of his armour. Cursing furiously, Zale could be heard groaning in pain and shouting, "WHAT THE HELL!"

When the dust had settled, he grabbed at his helmet and roughly pulled it from his head. "That's the second time that accursed Bomb Killer has blown me up. I'm gonna tear his soul out!"

"Bomb Killer?" Badrick repeated, completely aghast. Unwrapping his arms from around his partner, he stumbled back, fighting to remain upright despite the weakness overcoming his muscles. He noticed the other survivors, his heart dropping with anguish as he realised only two others had escaped the fire.

Though dust still clogged the air, Badrick was able to see through the murk and recognise the combination of red and blue as Mawr. He was crouched to the ground, helping the second survivor to her feet. He quickly realised this was a hopeless cause, and so lifted her off the ground.

The reason for this was obvious; the armour on her leg had been completely stripped and the burn across her flesh was almost black.

She groaned with agony as he set her down a safe distance from the destruction. Mawr also removed his helmet, revealing his stunned face. "What happened?" he demanded.

"Explosives!" Badrick breathed. "Is it just you two?"

"The others were too far from the door."

"Chri–" A tight grip from Zale stopped him finishing.

"The second team," the wounded veteran wheezed. Badrick followed his elongated finger and looked to the horizon, where an awful plume of black smoke was rising.

"Oh no," Mawr whispered. "Daniel."

"We have to go!" Zale roared. He rolled to his belly and forced his shaking arms to lift his weight.

"You can't—"

"I'm fine, Badrick! She's more hurt than I am. Mawr, look after her. We'll get to Reynolds."

With no other options, Mawr reluctantly nodded his agreement and bent to attend to the injured woman. She writhed appallingly at his touch, moaning with distress.

Badrick helped Zale regain his balance and led the way towards the smoke. Past the residential area, they rushed along the streets, no longer caring if they were seen. Their armour clanked as they carelessly pushed through the frightened crowds on the inner city.

Within minutes they were rounding a corner and the flattened office building came into view.

Badrick gasped in horror at the sight of the destruction.

And in the corner of his eye he could see the appalled look on Zale's face.

Where once walls had clearly stood now only powerfully hot flames crackled. The doors, of which they could see three, had been blown off their hinges and lay scattered across the street.

One was actually embedded in the window of the building opposite.

Bricks and mortar were scattered everywhere. There was so much of it there was no telling what could be buried beneath. Scared and shaking civilians were screaming and fleeing the devastation. Zale was almost knocked off his feet by a large, bulky armed man who was running ahead of his family, a look of terror on his butch face.

Ignoring them, Badrick pushed aside the useless citizens of Southampton and scrabbled to reach the building as fast as he could. Still helmetless, Zale did the same. Despite his wounds, he managed to stay his feet and reached the chaos before Badrick.

They dug their hands into the rubble and feverishly tossed aside bricks and glass and wood. The debris clattered as it rolled down the pile of clay, breaking even more so as they carelessly burrowed in as much as they could.

"Where is everyone?" Badrick cried when he failed to turn up any bodies.

"It was a big building," Zale responded, just as loud, his face as white as paper. "If they were spread out they wouldn't have all been incinerated. There must be survivors." He saw Badrick casting his eyes around in despair. "The plain-clothes agents won't be here for another five minutes. We have to keep searching. Keep looking!"

They continued searching, and Badrick had to fight the urge to use his powers to shift the debris en masse. Even in a situation this dire, nobody would thank him for revealing the existence of the supernatural to the civilian population.

"Here!" The shout came from behind a wall that still half stood, and Badrick scrambled gracelessly, tripping in his hurry. Reaching them as fast as he could, he helped Zale uncover a blue body and pull them from the chaos. Zale yanked the helmet off the agent and felt for a pulse.

Badrick was saddened to hear the man was gone.

"There has to be more," Zale whispered, casting his gaze over the rubble. "This can't have happened," he added. "This wasn't supposed to happen."

"Keep digging!" Badrick shouted. "We have to find survivors

before the police show up." They separated and once again plunged their hands between the rubble.

This time it was Badrick who located a body.

Recognising the familiar touch of flesh, his mouth fell open and he bolstered his efforts, chucking bricks so hard they smashed into dust behind him. He couldn't tell who the casualty was at first; the hand he uncovered was bare, stripped of its glove and armour.

It was only when some of the mortar avalanched and revealed a red chestplate did he stop and feel the breath catch in his throat.

"Zale," he tried to say, but his voice came out in a hoarse croak. Clearing his throat, and desperately fighting back tears, he tried again. "Zale!"

His partner sprinted from behind a large pile of devastated chairs and tables, slipping on a sheet of cracked glass in his haste to approach. "You got someone?" he called as he caught a hold of a doorframe and pushed himself up.

"It's . . ." Once again Badrick's voice failed to work and all he managed was a small, pained squeak. "It's . . ."

In the end, Zale was the one to say it aloud.

"Reynolds?" He fell to his knees and freed the Dominus' head from his helmet. When his white, unmoving face came into view, cuts and streaks of blood covering his forehead, Zale's eyes creased and began to water. "No . . ." he moaned. "No . . . not again."

It was then that they heard a groan and twisted sharply to see a shape emerging from beneath the bricks. It pushed the rubble from its back and weakly got to its feet.

Seeing the two of them, it stumbled over, reaching up to remove its helmet.

"Zach?" Zale gasped in disbelief. "How the hell . . . You!? Of all these people? Why are you the one who gets to live?!"

His rage was terrible to behold. Badrick had to grab his shoulders just to stop him lunging at the weakened detective.

Falling to the bricks, Zach winced in pain and grabbed his side.

"I wasn't allowed in the building. Reynolds told me to stay by the door. He didn't trust me . . . He should have trusted me!"

Zale's face flushed bright red and he escaped Badrick's grip with a vicious jerk, dashing forward and grabbing Zach by the throat. "Nobody should ever trust you!" Badrick gasped when Zale's fist met Zach's cheek. "The Bomb Killer did this! The guy *you're* supposed to be catching!"

"I know," Zach moaned. "I know. I don't know how . . ."

Barely audible over Zale's shouting and Zach's moaning, Badrick sensed rather than heard a very strange—very tiny— electrical spark.

Without warning, Zach stuttered and gaped, his hand clutching at his chest. When his fingers couldn't reach through the metal, he pulled at his collar, still choking.

"What . . ." Badrick leapt forward and grabbed him as he tumbled onto his back, writhing and flailing his arms in a blind panic. Zale didn't move. He was staring at Zach in shock, caught completely off guard by this sudden change of behaviour.

Badrick opened his mouth and cried, "What's happe—" He never got to finish.

Zach's hands fell to his side.

The life left his eyes.

And with one last convulsion, his body fell still.

"What?" Badrick spluttered.

Zale still didn't speak. He knelt beside them, and turned the lifeless detective onto his stomach, revealing a bright green handprint burned onto the back of his chestplate.

"The Bomb Killer," he sighed. Badrick saw his legs begin to shake and the electrical Enthraller fell to the dirt. "He killed them all."

chapter
THIRTY THREE

Tending to their patients in silence, the medics and doctors did not converse. The entirety of the Medical Wing was silent. Not even the burned agent Mawr pulled from the ashes of the house made a sound.

Badrick watched sombrely as the medic Melody inspected Zale for damage. She gently removed pieces of his armour, one bit at a time and checked each and every skin cell for wounds.

Clearly she took her job very seriously.

Or maybe she just wanted to prolong the only thing she had to distract herself from their reality.

Zale didn't protest as she overdid her job. He didn't once complain, wince or even tell her off for dawdling.

His face was blank and emotionless.

His eyes were dead.

It was still the middle of the day. The sun outside was beaming brightly and with great warmth, yet the world felt cold and threatening. The shadows in the corners of the room seemed deeper than usual, the lights dimmed as though they were being choked by the dark.

Nothing felt real anymore.

A metal scraping made Badrick wince and he scowled at Melody as she scratched at Zale's left pauldron. "Structure isn't compromised," she eventually whispered. She ran a hand over the skin of Zale's arm and gave him a soft smile. "You're lucky this time."

"No damage?" a deep voice enquired.

Mawr.

"No burns this time."

"Well, that's something," Badrick found himself muttering blithely.

Ignoring him, Melody took a nervous step forward. "Can I ask . . ." She licked her lips when she faltered, trying again. "What happened?"

"I don't know," Zale answered her. "I just don't know." His palms met his forehead with a slapping sound. "I've gone over it a hundred times and I . . . I just can't figure out how those bombs got there!"

Badrick only half listened—he was too busy watching Mawr. Prompted by her questions, the ex-soldier had released his port-pad from the slot on his arm and was busy typing on it. When he spoke, his voice cut into the silence following Zale's outburst. "I had a look at our systems." Approaching Badrick, he handed over his port-pad. "If you don't know, our scanners are designed to do two things. Locate new energy as best it can, and identify energies we've told it to. For example, we create a file entitled *Resurrected* and put in that folder an example of an energy reading from said being. We do the same when we want to identify an individual's signature."

"Yeah, Mawr," Badrick tutted. "From that point on when a Resurrected pops up our scanners know what to identify it as. Why are you giving us a BCR lesson?"

Mawr tapped the port-pad, bringing Badrick's attention to it. "I found this in the files on the Bomb Killer. Do you recognise it?"

Displayed on the screen was a render of an energy signature. Badrick recognised some of its patterns immediately, despite the vast number of sections alien to him.

With a hoarse voice, he croaked, "That's the New Evil's energy."

Mawr swiped the screen with his finger. Like a page in a book, the image flipped to the side to be replaced with an ever changing series of numbers and letters. "Zale's algorithm."

"My algorithm?" Zale snapped from the bed. "The algorithm I made to predict the Primordial's growth?"

"Aye." Mawr flipped the screen again onto another render.

Then again . . . and again.

"Every confirmed scan, render and prediction." Without giving Badrick any warning, he snatched his machine back and worked on it a second time. "This was in the New Evil's file."

It was another render, though the energy was far smaller.

Much less intimidating.

"Let me guess," Badrick sighed, his stomach dropping. "This is the Bomb Killer's energy?"

All of a sudden, he was feeling quite sick.

"Yes."

"Are you trying to tell me," Zale blurted indignantly, "the scanner's files were mixed up?

"Only recently," Mawr told them. "We always encountered the

New Evil when we expected to, up until—"

"The Captus Memoria," Badrick finished. "That was the last time. After that we . . ."

When he failed to finish, Zale did so for him. "After that we let Zach update the file."

Badrick's fists clenched so tightly he was surprised the port-pad he once again held between his fingers didn't crack. "Zach mixed them up," he snarled, rage filling him like boiling water.

They trusted Zach to input their data into the relevant folders. They allowed him to update their systems with the readings so that the scanner would detect the New Evil when it next struck.

But in the last few days of his life, the detective had not been right.

Driven by a transparent and desperate need to prove himself, Zach had become a mess. Jittery, obsessed, stretching himself too thin between what he'd been ordered to do and what he wanted to do.

Too eager to show the world he could catch the Primordial, the moron utterly failed to take care in his work . . . and had mixed up his files with theirs.

He'd . . . ruined . . . everything.

His newfound hatred for the dead detective was visibly shared between his friends. Their faces were sheens of odium, their fists tightly squeezed.

Noticing their fury, Melody clapped her hands and said, "That's enough, boys." She handed Zale his armour. "You need to go to bed, Zale. Rest is the only thing you need to focus on for tonight. Promise me you'll go straight to your room and sleep."

Zale nodded sombrely.

"You boys," she addressed Mawr and Badrick. "Same goes for you. Take the night. Doctor's orders.

"We can't." Mawr shook his head roughly. He slapped the

back of his hand into the palm of the other. "The Bomb Killer has taken out some of our best agents . . . Not to mention our Dominus . . . We can't stop."

"Nothing good will come from denying yourself rest."

"I can't." He waved an angry hand at her. "Daniel said there'd be repercussions. This was a trap by the Bomb Killer and we walked right into it."

"A sloppy trap." Zale's growl rumbled so deeply Badrick felt it in his heart. "We wouldn't have fallen into it if we didn't think we'd tracked the Primordial."

"Quite right," Mawr nodded.

"The Daemonium," Melody tutted impatiently, "isn't going to fall apart while you sleep. It'll be here when you wake. But if you don't rest, you'll all collapse when you're most needed. Do you understand *that?*

"Go to bed. That's an order."

With that, she ushered Zale off the hospital bed and commanded him to his room, telling him what repercussions *he'd* experience if he made any detours. With a dejected nod, Zale did as he was told.

"I'll see you guys later," he murmured as he disappeared through the exit.

With his departure, the Medical Wing fell into general quiet once more. The staff continued their care of the burned agent, who now emitted the occasional moan as cooling salves were applied to her damaged flesh.

As for Badrick, he was watching Mawr. The eldest member of their team had his hands against the wall, his head bowed. Badrick could see his shoulders beginning to sag.

"Mawr . . ."

The ex-soldier heaved a heavy sigh. "Daniel is dead." To his shock, Badrick caught a glimpse of something wet and reflective.

"Leave me be."

Understanding that completely, Badrick closed his mouth.

Zale had been expecting Horas to manifest at any moment, but utterly failed to foresee just how livid the demon would be when he finally did appear. His rage seemed to melt the walls and boil the air, it was so intense.

The Primordial was delighted to see it.

"S'up, Horas?" he grinned his way.

"That *was* your energy at those sites," the hellspawn stated. "It was *not* the Bomb Killer."

Chuckling, Zale simply responded with, "Was it?"

His anger appearing to grow even hotter, Horas growled, "You have some explaining to do."

chapter
THIRTY FOUR

The door had barely finished closing before Zale's demon materialised in his way and demanded an explanation for a second time, and, for a brief moment, Zale wondered whether he should punish Horas for his disrespect.

He, of course, decided not to.

Zale had *wanted* this reaction from Horas. He'd been giddily excited for the moment he exploded with confusion and desperately insisted he be clued in to what was going on.

"What was the Bomb Killer doing there?" Horas asked of him. "I watched you kill those three people. It was *your* energy that you dumped to draw the Daemonium in.

"Explain to me how it was the Bomb Killer. We both know Zach did *not* input the data incorrectly." The demon huffed angrily and paced back and forth across the room. "Is the Bomb Killer working for you?"

"Horas—"

"Or did you trick that murderer into doing your killing for you?"

"Horas—"

"It is time you explained what you have done—"

"HORAS!"

Zale's demon stopped pacing and ceased his flurry of questions in quite the hurry. Recoiling from Zale, he bowed his apologetic head and placed his hands together in complacent obedience.

"You silly creature," Zale smiled, approaching Horas. "I'm not going to tell you anything."

"But—"

"However, it *is* time I showed you everything." With that, he placed a hand on Horas' head, making impossible contact with his holographic visage. Accessing the demon's soul, he poured memories into his mind. Horas spasmed abominably as his head was filled with Zale's thoughts.

The room began to melt.

Colours blended together and ran down the walls like paint.

And then everything changed.

They were standing outside now, beneath a shining sun and surrounded by gloriously beautiful mountains that caught the sunlight and reflected it into gorgeous concentrated beams.

Stunned and afraid, Horas spun on his heel and stared at the scene unfolding before them.

What must have been hundreds of Daemonium soldiers were scattered all over the area, some patrolling, others organising machinery, and many striking pickaxes into rocks.

"Is this . . ." Horas began, pausing only briefly to double check. "This is the platoon that died. This is where the Bomb Killer first struck—"

The tranquil scene suddenly became very violent. As a soldier brought his pickaxe down upon the demonic metals they were mining, the quarry quite abruptly went up in brilliant orange flames.

Nearly the entire platoon was scorched, hundreds of bodies vanishing beneath the fire.

Only a handful survived the blast, however this was no mercy. As Zale and Horas observed, a hooded figure darted out from the smoke and slapped his hand onto the helmet of a disorientated soldier.

Flailing wildly, he was unprepared for what happened next; the hooded man lifted something large and black into the air before plunging the sharp end into the man's abdomen.

Zale could tell Horas expected the man to be dead, however when the spike was retracted he appeared to be unhurt.

That was until the attacker pressed his thumb into his device and the soldier was struck by a sudden fit. Writhing in agony, it didn't take him long to die from the cardiac arrest now savaging his body.

As the soldier passed from this existence, the world once again melted, colour and shapes warping into new images.

The pair reappeared in a forest, amidst a scene of chaos. A helicopter cut across the sky overhead and a carbon copy of Zale flashed past at speed.

Out of nowhere, a black mass of shadows materialised in the darker part of the forest. In fact, this position was so well hidden that the only reason Horas saw it manifest at all was because Zale's memories focused him on its presence.

The shadow fired a devastating blast of energy at the chopper, which knocked it from the heavens. A dozen figures leapt from the blazing wreck just in time to avoid going up in flames.

A flash of energy and they were transported several metres to the right. Zale allowed Horas to watch as the same hooded man appeared—as if forming from nothing but the air—and chucked two bombs fabricated from nothing towards the memory version of Zale.

The real Zale could sense Horas beginning to understand what he was being shown.

But he wasn't done yet.

Zale moved the slideshow along, summoning another memory from the recesses of his brain.

He was now injecting the gas from his heart-attack device into the coffee machine, altering the smoke into liquid form with his unmatched powers while remaining completely unnoticed by those occupying the cafeteria.

Next, they saw Badrick hand a mug of coffee to Zach.

They didn't need to watch him drink it to understand that he was now infected with the deadly poison that allowed Zale to cause supernatural cardiac arrest.

This time they materialised in the prisons, just in time to see a Kalik approach the cell within which was a trembling Charles.

Hello, old friend.

Charles' head shot up at the sound of his master's voice and his eyes widened at the sight of the Kalik. He rose to his feet and approached the forcefield, his fingers twitching nervously.

That's right. Your God is here. Ah! Zale's voice added quickly when Charles tried to open his mouth. *Don't speak. Just listen.*

Without warning another Zale appeared behind the Resurrected. With the same black device, he rammed it between Charles' shoulder blades, and then disappeared once again.

As the wound healed without fail, the New Evil's presence was felt again. *Did you feel that, Charles? That's what it feels like to be injected with the gas you stole from Koreath. That was good work, by the way. I've had fun with this device. You built my toy very well, indeed.*

Consider this an opportunity, Charles, as well as a warning: If you ever return, I'll activate the gas within you and you'll suffer a very painful death. That's right . . . this power works on even you.

No one knows this device exists. No one can trace it back to me. You'll die and never be avenged.

If you ever interfere with me, I'll kill you.

If I ever see you again, I'll kill you.

If I even figure out where you are, I'll kill you.

You will run and never return.

When the shield drops, follow the path I'm leaving in your consciousness.

The next instant, the Kalik pounced away into the jailor's office, killing him in seconds. The forcefield dropped and Charles bolted. As the Resurrected vanished down the corridor, Horas looked up at the cameras and Zale heard him think, *He altered the footage.*

Laughing his glee out loud, Zale let Horas see that he killed Charles by using the demon's own electrical powers to activate the gas.

Next he showed himself switching the data in the system, mixing up the different signatures in the computer files.

When the scene altered yet again, they saw Zale kill a random person on the street, ripping the heart from his chest and purposefully dumping energy at the site.

Horas now understood—though he'd believed at the time of these murders that Zale was leaving behind his Primordial signature for the Daemonium to follow into a trap, he'd actually dumped Bomb Killer energy.

"Impossible," Horas mumbled with disbelief. "You fabricated an entirely new demonic signature. A new identity. Like some kind of God."

"One that has no connection to your energy," Zale cackled,

"or mine."

The final memory was of the office building, however Horas turned away, apparently no longer needing an explanation.

"I can guess, Zale," he sighed. "As you approached, you used your power to burn a hand print on his back from afar, then had Zach die like he was murdered by the Bomb Killer."

Both their visions blurred.

A tugging sensation pulled at their minds.

And Zale's bedroom reappeared.

"It was you." Zale could feel how revolted Horas was and took great pleasure in the waves of revulsion the demon sent his way. "That is what you did when I had those blackouts. You caused those to hide the truth.

"The Bomb Killer is *you*."

"I've got to say, Horas," Zale smiled, "it's so good to finally show you everything. You *finally* have a chance to admire my brilliance."

Horas ignored his arrogant remark, choosing instead to continue voicing aloud every realisation that came to him. "You invented a fake villain with which to disorientate the Daemonium. Someone you could blame for murdering our friends and allies."

The demon spun to face him. "But why, Zale? Why go to all this trouble? What did it matter if they knew the New Evil was behind everything? You are undetectable! You could have stayed in this room and never been found."

Zale felt somewhat annoyed by this.

Of all the demons in the Universes, he had to be lumbered with one who had no appreciation for the fine art of deception. "Because, Horas," he drawled, "in enacting this ruse, I have eliminated my enemies without any suspicion falling on me whatsoever. I'm a goddamn genius."

"No, Zale," Horas disagreed. "You could have taken them out

as the Primordial without anyone discovering you. All of *this* was just a way for you to prove how smart you are. You created a game that you could control to prove you are the most intelligent man in the room.

"Using the machine you had Charles create for you . . . You could have mimicked the heart-attack power for yourself. But no, Zale, you *wanted* the danger of using something that could be found. Using something that left behind evidence."

Zale sneered. "What a weird thing to say to me."

"The longer the most vital piece of evidence went undiscovered, the smarter you felt." Horas sighed in dejection. "You wanted the excitement of being smarter than your enemies. You are a sociopath."

With a grin, Zale chuckled, "Listen, Horas, you strange fool. I needed to create a separate identity to confuse the Daemonium."

"No—"

"Yes! At the end of it all, I needed to lure Reynolds and Zach to either those offices or that house. This hinged on the three murders, but if the New Evil had already acted too much outside of that locale I ran the risk of them not being so confident I could be found *within* the black circle Zach drew.

"I had no choice with the Captus Memoria. I had to risk it. After all, why would the Bomb Killer destroy it? If I had acted as such, the agents would've linked him and the Primordial immediately.

"The Bomb Killer persona allowed me to execute certain aspects of my plan without jeopardising the required ending to this game."

"How . . ."

When Horas failed to continue, Zale said, "Ask your question, Horas."

Hesitating only a second, Horas blurted, "How could you

know Zach would drink the coffee? That is beyond coincidental. You could not have planned that."

"It's not as elaborate as you believe, Horas," Zale cackled. "All I needed to know was that Zach drank coffee. I didn't poison it with the plan that only he would drink it."

With a gasp, Horas bawled, "You did it more than once. You did it until Zach took some regardless of how many others did the same. My God, Zale. How many people here have the gas in their veins?"

"Hundreds."

"*WHY!?*" Horas clenched his fists and roared unintelligibly, but after a moment he appeared to regain control of his emotions. Taking unnecessary deep breaths, the demon once again spoke in his natural formal tones. "How did you know he would survive the explosion and not anyone else?"

Zale was glad Horas asked this question—it was his favourite part of this whole elaborate scheme.

"Everything I did to Zach was carefully planned. I vigilantly cultivated him into becoming a mess until—"

"He acted so callously that Reynolds no longer trusted him," Horas finished. "And with the seeds of mind-control you planted in the Dominus, you *knew* Reynolds would keep him back, believing him a risk.

"You planned for him to be outside the blast radius."

Flicking a finger the demon's way, Zale quipped, "Exactamundo."

Horas turned his back on him, his revulsion so very evident. Zale found his disgust both absolutely delightful and, at the same time, highly rude. "There was no need to humiliate your friends as you killed them," his demon snarled. "That was cruel and unnecessary."

"But fun."

"Sociopath!"

"Oh, be quiet, Horas." Zale poked a small but painful surge of power into Horas and smiled at his gasp of pain. "This is the last time you're allowed to talk to me with such disrespect. The only reason I allowed it today was because it was so fun to watch."

Horas took a moment to recover from the sharp stabs Zale sent through him and calm himself before daring to speak again. With one last exhalation, Horas half turned and murmured, "What do you intend to do now?"

"The fun is over," Zale admitted, wishing he didn't have to. "The last obstacle in my way has been removed. The Daemonium is leaderless. My competitor is gone. The survivors are split between two enemies they don't realise are the same.

"I just have to do one last thing before I raze this place to the ground."

"You are going to kill Badrick."

It wasn't a question.

"I'm going to *destroy* him." The dark sneer Zale enjoyed seeing on his face broadened across his perfect features, and he took a half second to admire the aura of his evil in the mirror. "He's going to know it was all my doing and he will die in despair."

"So that is what this has all been about," Horas said softly. "You wanted to create an elaborate mystery no one could solve and then watch their disbelief and pain as you revealed all the secrets.

"Their despair is your ambrosia."

"Poetically put, Horas." Zale cackled in delight. "Just imagine it, though . . . The look Badrick will slap on his idiotic face when he realises I'm everything he's afraid of. It'll be perfect, Horas." This time it was Zale's turn to pace the room. "But this can't be done any simple way. The setting has to be perfect."

"All the world is a stage," Horas quipped dryly.

That made Zale laugh again. "We will need a distraction for the rest of the rabble," he declaimed boldly. "Ensure we have the privacy and prepare the theatre for the Daemonium's fall."

"You have an idea?"

Zale's grin enlarged.

His eyes went dark.

And he sang, "Oh yes, I have an idea."

chapter
THIRTY FIVE

Never before had Mawr felt so lost.

The wreckage and desolation he experienced in the aftermath of the Devil's ascension hadn't even come close to this.

So many friends were lost that day, when the Devil stormed into the Daemonium and ripped their demons from their souls. So many comrades died in the fight to stop the greatest evil committed by a creature from Hell.

He'd had to do terrible things.

Things that haunted him to this day.

But . . . they didn't even come close to how he felt now.

The only true friend Mawr ever had was gone.

The single, solitary man who somehow understood the pressure Mawr constantly endured having to live up to his ancestor's names.

Their great deeds and honourable intentions.

A legacy he'd never managed to equal.

And without Daniel, how would he ever live up to expectations?

Combined, the New Evil and the Bomb Killer had brought the Daemonium to its knees.

They were leaderless.

Defenceless.

Was this how it was to go down?

After all these centuries, the most powerful organisation in the world—the only defence against demonic calamities—would be destroyed, never to be seen again.

Mawr never thought it possible.

But after everything they'd lost, how could they possibly prevent it?

Badrick was doing his best to shut out Mawr's inner turmoil, but it was *so* loud that ignoring it was proving utterly impossible. He'd believed his own messed up mind was capable of stirring up the most intense misery, but this was on a whole other level.

It was deafening.

Badrick never realised just how close Daniel Reynolds and Mawr Burakka truly were, but hearing the latter's pain helped him understand that no truer friendship had ever existed.

Inside his soul, he could feel Daemnos recoiling from the melancholy with such odium it was tainting Badrick's mind. He too was feeling a mild level of abhorrence towards the very notion of sadness, all because Daemnos couldn't fathom how emotions as deep as this were possible.

Badrick deeply wished his room offered some kind of

supernatural dampening technology, not just soundproofing. Then he wouldn't have to listen to Mawr's hopelessness.

In truth, it was Badrick's fault; his control over Daemnos' powers was linked to his ability to manage his own stupid emotions. The only reason he was unable to block out Mawr's thoughts was because he too was suffering.

Misery loved company, and, stimulated by the depression darkening his mood, the energy within him was reaching out, unchecked, and instinctively tuning into a similar frequency.

The only other thought that interrupted these awful musings was a worry of how Zale was feeling.

He'd barely held together when Carla died.

Now that he'd lost Reynolds too ... it wouldn't surprise Badrick if he was sitting on his bed, desolate and inconsolable.

Her moans of pleasure sent waves of irrepressible desire shooting through Zale. Watching Lora writhe rhythmically on top of him, mouth open and smiling widely, eyes closed and smooth neck gloriously visible as she stretched backwards, he lost himself to the kind of lust reserved exclusively for divinity.

He couldn't take his eyes or hands off her supernatural perfection.

Beauty unparalleled.

Sex incarnate.

With one last gasp of gratification, she trembled and fell to the mattress beside him. Rubbing herself on the soft sheets, she wrapped her arms around his chest and laughed. "Miraculous!" she exclaimed. "I never realised it would be *that* breathtaking. To be completely physical ..." She let out a high pitched whine of excitement. "No wonder they want it like this."

Zale ignored her, far too preoccupied with his own enjoyment.

"Just you wait," she continued, oblivious to his disregard. "When I get used to this . . . The things I'll be able to do for you. You won't covet anyone else.

"I will be your loyal and venereal queen. Every man who survives your wrath will be jealous of you."

"And every woman will be jealous of *you*," Zale deadpanned.

Another excited cackle. "That's for damn sure!" Her hands pressed into his chest as she pushed herself up and sat on his crotch. "You'll rule this Universe, my King, and I'll be there to . . . Well . . . let me give you an example." She leaned forward, smothering his face with her vast breasts. "Let's go again."

And so it was that the thrashing began for a second time and the room filled once more with moans of ecstasy.

It took two hours for Lora to be completely satiated. When her last whimper of indulgence stopped, she flattened herself against his chest and lay there, breathing raggedly.

"A true God, you are." She giggled and ran her hands along his waist. "Do you have any idea how arousing your power is?"

"I can't say I do," he said softly.

She lifted her head to gaze at him. "You pulled me from Hell without setting off a single one of the Daemonium's alarms. You did it without radiating any energy.

"I am here, on the Earth plane, one hundred percent physical. You shattered the unbreakable laws of the Universe and brought me up, not as a soul manifested as a body, but as a soul nestled within a flesh and blood vessel.

"I'm real, and the first demon to ever be so."

Zale listened to her voice as she spoke, observing how different it sounded without Reynolds' speech patterns ruining it.

He actually felt uniquely privileged to hear a demon's true voice—such a rare occurrence, most never experienced it.

She was still talking; "What you did takes power never seen

before. My King . . . you *are* God."

"I like the sound of that," Zale smirked.

Lora tittered, believing she had pleased her future ruler. She nestled into his chest and bit his neck, trying to incite more desire out of Zale. In his ear, she whispered, "Thrill me. Make me quake. Tell me what comes next."

Granting her wish, Zale said, "Tomorrow morning, I'm going to kill Badrick." He felt her shiver, but not with revulsion. "I'm going to tear him apart."

"Daemnos too?"

Speaking slowly, he whispered, "No one who learns my identity before I seize the Universes can be allowed to live."

A grin spread across her visage, Lora exclaimed, "I would expect nothing less."

Zale smiled. He pushed her into a sitting position and looked her in the eyes, drinking in the gorgeousness of their deep brown colour. He gently placed a hand upon her chest, which brought an impious smile to her face.

Lora didn't have time to protest as he dug his claws through her flesh and gripped her heart. A torrent of black blood flooded from her mouth and splashed across his chest. He felt one of his claws puncture her heart as he yanked it from her body and siphoned power into her soul, tearing it apart.

With a loud bang, the once arresting she-demon exploded in a detonation of black ichor, covering half of Zale's room with gore.

Within his grip, Lora's heart dissolved, nothing of her body capable of existing in this world without a proper anchor.

Licking blood from his fingers, Zale gazed into his mirror, regarding his black eyes and sharp fangs with glee.

"No one."

chapter
THIRTY SIX

The lack of anguished bereavement surprised Badrick when he awoke the next morning, opening his eyes with difficulty and straining to remove his sore body from the entanglement of his sheets. The entirety of the previous evening had been spent listening to Mawr as he remembered the good days with Reynolds and grieved for the loss of his only friend.

However, this morning, there was only silence.

A little shocked, and as rude as it was, Badrick couldn't help but purposefully go searching for the sorrow just to make sure something hadn't happened.

But no, there was no trace of Mawr anywhere near his room.

There was no doubt the man had gone down to the BCR to recommence an obsessive need to find the New Evil. With his friend murdered by the monster, it was likely Mawr's motives would change to those of revenge.

Dreading what he'd find when he arrived, Badrick pulled on his uniform and left his room.

There was a definite depression lurking in the air when he entered the HQ. He could practically taste the sorrow that saturated the Daemonium as he briskly walked in the direction of the BCR.

Mawr was exactly where he expected him to be; hunched over a console. Badrick stepped out of the way as an agent tried to exit the BCR and did his best to approach the ex-soldier. This proved to be somewhat difficult as this was the moment more and more people decided they wanted to leave the room.

Eventually, he reached his teammate and spoke softly to let him know he was there, not wishing to give Mawr a fright. The older man turned his way, his eyes pools of exhaustion, the colour in them dimmed to near grey.

"Badrick?" he asked. "What are you doing here?"

"It's morning, Mawr," Badrick replied, throwing a hand to the BCR. He noticed more people leaving, their movements practically robotic, no doubt because of the sorrow affecting everyone at the moment. "It's my job to come here in the morning."

Mawr's dead expression turned to one of surprise. "I didn't realise it was morning."

"What have you been doing?" Badrick queried. "Were you down here all night?"

"Not *all* night."

Mawr straightened and beckoned Badrick to a corner of the BCR. Frowning with curiosity, Badrick followed him, questioning what they were doing. Mawr glanced around the room, seemingly checking to see if anyone was listening.

When he was happy no one could overhear, he leaned in close and said, "I spent most of last night thinking."

"OK?"

"Zach got the files mixed up, so when the Bomb Killer attacked, the scanners saw the New Evil . . ."

"And when the New Evil attacked, they saw the Bomb Killer," Badrick finished.

Mawr gave him a look that suggested he wasn't impressed with being interrupted. "Something about it has been bothering me all night."

"What?"

"The last time Zach touched the files was after the Captus Memoria, which would be when he mixed them up."

"I agree," Badrick stated bluntly, unsure of where this was going.

"Badrick, if the files were mixed up *before* the Bomb Killer murdered the guard outside the walls, why didn't the alarms go off?"

Badrick sucked on his teeth in thought, eventually having to say, "What do you mean?"

Mawr tutted and tried again. "If the scanners thought the Bomb Killer was the Primordial, they would have set the alarms off when he used his power."

With a start, Badrick understood what Mawr was saying. "But they didn't."

Mawr shook his head. "The scanners didn't pick up the Bomb Killer as the New Evil when he tried to attack the facility. I've checked, Badrick. They detected the Bomb Killer, not the Primordial. So if they got it right then, why did they get it so wrong later?"

Badrick's mouth dropped as Mawr straightened, looking confident that he'd got his point across. "The files . . . somebody switched the—"

"Badrick," Mawr suddenly said, stopping him from finishing. "Does it seem . . . quiet to you?"

Frowning, he spun to face the expanse of space that was the BCR. The usual sight of computers, monitors and chairs greeted him, illuminated, as always, by blue overhead lights.

Everything looked normal.

Except for the fact that the place was empty.

It was more than quiet—except for Mawr and Badrick the BCR had been entirely evacuated.

Mawr stepped into the middle of the room, spreading his arms in confusion. Facing Badrick, he voiced, "Where is everybody?"

A smashing noise sounded to Badrick's left at that exact moment, and he swivelled sharply at the surprising clatter. Dropped from the table was a broken mug, the pieces rocking in a puddle of cold coffee that stained the originally pristine floor.

"Why'd you do that?" Mawr scolded him.

"I didn't . . ." He railed off, his eyes widening. He hurried to the remains of the mug, crouching down to stare as close as possible.

The mug was quivering.

And now that he'd clued in to something odd, Badrick realised that the entire floor was vibrating like an electrical current was flowing through it.

"You feel that?" he spat, jumping to his feet with alarm beginning to rise in his chest.

Frowning, Mawr gazed at his feet in confusion. After a moment, he crouched and spread his fingers across the floor, taking a moment before confirming, "I can . . . What the hell is that?"

Before either could provide a theory, the vibration intensified until it was no longer a soft trembling. Within seconds the room was quaking so violently it had begun to move. Losing his balance, Mawr was forced to throw himself into a console just to keep his feet. Even Badrick went sprawling to the floor, Daemnos' power somehow not strong enough to keep him upright.

"What's happening?" Badrick roared as one of the monitors shattered of its own volition. Scrambling to his feet, he gazed at the room in fearful astonishment as chairs fell to the floor, tables cracked, and computers smashed apart.

"Get to cover!" Mawr roared as one of the larger screens situated on the wall lost grip and smashed onto the consoles below.

However, his warning turned out to be entirely unnecessary.

Faster than it began, the devastating earthquake stopped.

A tense silence followed, disturbed only by Badrick's panting.

Regaining his feet, Mawr tried to speak. "What—"

Badrick caught sight of the shockwave of energy a split second before it hurled him into the wall. Originating from the South West, it phased through the walls of the facility and striking any loose objects it met, including people.

Mawr was also pitched into the air. He crashed noisily into a group of computer monitors, knocking them from the desks. Following them on their journey to the floor, he collapsed among the glass that shattered across it. Thankfully, he was unharmed, and Mawr quickly jumped to his feet, crushing shards of monitor beneath his boots.

Also pulling himself off the floor, Badrick slammed his hands over his ears as the BCR's scanners picked up the shockwave and blared so shrilly he was genuinely amazed he could still hear at all.

The blue illumination also flicked off, replaced by vivid, red warning lights.

Terror shot into Badrick's heart as they flashed, his mind racing at what it could mean.

Was the New Evil *finally* attacking the facility?

Mawr reacted to the commotion more usefully; he pushed aside fallen chairs and dashed to a blinking console. Checking for damage, he called up the scanning software, working so fast he rivalled even Zale's speed.

Badrick took a moment to side-step and slam a fist on the shut-off button for the alarms, thankful for the silence that followed. He drew up next to Mawr, desperate to find out what the cause of this chaos was.

"Is it the New Evil?" When Mawr didn't respond, Badrick's frustration led him to shout his name.

"I don't know what it is," the ex-soldier snapped. "The scanners can't identify what that shockwave was and I . . ." He worked on the keyboard a few seconds more. "I can't find anything remotely similar in the system."

Badrick saw the software finish contrasting the render of the energy signature belonging to the shockwave and watched as it confirmed Mawr's statement. Their computers hadn't a clue what just struck the facility.

"It's not Primordial," Mawr whispered, "It's not Bomb Killer. It's not anything we've seen before. This is new."

"God!" Badrick croaked. "What new bad guy is after us now?"

At his demand for information, a second set of alarms whined on. Just as interruptive as the first, their blaring drowned out all other noises.

Mawr's response to this new racket was a simple breath of, "No."

"What now?" Badrick screeched. Once again, he stomped to the switch and punched it off.

"The siege alarm." With seconds, Mawr was by a different computer. At his command, the monitor signalled in to the cameras viewing the grounds. The image changed from a disturbingly vacant shot of the Main Hall to one of vehicles, green grass and . . .

Badrick's jaw dropped.

Brown spiky bodies were swarming the Wall, cresting over the top, their jaws wide in what were no doubt monstrous roars. The Daemonium soldiers that stood guard atop the Wall were firing their weapons at the invaders, some in a panic, but others with more wit.

A bulwark of red armour was building against the army of Kalik to the West but Badrick could already see it would make no difference. Moments later, the demons horded over them. So many of the beasts charged the group that the bullets from their weapons caused very little damage, and did nothing to slow the onslaught.

"They've taken the Wall." Mawr's voice was almost inaudible. He appeared to be in shock, his body stock still, his face lacking all colour. He typed absently, switching the camera feed to another on the other side of the facility.

The same sea of death greeted them. Having cleared the Wall on this side, the Kalik were already pouncing upon the Enthrallers in the grounds and slaughtering them without mercy.

Badrick watched in stunned shock, unable to move, as the Kalik decapitated the last Enthraller with a vicious swipe of its claws, and the huge force moved to encircle the building. Forming a dense ring, the demons retracted their wrist blades and relaxed their jaws.

Now they simply stood there, as though waiting for something.

Finding his voice in the face of this odd behaviour, Mawr muttered, "Why aren't they trying to break in? What are they waiting for?"

Badrick couldn't respond.

His voice was no longer working.

Never had he seen so many Kalik in one place. Even when the Daemonium fought to defend a human military base from an army of the subspecies, there had not been this many. Here, standing in the grounds as if they owned the place, were too many for just one clan.

The horrible truth of that numbed Badrick's body in fear.

The Kalik had united.

"What . . . the . . . hell . . . could have done that?" he spoke aloud. The monsters were standing shoulder to shoulder with what had to be foreign clans, showing no signs of aggression towards one another and acting as though they were brothers in arms.

Never in the history of the Daemonium had this happened.

"Badrick," he heard Mawr say. "I don't know what to do."

Finally managing to open his airways, Badrick coughed his throat clear and moaned, "Neither do I."

Maybe it was time to call for help. The Daemonium had outposts and smaller facilities all over the world. They weren't limited to this one base, so unless the Kalik were assaulting those locations as well, it was most likely a good time to contact them.

He indicated to the console, opening his mouth to make this suggestion.

Unfortunately, for the third time today, something dreadful and unexpected prevented him speaking.

Agony flared inside his skull. Badrick screamed and gripped his scalp as a pressure compressed his brain. Grabbing his hair and practically ripping it out, Badrick's suffering was so great he lost all awareness of his surroundings and tripped over his own feet, tumbling to the floor in a mess of limbs.

He was vaguely aware of an alarmed Mawr calling his name.

With an extra push of pressure, Badrick's eyes conked out and he was thrust into a world of darkness.

And then images began to appear in his mind . . .

There was nothing funnier than seeing the Enthrallers of the Daemonium marching like zombies into the Quarters Tower, their faces blank, and movements sluggish as their broken minds obeyed Zale's powerful psychic commands.

Standing slightly apart from the orderly lines forming at the entrance to the Tower, Zale watched them evacuate to their rooms while simultaneously issuing power to the security cameras to prevent them seeing what he was doing.

As the procession of mindless drones continued marching to their beds, Zale caught sight of their dead leader's Eminent. They moved among the others, faces just as vacant as the rest.

Spotting them sent waves of excitement flowing through Zale.

He couldn't wait to see how they would react when they awoke to find an unbeatable army of Kalik tearing the place apart.

With the thought of those mindless beasts at the forefront of his focus, he reminded himself that it was time to get the next part of his plan going.

Much to his irritation, he heard the self-proclaimed voice of reason speak up inside his soul. *You cannot free him, Zale.* Apparently deciding his argument should be put forward in person, Horas manifested and added, "You must leave him in the cage. He was imprisoned for a reason."

"The plan is already in motion, Horas. It's too late to change course now."

Shaking his helmeted head, Horas attempted to convince Zale once again. "I do not know why you want to do this, but I cannot condone it. Please listen to me. Do not do this."

He felt the demon's sheer, unparalleled dismay as Zale raised a hand and, with a mocking sneer, clicked his fingers.

The sound reverberated impossibly loud throughout the Main Hall, and at its beckoning a vast pulse of energy exploded several miles to the East.

They could both feel it.

The resulting shockwave struck the facility seconds later and Zale had to concentrate to ensure his puppets didn't get lobbed into the walls.

"It's done, Horas. No turning back."

With a cry of despondency, the demon retreated to his Enthraller's soul just as the last Enthraller passed the threshold and stepped into the Tower's foyer.

Satisfied that all were accounted to, Zale clicked his fingers again and activated the lockdown sequence. At his command, a thick door built from concentrated demonic materials shot from the top of the doorframe and slammed to the floor.

He smiled widely, exhilaration coursing through his veins and electrifying his senses.

The game was coming to an end.

With every obstacle imprisoned or dead and the Kalik set to murder any loose ends, Zale was finally free to trap Badrick, reveal himself as the Primordial, and then take his life.

And he'd do Mawr too, for good measure.

That *gnat* had annoyed Zale quite a few times with his interfering and talk of machines that could undo everything he'd worked to achieve. It was definitely time to remove him from this world.

Taking a moment to spread supernatural feelers into the local area, he enquired as to the Kalik's progress, wondering if they'd made it to the facility yet.

He was gleeful to see they'd already despatched the guards and were standing in wait.

Zale took three breaths to prepare himself for what was to

come.

Now to act panicked, kill Mawr in secret, watch Badrick lose all hope and then . . . kill hi—

Click!

Frowning at the curious sound, Zale turned on his heel . . .

And froze when he realised he was staring down the barrel of a gun.

In a voice that perfectly communicated his fury, Badrick snarled, "Don't you dare move."

chapter
THIRTY SEVEN

"Badrick," Zale spoke in a forced questioning voice, "what are you doing?"

The look on Badrick's contorted face was one of utter hatred. Zale had never seen such detestation in someone before in his life, even when the hateful Stefan had attacked the place.

"We know."

Frowning, Zale went, "What?"

Badrick shouted this time. "We know, Zale!"

Putting on an act of ignorance, Zale mirrored his agitation, bawling, "Know what!?"

It was Mawr who responded this time around. "All this time," the furious operative barked. "Everything we went through . . . It was you this *entire time*."

Throwing his hands into the air, Zale's eyes widened in fake incomprehension. "What are you talking about?"

"You're the Primordial!" Badrick's grip on his single-rifle tightened and his body shook with barely contained wrath.

"*And* the Bomb Killer," Mawr added, hissing like a snake.

"You killed everyone!" Badrick cried, a fleeting moment of anguish replacing the anger. "Zach, Reynolds, Charles . . ." His angry red face suddenly fell and turned white as snow. "Carla . . ." he wheezed. "Zale, you had Carla murdered!"

Zale prepared to deny these allegations—refute any and all accusations thrown his way—but something stopped him before he'd even opened his mouth.

What was the point?

Letting his arms fall to his sides, Zale dropped the pretence he'd cultivated for so very long, allowing his features to darken, his eyes to blacken, and his canines to grow into inhuman fangs. Despite knowing the truth, seeing the New Evil's form manifest from someone they knew came as quite a shock to those hefting rifles.

In a voice dark as night, Zale growled, "How did you find me out?"

"It was me."

Disbelief flared inside Zale, his heart skipping a beat as he rotated sharply and glared at the demon standing behind him. "Horas . . . what did you just say?"

Badrick spoke for the demon. "He sent me your memories. I saw everything."

The very air surrounding Zale seemed to suffocate as shadows began to dance dangerously on the floor. His wrath becoming so great it was manifesting in the world around them, Zale snarled, "You . . . did . . . what?"

"You heard your friend, Zale."

"HOW!?!"

Rolling his shoulders in a way very reminiscent of the late Dominus Reynolds, Horas said to him, "You forget what I was before the Enthrallers, Zale."

"You were a conduit."

"That is right." The demon nodded. "A conduit for the darkest ancient power of Hell. Long gone now, as you surely remember, but I still have my skills."

"You channelled my power." Zale took a dangerous step in his direction. "You hijacked my energy and told Badrick the truth."

"It has taken a very long time to gather the strength to do so, but yes . . . that is what I did."

Realisation hit Zale like an angry horse kicking him in the stomach. "Those discharges!" he roared in ire. "Your powers weren't reacting to mine, you were stealing my energy."

"That is right."

Zale clenched a fist and fired a blast of devastating energy Horas' way, momentarily forgetting he was not yet strong enough to hurt what was nothing but a hologram. When Horas' visage only flickered, he screamed and shouted, "How did I not notice? Why didn't I sense you invading me?"

"As the Primordial, you are arrogant," Horas spat. "You believe no one can possibly beat you. As a result you ever even considered I would be capable of anything like this.

"You were wrong."

"TRAITOR!"

At this accusation, Horas vigorously shook his head in disagreement. "I am no traitor. I remain as loyal as ever." He stepped closer and abrasively shoved his visor in Zale's face, taking him aback at his daring. "But not to this perversion you have become. I remain loyal to the real you."

"Unless you're quite finished," a deep voice interrupted Zale's screams and Horas' arguments, "you'll give yourself up, Operative Hood. This cruel game of yours is over."

Annoyance the likes of which Zale had never known before rushed through him as he returned his attention to the bacteria still pointing guns in his direction.

"The game?" he muttered softly, dangerously. Suddenly, he raised his head to the sky and hollered a shrill, maniacal cackle. "The game isn't over, *Operative Burakka!*" he screamed. "The game is at its climax and *I* will finish it. *NOT YOU!*"

A demonic screech escaped his mouth, and Zale spread his hands as wide as he could. Dark shadows spread at his command, suffocating the air and choking the lights high above them. A stray shot of blackness struck Mawr on the side of his head, and he fell to the floor, bleeding profusely.

Badrick shouted his name in panic, but the ex-soldier did not wake.

Another laugh burst from Zale's lips as he commanded his body to rise into the space above and float towards Badrick, held aloft by his dominantly powerful shadows. "Don't worry. He'll wake up in a few moments and I'll get to kill him again.

"But first, *Badrick* . . . you're going to die, suffocating, in darkness."

Terrified out of his wits, confused and dismayed, Badrick backed away from the monster converging on him. He gaped in disbelief at what his best friend had become, wishing he could clamp his eyes shut and pretend it wasn't real.

How could Zale have done all this?

So much death . . .

What had it achieved?

"Are you afraid?" the New Evil jeered. "Do you fear death?"

Badrick refused to give him the satisfaction of receiving an answer. He ensured to keep his mouth shut and, in an act of horrified bravery, pulled the trigger on his rifle.

A single round shot from the barrel and rocketed towards Zale's forehead.

If he'd been anybody else, Zale would have died.

But to Badrick's alarm the bullet vanished as it approached, swallowed by the shadows swirling around Zale's suspended form.

"Nice try," he smirked, his dark eyes appearing to glint in excitement. "But nowhere near good enough."

Badrick expected the Primordial to speak further mockery—take the opportunity to taunt him as much as possible. But Zale only reached out a hand and Badrick could already sense the awe-inspiring power generating in his palm.

Sensing the end, Badrick clenched his eyes shut and waited for the pain to begin.

But when nothing happened, mystification dominated his emotions and he dared to reopen one of his eyes.

What he saw shocked him to his very core.

Zale was frozen in place, the cruel deranged grin stuck still, and the shadows that were writhing only seconds before had ceased their thrashing.

Taking a wary step back, Badrick couldn't help but exclaim, "What?"

"I have frozen time."

An unfamiliar figure appeared inches from him, too suddenly for Badrick's shattered nerves to handle. He instinctively lashed out in an attempt to strike the new arrival down, only to have his fist phase through its body.

"Badrick, calm down. It is I, Horas."

"Horas?" Badrick lowered his fists and studied the figure warily. However, he didn't disbelieve the demon; he recognised the shape of his armour from the memories forced into his head. "How . . . How am I seeing you?"

"I have channelled the Primordial's power," the demon explained, "and have projected my visage into the vision centres of your brain and my voice to your ears."

"You saved me," Badrick stated, stumbling away from Zale.

"I am afraid I have not saved you. This is only temporary."

"Then why are you here?"

"I am here to help." He made two long strides in order to get close to Badrick. "We must defeat the Primordial."

For the first time, hope flared within Badrick. Something sounded so resolute in Horas' voice that it seemed like he had some sort of plan.

Was he naive to wonder if they could survive this?

"What do I do?"

"You need to periodically hit him with your powers."

"Why?"

Horas glanced at Zale, his movements nervous and urgent. "Time is running short. Badrick, you need to run. Keep away from him, but strike him when you can. You cannot hurt him, but Zale's power will instinctively gather to defend him from the blasts.

"When you do this, he will be unprotected at his rear and I can siphon more power each time. Zale's power is growing. We have a very small window. We must do this now. Can you do this, Badrick?"

Stuttering like an idiot, Badrick 'ermed' without end, too flustered and alarmed to speak. Horas clicked his fingers to regain his attention and repeated, "You *must* do this. Please." Badrick sensed a strange kind of shift in the atmosphere, and instantly Horas shouted, "Badrick, you must run. Remember what I told you."

Badrick didn't budge, his broken emotions leaving him too scared.

Several feet away, Zale began to stir.

And Horas screamed, *"RUN!"*

His shout inspired Badrick to move. The exact same moment that Horas vanished from sight Zale bounded forward, his face a sheen of rage, black eyes glinting hatefully.

Instinctively, Badrick threw a hand in his direction and hit him with as powerful a laser as he could. Zale grunted with exertion as the energy slammed into the shadows protecting him, and Badrick utilised his hesitation to peg it in the opposite direction.

Having no choice but to leave the temporarily deceased Mawr where he lay, Badrick sprinted up the ramp leading to the lowest walkway.

He cried aloud as a shadow carved the bridge in half, cutting through it like it was paper. Debris tumbled to earth, smashing into dust, and Badrick was forced to leap the gap left behind lest he too plummet to the floor.

He ducked as another dark tendril tried to take his head off, swiping the air where his neck had been only seconds before. As he bolted through an arch, he sensed Zale leap onto the walkway, and spun in the air in order to strike him a second time.

The laser exploded harmlessly off Zale's unhindered form, but did serve to make him even angrier. Another inhuman screech followed Badrick around the corner and he felt the air sizzle behind him as more deadly shadows tried to impale him against the wall.

He hurled an energy bomb to the floor and ducked behind a large plant pot. Zale rounded the corner just as the bomb detonated, showering him with molten hot plasma.

Badrick tried to get to his feet, but was unexpectedly thrown to the carpet by a shockwave of power. He choked as he skidded along it, his skin burning against the material, and he hit the door at the end of the corridor.

He winced as his hair was pulled from his scalp when it tried to react to his presence by opening. Scraping his body over the threshold, he only just managed to dodge the explosion that utterly destroyed the door. Badrick clenched his eyes to avoid letting shards of metal and wooden splinters cut his eyes, jumping up at the same moment and blindly stumbling back.

Through the chaos he could see the Primordial approaching, his cruel, dark form truly livid. The murderous look in those grotesque, black eyes was shocking. Badrick had never seen such cruelty in a person before.

Hitting Zale with another blast, Badrick threw himself through a window to avoid the responding discharge. Roaring with rage at his own inaccuracy, Zale's mass of shadows surged ahead, crushing through a wall like it was made of plastic, and stopping right where Badrick was going to land.

He only just dodged the spike of shadows that tried to use his own fall to impale him. Crying for help from Daemnos' powers, Badrick utilised his momentum to soar like a panicked, flailing eagle back to the upper levels.

However, it wasn't a perfect escape.

The razor sharp blade of darkness sliced open his left leg, splitting the skin and leaving blood spattered down his trousers. Landing awkwardly on a fourth floor bridge, Badrick limped through another archway, cursing as a jagged pain shot through his limb

Having witnessed what had to have been only a percentage of Zale's power, Badrick now understood that this was a lost cause. Hitting him with energy just wasn't working. The Primordial didn't seem even slightly fazed, even when he was struck head on.

He was too powerful.

Ramming his shoulder into a wooden door, Badrick panted as he fell into a storage unit attached to the RCR. The red light disappeared as he closed it behind him and trembled back against the shelves behind, his hand at the cut on his leg.

Having Daemnos in his soul, this minor wound would heal quickly, however it wasn't the pain that was crippling him—there'd been power behind the strike... such power... He'd sensed it burn the very air as it cut his leg open.

His very soul had trembled at its touch.

Daemnos had too.

What now? The Royal spoke quietly, the danger of their situation actually enough to sober his usually manic personality. Badrick gently shushed him, holding his breath as he sensed the New Evil reach their floor.

His beating heart intensified when he heard an alien voice in his head.

Charles tried to hide from me. Dhornji did as well. Are you so naive to think you'll have better success?

Badrick strained to keep his mind blank and quiet, nudging Daemnos to do the same. The Royal was already trying to respond in kind to their enemy, and Badrick had no doubt that, with his immense power, he'd actually break the rules and hear the Royal.

Maybe you think, because you're a powerful Enthraller, you'll be different. Your situation is nothing like those failures. You'll survive.

I look forward to showing you how wrong you are.

Badrick actually screamed when the door buckled with a loud bang. He slapped his hand over his mouth, redundant as this action was. The wood splintered with the next impact, tiny shards flying Badrick's way. The next strike left a hole, through which he could see the RCR.

Badrick knew that Zale could tear that door from its hinges with a flick of his finger. There was no doubt he was strong enough to melt the walls around Badrick and get to him in seconds.

It was clear he was destroying the door purposefully slow.

Zale wanted Badrick to fear him.

He wanted to be terrifying.

A shadow covered the hole and Badrick saw a black eye staring at him with keen and eager malevolence. Badrick's heart skipped a beat as he realised in his terror and panic he'd only gone and cornered himself.

Stupid!

The monster spoke, his rumbling voice low and evil. "Badrick, are you afraid of the dark?"

Shadows began seeping through the hole. They oozed down the door like blood, but also swirled menacingly towards him as though made of gas. The bulbs began to flicker. Darkness dominated the room. Badrick's throat tightened as the power suffocated the air and his lungs fought to find oxygen.

Knowing that he would die if he stayed in this glorified cupboard, Badrick did the only thing he could.

Screaming hoarsely, he rammed the door with all his might, shattering its remains to splinters. Zale was caught off guard as Badrick's shoulder met with his chest and they both rolled to the floor. Having been the one to make this happen, Badrick's wits were still with him. He was first to his feet and was running for the door before Zale could even blink.

He was a breadth of a second from escaping when an unseen force gripped him by the throat and halted him in his tracks. Choking, unable to breathe, tears blinking from his eyes, Badrick was pulled back to the monster that wanted him dead.

"Enough games," the demon snarled.

Badrick was so transfixed on the darkness of Zale's eyes and his inability to catch air that he almost didn't react when he heard a different voice scream, *AGAIN, BADRICK!*

Acting on instinct and trying to ignore the protests of his oxygen-deprived lungs, he slapped his hand on Zale's chest and summoned as much demonic energy as he could. Bright red light drowned out the shadows surrounding them and Zale roared as he was blasted back, his grip on Badrick failing.

He threw out his hands as Badrick fell to his knees, commanding the shadows to support his weight and skidding to a halt before he could fall.

And with rage unparalleled, the Primordial raised a hand, elongated the black claws on his fingers, and darted towards Badrick like a Kalik lunging to gut its prey.

The claws were inches from his stomach when a pair of grey arms wrapped around Zale's chest and aggressively dragged him away, despite the Primordial's screams of protest. The monster tried to wrestle against his sudden captor, but to no avail. The arms were too strong and held him fast, no matter how hard he tried to struggle.

Gulping air hungrily, Badrick painfully rose to his feet and gazed in astonishment at the sight before him.

Zale's captor spoke in his ear, "Enough, Zale. It is over."

The New Evil's surprise at having been overpowered by what was supposed to be an incorporeal entity was so vast it was a stark contrast to his earlier wrath. He gazed down at the gloved fingers interlocking across his chest, his mouth stunned open.

Abruptly, the rage returned. Zale's fury at being conquered by his own demon was evident in the way he shook his head, then roared like a beast, such loathing in the noise it hurt Badrick's heart to hear it.

Ignoring his Enthraller's odium, Horas spoke again.

"Calm down, Zale. I said, it is over."

chapter
THIRTY EIGHT

The sight of what was once his best friend tied remorselessly to a chair was almost too much for Badrick to bear, despite knowing that taking his eyes off Zale could be catastrophic.

If he got a chance to escape . . .

Badrick did his best to forget about what was surely inevitable as he used an RCR computer to monitor the Kalik that were still holding position, encircling the building with a serenity about them never before recorded in the species.

"What's going on?" he voiced his concerns aloud, wondering if the Primordial really had learnt to control them.

Of course, he had to remind himself that was not likely; were Zale commanding them, he would surely have summoned them to his rescue.

Unless he didn't consider himself trapped . . .

That pondering sent worrying shivers down Badrick's spine—what was Zale planning?

"It is not Zale who commands them," a voice interrupted his fears. Turning on his heel, Badrick saw Horas, perfectly visible, watching the screen, his body still and shockingly tense.

"Then what are they doing?"

Horas approached to stand near Badrick, never taking his eyes from the screen. His vivid blue visor reflected the soft red light that bathed them, turning it a sickly brown. "Zale released something," he said slowly. "Something to command this army . . . And what confuses me is that the idea stemmed from his human side."

"What'd you say?" Badrick asked in confusion, instantly picking up on this last comment and failing to prevent it dominating his morbid curiosity. "Human side?"

At first Horas did not respond to the question. He seemed to glance at the sneering Zale and muttered, "I cannot hold him long. This is, again, temporary. Zale is too strong to keep this up."

Too strong. The simple ludicrousness of this statement had Badrick grimacing. He turned to Horas' visage, eyeing up the demon's similarities to Zale's armour and beginning to wonder just exactly what he'd gotten himself into by helping the demon.

"What is he?"

Before the demon could speak, Zale suddenly roared, *"YOUR DEATH!"*

Horas sighed, placing a hand over the metal above his visor and using his palm to support his head. "He is the product of a human and demon coupling. Zale is the first ever combination of DNA from both realms."

"He's half demon?" Badrick squawked indignantly. "Is that even possible?"

"The evidence that it is sits before you."

"Then *how?*"

Horas responded with a very human-like shrug, a gesture that communicated his sheer exhaustion so clearly Badrick began to feel pity for him. "I do not know how his mother did it, but a demon we do not know gave birth to him, most likely after raping a human."

"She had the right idea," a snarl came from the chair.

Disgusted, Badrick turned his back on the *thing* sitting in the chair.

"You keep an eye on him," he snapped. "I need to try and wake Mawr, if I even can."

When he began to ease away, Horas called, "Badrick, Mawr cannot be woken until he heals, and the rest of the Daemonium is locked in the Quarters Tower. Zale activated the lockdown."

"Fine!" Badrick bawled, spinning back around. "Then you can tell me how to kill him."

Though he couldn't see Horas' eyes, he could sense their piercing gaze. "Is that what you think is best?"

"Of course," Badrick snarled, throwing a hand in Zale's direction and trying to ignore the wolf-like growling coming from his throat. "He's a monster."

Horas' voice was but a low rumble. "Are you sure that is how you really feel?"

Badrick wanted to confirm these feelings.

Desperately wished he could tell the demon to just execute Zale and be done with it . . .

But at Horas' prompt, Badrick's stomach lurched and his heart tightened. A sob rapidly travelled its way up his chest, and with a wail of shattered emotions, he cried, "He's killed everyone!" The strength in his legs failed and Badrick almost collapsed to the floor. Using the nearest console to steady himself, he moaned,

"He murdered Reynolds. Carla is dead because of him. Mawr's lying in a puddle of his own blood."

"He will awake."

"That is *so* not the point!" Badrick glared at the demon. "He's a monster. He doesn't care how much pain he's caused and deserves no mercy from us."

Horas watched Badrick panting painfully and gripping his chest in an attempt to stifle the agony in his heart. He stumbled into a chair, falling into the cushion with a heavy thump, and sat there in silence, small tears running down his face as he thought about all the people they'd lost.

Audibly, Horas sighed, and brought his hands together. "The Zale that you see before you is not the Zale you know. It is a perversion of him. His soul has been corrupted by the demon power within him."

"So?" Badrick snapped. "Whatever he is, it doesn't change what he did. He killed so many."

"No," Horas argued. "Zale has killed no one. All this time, it has been the Primordial."

"Are you trying to tell me they're two separate people?" Badrick scoffed derisively, acting on instinct despite his better judgement. "Like a Jekyll and Hyde piece-of-crap situation?"

With the tips of his fingers touching, Horas huffed with frustration. "It is difficult to explain."

"Try!"

Huffing a second time, Horas said, "Zale's human soul and his demon soul are not two separate consciousnesses. No matter what portion of his being is dominating, they are both parts of Zale."

Bawling with impatience, Badrick hollered, "Then how can you say it *wasn't* Zale who killed our friends?"

"Listen to me, Badrick. These halves may both be Zale, but there are times when they talk to each other. As though they *are* separate."

"And what's that like?" Badrick queried with genuine interest. He tried to wrap his brain around how such a mental thing was possible and utterly failed to imagine it. Hearing a derisive sneer, he glanced at his partner—*ex-partner*—and saw him leering in their direction, giving Badrick the impression that the evil bastard knew exactly what he was thinking.

"It is difficult to observe," Horas admitted. "Both halves refer to Zale's actions in relation to them both. They use words like *'we'* as opposed to *'I'* or *'you'*"

"Except . . ."

With his stomach growling nervously, Badrick dared to ask, "Except?"

"Except for the odd moments that his demon side refers to his human side as *Zale*." Horas faced his Enthraller, his body language screaming intense distress.

It couldn't have been easy to see someone he obviously cared about looking like Zale did now. The New Evil had refused to let his eyes ease on the darkness, his canines were still razor sharp and black claws still covered his nails.

He looked totally *inhuman*.

Blinking dumbly and feeling remarkably useless, Badrick blurted out, "What does that mean?"

"It says to me, Badrick, that in their own way they *are* separate. There is a Zale that lives inside that darkened soul that is the one we know. The Zale who defends us. The one who is our friend. A soul of goodness and who is *not* the Primordial."

Badrick jumped to his feet, placing a finger near Horas' chest and saying, "Sounds to me like you're letting your attachment to Zale cloud your judgement."

"That was a mighty grown-up sentence there, Varner," the beast snarled cruelly. "Did Daemnos have to help you string the words together or did you use a thesaurus?"

Grinding his teeth and doing his best to refrain from retorting, Badrick pointed at Zale and muttered, "He *is* a monster, and we have to deal with him before anyone else dies."

Horas nodded. "I agree. The Primordial must be defeated."

"Good," Badrick stated. "Then we're on the same page. We have to take care of Zale."

"We are not going to hurt Zale."

Badrick groaned in frustration. "Horas, he's too dangerous to let live!"

Horas turned from Badrick and regarded Zale. His hands were curled into fists, the material around the knuckles looking stretched from the tightness of his clenching. Horas' body was as rigid as his grip was firm, and, as he took several steps towards his Enthraller, Badrick could see strong determination practically emanating from his holographic form.

"When he struck Mawr down at the Captus Memoria, he could have killed him. But he did not. He pulled his punch. The Primordial claims it was part of the plan but I do not believe that he really wanted to kill anyone.

"In that moment, his better half prevailed.

"He has been having dreams, Badrick. Dreams of days when he helped people. Uncovered mysteries that saved lives. I felt a stirring during the last one. Zale's subconscious was trying to remind itself how effective it was as a force of good. How amazing it felt to *be* good."

He sighed again, and through it Badrick realised just how much pain Horas was in as he did his best to keep Zale contained. He could hear the strain in his breath, the sorrow in his voice . . . and his resolve to fix everything.

"The real Zale—our friend—does not deserve to die." With what seemed like great effort, Horas forced his fingers to uncurl and relax. "We will defeat the Primordial, Badrick, but we are not going to kill Zale."

His visor locked onto Badrick's gaze.

And he proclaimed, "We are going to save him."

<u>**And some final words:**</u>

As this book is self published and I lack the advertising and marketing budget of more traditionally published books, my main form of advertising comes from you guys (the readers).

So please, if you liked, loved, hated, despised or felt/thought anything about this book at all, leave me a review and let me and others know what you thought.

For more immediate updates on new releases and works in progress you can follow me on:

http://www.facebook.com/JavscoBooks

or

http://www.wattpad.com/user/Josh_Brookes

9 781912 663040